MORE
THAN A NOTION

PATRICIA HOPKINS

More Than a Notion

Visit our website: http://www.wanderlustbooksllc.com

Library of Congress Cataloging-in-Publication Data

LCCN: 2011943140
Hopkins, Patricia.
More than a notion / Patricia Hopkins
p. cm.

Published by Wanderlust Books

ISBN-10: 0615554172
ISBN-13: 978-0-615-55417-4

In loving memory of my father, John R. Hopkins, Sr. He used to always tell me to "be still", give my blessings a chance to find me. To my children, Anthony and Zak, don't ever give up on your dreams. They do come true.

ACKNOWLEDGMENTS

God gives us all a unique gift and it's up to us how we choose to use it. Thank you for mine. Mom, thanks for giving me wings and encouraging me to fly. To Papi, without your inspiration and encouragement this novel would have never come to fruition. And to Aunt Sissy, thank you for helping me learn the awesome power of forgiveness.

A Dream Deferred

What happens to a dream deferred?
Does it dry up
like a raisin in the sun?
Or fester like a sore—
And then run?
Does it stink like rotten meat?
Or crust and sugar over—
like a syrupy sweet?
Maybe it just sags
like a heavy load.
Or does it explode?

--- Langston Hughes

Also written by Patricia Hopkins

Living In The Offbeat

I Am The Shadowman

PROLOGUE

The alarm clock came on again at 5:33. John Legend singing *Wake Up Everybody* filtered through the radio, breaking the silence and gently reminding me it was time to get up. Another restless night, filled with tossing and turning, left me in no mood to crawl out of my warm comfortable bed for another week filled with the same old stuff. Why did the weekends always have to go by so quickly? I listened to the rest of the song, wondering why anyone felt the need to remake one of Teddy Pendergrass' signature hits.

After hitting the snooze button for the third time, I slowly drifted back to sleep in a desperate attempt to recapture a few more moments of the tantalizing images that swirled in the depths of my subconscious mind.

~~~~

Standing on the balcony of an island hilltop villa located somewhere in the Caribbean tropics, looking out over the magnificent scenery below, everything seemed to be right in the world. I had an unobstructed view of the turquoise water. The midday sun filtered through white fluffy clouds and was reflected back in the deep, blue green of the ocean. Luxuriously thick grass carpeted the mountain and complimented the lushness of the surrounding landscape. A steady ocean breeze blowing across the water gently bent the branches of the palm trees. Sun bleached stucco houses with terracotta roofs peeked through the vegetation. The air was thick with the sweet, heavy scent of jasmine and other tropical fragrances.

The unmistakable sounds of jungle creatures pierced the quiet with mating calls. Beads of perspiration gathered on my forehead as the island humidity built up its strength for the day. In an attempt to ward off the oppressive heat, I was dressed coolly in a linen, ivory-colored, ankle length dress. My feet were bare.

The hot air brushed against my face and the sun's warm rays caressed my skin. I inhaled the island's fragrance as if it were the delicious scent of a lover's breath. I was so content and there was no other place I wanted to be. As I took in the entire view, my gaze settled upon a very handsome, dark brother standing on the sandy beach. He looked up and after what seemed to be an eternity, he slowly started walking towards me...

Wouldn't you know it?! That damned alarm clock went off again. Poof! All the images magically disappeared just as quickly as they came. In one fell swoop, I threw my pillow at the clock, knocked it off the dresser, pulling its cord free from the wall. I gathered the covers of the down comforter over my head and went back to sleep for what ultimately ended up being the first day of the rest of my life.

PART ONE

CHAPTER 1

I didn't know where I was, but it felt familiar. Like déjà vu. The landscape reminded me of those office calendars teasing you with the promise of a tropical island getaway. Palm trees, weighed down with ripened coconuts and anchored in fine white sand resembling sugar, bordered the shore. The lone stretch of beach went on for miles.

A woman stood about 20 yards away from me, smiling and waving her arms, trying her best to get my attention. She was dressed in an oversized white t-shirt with a big yellow smiley face on the front and cutoff blue jean shorts. Her face was partially hidden by a huge, floppy straw hat. I shielded my eyes from the rays of the sun and headed in her direction. As I got closer, I thought she looked like a hippie or a flower child from the 60's.

"Lena! Hey girl, I see you finally made it! It's great to see you again. How long do you plan on staying this time?"

I was close enough to see that she was an older black woman with hair hanging well past her shoulders, locked in a cascade of black and silver tangles. Her skin had the ageless glow that indicated she had been blessed with good health and even better genes. She was breathtakingly beautiful.

"Uh, uh, excuse me?"

"Oh, I'm so sorry. Where are my manners? Please pardon me for being rude. Let me introduce myself. My name is Simone and you can consider me as your tour guide. I'm sort of like that Mr. Rourke character on *Fantasy Island* from way back in the day. But I'm a whole lot more fun and much livelier than he could ever be." She reached for my hand, showing a mouthful of pearly whites.

"W-w-where am I and h-h-how did I get here? Do I know you? Am I d-d-dead?" I stuttered, looking down at the field of pale white flowers surrounding us. I recognized the fragrance.

"Walk with me and I'll explain everything." She wrapped her arm through mine and nudged me along.

A flock of seagulls flew overhead calling out to each other, flying in a perfect formation, much like soldiers marching. They were headed towards the water. As the thought of soldiers entered my mind, the noise of the seagulls grew faint, until I could barely hear them at all.

Thinking of soldiers caused me to reflect upon the current state of my life sending me back to a place I did not want to be.

Simone spoke gently, "Honey, you must only think of you for as long as you are here. Let the real world take care of itself for now. This time is for Lena to take care of Lena and no one else. Now let's go!" The noise of the seagulls returned to their original strength.

We walked silently, arm-in-arm, down a dirt road until we came upon a charming little bungalow nestled in a clearing. It looked so familiar, as if I had been there a thousand times before. The Spanish styled cottage was perfect in every respect, from the faded green shutters, weathered from years of sun and sea, to the handmade terracotta tiled roof. Two wicker chairs sat on either side of the oversized wooden door. Flowerboxes brimming over with red bougainvillea, rested on the small windowsills.

"Oh, my goodness! This is my house! The one I have dreamt about since I was a little girl."

I ran around to the back yard and knelt into the greenest, thickest grass imaginable. Rickety stairs, bleached white by the sun, led down to the sandy beach. Waves broke against the shore in gentle, almost hypnotic sounds. Awkward looking pelicans dove headfirst into the water, scooping up small fish swimming near the surface, in their huge pouches.

Towards the back of the yard was one of those infinity swimming pools, the kind where you can't tell where the pool ends and the ocean begins. A small guesthouse that served dual purpose as a dressing room, bordered the other side.

"Simone?" I looked at the smiling woman. "Where am I?" Amazement, laced with trepidation filled my voice.

"You are exactly where you need to be at a time you need to be here," she responded. "Come inside. We'll have a drink and I'll answer any questions you may have."

I followed Simone through the back door. The kitchen was absolutely gorgeous! It was literally the kitchen of my dreams. I ran my hands over the cool beige flecked granite countertops. Brightly colored tiles depicting Italian villa scenes were arranged amongst natural stone tiles on the backsplash. The stainless steel appliances were top of the line, including a gourmet gas range with six burners and a built in grill. It was the one I had always wanted, but could never afford.

The hardwood floor was polished to glossy perfection. I opened the cabinets and discovered Calphalon, *All-Clad*, and *Le Creuset* pots, pans and crockery suitable for cooking meals of every kind imaginable. The refrigerator and pantry were fully stocked with exotic culinary ingredients from all over the world. Ah yes, the foods I love and loved to cook. I felt like I really had died and gone to *Williams-Sonoma* heaven.

The spacious family room contained a wood-burning fireplace that took up almost half of one wall. An oversized armchair, large enough to cuddle up in and a matching ottoman were placed close enough to feel the warmth of the fire. In the far corner stood an antique desk and chair, just like the one my grandparents had when I was a little girl. A computer, printer, fax and telephone sat on the desk. All the equipment I ever needed to run my own business was right at my fingertips.

The bedroom was simple. A king-sized sleigh bed covered with a goose down comforter and several multicolored pillows, helped to offset the coolness of the eggshell painted walls. A fireplace, on a much smaller scale than the one in the living room, took up one corner. I peeked in the closet filled with clothes from casual to classic in all my favorite styles. Dozens of pairs of shoes lined an entire wall.

The master bathroom reminded me of a spa. Scented candles were placed virtually everywhere a plant wasn't. A thick white terry cotton robe hung on the back of the door. I wrapped my body in its luxurious warmth and wandered through the cottage several more times before heading back to the kitchen.

Simone waited patiently at the counter, perched on one of the stools, looking too much like my long deceased Aunt Shirley. I had to look twice to make sure it wasn't her. Simone set out my favorite red wine, assembled a tray of various fruit, cheese and crackers, and was fully prepared to clue me in on what was going on.

~~~~

Mark entered the bedroom to get ready for work. For about the past six months or so, he'd recently taken to sleeping on the living room sofa. Told me it was because I kept him awake with my nighttime restlessness. Anyway, noticing that I was still in bed, he came over to find out why I wasn't up.

"Lena, wake up. You're going to be late for work," he called out.

I mumbled something in my sleep and turned over. Fifteen minutes later, Mark had finished taking his shower and was dressed in his Army uniform. He noticed I still hadn't gotten up.

"What's wrong? Aren't you feeling well?" He asked, lightly touching my forehead.

I apparently said something to convince him I wasn't dead or seriously ill, because he felt it was all right to leave me alone. He went to each of the boy's rooms to make sure they were up and dressed for school and to let them know I wasn't feeling well and wasn't going to work. He also told them not to bother me. The boys got up, fed themselves, gave me a goodbye kiss on my forehead and left for school.

Ever since moving to Salinas, Kansas, almost three years ago when the Army transferred Mark from his last assignment in northern Italy, I worked on the local military post in a tank repair factory. The town of Salinas had less than 50,000 people and was smack dab in the middle of the state--in the heart of the Bible belt. Open the dictionary to "conservative" and the town of Salinas would be listed first.

It took over six months before I finally found a job paying barely more than minimum wage. Unfortunately, it was in the tank factory. Fort Salinas' Army post was the largest employer in the area. Practically the entire town worked in the factory. After sending out dozens of resumes and going on just as many interviews, I was hired to install bolts into the floor assembly of army tanks.

It wasn't the most glamorous job. In fact it was extremely tedious and I hated it from the get go. But, since we needed the money, I kept getting my ass out of bed every morning, dragging myself through each and every day for the past several years. After work, it was the same routine day after day. Errands, dinner, help the kids with homework, do laundry, watch TV or read a book, and in bed by 10. Very routine, very predictable, very boring.

James was almost 18. Grown as far as he was concerned. He was in his final year of high school with thoughts of college on his mind. James was also a talented musician who played guitar and piano. Neil was fifteen and Carlos was eleven. The younger boys were into anything that had to do with sports. They were all so busy that they had no time to spend with old Mom. Which was very normal and very understandable. It was difficult to do, but little by little I let them spend more time with their friends and didn't demand they report home every hour on the hour. Despite our busy lives, we still had dinner together at least twice a week.

I knew my life was in a serious rut, but for the life of me, I could not see a way to get out of it. I felt like those pathetic little hamsters, stuck inside a cage running on a wheel, never getting anywhere, no matter how hard they tried. Topping things off, the relationship with my husband had gotten to the point where we barely talked to each other. Our marriage had evolved into something more akin to roommates. Conversations became perfunctory, concerning mostly the trivial rituals of everyday living. The fire had truly gone out a long time ago.

~~~~

I pulled up the kitchen stool next to Simone, picked up the glass of wine and took a sip. It was good. After several moments had passed, I asked again, "Why am I here and how did I get here?"

"Like I said earlier, Lena, you are here because you need to be here." Simone took her wine into the living room and looked out the picture glass window. She motioned for me to follow.

I slipped off the seat and went to stand besides her. I was started to get frustrated and more than a little irritated by her cryptic answers.

"What do you see when you look out this window?"

"What do you mean? I see outside. Lots of trees, flowers, grass… You know, just regular outdoorsy stuff."

"How do you *feel* when you look through this window? And before you answer, I want you to focus on how you *really* feel." Simone smiled.

I took in the breathtakingly beautiful scenery. On the front porch, I sat in one of those wicker chairs and inhaled the fragrance of the flowers mingled with the dewy scent of the freshly cut grass. Birds soared through the air, swooping and diving between tree branches. A couple of little girls rode their bicycles past the cottage. They were laughing and having a good time just being kids. I looked up towards the blue sky then closed my eyes. An overwhelming sense of calmness suddenly overtook me.

"I feel absolutely, positively free! So alive! That's the best way I can describe it. Like I don't have a care in the world. I feel content, something I haven't felt in a very long time." I looked towards Simone who had only come as far as the front door.

7

"Magnificent! That's exactly how you're supposed to feel! Otherwise, this would all be a mistake." She walked out the door and took the other chair and turned it to face me. "Lena, you are here because you choose to be here. This place doesn't feel strange because you are the one who envisioned it. You've come here many times in your life and until now, you never felt the need to stay."

"I don't understand. How did I get here? And where is here?"

"Sometimes life just gets so difficult that some of us simply need to escape. Although, the fortunate few have the ability to take exotic vacations and go off somewhere for weeks or even months at a time, others simply don't have the means or the know how to get away from the everyday grind. They are so busy taking care of everyone else's problems that they often forget themselves in the process of everyday life. Every so often, our bodies and minds know what's better for us than we do. The mind takes over and gives us a well-needed rest, whether we want it or not. This little trip of yours is your mind telling you that you need some down time. Some Lena time!"

"Have I gone crazy? You mean to tell me that I'm making all this shit up? None of it is real?" All of a sudden, I really did feel the need to get away.

"Lena, sit down. You have not gone crazy. Your mind has just decided to give you a vacation from your life. You would not believe how many people have come "here". Most come only for a few hours, some decide that they never want to leave. How you got here is not as important as why you decided to remain this time. Like I said before, you've made short trips many times before, but you always left. You weren't able to see me then, because you didn't need to stay. This time is different, when I saw that you could see me, I knew it was your time."

"You're telling me that I am in some kind of dreamscape, third dimension or *Twilight Zone* type of place?" I calmed down to try to figure this situation out.

"I guess you can say that. I know that this will be difficult for you to accept and even harder to wrap your mind around, but try to understand. This place is another dimension that has successfully merged both the conscious and the subconscious world. It's the same, but absolutely different. You can and will interact with others in similar situations as yours, as well as everyday ordinary people. No one will know your true state and you won't know theirs because you will appear to be just like everyone else. And because these two dimensions have merged into one, your encounters will be very similar to the waking world."

Lena continued to listen.

"The major difference here is, the interaction you have with others is on a spiritual level, although it will and can seem to be physical. For all intents and purposes, you are still asleep in your bed at home. But your mind is free to project a physical image to allow you to do whatever it is you choose, for as long as you want to stay. You can go practically anywhere you want to go, do what you want to do and see whoever it is you wish to see. The only exception is, you cannot and will never be in the same setting as "the real you". It's impossible because that truly does defy the laws of nature."

"Lena, this is nothing new. People have been projecting themselves for centuries. Your out-of-body experience isn't as unique as you may believe. Unfortunately, when and if you decide to tell anyone in the "real" world, they will probably think you are insane. What you are experiencing lies in the same realm as seeing UFO's, cloning humans, or some may even say believing in God. You have to take a leap of faith and trust what is happening as real"

"What do you mean? I asked.

"Physically, you are sound asleep. Your body will carry out all its functions and your heart will continue to beat. Be aware that a day here is unlike your normal day in the real world. What used to be 24 hours there, can take up to two or three times the number of hours here. Time is irrelevant and easy to lose track of. You may think you've only been here for a week, but in reality it can actually be two weeks, a month, even a year. Don't worry, your family will find a way to take care of you while you sleep. Just know that you are free to leave whenever you choose." Simone removed her hat, freeing the locks trapped under the cloth.

"I don't understand, Simone, you say that it was my time. How do you know that? And how do I know that this is real?"

"Think back to the current state of your life. Haven't you been feeling unappreciated and taken for granted by your family lately? The marriage you're in has left you totally dissatisfied. You have been wife, mother, caretaker, nurse, teacher, maid, chauffer, cook... The list goes on and on. You've devoted your entire life to others, foregoing yourself. Most of your adult life has been spent traveling all over the world, dropping your life when your husband was transferred, only to begin anew each time you moved. It was your responsibility to make a home out of dreary little apartments and remain cheerful and accepting whenever he told you he had to deploy for six months at a time. You stretched meager paychecks your husband brought home and found creative ways to entertain on a budget. You practically raised your sons on your own."

"I did what I had to do." I said."And it was never easy."

"Despite having gone to college, you were never able to find a decent job, because no one wanted to hire a military wife. Look at yourself! You're holding on to a job you despise, but have to keep because it helps to pay the bills. You stopped making friends a long time ago because it was just too difficult always having to say goodbye. You've forgotten the things that used to make you happy, like painting and music. Whatever happened to that million-dollar smile of yours?"

I dropped my head in shame, embarrassment, perhaps disappointment, but continued to listen.

"Damn it, girl! You don't even dance anymore and you used to love to dance. Remember?" Simone replied with the conviction of someone who knew it to be true.

"Are you my imagination? Or my subconscious speaking to me, reminding me of what I've let myself become?" By now tears flowed freely. Everything she said was true. I had let "me" go, little by little, until very little of me remained.

"No, I am not in your imagination, nor your subconscious. Remember earlier when I told you that I'm kind of like Mr. Rourke on *Fantasy Island*? Well, I'm really more like your spiritual caretaker. I suppose you can call me a spirit of the dreams. Lena, there are many spirits that exist in your everyday life, watching over and taking care of you, making sure you're safe. In those situations, when you find yourself in imminent danger, we are there to help guide you and give you strength. We are everywhere. We are what makes you avoid driving into the dangerous part of town when you know the car has been acting up. You know that little voice that you call your "inner voice" or intuition, your guardian angel...?"

"Yeah, I think I know what you mean. I call it my "inner spirit"— how God sometimes uses my thoughts to communicate to me. I used to listen to it all the time. It's what got me through the past decade of my life. All those times when I was alone with the boys, in a foreign country. When Mark deployed off to a war zone, I called on that inner spirit to give me strength to get through the difficult times. It never let me down. I don't know what happened this time. How did I let myself get so far gone?" I posed the question more towards myself than to Simone.

"What's important now is for you to find out why you decided to stay this time. Only you can answer that question. I'm here only to help guide you towards rediscovering your own truth." Simone drank the remaining wine and got up for more.

"Simone, I just have a couple more questions. You said some people decide to remain here and not go back. What makes some people stay for only a few hours while others decide never to leave?" I eased out of the chair and followed Simone inside as she made her way to the kitchen, refilling our glasses with wine.

"Most people come here and stay only a short while. They find that the time spent is enough to refresh their minds and they go back to their everyday lives. It's what happens when you dream. Then there are those unfortunate few who arrive involuntarily, either through a major illness or accident. Their bodies need time to recuperate, but their minds are endlessly trying to find ways to occupy itself. When these people begin to dream and involuntarily project themselves, they are often very confused about what's going on."

She continued, "One moment they're enjoying life to the fullest and the next they end up here in this "altered state of reality". Those are the ones who have the most difficult time accepting what's happening. They don't know what to believe. At first, most assume they have died and gone on to heaven. I explain to them that they are here only for a short time until their bodies are capable of functioning properly again. Some enjoy the time and can't wait to get back to the "real world". Others find this world so accommodating; they choose to spend their entire lives in this state. I remember there was one woman whose body was asleep for almost 16 years before she finally returned. One day she just decided it was time to go, so she went back. There was nothing physically or mentally wrong with her, although the doctors declared it a miracle that she'd woken up at all."

"I think I remember hearing about her. Wasn't she from New Mexico or something like that? She was a grandmother by the time she finally woke up. Right?"

Simone laughed. "She was so full of life. Carmelita, that was her name, said she was so tired of taking care of everyone and everything that she just needed to get away. She had no money and no place to go for vacation, so one day she just decided to not get out of bed. Kind of like how you felt. Anyway, when Carmelita was here, she laughed and danced the nights away. She was the life of the party. You know, she didn't intend to stay as long as she did. Every so often, she would drift back to the real world to check on her family without their knowing. She'd find out how everyone was doing and that they could get along without her. As long as everyone was all right, she felt it was okay to remain."

"During one of her "visits" back home, she heard her daughter speaking to her about her grandbaby and how she wanted her Mama to see him. After hearing about her first grandson being born, Carmelita came back one last time to say good-bye and to tell me that it was time for her to go. I told her I understood. Shortly thereafter, she awoke and the doctors and her family proclaimed it was a miracle. I see her every now and then, but she can't see me. Now she only spends a few hours here before she goes back. It took all that time away before she finally realized what her life meant to her and to others."

"Damn, 15 years! How could she stay asleep for that long? Didn't she consider how her kids would feel growing up without a mother?" I took a long sip of wine and wondered how her children must have felt.

"There is no time table here. Each person must individually decide how long is long enough. Just remember that while you are here, only you have control over yourself. You are the driver of your own destiny." Simone emptied her glass and placed it on the granite countertop.

Surveying the kitchen, I noticed even more than before. Hanging neatly on a pot rack over the kitchen island, were shiny copper pots just like the ones I bought during a trip to England way back.

Gathered neatly on a corner shelf above the sink was a group of black *mammie* dolls I started to collect after I discovered the first one in my Grandmother's basement. They were arranged just as they were in my kitchen – watching over me as I cooked my family's meals. A baker's rack held plants and cacti of all sorts. Some of the leaves were beginning to turn yellow, just like my plants at home. As I picked off the discolored leaves and threw them in the trashcan below the sink, I heard the kitchen door close.

Simone was heading towards the rickety, wooden staircase that led down to the beach below. I watched her descend the steps and walk off to speak with a man standing at the edge of the water. He looked distraught, much like I had when I first met Simone. She reached out for his hand and I watched them stroll down the sandy beach. Well, well, well, guess I was on my own.

~~~~

James was the first to arrive home from school. He opened my bedroom door and called out. When I didn't answer, he came over and shook me. I moaned, which was a relief to him to know I was at least still alive. But when I didn't wake up, he called his Dad at work because he realized then that something was definitely wrong.

CHAPTER 2

Having all the time in the world to do what I wanted, I still didn't know what to do. Wandering from room to room looking at items that were foreign, yet very familiar, was slightly disconcerting. On the living room mantle sat a picture of my boys and me standing in front of the coliseum in Rome. A silver frame I picked up at an Indian craft fair in Santa Fe held a picture of me when I was 25 years old and at least 20 pounds lighter. Dressed in green, I stood on the rocky outcrops of a Hawaiian beach surrounded by aqua colored water. Both pictures represented some of the happiest times in my life. A lone photo of Mark and me on our wedding day sat tucked away behind the others. I thought back to how happy we used to be. Ah, memories. I let out a very long, deep sigh, set it down and decided to take a walk.

Not yet knowing how things worked, I decided to explore my surroundings. Though the midday sun shone brightly, it was cool enough for a light sweater. I pulled on a sweatshirt hanging in the closet. Stepping back outside, I followed the road to see where it would eventually take me. I marveled at the absolute peacefulness. No loud airplanes or traffic in the background, just the melodic sounds of nature and an occasional child playing.

After about a mile, I wandered into a town that reminded me of a northeastern Italian coastal village named *Gorgazzio*. I spent nearly five years of my life in Italy and loved every moment. Could it really be the same place? Grand old buildings, draped in ivy and decked out in spring flowers, were nestled tightly together forming the town center.

Towering high above the town center stood a massive clock tower, chiming out the hour, day after day, year after year. Shops selling fragrant meats, pungent cheeses, sinfully rich chocolates, freshly-cut flowers, and a variety of exotic foods all stood with their doors open releasing their enticing aromas. Older women, some of them my grandmother's age, rode into town and parked their bicycles in the bike rack to do their daily food shopping.

A *gelato* cafe, nestled towards the end of the street, beckoned me with its aroma of freshly churned ice cream. I ordered *copa spaghetti;* a wickedly rich concoction of creamy, soft vanilla *gelato* topped with juicy red strawberries, shaved gourmet white chocolate, and freshly whipped cream.

The shopkeeper replied *"Buon appetito"*. I found an open seat under the store awning and anticipated the smoothness of the *gelato* melting in my mouth. Taking that first spoonful was as close to having an orgasm as I could get without actually having one. Closing my eyes in anticipation of the rich sweetness, I heard someone call my name.

My eyes flew open at the sound of his voice. I hadn't seen Keenan Jones in almost twenty years. He looked as good as he did the day we said goodbye in the St. Louis airport, when he left to join the FBI.

Keenan was my high school sweetheart and my first love. He was the man I gave my heart to. He was also my "first" and you never forget your "first", whether it was good or bad. This was the man I dreamt about and said a prayer for every single day of my life. We kept in touch for about a year after he left, then slowly, ever so gradually, the long letters gave way to postcards from countries all over the world. There was never a return address. Eventually, the postcards arrived further and further apart until I couldn't remember the last time I received one at all. Although I married Mark, I had never forgotten Keenan and what he meant to me. I suppose I had never truly gotten over him.

"Lena? Lena McAllister? Is that really you?" He smiled, showing his familiar grin. His eyes seemed to glisten over with emotion as he opened his arms to give me a hug. I looked up to see that gorgeous specimen of a man reaching for me. I dropped the cup of gelato on the table. If there were flies nearby, they surely would've flown directly into my mouth the way I left it hanging open.

"Keenan? Oh my God! Look at you!" I pushed the chair back from the table and stood, momentarily unable to move. I quickly found my bearings and stepped deep into the span of his arms. He smelled of masculinity and exotic spices. I hugged him, resting my head against his muscular chest, enjoying the feel of his arms.

"Lena? It really is you! What are you doing here? I haven't seen you since forever! Lena, do you have any idea how much I've missed you? I called your house a few years after we last saw each other. Your Mom said you married some guy in the Army and had moved overseas. I told her not to tell you that I called, because I didn't want to interfere in your marriage," he whispered and held me tighter.

Although I knew this wasn't "real" I was thrilled! "I thought you had forgotten about me and went on with your life. When I stopped hearing from you, I didn't know what to think," I replied, holding back the tears.

"Don't you know I could never forget you?" He tilted my face to meet his. We kissed timidly at first exploring each other with soft gentle caresses. He parted my lips with his tongue releasing the passion I had kept pent up for so many years. We remained embraced, for what could have been only mere seconds or as long as an eternity.

He released me only because we were starting to draw attention. He took a step back and said, "You are even more beautiful than I remember. I love your hair. That style really does flatter you."

I blushed as I mouthed, thank you. I looked into Keenan's eyes and felt all those lost years wash away. He was just as I remembered – just a few more lines on his forehead and his hairline had managed to show those tell tale signs of starting to recede.

The smile never left his face as he kissed me once more. "Woman, you sure do taste good. Umm, strawberries and chocolate. My favorite combination."

I thought to myself, Simone said that I am in control and whatever I want to happen, will happen. Keenan looks so good and it's been so long since I felt this way about any man. I think I will just play this out and let it go wherever the feelings take me. I wrapped my arm through his. "Let's go for a walk."

~~~~

Mark rushed home to find me still lying in bed, softly moaning and quietly sighing. He desperately tried to wake me. When he couldn't, he picked up the phone and dialed 911. Minutes later, the ambulance arrived. The EMTs checked my vital signs, determined I was stable and took me to the nearest hospital for observation. He loaded the boys in the car and followed the ambulance.

"But why won't she wake up?" Mark asked the emergency room doctor when he finally returned. "She was fine when I left her this morning."

"I'm sorry Mr. Delgado, but we haven't found anything physically wrong with her. All the tests have come back negative. Of course, we'll keep her here under observation, and we'll continue to run a few more tests. But, as of now, we simply don't know." The doctor shook his head as he relayed the news to Mark.

"I don't know what to tell the boys. They'll be so upset." Mark looked towards the waiting room where the boys sat.

"Just tell them what I've told you. It's best to be honest. Remember, because there is nothing physically wrong with Lena, she could wake up at any time. Now, why don't you take the boys home and get some rest? I'll call you if there is any change." The doctor turned and walked towards the nurse's station providing additional instructions on my care.

Mark returned to the waiting room to speak to the boys. All three jumped up and ran towards Mark. He gently guided them to the sofa and repeated the diagnosis. They sat there looking at Mark for clues about what they should feel.

The first one to speak up was Carlos, the youngest and most precocious child. "Don't worry Dad. Mom is just taking a long nap. You guys know how she's always talking about how tired she is? I know she'll be okay and she'll wake up when she's had enough rest. Let's go see her and tell her to have a good sleep."

Carlos went to Mark and gave him a big bear hug. James and Neil joined in. The four of them walked into my room, kissed me one-by-one, told me they loved me and went home.

~~~~

Keenan and I meandered through the cobblestone streets, passing stores, looking in windows, pausing to speak with shopkeepers about their wares. We came upon a *pasticceria* and went in for a cup of coffee. Stepping inside, we were greeted by the woman behind the counter. I had previously learned a bit of Italian, so I responded that we'd order in a moment. Keenan guided me to a small table towards the back of the shop. Since there were only a few men at the counter, we hoped we would be able to have a private conversation without being disturbed.

"I'll have a *cappuccino* with two sugars, *por favore*," I told the waitress who had come to take our order. "And we'll also have two of your almond pastries."

"I think I'll have a double espresso. I have a feeling that I'm going to need to be as alert as possible this afternoon." He winked at the waitress who returned the favor with a smile.

"Oh, so you think you need caffeine to help you stay awake?"

"No, not just to stay awake, but I want to be alert for everything that's about to happen," he replied in a serious tone, reaching across the table for my hand.

Keenan had a faraway look in his eyes, a look that said there was something he hadn't told me. I'd seen it so many times in the past. I remembered that anything following this look was never easy to handle. I began to feel uneasy. After all, this was my time and whatever I wanted to happen was going to happen without interruptions from anyone--not even Keenan. At least, that's how I understood Simone's explanation.

"Lena, there's something I have to tell you, but I don't know how to begin." He removed his glasses, laying them on the table.

"What is it Keenan?" I was confused. He wasn't supposed to be able to change the course of events I had set in motion. I guess I didn't understand how this thing worked after all. I definitely had to get with Simone later on for an explanation.

"When I saw you sitting at that table, I didn't know what to think or feel. I just know that I've been wandering around lost for the past several days. I thought I had amnesia until I saw you. I'm not even sure where I am or how I got here. The last thing I remember is being in a 26K bike race through Yosemite. I was coming up on the last 5 miles, when all of a sudden I found myself in an airplane full of people. They all seemed happy. Like they were headed off to some great vacation destination. I don't know how I ended up on that plane, or where I was headed. A short time later we landed in Italy. I've been wandering around ever since, trying to figure out what happened. Why Italy? I remember you always wanted to visit Italy. In fact, it's all you ever talked about. So I bought a train ticket and somehow ended up here in *Gorgazzio*. And when I saw you, I just knew everything would be alright." He took a sip of espresso, sat back in the chair and closed his eyes.

As I sat looking at Keenan, I recalled my conversation with Simone that some people get to this "place" through accidents or illness. I assumed Keenan was involved in an accident and that's how he ended up here. But how could our paths have crossed? I thought this was supposed to be my dream. Yeah, I thought about Keenan a lot, but to have him appear like this? I don't think he was here because I "thought him up". If he did have an accident, then how badly was he hurt and how long would he be here?

"Uh, Keenan? I think I know how you got here," I stammered.

"You do?" He opened his eyes.

"Well, it's going to sound really crazy. It did at first for me, too. But, we're not really here, at least not in the way you think we are."

He looked at me like I had suddenly gone nuts. "What are you talking about?"

"Okay, let me try to explain it like it was explained to me. This is going to sound weird, but stick with me for a moment. Sometimes when our bodies get overly tired – you know, stressed out from overworking or when you just need to take a break, apparently, there is this place where our subconscious minds go. Kind of like a spiritual resting place. Well, it's not really a physical place that we go to. It's more of a collective state of mind," I knew how I sounded. I only hoped he wouldn't get up and walk away.

"You mean, like, Heaven? Are you saying that I've died and gone to Heaven? Is that it?" Keenan stood up, looking wildly around the room to confirm his suspicions.

"No, no, no. This isn't Heaven--or Hell or anything like that. This is just a place we go when we need to chill. It's a vacation of the mind for the weary, worn out, and just downright tired folks who are fed up with the bullshit we have to deal with on an everyday basis. Dreaming was how it was explained to me. Whenever we dream, our bodies stay in the physical world while our minds are free to go and project our images to wherever we want. And there is no limit to where or what we can do, as long as we leave our physical bodies behind." I pulled him back down and offered him the almond pastry.

"You're saying that I'm dreaming?"

"Yes and no. It's more than dreaming. During a dream, you pretty much stay here for a few hours and don't really interact with others. You're here, but you're not acutely aware of your existence. When you're dreaming, you think "this" exists only in *your* mind. But it's so much more. Here, you can go, see, and do anything you want without the consequences of having your physical body tied to you. In this world, *you* get to decide how you want your life to go. At first, I thought I brought you here. But, now I realize that you must have had an accident that banged you up pretty badly. But your mind is still active. I think that if you had died, you'd have gone somewhere entirely different. Sweetie, you're here so your body can get its rest and heal properly." I stroked his face.

"Lena, if I'm to believe what you're saying is true, that means that I probably wrecked my bike and I'm lying unconscious in some hospital. How do you know all this?"

"When I first arrived, I didn't know where I was either. I thought I was dreaming my usual dreams. I saw this woman waving at me, so I went over to talk to her. She told me her name was Simone and she was kind of like a "spiritual tour guide". She also said that just by the mere fact that I could see her meant that I'd chosen to stay. I wonder why there was no one there to meet you. Don't worry Keenan. Everything is going to be alright. I promise." I took his hand.

"Not to change the subject, Keenan, but you should see my house! It's everything that I ever dreamed of. Remember that I always talked about living in a small cottage near the beach? Well, here I've got that and much, much more. I know I'm not going to stay forever, so I want to have fun while I am here."

"Your place sounds great. Can't wait to see it. Lena, thanks for the explanation. That explains some of it. I don't know whether to believe this or not, but I guess it's better than the alternative. Hey, why are you here? Were you also in an accident?" He remained skeptical.

"Umm, try some of this pastry. It's delicious," I replied, stalling for time, suddenly feeling very foolish. I didn't want to admit that my life was so dull, I voluntarily chose to stay asleep.

"I know when you're stalling. Did you forget all the years we spent together?" He took the pastry I offered and reached over for another piece.

"No, I didn't forget. All right, I'm here because I just didn't want to get out of bed. I was sick and tired of my life and I just needed to take a break. I know that sounds foolish compared to what's happened to you, but it's the sad truth. My life has become so depressing that the only comfort I find is when I am asleep and dreaming," I looked down, embarrassed how I handled the problems of my everyday life.

"Hey, it's nothing to be ashamed of. Everybody needs a little escape every now and then. I'm just happy that you wanted to see me." He leaned over to kiss my embarrassment away.

"Thanks for understanding. At first, I thought I had conjured you up. But now that I know I don't have total control over you, it might not be quite as fun."

"Don't be so sure about that. You still may have total control over me. You always did before. Now that we're together, let's see what kind of trouble we can get into." Keenan pulled his chair closer. We finished our coffee and fed each other what remained of the pastry.

CHAPTER 3

Leaving the coffee shop, we explored the village of *Gorgazzio*. Somehow, somewhere along his journey, Keenan had picked up a motorcycle. He was always the resourceful one and I never knew him to pass up an opportunity for excitement.

We rode through town slowly making our way towards the beach. It was fun wandering the narrow passageways of the ancient town, zigging and zagging between cars left parked in the street. Young Italian men would throw kisses shouting out, *"Ciao Bella!"* Keenan found their interest in a Black woman fascinating. We stopped at a local food store and picked up a couple of bottles of *Sangiovese* wine, a hunk of smoked gouda cheese, a loaf of hearty Italian bread, packed it all up in the motorcycle saddlebag, and headed the short distance towards the beach.

Sitting on the back of that motorcycle with my arms wrapped around Keenan, feeling the wind on my face, I couldn't believe how happy I was. It was the way I always wanted to feel with Mark, but somehow never seemed to make it there. I could have stayed in that position forever but within minutes, we were at the beach. We dismounted the bike, his hand accidently brushing against my breast. A mischievous grin lit up his face. Well, maybe it wasn't by accident, but I wasn't bothered.

Keenan walked ahead of me. I watched his muscles strain against the fabric of his jeans. He was just as fine as I remembered. Keenan always was a good-looking brother, reminiscent of a young Denzel Washington, the way he looked in *Glory* or *A Soldier's Story*. In fact, whenever I watched any movie with Denzel, I didn't think about Denzel, but instead imagined I was seeing Keenan all over again. Yes, we ladies love us some Denzel, but I figured my chances of ever being with him were about as good as a snowball's chance in hell. So while I may occasionally fantasize about Mr. W., I placed my hopes and dreams where they would most likely come true.

I loved how Keenan kept his hair short and neat. And he must spend a small fortune on skin care products to keep his pecan-colored skin looking so great. He wasn't considerably tall. In fact, at 6'0", he was only a few inches taller than me. There was also something about the way he spoke to women that made them melt and turn into putty in his hands. I knew because I was one of them. He was no player, but Keenan could basically have any woman he wanted. I ran my hands across my soft belly and drooping breasts, wondering if he would want to be with me again.

"Hey Lena, check that out!" He pointed towards the horizon.

I turned to watch a couple of dolphins playing in the water less than 20 feet away. Plumes of water spurted up high from their blowholes as they swam. I watched until I could no longer see them.

"That was amazing!" I gasped, turning to find him staring at me. The look on his face spoke volumes. He pulled me into his embrace. And like a scene from so many sappy movies I've watched in the past, we stood in the water, locked in a kiss as the sun set behind us.

We eventually let each other go and headed back towards the beach, where Keenan had spread out a blanket. Although the day had started out warm, there was now a noticeable chill in the air. As if by magic, the wine we picked up earlier, two wineglasses and a corkscrew mysteriously appeared while I was frolicking in the water. Keenan draped another blanket across my shoulders to ward off the cold.

"You know, a woman could get used to this. You make me feel special—like I'm the most important person in your world." I clamped my teeth together, trying hard to keep them from chattering.

"Still cold, huh? And what do you mean? Why wouldn't I treat you like you're the most important person in the world? After all, didn't you used to say you would only be with a man who treated you like a queen? What about that guy you married? You still with him?" He expertly opened the bottle of wine.

At the mention of marriage, my mood immediately darkened and I lowered my head. Technically I wasn't cheating on Mark, but my heart told me differently. Strange as it may seem though, I didn't feel an ounce of guilt. I wanted to be with Keenan. I always had. My marriage with Mark had long ago ceased to exist, except for on paper.

"Yes, I'm married and still with him, but it's not what I hoped it would be. I think I simply settled when I met Mark. He was a good person and although I wasn't head over heels in love with him, I thought we would be good together. Our marriage was fine in the beginning, but very quickly I realized he wasn't the right man for me. I stayed with him all those years because we were a good team. Not great as husband and wife, but a good team nevertheless. Anyway, I guess I never really got over you. I married him because I couldn't have you."

"Want to talk about it?"

I looked towards the horizon. The sun had almost set. High thin cirrus clouds in colors ranging from red and pink to orange, formed in the deep blue of the western night sky. Sea gulls called to one another as they prepared to settle down for the night. The waves lapped gently against the shore, hypnotizing me with their motions and sounds. Sitting on that beach wrapped in the blanket, drinking wine with Keenan, I couldn't imagine a more perfect moment and I didn't want to ruin it talking about my life with Mark. Unfortunately, this time I wasn't able to push the memories away.

~~~~

My sisters convinced me to go to opening night for an ultra lounge in West St. Louis. The lounge was supposed to be primarily for the "upscale mature crowd", which meant the $20 cover charge with a two drink minimum was supposed to keep the lowlifes away. Can you say *bourgeois*? While my sisters were out getting their flirt on with two men at the bar, I kept vigilance at the table, bypassing numerous attempts to get me on the dance floor. During a lull in the music, I heard some of the women buzzing about a fine brotha who had just walked in.

Mark Andre Delgado was what women referred to as "eye candy". He was the kind of handsome most women fall all over themselves for. Mark stood 6'2" and had the build of an athlete. He was light brown with very keen features and wavy hair he wore shortly cropped to his head. His eyes were so dark they looked almost black, yet his smile could light up a room.

When I first saw Mark, I must admit I was slightly taken aback by his good looks. However, I was still so hung up on Keenan, I glanced at him briefly and turned away. I suppose he thought my behavior so unusual, he took me on as a challenge. What he mistook for "playing hard to get" was actually disinterest. He hovered by my table, persistently asking me to dance. Despite my refusal through four songs, he never gave up. Numerous other women were trying to get his attention, some so shamelessly it was embarrassing, but he turned them all down waiting for me. Finally, just to get him away, I acquiesced. We danced together exclusively for the remainder of the night, much to the other women's chagrin. Mark thought they were too pushy and clingy, which turned him off completely. Before we left the club that night, we exchanged numbers.

I discovered he was in the Army stationed at Ft. Bragg, North Carolina. He was on a month long duty in St. Louis. He and a few of his friends came to the club to check out the nightlife. As far as I was concerned, his being from out of town was not a good sign. The last thing I wanted was to be involved in was another long distance relationship. In spite of my reservations, I agreed to see him the next day. We hit it off and for the month he spent in St. Louis we were practically inseparable. Thoughts of Keenan were pushed to the back of my mind. After Mark returned back to North Carolina, he and I kept in touch via letters and phone calls. He wrote me when he was sent on temporary assignments overseas, detailing the excitement of his travels. Our relationship grew and we started making plans for a future together.

The first year of marriage was good and filled with all the things we spoke of on the phone and in our letters. We took trips on the spur of the moment, stayed in bed all day making love, took long showers together. It was an adjustment getting used to being a soldier's wife, but I persevered. I loved my husband and I believed he loved me. The babies started coming a year after we were married. One after another. And before I knew it we had three sons. I enjoyed being a mother, but didn't too much care for being a military wife.

As the years passed, I became more and more frustrated with the restrictions the Army placed on me. This frustration only fueled the discontent within our marriage. Mark started staying out all night. We argued constantly about not having enough money, raising the kids, my not working, him not helping out more around the house. You name it, we fought over it. We couldn't even have a conversation without it ending in an argument. Pretty soon we stopped speaking to each other all together. At least it was quiet in the house. Despite our strained relationship, on weekends especially, I still wanted him home. But he seemed to prefer hanging with his partners more so than with his family.

Regrettably he started to drink. Mark went through two cases of beer every week. I suspected and accused my husband of being an alcoholic. He always denied it. Told me he drank because I wasn't a good wife.

Ultimately, I came to tolerate his drinking, shielding my sons from his drunken behavior, taking the wheel when we went out to dinner, hiding bottles of liquor. I resorted to pouring bottles of liquor down the drain to avoid his drunken flirtations. I avoided his advances with every viable excuse I could muster. Not knowing what to do, having no control to stop his decline, I stopped drinking entirely. One of us had to be sober - for the children's sake.

Eventually, I turned into "the Bitch" constantly monitoring how much he drank, stopping him from driving with my kids in the car, pulling him out of the car so the neighbors wouldn't see him passed out behind the wheel in the morning.

As soon as my children were old enough to understand that Daddy was passed out drunk and not just sleeping was the time I should have packed our things and left him for good. Why didn't I leave? Why did I continue to put up with his behavior for so long? What made me stay? Why didn't I leave years ago? I asked myself those questions then and I continued to ask those same questions every day of my life. There's no right answer. I suppose it was just easier to stay.

The love I initially felt in my heart for Mark turned cold as ice from the anguish I suffered at his indiscretions. Over time I built up a wall of defense against the pain he put me through. I stopped worrying about him dying in a fiery car crash caused by his own drunken hands. My heart became numb. I no longer trusted him with my love, so I withdrew emotionally. Not only from him, but also from almost everyone else. Yet, I remained. Now look at me, pathetically escaping into myself to find some mystical eternal semblance of happiness.

~~~~

"No, not yet, not here. This feels so perfect. I don't want to spoil the mood." I snuggled closer and pushed all thoughts of my present life back towards the hidden recesses of my mind where they belonged.

We sat quietly on the beach until the stars lit up the night sky. The heat from our bodies, fueled by the wine, kept us warm. We didn't speak because there was no need for words. We were totally comfortable with our silence.

Keenan took my hand in his. There was just enough light from the moon to see his face. He said, "All those years I spent living overseas and traveling the world, I never, ever stopped thinking about you. I never stopped loving you. Lena, you were on my mind every single day. Listen, my job with the FBI kept me so busy… I didn't have time for a social life, much less a personal one. It was so damned hard not being able to be with you so I chose to cut all ties. A few years ago, when I was back in St. Louis on business, I called your Mom's house and asked about you. She told me you had gotten married. I almost – well, I didn't know what to do. I knew you wouldn't wait around for me forever, but to think that you could marry someone else… I've been in several relationships – some serious, but I never found anyone who made me feel the way you did. You know, you ruined me forever being with anyone else!"

"Hey, you're the one who left remember? I know that joining the FBI was a dream come true for you. All you talked about during high school and college was how you were going to join the FBI and become a special agent. You had a plan and knew what you were going to do before graduation. I didn't know what I wanted, that's why I went back to St. Louis. Lord knows I had no intention of staying there, but I didn't have anywhere else to go after college. I ended up staying and found a job at an insurance company. I hated the job, although it paid pretty well. After a while I got sucked back into the drama that comes with living at home. The only thing that kept me going was the letters from you and knowing that you'd be back. When I stopped getting your letters, I eventually started going out. That's when I met Mark. He was home on leave from the Army. One thing led to another and before I realized it, we started dating and he asked me to marry him, so I did." I reached down into the sand, picked up a stone, and tossed it into the ocean.

"I'm sorry for hurting you. I know I can't make up for all those lost years, but let's work with the time we have now. Okay?" He helped me up.

"That sounds like a good idea to me, too." I hesitated slightly. All of a sudden and out of nowhere, I felt a subtle uncomfortable shift in my feelings. Uh oh, that didn't feel right. I had waited for this moment for so long, so why am I experiencing these inklings of doubt? I supposed it's normal to feel uncertain after all these years. Well, I am not going to blow my chance of getting to know him again. After all, who knows what will happen in the future? I dismissed the feelings as quickly as they came. Further down the beach, someone was having a party.

Faint strains of music filtered through on the currents of the breeze. We both heard it at the same time. It had a funky reggae beat. The music became louder and seemed clearer. I wanted to dance, although I hadn't danced in a long time. I thought I had forgotten how. But watching Keenan's hips move to the beat, I fell in place right alongside him. We laughed and danced until we no longer heard the music. Afterwards, we swayed a sensual slow dance to a song only the two of us could hear.

With my head resting against his chest, I spoke aloud a poem that swirled in my head:

Who is the girl dancing on the beach?
Nothing but a cool breeze covers her skin.
The soft light from the full moon
and the sound of the waves crashing against the shore
are her only companions.
Not a care in the world.

Now there are few free moments in the day,
cookies to bake, floors to scrub, stories to read,
laundry to hang outside on the line, awaits.
Suddenly a breeze as quiet as a whisper brushes against her cheek.

Images of a young girl dancing on the beach slowly return.
Memories long lost and slowly forgotten.
The girl dancing on the beach was once me.

"You know you can bring back that girl hiding inside of you. It's not too late. C'mon, I think it's time for us to go." Keenan's voice grew husky, as he attempted to hide his arousal.

"Yeah, it's getting pretty chilly." I wanted nothing more than to jump on top of him and get back what was mine so many years ago, but instead I helped put away the blankets and pick up the trash.

I gave Keenan directions to my cottage. It was only a few miles up the shore. He had no trouble finding my place, as I had described it hundreds of times in the past. He parked the bike near the front door.

"C'mon in. I want to show you around."

He "oohed and aahed" in all the appropriate spots. We ended up in the living room. I showed him the stereo and the CD's. Pulling off my still damp sweater still feeling chilled to the bone, I headed for the bathroom to take a hot shower.

Twenty minutes later, I stepped out to hear one of my favorite jazz guitarists, Jonathan Butler, playing in the background. I hummed along as I applied fragrant Victoria's Secret lotion, jelled back my short fro, put on a little bit of makeup and stepped into a pair of silk pajamas. I quickly rechecked my reflection in the mirror before I went back to the living room. Not bad, if I do say so myself. Keenan was scanning my book collection, which ranged from Maya Angelou's *I know why the caged bird sings*, to several off the wall Dean Koontz novels, to Nathan McCall's autobiography, *Makes me wanna holler*.

"My, my, my, don't you look and smell fresh and clean? Uh, well, I think it's time for me to go 'cause if I don't I may just do something we both may regret."

"You are not going anywhere except into that bathroom to freshen up. I left a clean towel on the rack and there's a pair of sweats for you on the bed." I nudged him towards the bedroom, ignoring his last comment.

"Thanks, I really appreciate the offer, but I think it's best if I leave…"

"You have no place to go. Remember? And it's no trouble with you staying here. There's a guesthouse out back if you don't feel comfortable spending the night inside. I want you to stay. Please?"

"Okay, okay. You win. I'll be out in a sec." He gave me a quick peck on the cheek and headed towards the bedroom for the master bath.

Damn! He even walks like Denzel! "Lord, please help me resist the temptation that's been placed in front of me," I silently prayed. I turned up the volume, lit several candles, and fell into the rhythmic sounds of *fourplay*.

I went to the kitchen for a glass of water. As I passed the window, I saw the shadow of a woman approaching the cottage from the back yard.

"Hello! Can I help you?" I yelled out the back door into the darkness.

"Lena, it's me, Simone. Just stopping by to see how you're doing and if there's anything you need." She continued towards me.

29

"Oh Simone! I've got the most wonderful news. You'll never guess who I ran into today!" I met her halfway up the walk.

"I don't suppose it's a long lost love coming to take you home, is it?" She smirked.

"Of course, you know! Well, to be perfectly honest, I don't understand how this is supposed to work. I mean, I haven't seen Keenan in over 20 years, yet it feels like we were never apart. Is he part of this fantasy or is he real? He doesn't know why he's here. We assume he was in an accident like you told me about earlier. He said he's been wandering around lost," I attempted to explain, despite my own lasting confusion.

"I see," Simone replied, "usually, I am able to meet everyone when they first arrive, but sometimes it takes days to find them, especially the injured. They are often confused and are always on the go trying to make sense out of the situation. I see he's found you though?"

"Yes, he has. Or I've found him. Either way, I'm extremely happy, yet sad, both at the same time. Does that make sense? How do I know that this is real and not part of this crazy dream I'm having?" I looked back at the cottage.

"Honey, this is more real than real. You two have found each other's soul. Your subconscious minds have bonded in spite of the physical distance between your bodies. This doesn't happen too often, where two close friends are in the same metaphysical state at the same time, but trust me when I say that you did not bring him here. Somehow your paths have crossed. Is it fate? Possibly. But he is no more in control of you than you are of him. You still have your free will to do as you please. This is your time, but now he is a part of it. As long as you allow him into your reality and he permits you in his, you two can do whatever it is you choose to," Simone explained.

"You're saying I didn't bring him into this "world"? You mean I'm really interacting with him? This is wonderful!" I reached out and hugged the bearer of good news.

"Yes, it can be wonderful. Be very careful, sister. Although you are not physically together, it will feel like you are. Every emotion is authentic. When you reach out to touch Keenan, it will be flesh you feel. When you eat, you will have the full experience and sensation of eating. And when you make love… well, I'll let you complete that thought on your own. However, you must always remember that when you leave here, you will have to deal with the consequences of your actions. Do you understand what I'm telling you?"

"Yes, I do. I will be careful. I know I'm not going to stay here forever, but Simone, I've got to tell you, I let him get away once, I don't know if I can do it again... I do know one thing though; this is going to be one helluva good time for me."

I heard Keenan calling my name. Because Simone was already here, I asked her to meet and explain the situation to him. She agreed, following me back to the kitchen. I entered through the back door. Simone trailed a few steps behind.

"Hey, where did you go? I thought you ran out on me," he joked.

"Uh, Keenan, I have someone I want you to meet." I motioned towards Simone and said, "This is Simone. She's the woman I told you about earlier. My uh "tour guide". She has a few things to cover with you. I'll be outside if you need me."

I left them alone in the cottage. Through the window, I watched Keenan nod his head as she explained. He looked out towards me occasionally rubbing his face. It was the same gesture I'd seen him do years ago when he worked on difficult trigonometry problems. I nervously wrung my hands as I kept watch on the back door waiting for either one to come out. There was a good chance that he wouldn't accept her explanation. Keenan was a levelheaded man who didn't believe in things he couldn't explain.

Several more minutes passed. They moved from the kitchen and were no longer in my sight. If he didn't believe her, he could return at any time to his physical body and I may never see him again. I promptly realized I had no clue where he lived. Hell, I didn't know if he even lived in California! All I knew was, he was in a bike race at Yosemite National Park when he had his accident.

Finally, the back door opened and Simone stepped out on the deck. She stretched her arms out towards me. I immediately got up, alarmed at what she was about to say. I stepped into her embrace, preparing myself for the shock that was about to follow.

"Honey, you have got a very strong-willed man there. I explained his current situation. I don't think I totally reached him, but that's all right. He has the strength and the courage to see things on his own. I told him if he needs me, to just call. That goes for both of you. He spoke about what you meant to him – then and now. I must admit it's been a long, long time since I've seen love this strong. Remember that you two have to be careful with how you handle this. Keep in mind this "reality" is only temporary and eventually one of you will have to leave." She stroked my hair as she spoke, "I'm going to leave now, but I'll be back to check on you. This is your time to be free and do what is in your heart – that is what this place is about. And like the song says, 'don't worry, be happy'!"

She released me, looked me squarely in the eyes and asked, "Lena, do you still love this man?"

So many years have passed by. Too much of life has gotten in the way. "Honestly, I really don't know if I still do or not. I think so. But I gotta admit, earlier this evening I felt inklings of doubt. Well, not necessarily about him, but the feelings I have carried all this time."

She nodded, accepting my reply, then turned and walked away. The cool breeze chilled the tears on my cheeks. I had been crying. Looking towards the cottage, I saw Keenan headed in my direction. Thankfully, he was smiling.

"Okay, I admit I don't understand everything, but I'm willing to give it a try. It just sounds so…" he muttered, shaking his head in bewilderment.

"Weird, strange, whacked out, kind of like being in a drug induced stupor?" I finished his sentence, managing to gain my own composure.

"Exactly! I feel like I've entered the *Twilight Zone* and can't wake up. Simone told me some pretty wild stuff. Lena, I'm an FBI agent. How am I supposed to believe that I've entered into some metaphysical alternate dimension that exists mostly in my mind?"

"I don't know. I'm not even sure I believe it myself. I know I'm not dreaming. My dreams are realistic, but none have ever been this real. Look, we're standing here having a conversation like we could anywhere on this planet. According to Simone, the only thing *real* about this whole situation exists within our subconscious minds. We've constructed all the rest of this through our wishes and desires. Yet, as I stand here before you I can touch you. You feel my touch. How is it possible? I don't know. I do know there are things in this world that can't be explained and maybe this is one of them. You're not from my imagination, nor am I from yours. We're as real as we want to be, and can do whatever it is our hearts desire. I say let's go for it and enjoy the time we have together. Some things are just meant to be enjoyed – not understood."

"You want to just go for it? Let our minds be as free as our spirits will allow? Okay. How about we seal this with a kiss?" he asked.

"I thought you'd never ask," I replied.

CHAPTER 4

"Hey, where do you think you're going?" I blocked the door.

"It's probably not a good idea for me to spend the night. Besides, I'm beat. It's been a very long day, Lena." He yawned.

"That's exactly why you should stay. We're both grown folk--*tired* grown folk. All kidding aside, I'd love for you to stay and I don't want to be alone tonight."

"Are you sure? It's not a problem for me spending the night out there. On the other hand, I wouldn't mind holding you all night long. I promise I'll be a gentleman."

"C'mon in. I might even promise to be a lady." I patted him on his butt as walked through the door.

We ended up in the bedroom. Having him so close was torture. I'll admit that the temptation to do more than sleep was very strong, but in the end, sleep won out. Disrobing down to our underwear, we slipped under the down comforter and held each other tight. We kissed and said our good nights. I must have gone asleep first because I didn't hear anything after my head hit the pillow.

The sounds of barking dogs and the brightness of the morning sun streaming through the window awakened me. I reached over for Keenan. He wasn't there. I retrieved the cotton robe I wore yesterday and slipped it on. A magnificent sight greeted me as I walked into the kitchen. Keenan was already up and dressed. Damn, he could even make an old pair of jeans look good! He was in the midst of preparing freshly squeezed orange juice made from oranges picked from the trees in the back yard. He stood over an electric juicer, holding the power cord in his hand, searching for an outlet.

"Good morning, beautiful. How did you sleep?" He kissed me fully, morning breath and all.

"Well, good morning yourself! You sure are full of energy! When did you have time to pick oranges?"

"I've been up for a couple of hours. I'm an early riser, remember? How about some breakfast? I can whip us up a really mean omelet." He was all smiles as he removed veggies and cheese from the fridge.

"You mean *you're* going to cook our breakfast?" I asked.

"Of course, but you can help if it'll make you feel better," he teased.

I almost lost it right then and there. In my house, the only ones who cooked in the morning – or evening for that matter, were the older boys and me. Mark fixed breakfast only on special occasions, like Mother's Day, and it was never a for real cooked breakfast. Although he was more than capable, he never went through the trouble of preparing an actual meal. I always felt he didn't care enough to spend the time doing anything special like that. He considered cooking to be woman's work. Taking all of that into account, Keenan cooking breakfast felt extra nice and special. I gave him a full body hug. Oh my, he felt good! Strong, yet gentle—smelling like soap and freshly cut oranges.

"I'm so happy you're here! Let me freshen up a bit and I'll be right back to help," I kissed him and ran to the bathroom to get rid of my morning breath.

"That was fast. You must really be hungry. All right then, what would you like in your omelet? I can make western, Denver, veggie, lite...? Your choice." Practiced hands went about cracking eggs into a dish. A chopping board with vegetables and a tray filled with ham and cheeses sat on the counter.

"They all sound great. Surprise me. Now, what can I do to help?" I picked up a paring knife.

"You can put down that knife and go pour yourself a cup of coffee. It's your day to be waited on. You are a queen and I intend to thoroughly treat you like one. Today is your day, sweetheart."

This time the tears came not from sadness, but from joy. I had always heard of people crying because they were so happy. I didn't think it was possible, but there I stood smiling with tears streaming down my face. Damn! All this drama over a simple breakfast! Not knowing what to say, I didn't say anything. Keenan handed me a mug of steaming hot coffee. Using the sleeve of my robe, I wiped the tears away. Happily content, I pulled a stool up to the counter and watched as his expertly deft hands assembled a western omelet with all the fixings.

"My mother taught me how to cook. She always told me and my brothers to never depend on a woman to fix our food or wash our clothes. All men should be able to take care of themselves." He smiled at the thought of her. Although his Mom was still alive, he mentioned that he hadn't seen her in years.

Keenan placed a plate filled with an overstuffed omelet, two flaky hot biscuits and golden hash browns in front of me. A pitcher filled with the orange juice he squeezed earlier, sat on the opposite counter. I poured two glasses. He motioned for me to go ahead and eat while he prepared an omelet for himself. The food was as beautiful as it was delicious. Minutes later, he joined me at the counter. We fed each other off one another's plate. Laughing and enjoying our breakfast, we planned our day.

The village of *Gorgazzio* was in the midst of its annual Spring Solstice Festival. It was held to celebrate the end of winter and the beginning of spring. For centuries, Italian villagers decorated their homes and businesses in brightly colored fabrics and freshly cut flowers to celebrate their good fortune and encourage the success of their crops. And although the town no longer relied purely on agriculture for its survival, the festival had become a long anticipated tradition. Most agreed it was really just another excuse for a party, which the Italians were so famous for, and somewhat similar to Venice's annual *Carnavale* celebration.

A parade to launch the celebration weaved through the town's center spreading cheer to all. Colorfully clothed caricatures, representing the patron Saint of the Crops, threw candy into the crowds of children gathered to watch. Loud music blaring from speakers mounted on streetlamps helped to make the atmosphere even more festive. Clowns on stilts, boys riding tiny unicycles, and dancing girls dressed in skimpy outfits, helped to entertain the crowd. It was truly a sight to behold.

We made our way through the growing crowd to a refreshment stand located in a large parking lot. I bought two bottles of *San Pelligrino naturale* water from an old man working behind the counter. The old man winked and gave me a toothless grin as I paid him with 2 euro coins. An ancient looking woman, most likely his wife, shoved him playfully and said something meant to be shared by only the two of them. As I looked on, the old man pecked his wife on the cheek and she immediately blushed. Not wanting to intrude any longer on their personal moment, I turned and went to where Keenan stood.

"Did you see those two? It is so sweet to see people their age still in love." Why can't it be like that for me? I thought to myself.

Thoughts of my marriage entered my mind, temporarily bringing down my mood.

~~~~

Mark and I hadn't been affectionate with each other for so long. In fact, we behaved more like roommates than husband and wife. We kissed only to say 'hello' or 'goodbye' and then it wasn't really kissing. Our lovemaking had become infrequent. Truth be told, it was almost nonexistent. It's not that we didn't have the desire, it's just that we didn't desire each other. And any attempt at conversations usually ended in an argument.

Eventually, after years of watching Oprah and reading dozens of self-help books, I decided my opinion really did matter and should be heard. Unfortunately, too many years had passed and the damage was already done. Now, whenever I voiced an opinion different from his, he dismissed my ideas as ridiculous, leading to constant arguments. Although I wasn't physically abused, I was emotionally exhausted. I knew the marriage was over, yet I continued to stay.

~~~~

"Thanks for the water. C'mon, there's a couple of empty seats over there." Keenan pointed to two chairs set up facing the band. "Let's get them before someone else does."

We made our way to the chairs and sat down just as the group made its way to the stage. The crowd grew quiet as the MC welcomed everyone and introduced the band. We didn't stay in our seats very long after they began to play all my favorite songs from the 80's. They were really good. No, better than good. They were excellent! The crowd thought so too, because once the music started, all the chairs were pushed aside to make room for the dancers.

We had a great time bumping and grinding to both fast and slow songs. I even danced with a couple of really cute local Italian guys. Those guys could dance their asses off! I must have danced four or five fast dances before I had to take a break.

During a break between songs and in between their incessant flirting, they introduced themselves as Lucio and Giovanni. They invited both Keenan and I to a party at a local pub later that night. I told them we'd try to make it. After I received two sweaty double-cheeked kisses, they grabbed a couple of women from the crowd and began partying with them.

"Wow! That was too much fun! Thanks for letting me dance with them. Those guys could really move!" I wiped the sweat from my brow.

"Hey, no problem. And I didn't *let* you do anything. You wanted to dance and they wanted to dance with you. It's not a problem at all. In fact, it gave me a chance to check out your moves from a different angle. Baby! You sure do have the moves!" He attempted to check me out from head to toe.

"Oh stop it!" I teased and gently guided him back towards the dancing crowd. "You know you're the only one I really want to dance with. Listen. They're playing our song."

"I'm listening, but I don't recognize the music. You did say this was our song, didn't you?"

"Well, to tell you the truth, I don't know what song this is. I just wanted to get close to you. I think dancing is just an excuse to snuggle and get close out in public."

Swaying to the music, he lowered his arms around my waist. I reached up and hugged him close, snuggling my head to his chest. We danced the remainder of the slow set, feeling the heat from each other, becoming intoxicated with the promise of what was yet to come.

"Lena? Lena, sorry babe, I have to go somewhere for a little while," Keenan whispered in my ear after checking his watch. He touched his delicious lips to my face.

"Go? Where are you going? I thought we were going to spend all day together?" I started to panic, but the look in his eyes told me everything was alright.

"I just need to take care of a few things before I see you tonight. That's all. Don't worry. I'm not going anywhere. Stay here and have a good time. I'll pick you up from your place around eight. Is that ok?" he asked, looking like he had something mysterious on his mind and up his sleeve.

"Yeah, sure. If you need to go… I'll be fine. Since it's still early, I think I'll go shopping. I'll catch the train to *Pordenone* and be back before you know it. I need a new outfit anyway, especially if we go to that club tonight." The old Lena might have panicked at the thought of being left alone, but of course there was no need to be afraid. Keenan took me in his arms again kissing me long and slow, leaving me lightheaded when he finally pulled away.

"8 o'clock," he repeated as he turned and walked away. Within moments he was gone from my sight.

Several minutes passed before I realized I was still staring in the direction from which he disappeared. People danced all around me, moving to the deep beat of the drummer's frenzied rhythm. Suddenly, the youthful crowd formed long lines for the electric slide. Dozens joined in. Feet stomping, hands clapping to the beat, and dancers of all ages soon filled the square with their hypnotic movements. Anyone who hadn't or didn't know the steps also jumped in. I was amazed that even the Italians did this universal dance.

When I could dance no more, I walked the short few blocks to the *Vivaro* train station and purchased a round trip ticket for the 25-minute trip to the town of *Pordenone*. The train wasn't scheduled to arrive for another 30 minutes. To pass the time, I bought a Coke from the machine and took a seat on a nice shady bench to wait.

Sooner than expected, I boarded the train and found an empty seat. I lost all track of time as the countryside passed by much too quickly. The rhythmic motion of the high speed train was soothing and I must have dozed off. Before I realized it, the train pulled into the *Pordenone* station and began picking up more passengers. I hopped off mere seconds before the conductor yelled out to clear the doors. I checked the departure schedule to confirm how long I had to shop. I flagged down a taxi.

"*De dove, Signorina?*" asked the taxi driver.

"Please take me to the town center near the shopping district," I replied in broken Italian. I sat back and enjoyed the ride listening to one of Italy's most famous tenors, Andrea Bocelli, sing one of his famous ballads. The driver occasionally joined in with a "not too shabby" rendition of his own. After a short drive, we arrived in town and he stopped at the entrance to the shopping area. No cars or mopeds were allowed past this point, only shoppers and bicyclists. I paid the driver and set out to find the sexiest outfit possible. I headed directly to my favorite clothing store.

"*Ciao* Lena. Girlfriend, I haven't seen you in years. Where ya been?! I thought you moved back to the states!" Cristina and I clicked instantly the first time we met. Her father was a Black American and her mother a local Italian. Although her parent's marriage didn't survive the cultural differences, Cristina managed to merge both cultures into one of her own. Though she was a biracial woman, she had the "bones" of a very healthy sistah. According to all who knew her, God took the best from both her parents and packaged it all in a gorgeous long, lean – yet curvy body. Cristina was blessed with brains as well as beauty.

As a college graduation gift, her maternal grandparents purchased this boutique and offered it to her to manage until she decided what she wanted to do with her life. She lived on the money earned from the shop and took modeling jobs on the side to supplement her income. Her dream was to be a fashion designer and from the look of her current line of clothes, she was going to be very successful.

"What's up Cristina?" The day was turning up one surprise after another. I was actually speaking and interacting with Cristina. This whole scene was becoming stranger by the moment. I was going to definitely have to get with Simone. I thought I was in control of this "reality", but maybe I was only in control of me.

"Don't tell me you came all the way back to Italia to visit my boutique?" She teased.

"Girl, you have no idea! I couldn't find any decent outfits in Kansas – all the clothes look the same. Boring! You know you spoiled me with all your wonderful designs. When I first got back to the states, everyone wanted to know where I shopped. When I told them I bought all my clothes in Italy, they just thought I was bragging."

I loved the personal attention I received while shopping in her store. She picked out outfits and coordinated separates that flattered my body and emphasized all my best assets. Cristina appreciated having Americans shop in her store and encouraged me to bring in more friends to experience "real" Italian designs – not the pseudo Italian labels being sold in the base clothing exchange.

"Come. I will show you my latest fashion designs," she said.

I followed Cristina towards the back of the store and spent the next two hours trying on different outfits. Like old friends, we laughed at each other's clothing mistakes and indiscretions made while we were younger and into fashion fads.

I tried on a very nice, sexy looking dress Cristina had designed particularly with me in mind. I tried it on and it fit perfectly – hugging in all the right places. I bought the dress, a casual pantsuit, and a super sexy two-piece skirt set, that showed off the legs I worked so hard to maintain.

I thanked Cristina, paid her and left with my new outfits in hand. A couple of hours remained until I had to catch the train to head back. I needed to get my hair done before my date. I still had time.

Being so close to Africa, Italy was a natural destination for African immigrants traveling across the European continent. Many arrived as tourists, decided they liked the laid back Italian lifestyle and decided to stick around a while. Others came illegally, in search of a better life than the one they left behind.

Nevertheless, I was incredibly surprised to discover that there was a large African population living in Italy. The disheartening realization was most of the work they could find was purely in the service sector. Many worked as hotel maids or laborers. Sadly, all too many of the younger women were prostitutes.

In larger cities, you could always find groups of young men working on the streets selling everything imaginable to passing tourists. Their wares were typically laid out on a cloth to make it easier to scoop up when the police came by. It was very easy to spot the tax dodgers for they all carried large black bags, slung across their backs. I used to think they were very enterprising men selling all kinds of knick knacks – that is until I found out they worked for unscrupulous Italian businessman who sponsored them to Italy. To pay off the "sponsorship" debt they had to work the streets selling crappy merchandise to unsuspecting tourists. The vast majority of them had to work several years to pay off this debt. Those who couldn't or wouldn't put up with the crap returned to their homeland, more broke than ever.

I walked the short distance to the beauty shop, *Somalia's Finest*. Ojuma, the owner, was a lovely woman from Somalia. She met and married an Italian man who was on holiday in her country. He saw her and immediately fell "head over heels" in love. And despite objections from both families, they got married and he moved her to Italy to live in a true to life Italian villa.

Ojuma was from a proud, affluent family. Her father was a high-ranking, important diplomat in the Somalian government and he did not want his oldest daughter to marry a foreigner and move away. However, with quiet grace and persuasion, she managed to convince her parents that she was in love and wanted to leave. Her father agreed with only one stipulation that if she ever felt unhappy, she should immediately call him and he would send for her. Ten years had gone by, two children had come and yet she never made the call.

Ojuma specialized in natural African hairstyles. She believed Black women should emphasize their natural God given beauty and not emulate other cultures. Although her Somalian heritage gave her long, wavy, black hair she did not encourage others to have hair like hers. She made all who entered her shop feel beautiful by the time they left. Ojuma possessed a charm that made everyone comfortable. She was fluent not only in Kiswahili and Italian, but also spoke English in the dialect of a proper British aristocrat.

I was happy to see the shop was still there and even more so that it was open. I opened the door and shouted out *Ciao* loud enough for them to hear from the back room.

"Lena, it is so nice to see you again! Please come in and have a seat." She motioned for her assistant to bring tea.

I saw that the shop was empty except for the three of us.

She noticed me noticing and replied, "Business has been very slow. It seems that the women prefer to use the chemicals to straighten their hair again. Not too many want the natural hair anymore. Most of my clients seem to be Italian teenagers who watch too many American videos. They want to have the hair that looks like the black rappers on MTV," Ojuma sighed then snickered when she saw my reaction.

I hung my new clothes on a coat tree near the door, and sat down at a small table with Ojuma. I heard her assistant preparing tea in the next room. Ceremonial masks hung alongside sketches from local artists depicting historic Italian landmarks. Fragrant smoke emanating from sandalwood incense perched on a bookshelf, curled up towards the ceiling. This was the most relaxing place I'd ever been in my life to get my hair "did".

A younger version of Ojuma walked in the room, balancing a tray filled with all the fixings for a proper cup of tea. She sat the tray down and quickly returned to the back room. It was only after Ojuma motioned for me to drink my tea, did I speak.

"It is so good to see you! And I actually did go back to the states. It's just that I missed beautiful Italy so much that I couldn't really get it out of my system. I never imagined I would miss living here, but I do. You remember all those times I came in here bitchin' and groanin' about how some local treated me? Well, after I moved back to the United States and had a chance to visit my parents and then move to Kansas, I decided you all weren't any worse than my fellow Americans.

I learned to appreciate your passion and love of life." I drank in the warmth of the hot liquid. Umm, it was good.

"Yes, I understand what it feels like to live outside your country. I too miss the ways of my country. It's the small things – the way the wind always blew, leaving a thin layer of dust on everything, no matter how often I dusted," she smiled wistfully, "I miss going to the market and seeing the women dressed in magnificently colored clothing, shopping for food while keeping the children in line. But most of all I miss my family... Oh, what am I saying? Of course, my family with my husband Daniele and my children. I am blessed, truly I am. You know Lena, I see pictures on the television showing how poor my people are. How so many of them are now starving and dying in the streets. I ask myself, what can I do? I am not rich. I am not a leader of men. So once a month I send a few hundred Euros back to my parents to help buy food for the people in my village. It's not much, but it's something. Imagine how many we could help if we all chose to do this." Ojuma stopped speaking and took a drink of her tea, trying to calm the fire that had built up deep inside her within those few moments.

I didn't know what to say, so I said nothing. I let the awkwardness of the moment collapse upon itself, until it was as transparent as the incensed smoke filtering up towards the open window. There was no way I could know the feelings she spoke of. I heard the despair in her voice give way to acceptance. This is how things are and there was nothing she could do to change otherwise. She had to somehow console herself by hoping the money she sent home actually helped to feed the hungry. After I drained my cup, I watched Ojuma drink her tea and eat the fruit filled pastry the girl brought out.

"Well, that's enough about me. Here I am just going on and on about inconsequential things. You came to get your hair fixed up. C'mon over here to my chair and let me take a closer look. It sure has grown. Lena, are you all right? You've barely said a word since you've arrived."

"Yes, I guess... I'm fine," I replied in an emotionally charged voice I didn't recognize as my own. And then ever so gradually, the tears came. There were no gut wrenching sobs, just quiet tears that ran down my cheeks, dropping from my face to hands folded in my lap. I didn't know why I was crying, but it felt good--like something that needed to be done without prompting. Ojuma came and stood above me, gently holding my head, as the tears found a new home on her native dress. I have got to get a grip on myself, I thought. I am in a place where the whole purpose is to make me happy. Yet, why do I continue to feel so sad?

"Ojuma, I feel so lost. I have no place to call home and I feel like I don't belong anywhere. My marriage is a joke… I hate my job and I have no real friends. I go through each and every day wondering how I ended up where I am. This isn't how it was supposed to be. I was supposed to be a happily married, successful career woman raising my children, maintaining a house and loving my man with a passion so strong no one or nothing could break us up. Instead, I ended up in a mediocre marriage. In debt up to my ears. Working in a job I can't stand and living in a city where I don't want to be! How did I end up like this?! The only good thing that's happened lately in my life is having my kids. And even they sometimes drive me crazy!" I exhaled and continued, "My husband feels more like a stranger to me than my man and he treats me even worse. Do you know what it's like to be married to someone you're not in love with? It's worse than horrible."

I continued, "You spoke of what you missed about home? Well, at least you can go back. I feel like a visitor when I go home. I don't connect with anyone in my family. I'm like a stranger looking through a distorted window. The people I grew up with – I don't know them anymore. I've been away for much too long and I can't relate to their ways of living. When I talk about my lifestyle and the places I've been, they look at me like I'm some sort of bourgeois freak! It's my life and I can't even talk to my family about it! What am I supposed to do? Pretend that I've never done anything or been anywhere? My world has gotten so much bigger and there is nothing I can do about it. I try to fit in, but they know it's all an act."

Ojuma listened, nodding in appropriate places, holding my hand when needed.

"The problems I have are more closely associated with being "white". I don't have the Black melodrama relating to who's having whose baby, who lost their job and had to go on welfare. And I don't have a house full of grown assed kids living under my roof using up everything that I have! You know Ojuma, my family only sees my big house, the nice cars I drive and the things I am able to give to my kids. They assume I have it made. They don't see how lonely and unhappy I really am. I'm living a lie and feel like such a fraud!" I took the napkin she handed me and wiped the tears from my eyes. Once I'd gotten all that emotion out of my system, I actually felt better.

"You know, it is true that we all have our own pains and sorrows. Everybody has a story. Unfortunately, we tend to believe that all the world's unhappiness is reserved only for our individual suffering. We all suffer in one way or another, and who is to say that my pain is any greater than yours or vice versa? I'm sorry to hear of the turmoil you have within your family. You must always remember that they are your family and even when you think you're alone, you're not. They recognize how traveling the world has changed you. It is inevitable that those experiences would reshape your life. I know you've heard the expression that a rolling stone gathers no moss.... Well, you are like that stone – always moving and gaining new experiences. I know that you don't think you're better than anyone and I'm certain they know it also. Lena, you've got to stop beating yourself up for what's happened in the past. Don't you know that nothing happens by chance? You are part of a link in God's master plan." Ojuma pulled up a chair directly opposite me.

"How did you get to be so smart?" I laughed, looking at the woman who couldn't have been more than 5 years older than me.

"It's not that I'm any smarter than you are. It's just that my heart is open to accept the lessons that life has to teach me. Lena, I know why you're here. I freely admit I don't totally understand it, but I accept the fact that you are sitting here drinking tea and having a conversation with me. I guess this is some strange "time paradox" kind of situation. I've read about it in some of my father's science journals, but never in a million years could I imagine that it was possible."

"But, b-b-but, how do you know?" I stuttered.

"Well, your friend Simone stopped by. I thought she was just another customer needing to have her locs tightened… We started to talk. I knew she wasn't from around here. She had a mystical, ethereal aura. She eventually told me the purpose of her visit was to prepare me for your arrival. She said do not be frightened. You are neither a ghost nor spirit. I admit I thought she was some crazy woman who wandered in. All that talk about being in two places at once… But Simone made me believe. She explained how it could happen and that it has happened more often than any of us would imagine. When you showed up, I knew it was true. My little sister is frightened. She thinks you came from beyond. It's all right. She just needs a little extra time to sort this out in her mind. After all, how often does one hear of someone's spiritual body traveling through an alternate dimension to get to my real one? It does sound a bit strange." Ojuma chuckled at the absurdity of it all.

So that's who the girl was – Ojuma's sister! I thought she was a servant because she quickly disappeared in the back room shortly after I arrived. No wonder she didn't sit down and have tea with us. She was afraid! This whole people interaction thing was becoming more confusing as time went on. This was supposed to be my fantasy, not me walking around scaring people out of their minds, having them think that I was some kind of spirit or something. On the other hand, I must admit, the girl did have a point!

"Yeah, it does sound crazy. I don't really understand why I'm here. I just know that I'm going to take advantage of all the freedom this time brings." I looked at my watch. It was already past 4.

Ojuma saw me take notice of the time and began clearing the dishes from the table. She motioned for me to follow her to the backroom to the shampoo sink. I leaned back in the chair, laying my head on the hard molded plastic sink. She tested the water and when it was the perfect temperature, she began spraying the warmth through my tangled roots. Wow! That felt good! She gently worked a tropical scented shampoo through my hair, followed it up with conditioner, and sat me under the dryer.

While the conditioner worked its magic, I watched the young woman walk out of the back room. Ojuma spoke to her, pointing in my direction. I could see the look of fright in her eyes as she stole glances at me. Eventually the girl found the courage to gently touch my hand. I guess she wanted to make sure I was real and not a ghost. When she was satisfied that I wasn't going to dissolve into nothing, she smiled timidly and retreated to the room from whence she came.

The timer on the dryer went off and Ojuma directed me to the sink for a rinse. I sat up awkwardly while she wrapped a warm towel around my head. I held unto the towel and followed her to the so called "chair of magic". She nicknamed it that because she insisted that she could work magic on her client's hair and give them exactly the style they wanted. I just needed a trim to keep my short looking stylish. There was nothing I hated worse than seeing someone sport an unkempt nappy looking afro.

I recently started seeing a few sisters sporting a new texturized look and thought I'd eventually go to that. Ojuma was really the only beautician I'd ever known who didn't like to chit chat while she worked. After asking her client her styling preferences, she only spoke when she had a question concerning the hair. She worked in total concentration to get the best results. She handled those clippers, combs and scissors like the true professional she really was. After 20 minutes of cutting, trimming and lining my "kitchen", she finished off with a cloud of hair spray. She gave me the mirror to check out her work. As usual, she did me proud.

I admired the way my short hair framed my face, causing my cheekbones to prominently display both the Native American and African heritage I gained from both sides of my family. Yes, my cheekbones. They were the bane of my existence until I turned 18. Unexpectedly, I began to receive comments from men and women alike on how beautiful they were. I started to appreciate what some women tried to gain from implants and makeup.

But like every other sister friend I grew up with, I was a slave to the relaxer. I tried relaxers with lye, those that promised no-lye and others that practically lied to my face. From the tender age of 12, I sought out hairdressers in an effort to get the straight, breezy hair displayed on the beautiful stick thin models. Me and every sister I knew thought nothing of spending our entire Saturday in the beauty salon. It was a tortuous ritual all black women endured. In my search for the straight look, the chemicals caused my hair to become dry and brittle and break off by the handful, despite all the moisturizing and hot oil treatments. My scalp itched constantly from the styling products I used in an effort to keep my hair fly. And I'm not going to even mention how expensive it was! Just like having another utility bill!

One day I just got sick and tired of all the chemicals and went to the nearest barbershop and told the barber to cut it all off. He asked me if I was all right and if I was sure I wanted to do this. I told him that I was never surer of anything in my life. I remember the first time Mark saw me with hair this short. You would've thought I cut off my right breast with the way he reacted. Said I didn't look like a real woman anymore and that women shouldn't cut their hair because it made them look too masculine. Months went by before he would even touch me, much less make love to me. I think he only gave in because he was too horny to hold out any longer.

"Oh, my hair looks so good! Thank you Ojuma for everything." I gave her a hug. It was then that I noticed the time. I had to be at the station by 6 to catch the next train. I pulled out a € 20 euro note and told her to keep the change.

"Well, you are most certainly welcome. Lena, whatever you decide to do, I really hope he's worth it…" she said with a knowing smile on her face.

"Yes, he's definitely worth it." I picked up my new clothes and started for the door.

"Lena, I know you're still probably feeling a bit lost with everything that's happening, but just remember to listen to your heart.

Only you really know what is best for you. Now go before you miss your train." She shooed me towards the door.

Just as I was about to leave, the young girl rushed out from the back room and hugged me. She placed a flower behind my ear and said in Italian, "Until we meet again…"

I stepped into the rushing crowd of people. And through the glass door, I waved good-bye to my friend. I was sorry I had to leave. And yet so happy I stopped by.

CHAPTER 5

The taxi arrived at the station just as the train was pulling in. I validated my ticket. In less than an hour I was back at the *Vivaro* station, wondering how I was going to get to my cottage. It wasn't that far, only a couple of miles, but it was starting to get dark. I wasn't looking forward to walking home alone on the dark, narrow streets. I decided that a taxi was my best bet to get home not only safely, but also in a reasonable amount of time. After all, I had my date with Keenan to get ready for.

As I walked towards the bicycle rack, a motorcycle zoomed up out of nowhere and scared me. I was prepared to give the asshole a piece of my mind. The driver took off his helmet. It was Keenan.

"You need a ride?" He shouted over the roar of his engine, showing that gorgeous smile I'd fallen for each and every time.

I quickly recovered and responded, "Well, I've got to get home to change for a hot date. How soon can you get me there? I don't want to keep him waiting."

"Oh, I'm sure he won't mind waiting, especially for you" He produced a spare helmet.

I pulled the helmet over my head and straddled the motorcycle. His scent was intoxicating and drove me wild. I threw my new clothes over one arm, rested my face on his back, and held on as we drove off into the twilight. A short while later and before I wanted to let go, we pulled up to my cottage. He turned off the engine and held the motorcycle upright so I could dismount. He followed me to the door.

"Are you hungry? I haven't eaten since this morning and my stomach feels like it's touching up against my back." Keenan wiped his dirty boots on the door mat.

"Yes, I guess I am. I've been so busy that I'd forgotten all about food. But now that you mention it, my stomach is starting to speak to me." My stomach growled on cue loud enough for both us to hear.

"Ok. I hear ya," he laughed. "I'll wait here while you freshen up. And by the way, I like your hair."

"Thanks for noticing." I touched my hair, trying to smooth it back into place. I carried my outfits into my bedroom trying to decide on what to wear.

"Hey, Keenan?" I shouted towards the living room. After a few moments passed with no response, I went out the back door looking for him. He held a glass of wine and was standing on the deck, looking out towards the ocean. I went to him.

"It's beautiful, isn't it? Look at how the moon reflects off the water." I didn't know if he was talking to me or making a comment to himself.

"Are you okay?" I asked, gently touching his arm.

"I went back there today."

"You went back where, Keenan?"

"You know when we were at the town square and I told you I had something to do? Well, I saw Simone in the crowd and decided I had to find out what was really going on. I went back to see if what she said was true – you know, about me not being here by choice. She led me to some little old hotel and told me I was going to take a short nap. She said that once I awoke back in the real world, it would be my decision if I returned. I don't know if she hypnotized me or what. The next thing I knew, I was laying up in some hospital bed back in California. My parents were there and so were some of my friends. It was wild and very strange, but I wasn't afraid," Keenan replied, fascinated.

"What happened that brought you here?"

"From what I could make out – the docs had given me lots of sedatives to knock me out so I wasn't too coherent, I found out I was hit by a car when I was in that bike race. I'm actually in pretty bad shape. Lots of broken bones… I've been in a coma for days. They weren't sure I'd wake up at all. My Mom was pretty shaken up and it tore me up to see her like that. Anyway, they called the doctor to the room because I finally came to. The funny thing was, I kept fading in and out, but I heard everything they said. The doctor told my family that I was still in critical condition, but because I had regained consciousness, chances were very good that I was going to pull through." He relayed, matter-of-factly.

"Oh Keenan. I'm so sorry. It must have been awful." I used my sleeve to wipe away the lone tear that slid down his cheek.

"Before I went back, Simone told me that I had a choice about returning. I could stay there with my family or I could come back to you in this "alternate reality world". I chose to come back to be with you. I whispered to my Mom that I was going to be fine and that I was going to sleep for a little while longer. I told her not to worry."

He continued, "The last thing I remember is her kissing my forehead. When I awoke, I was in that hotel room all by myself." He took a sip of wine and looked at me like he was seeing me for the first time. He sat the wine glass on the rail.

"Are you saying that you came back to be with me?" I was frightened anyone could care so much about me. Amazed that he still cared at all.

"That's *exactly* what I'm saying. I let you get away once. I'm not going to let that happen again. I love you, Lena. I always have."

There were no words that could express how I felt. I'd never felt more love from anyone than I did at that very moment. With joy spilling from my heart, I sank into his arms in an embrace that could carry me from one lifetime to another.

Keenan kissed me fully and I returned the kiss with a fervor I didn't know I possessed. Our breathing deepened and I could feel his heart pounding against my chest. He pulled back and gazed deep into my eyes. I knew that look. The years hadn't changed us that much. I felt all the old familiar feelings rushing back.

His mouth found mine once again. The rush of adrenaline I felt as our skin touched was almost worth the many years of waiting. He kissed my neck, my shoulders and his hands found each breast. I moaned in pleasure and arched my back as he gripped me around my waist. I removed his glasses and placed them on the counter. We quickly undressed each other. His erection bobbed up and down as he moved. I couldn't stand it any longer. I had to have him inside me.

He was an expert lover who took his time. There was no need to rush and he made sure I was more than ready to receive him. He laid me back on the bed and lightly planted kisses on my stomach, down my thighs and ended up at my feet. He kissed the soles of my feet and placed each toe in his mouth, one-by-one, sucking each toe along the way. This drove me absolutely wild because no man had ever sucked my toes. It was an exquisite feeling. I came with such intensity, even I was surprised. He then proceeded to make his way back up again, tonguing me along the way until he made his way between my legs. He licked away my nectar and began to tease me with his tongue. I looked at him as I moaned in pleasure.

Keenan smiled at me and continued on his quest. I came again in his mouth. I pulled him towards me and kissed him fully, tasting my own aromatic honey. I writhed in pleasure trying to get him inside me.

Finally, he entered me, moaning as he did. He began stroking me, telling me how much he missed me. How much he loved me. And after neither of us could hold back any longer, we came together in an explosive orgasm.

"Baby, you still knows how to get me there. I can't remember the last time I felt this good. And I must've come at least three times," I whispered, caressing his back as he rested on top of me. Some unknown feeling stirred inside of me and I felt a little uneasy. Maybe it was guilt. After all I was still married to Mark, even if this episode was only happening only in my head.

"Lena, with you, for you, I do this out of love. I want you to feel good and be happy. You deserve it and so do I." He rolled over, kissed me and quickly fell asleep.

I smiled in spite of myself. Yes, he was just a man after all. I watched him quietly snore, content in the knowledge that he'd just given me an experience I so badly needed.

After a quick nap, we decided to go to a local family restaurant, *Abrezzo's,* for a delicious home cooked Italian meal. The owners were an older couple who immigrated north shortly after WWII, opening the restaurant at a time when the country was desperately trying to establish itself in a new Europe. They were extremely successful and had managed to send their two children to England's prestigious Oxford University.

"Baby, just wait until you try the food there. I know you're not crazy about Italian food, but this will be like nothing you've ever had before." I led him to the garage where I kept a fully customized, metallic silver Porsche Turbo.

"Is this yours?! Girl, you really are living large!" He lovingly stroked the car with one hand and held out the other for the keys.

"Hey, if I'm gonna dream, I might as well dream large. Right? I suppose you want to drive it now, huh?" I handed him the keys.

Keenan acted just like any other man in this situation. He sat there listening to the purr of the engine, fiddling with the dashboard. It was only after he turned every knob and pushed every button that we finally drove off. And when we did, I felt like I was in the Indy 500 with the way he drove – hugging every corner, going way too fast.

I felt the wind on my face as we sped through the night, and the one thought that crossed my mind, other than crashing, was it was a good thing I had short hair. He was having fun and I enjoyed watching him.

"When I get back home, I want a car just like this! Now I know why race car drivers love their job! Thanks for letting me take it for a spin." He leaned over and kissed my cheek.

"You are more than welcome. Maybe we can take a longer driver tomorrow…"

"That sounds like a plan. Now, let's go have some of this delicious food you've been raving about!" Keenan turned off the car and helped me out.

Surprisingly, Mrs. Abrezzo recognized me instantly. She whispered something to the waiter that made him smile and caused her to shake her head whispering, "Tsk, tsk, tsk". I didn't think about what it looked like for her to see me with another man.

After we were seated, I explained to Keenan what had just happened. He thought it was kind of funny. The waiter brought bottled water and breadsticks. He winked at me and smiled at Keenan, like he knew some deep dark secret. All the while, Mrs. Abrezzo kept watching us, shaking her head, muttering something under her breath. We ignored the obvious and looked over the menu, although I already knew what I wanted.

"You seem to be really popular. Look, they're looking at you like you're some kind of movie star," Keenan teased.

"Snap! I didn't expect this. I've been in here so many times with Mark and the boys that I didn't think about what it would look like coming in here with you. Look at us! There is no way that I could pretend you are someone other than who you are. Anyone can tell what you mean to me by the way I look at you. We practically send out sparks every time we touch." I peered over my menu at Keenan, sitting across the table only a couple of feet away. He was still smiling, but not at me. It was directed at Mrs. Abrezzo. She started walking towards us.

"*Buona sera, Signora.* How have you been? You certainly look lovely tonight. Who is your new friend? Where are the *bambini*?" she asked and looked at Keenan, wasting no time in putting her nose all up in my business.

"*Buona sera, Signora* Abrezzo. I am well, thank you. This is my friend Keenan. I brought him here to try some of the best Italian cooking in all of Italy. I told him that not only is the food delicious, but the service is excellent as well," I replied, returning my gaze back to the menu.

"I see. Well, he certainly is a handsome fellow and I can see his eyes are only for you, *Signora. Alora!* I will take your order and you will have a nice romantic meal. You do make a nice couple, if I do admit it to myself. Many years ago, when I was a much younger woman, there was this beautiful young man who lived in the next village…" With a faraway look in her eyes, her tone softened. She took a book of matches from her apron pocket and lit the candle as she spoke. Before she could get too deep into her story, the waiter, who I soon discovered was also her grandson, came over and tapped her arm.

"*Nonna*, please don't tell that story again. Come, I will take the order while you help Papa in the kitchen." He guided his grandmother away and started to apologize profusely for her behavior. She swatted his hand away, muttering in Italian all the way back to the kitchen.

"It's all right, really it is. I've come here many times before and this is the first time she has said anything more than "Hello" to me," I told the waiter.

"She means no harm and she is a good woman who believes deeply in romance. When she sees a couple so much in love, she automatically reminisces about her own life when she was younger. If I let her go on, you would be here all night without your dinner. Now, what can I get for you?"

"Lena, why don't you order for the both of us, 'cause I have no idea where to even begin. It all looks so good."

I suggested we start off with *caprisce,* a delicious tomato and mozzarella appetizer, followed by *spaghetti all'amatriciana* for Keenan and a pumpkin ravioli dish called *ravioli di zucca* for me. The main course was veal served in a delicate mushroom sauce, followed by potato croquettes and buttered spinach. We also ordered a bottle of their local red wine with the meal.

"Very good choices, Signora. I will be back with your *primo corso* in *uno momento.*"

The very cute, but also very young waiter returned to the kitchen to place our order. Within minutes he returned with the appetizer and a bottle of wine.

"I think I'm jealous. Did you notice the way Mrs. Abrezzo kept looking at you? Old girl was practically drooling! Can't say I blame her though. You are so… Ummm, yummy!"

"Well, like she said, 'my eyes are only for you.' Hey, did I tell you how sexy you look tonight? If I didn't, I'm telling you now. Girl, when I think about our little escapade back at the cottage…"

"You're not the only one who's worn out. But then again, I feel like I have more energy now than I've had in years. Look, here comes the first course. I hope you're hungry!"

After dinner we were both sufficiently full, but not stuffed. We finished off our meals with *tiramisu* and coffee. The Abrezzo's said their goodbyes and wished us good luck as we headed out the door into the humid night. Mrs. Abrezzo had gotten over any ill feelings she had for me when we first arrived.

"That was the best meal I can honestly say I have ever eaten! That veal was so tender I could cut it with my fork. And the pasta… I think I could eat like this for the rest of my life." Keenan rubbed his stomach, signifying contentment.

"See, I told you it was good food. And *Signora* Abrezzo was a trip. She had me cracking up when she started going all into her "remember when" days. But you know what? They are really cool people. Not at all like what I expected. All I knew about Italians was how they were portrayed in the movies from when I was younger. According to *those* movies, they didn't too much care for us Black folks. But you know what? They're not at all like the *Sopranos*, *Goodfellas* or *The Godfather* or involved with the *Mafia*. I was afraid I was going to be treated like dirt. I've got to admit, I haven't been treated badly at all. They know you're not Italian and aren't trying to take anything away from them, so why bother treating you like scum when you come to their country? It's not like living in the United States where it's so territorial and every group is segregated inside their own little neighborhoods. I can just be me when I'm overseas," I replied feeling my arms break out in goose bumps, despite the warmth of the night air.

"Yeah, I know what you mean. Overseas, they see you as an American first before they see your race. In the past, when I visited foreign countries, I kept expecting to be treated as I had in the states. Now don't get me wrong, there will always be those ignorant folks who will treat you badly because they think they are better than anyone, but for the most part, I've been treated fairly well. Of course, my being an FBI agent may have had something to do with it." He winked and magically produced a single red rose.

"Oh, this is so sweet! Thank you." I leaned over to smell the flower. We simultaneously looked up when we heard the screeching tires of a car that turned much too quickly into the parking lot. It was a cherry red Ferrari. We both jumped back with surprise.

Through the open window, I recognized the driver as Lucio, whom we had met earlier in the day. A beautiful young woman with dark olive skin, almond shaped brown eyes and shoulder length black hair rode in the passenger seat.

"*Ciao Bella y Signori!*" Lucio happily sang out. He stopped the car just feet away from where we stood. Strains of American rap music, heavy on the bass, blared from his stereo. He lowered the volume and turned to his companion stroking her cheek, saying something meant only for her to hear. She glanced at us with indifference before dropping her head to focus on her manicure, all the while bopping her head to the music. He opened the door and got out to speak with us.

"*Ciao Lucio. Come va?* Where is Giovanni?" I asked, noticing that he was way too fine in his black leather pants and silk shirt. Although his body was of slender build, he was very muscular. Layers of dark wavy hair hung loosely framing his face. His mustache and goatee were groomed to perfection and whatever cologne he was wearing was simply intoxicating. On top of everything else, the bulge in his pants was just enough to distract me from Keenan, who obviously noticed that I was checking him out. I heard Keenan clearing his throat. I looked up to see him smirking at me. Lucio also saw where my eyes had gone, but he was too much of a gentleman to comment.

"He is at the club waiting for you—his dancing partner. I was on my way there when I saw the two of you standing here. Have you eaten yet? This is my Uncle's restaurant and my Aunt is a wonderful cook." Lucio beamed and winked.

"Yes, we did have dinner and it was very delicious. Your Uncle owns this restaurant? I'm sure business is excellent. Who is your friend?" Keenan asked returning his arm to my waist, rather possessively.

"*Si,* my family is very successful in many businesses. *Alora,* how about it? Are you coming to the party? I'm sure my friends would love to meet the beautiful, sexy American who dances so well." Lucio leaned back on his car and crossed his arms as if he owned the world.

I know he didn't just wink at me! I couldn't believe this man was standing there flirting with me right in front of Keenan, who I knew was pissed, because his arm gripped a tad bit too tight around my waist. I was almost ashamed to admit that I loved it. Here I was with two gorgeous men and they both wanted *me*. All the years of feeling ugly and undesirable melted away. I felt like I did when I was a single woman. Before I became married and fell into the grind of being a boring housewife.

Before I could answer, Keenan asked again, "Lucio, who is your friend? She looks a little, uh restless."

"Oh, that's just Maria. She needed a ride and I was happy to oblige a friend. Well, if you all decide to come party with us this is the address. I promise you will have lots of fun and excitement." He retrieved a business card from the car's console and handed it towards Keenan.

I took the card when Keenan didn't reach for it. Ignoring the intentional slight, Lucio returned to his car and drove off into the night.

"What was all that about, Lena?" Keenan was visibly angry — which both surprised and fascinated me.

"What was what all about?" I played innocent, secretly enjoying his jealousy.

"You know what I'm talking about. Why were you flirting with him and checking his package acting like you haven't seen some pretty Italian boy before?"

"I'm sorry Keenan. It's just been so long since anyone paid me that much attention. Of course, other than you. I just wanted to enjoy it for a little while. But you know you got my heart. Don't you?"

"Yeah, sure. But dude was all up in your stuff like I wasn't even standing here. I don't mind guys paying my lady a compliment, but I don't like it when they disrespect me," he said forcibly.

Keenan just called me his lady. I honestly didn't know how I felt about that. On one hand, this is exactly what I've always wanted—to be his lady. But, then again, it was exciting to talk and flirt with another man. The episode I went through with "Mr. Italian Stallion" made me rethink everything. Did I want to be with Keenan exclusively or was I ready to play the field? And what was this saying about me?

For as long as I could remember, I've been fantasizing about Keenan, imagining a life with him instead of Mark. I made him out to be the perfect man, but he was a man after all… Now, I wasn't so sure about this lifelong obsession that I'd kept going all these years.

"What's going through that head of yours? You look like you're a million miles away," he asked, back to his normal self.

"Oh, nothing", I replied, "I was just thinking how much I missed you and how much I enjoy being with you, that's all." Most of it was true.

"What's up? Do you want to go show these locals how to really get down? Or we can find some quiet little secluded area and get down on our own," Keenan whispered, nibbling at my ear lobe.

My knees went weak and if he weren't holding me up, I might have fallen. His hot moist lips on my ear, the warmth of his breath on my neck, and the smell of jasmine in the night air. Whew! What a sensation. I felt him grow erect against my thigh.

"Ooh, that feels so good!" I said huskily. And if we were any other place than standing in the middle of a restaurant parking lot, my decision would have been a whole lot easier to make. I reluctantly pulled back when I noticed other customers coming from the restaurant.

CHAPTER 6

Keenan agreed to go to the party only because I wanted to go. Part of my reason, although I wasn't willing to admit it even to myself, was I wanted to see Lucio again. I don't know why or how, but he stirred something in me that hadn't been awakened in a long time. Keenan would have preferred to spend a quiet evening alone with me, instead of in a club full of sweaty people dancing to what he called "euro trash music".

The party was held in a local pub named *Busco's*. It looked deceptively small from the outside. It was the typical bar setup. There were several booths and tables available for those wanting to have food with their drinks. Customers lined the bar, vying for the attention of the bartender while waitresses made their way through the crowds, expertly balancing trays of drinks without spilling a drop. The DJ sat high above the dance floor in a plexiglas booth, spinning vinyl records and popping in CDs as quickly as he could. In between songs, he'd get the crowd either pumped up or slowed down. He played a funky mixture of European techno house music and also a few popular American hits.

"Would you like something to drink, Lena?" Keenan had to practically shout, despite his being less than a foot away.

"Sure, I'll take a *rossa* beer," I yelled back, looking around the room for Lucio.

"One *rossa* beer coming right up," Keenan replied.

I scanned the crowd. I saw Maria, the woman who was in the car with Lucio, leaning against the wall looking just as bored as she had earlier. Giovanni was on the dance floor dancing with a very attractive woman in a manner reminiscent of the brothas back home. He stopped dancing and pushed his way through the crowd towards me.

"Welcome to *Busco's*. I am so happy that you have come to my club," he said in a heavily accented voice. Then, as is the custom, he took me by the arms and kissed me on both cheeks.

My mind immediately went into overdrive. Up close this man could have been a model, not your typical feminine "pretty boy", gay looking model, but a buttoned down shirt, jeans wearing macho "manly man" type model. Was it possible that he was even more handsome than Lucio?

He stood as tall as me. He wore his wavy black hair very short and brushed back from his face. Looking more closely, I noticed his eyes were dark green interspersed with gold flecks. Giovanni was one of those men who looked like he needed another shave five minutes later. Underneath the beard's shadow, his skin was a smooth, deep olive complexion which probably reflected a southern Italian heritage. Fashionably dressed, he wore stylish black slacks that accentuated his muscular body. A dark blue silk shirt, buttoned down only enough to reveal the hint of a hairy chest, completed the image of a sexy, yet confident man. Looking at him, I guessed him to be in his mid to late 30s. Yes, I was physically attracted to Giovanni. Like a moth to a flame, I was drawn to him.

"Well, you can thank Lucio when you see him. He's the one who talked me into coming. By the way, where is he?" I tried to be cool and hoped he didn't notice me staring.

"Oh, my brother? I never know where he is or what he's doing from one moment to the next. Did you come here alone?" He stepped closer and took my hand in his.

"You and Lucio are brothers? I should've known!" I didn't try to conceal my surprise. No wonder I felt such a strong attraction to them both, although with Giovanni it was even more intense. I think we both felt a mutual attraction. It was at that moment Keenan returned, holding two beers. He looked at me, slightly confused.

"Lena, are you alright?" he asked, handing me a beer.

"Yeah, I'm fine. Keenan, you remember Giovanni. We met him and Lucio earlier today. It turns out they are brothers and this is their club." I quickly let go of Giovanni's hand and took my beer from Keenan.

"Good to see you again, my friend. Yes, we are brothers and co-owners of this club. Lucio should be around here somewhere. *Scusa*, Lena, I must get back to make rounds with my customers. If there is anything you need, please tell Nicky, the bartender, to call for me. *Va bene,* for you both, drinks are on the house." He shook hands with Keenan and secretly slipped his business card into my hand before he walked away.

Without looking at the card, I slipped it into my purse when Keenan had his head turned. I felt simultaneously guilty and excited. Why was I sneaking some man's card into my purse? I didn't even know him. For all I knew, he indiscriminately passed his number out to all the women in the club. I looked at Keenan and suggested we dance.

He agreed. We placed our half full glasses of beer on the nearest table and made our way to the floor. After a few house songs, the DJ spun some slow jams that we easily "bumped and grinded" along with. I was feeling pretty good and had all but forgotten about Lucio when he appeared out of nowhere and politely asked Keenan if he could cut in. Keenan agreed and told me he'd wait for me near the front.

"I meant to tell you how beautiful you look tonight, *Signora*. When I saw you in the parking lot earlier, I wanted to pull you in the car with me and drive away."

With one fluid motion, Lucio placed his arms around my waist, pulled me to him and smoothly spun me around the dance floor. I asked, "But what would you have done with Maria? I really don't think she would've liked me sitting on her lap." I played along, enjoying his moves. I let him effortlessly guide me around the dance floor.

"Maria is just a friend. She cares about nothing except how she looks. She's all look and no substance. Unlike you, I can see there is much to learn."

"And with you as well, I didn't know you and Giovanni were brothers and that you both own this club." We stood face to face, momentarily gazing into each other's eyes.

"Giovanni? Ah, he works much too hard. I keep telling him that he should be more like me. It is not good to work so much, one must have fun also."

As if on cue, Giovanni stepped in and asked Lucio to walk the floor. I looked over to where Keenan was and saw that he was talking to Maria. He seemed to be all right, so I continued to dance. Just then, the DJ played a beautiful ballad. I suspected Giovanni specifically requested it, as he sang along in a fine voice befitting of a singer. He could really sing!

"That's a beautiful song. Who sings it?" I asked after he finished the last verse.

"That was Andrea Bocelli singing *Con Te Partiro*. You like?"

"Oh, yeah. I could listen to him sing to me all night long!" I became nervous all over again.

"*Bella* Lena, how long are you planning on vacationing in *Italia*?"

"Uh, I'm not sure. Why?" I stammered, unable to find my voice. Aware of how nervous I was, he smoothly maneuvered me through the crowd to a quieter, more private part of the dance floor.

"I would like to take you places that tourists do not know of, and show you the real *Italia* in all its splendid glory. Did you read the card I gave you?" He looked at me with such intensity – the golden flecks in his eyes standing out--almost glowing. He seemed to see right through me.

"I'm sorry Giovanni. I came with my friend Keenan and it would've been very rude for me to flaunt your card. Besides, you've probably given your business card to hundreds of women."

"It is true that I give out my business card to many, but you should know that you are the only one that I have given my home phone number. You see, in my business I meet many, many beautiful women, but until I met you, none of them managed to get my attention the way you have. After meeting you this afternoon, I prayed you would come tonight and offer me the opportunity to see you again. There is something very special about you I cannot place my finger on," he whispered the last sentence so softly, I barely heard him above the music.

"You speak English very well. A lot better than I speak Italian. But, I think your brother is also trying to "get with me". Is this some kind of game you two are playing? Trying to see who can get the Black American?" I was slightly annoyed.

"No, no, no! This is not a game. I do not play games. I am much too busy to bother with silly games. I think you are very special and I would really like to get to know you better. When you have time and we can really talk openly, please call the number on the back of the card. I see your friend is coming this way, and I prefer to not have any trouble in my club. *Bella donna*, I will await your phone call." He gingerly kissed me and walked away.

"What was that all about? Did I just see him kiss you?!" Keenan asked perplexed, with a hint of anger in his voice.

"It was nothing. Don't worry about it. He is just one of those typical Italian men always trying to see how many women they can get," I hoped I sounded convincing despite the butterflies fluttering in my stomach. "C'mon let's go somewhere else." I eased him towards the front of the club. As we made our way through the crowd, I noticed Giovanni standing behind the bar looking my way. He raised his glass to me and I briefly smiled at the gesture.

After pushing through the pumped up crowd of dancing, drunk partiers, we finally made our way outside. It was like stepping into a fog. The club must have been sound proofed because you could just barely hear the music when the doors were closed. I took a deep breath and watched Keenan stare off into the distance. Neither one of us spoke. He reached for my hand and brought it to his lips, where he planted a kiss. He started to say something, but decided against it. I didn't know what to say either. I was torn between needing to feel the comfort of his arms around me and wanting to explore the possibilities that were offered this evening. I needn't have worried because Keenan made the decision for both of us.

"Lena, you know I love you. I've always loved you." He tenderly put his finger against my lips to quiet me. "Please let me finish while I still can. I've been watching you all night and I understand why these guys want to get with you. I'd be a fool to think I'm the only man here who finds you attractive, but that's not the reason I'm upset. Like I said, I've been watching you and I see how much you enjoy being with Lucio and Giovanni. I can see it on your face whenever you're near them. The way your face lit up when you first saw me – well, you have the same expression when you look at them, especially Giovanni. And when I saw him slip you his number and you didn't mention it to me… Look, I'm not going to stand in your way. But, I want you to remember this, if you don't know what you're looking for you'll never find it. I'm going to take off for a while and give you some breathing room. When you decide what you want, I'll be around. Just don't take too long."

Keenan bent over, kissed me on the cheek, handed me my car keys and walked away into the night. He left me standing there in front of *Busco's* with my mouth hanging wide open. In total disbelief.

How did he know about Giovanni slipping me his phone number? I guess the man was more observant than I thought. After all he did work for the FBI. Now what was I going to do? I wanted to run after Keenan, but the possibility of being with Giovanni was too powerful to simply disregard.

As I watched him walk away, I questioned the obsession I held for all those years. In my mind, I made him out to be the ultimate man. I imagined him to be the perfect lover, the perfect husband - the perfect everything. Now, don't get me wrong. Keenan was a sweetheart and a truly wonderful man. Any woman in her right mind would want him. Problem was, I didn't know if I was truly in love *with* him or just the thought of him.

When I married Mark, all I could think of was Keenan each and every day of my life. Right or wrong, I compared my husband to the image I built up of my first real love. It was an image that no one could live up to. I finally realized the improbability of my obsession.

Keenan stopped walking, looked over his shoulder to see if I followed and continued on when I didn't move. I couldn't move. My feet were glued to the ground with indecision. At that moment, the door of the club opened releasing music of *Destiny's Child* out into the night. A young drunken couple, holding on to each other stumbled past – laughing and kissing, making their way down the street towards another pub. I watched their awkward stroll until they turned the corner and were no longer in my sight. I turned back towards the club when I heard my name.

"Lena, Lena?" Giovanni held the door open and peeked out, probably checking for signs of Keenan.

"Hey, Giovanni, I'm over here!" I felt my heartbeat pick up its pace at the sound of his saying my name. I looked to where Keenan stood last. He was nowhere to be seen.

"Are you alright, *Signora*? Where is your friend?" He stepped out into the night and stood beside me still looking around. Away from the crowd, his voice was rich, deep and velvety smooth. He spoke in a measured controlled manner, unlike his energy filled younger brother.

"I'm fine. Thanks. Keenan had a few things to do so he took off. Shouldn't you be inside, making sure nothing gets out of hand?" I asked.

"No, nothing will happen because tonight is a special night."

"What's so special about tonight?" I wondered aloud.

"Tonight is special because you are here." He smiled, showing dimpled cheeks I hadn't noticed before and continued. "Now that your friend has left you all alone, what will you do?"

"I don't know. I suppose I'll go home and just chill out. Maybe read a book or watch an old movie…"

"I have a better idea. Let me take you to my family's villa up in the mountains. It is about a three hour drive from here. If we leave now we can make it before sunrise. I promise you shall have a wonderful time." Giovanni seemed genuinely excited.

"To the mountains? I don't know Giovanni. We just met! I can't go away with a man I just met! Anyway, that's such a long drive. Aren't you tired?" The possibility of being with him was thrilling. It was true that I didn't know anything about him, but somehow that fact ceased to matter. I scanned the darkness wondering if Keenan was still around. Not seeing him made it easier to say yes.

"No worries, Lena. We can stop by your place and you can change clothes before we leave. Do not worry about me. I am typically up late every night working in the club. I am neither a rapist, nor murderer. I promise to treat you only with respect. Please say yes."

The warmth of his hands traveled throughout my body. All the excuses I would have given in my previous life flashed through my mind. It was late. I was tired. I had to work the next day. I didn't know him. All the excuses went out the window when I decided to take a chance and go for it. "Yes, Giovanni, I'll go with you."

"Good. I promise you won't regret this, Lena. I'll be back in *uno momento*." He quickly stepped back inside. Within minutes he was back holding a black leather jacket and his car keys.

"Whoa, that was quick." I followed him to a sapphire black BMW Z4 M Roadster. "That's what I call a beautiful car!"

"I'm sorry. I needed to let Lucio know where I'll be in case of emergencies. By the way, you look really beautiful tonight. *Alora*. Are you ready?" He opened the passenger door to let me in.

"Sure, I'm as ready as I'll ever be. Thanks for inviting me! I'm sure we're going to have a great time. Oh, and I love your car!" I sank into the luxuriousness of the Z4. He closed the door after me. I was relieved he hadn't tried to kiss me. I don't think I was ready for that. Not yet anyway.

Giovanni slipped into the driver's seat, buckled up and put on a CD filled with mellow jazz music. We took off.

As we drove away, I failed to notice Keenan standing in the shadows of a doorway. He stood back watching it all.

"Damn it Lena! What the fuck?! Do I mean nothing to you? It was only today you said you loved me!" Hurt, confused, and angry he left to find Simone. He had to get the hell out of there.

CHAPTER 7

Giovanni and I arrived at my cottage minutes later. Keenan's motorcycle was parked where he left it earlier in the evening. Feelings of guilt washed over me as I went in the bedroom to change my clothes. Giovanni said he'd wait in his car because I told him I would only be a few minutes. Evidence of this afternoon's delight remained tangled in the sheets of the unmade bed. I walked past trying hard not to look in its direction and went to the bathroom closet. Pushing aside any remnant of guilt that remained, I changed my shoes, stuffed a pair of jeans, a T-shirt and a sundress into a small duffel bag and ran out the door to start my adventure with the gorgeous Giovanni.

I must have fallen asleep because when I opened my eyes, we were parked in a clearing and the sun was just beginning to rise. Although I felt kinda groggy, I woke up enough to smooth down my hair, wipe the sleep from my eyes and pop a piece of gum in my mouth to freshen my stale breath. All this was done in the span of time it took for him to come around and open my door.

"It's beautiful!" I whispered, stepping out of the car to get a better view. Majestic mountains, blanketed in green grass with a sprinkling of yellow and blue wildflowers, bordered the valley. I looked towards the eastern sky and observed the sun was beginning to rise. I took a deep breath and inhaled the fresh cool morning air. Giovanni stood beside me. Watching. Smiling. Although there was still a slight chill to the morning air, I felt the beginnings of the sun's warmth on my face.

"You like *Signora*?"

"Yes, yes, I do like! I like it very much! Thank you so much for bringing me here. I've never seen anything so beautiful in all my life. Being up here makes me feel closer to God. Listen. Can you hear the angels singing? Well, I know it's not really angels, but the way the wind whistles through the grass, it sounds like how I imagine angels' voices would sound."

"I suppose it does sound a little like voices. Look, see that village down there? That is where I was born and raised. I used to ride my bicycle here when I wanted to get away from my family. This village has stood for hundreds of years through the ravages of war and the sands of time. My parents still live in the house where my Papa was born. He and my mother raised three children there." Giovanni spoke with the pride and passion of a person who knew his own roots. It was not a feeling I could identify with.

As I looked down at the small village, listening to him speak about his family, a feeling of sadness overwhelmed me. I'd never felt that close to my family and I didn't know anything about my history.

"Lena, what is wrong. Are you alright?" he asked in a gentle voice.

"I just can't get over how lovely it is. Absolutely breathtaking!" I accepted his touch, but I didn't want to bring up my family background. Not yet. I was afraid my telling would break the magical mood of the moment.

"If you think this is wonderful, just wait until I take you down to the village and then you will see how magnificent the mountains really are."

He started back for the car. I followed, marveling at the beauty in nature so many of us take for granted. It was the beginning of Spring and I could tell it was going to turn into a perfect day. I felt the temperature slowly rise, as we descended the mountain to the town of *Piano Montissimo*.

Clearly you would have thought Giovanni was a celebrity the way people came up and greeted him. Within the first few minutes, we must have stopped to say hello at least 10 times. Each time he introduced me, I was greeted with affection and warmth. A couple of the local women eyed me suspiciously, probably wondering what I was doing with their native son, but none of them were outright rude.

At the *pasticerria*, I excused myself to the bathroom to freshen up. If I was going to meet this man's family, I wanted to look halfway decent.

When I returned, I found a more mature, grayer version of Giovanni sitting beside his son. They were deep in animated conversation. Both stood and reached for my chair simultaneously. They laughed and I joined in. Like father, like son. We all sat down for coffee.

"Lena, this is my Papa. Can you believe he knew we were here moments after we arrived? That is one bad thing about small villages, everyone knows what you're doing even before you do," he laughed shaking his head.

"I'm very pleased to meet you, *Signore*, uh…" Only then did I realize I didn't know Giovanni's last name. I think we were both a bit surprised how little we knew about one another. After all, we only had the briefest of conversations in the club before leaving. My falling asleep during the drive left no time for details.

"What? This guy no tells to you his surname?" His Papa faked indignation and added, "*per favore* call me Papa Morelli. Our last name is Morelli, from generations before me. But I digress… Lena is a *bella Italiana* name. Do you have Italian family who give you such beautiful name?"

"No, I don't believe I have any Italian relatives. I think my Mother liked the way it sounded and it stuck," I replied, enjoying talking to him, although he spoke very broken English. I appreciated his making the effort to make me feel welcome.

"Ah, is okay. You are still *molta bella. Va bene, mangia* – eat!" Papa Morelli pointed to the pastries the waitress brought. He got up from the table, shook his son's hand, and said something to him in Italian. He then tipped his hat at me as he walked out the door to talk to his friends gathered out front.

"I think he likes you, Lena. He says you look like a beautiful African goddess and you remind him of his great *nonna* from Morocco."

"Wow, I'm learning more about you by the minute!" He wasn't so different looking than some of the brothers I dated in the past. His skin was just a couple of shades lighter than mine and his features were more Mediterranean than European. However, it was his eyes that mesmerized me most. I've often heard that the eyes are the windows to the soul and looking into his eyes I felt I could trust this man with my life.

As if reading my mind, he replied, "Listening to you, I can see you have many, many troubles in your life and you're not sure which path to take. But for today, when we are together, I promise I will show you things you have never seen before. I want you to simply enjoy being alive. Forget about all the troubles, because no matter how much you worry about them, they will always be there. Today, I challenge you to live in the moment, not the past nor the future, but live for right now. How about it?" He sipped his espresso.

I appreciated his insight. And he was right; I did have a lot on my mind, which was filled with worries and indecision. I deserved to enjoy the time away from my true reality. I wanted to dive in the water headfirst, without determining if it was safe. I needed to be impulsive at least once in my life – not always cautious and methodical, managing to talk myself out of most everything before I even tried it. I needed to live in the moment and decided to take him up on his challenge.

"Ok, Giovanni Morelli. I accept your challenge. I will live in the moment!" I quelled the fear building. Time to push my old dependable friend—fear, aside.

"My full name is Giovanni Fuglio Morelli. And you will do whatever it is that I say, correct?" He smiled a devilish grin and I wasn't as sure anymore.

"Yes, I'll do whatever you, say. But if you get freaky with me, I'll have to go upside your head," I leaned over and kissed his dimpled cheek.

"Ooh, what is this, 'get freaky'? It sounds very interesting. Maybe you will show me later?" He grinned again, as we stood to leave.

The first stop on my Italian adventure, as Giovanni called it, was to explore an underwater Italian grotto. Legend was that the Virgin Mary would appear to those brave enough to dive in the lake and swim to the underwater cave.

I had an intense fear of drowning and as I stood looking into the deep, blue water of the small lake, my old fears began to resurface. Giovanni assured me that all would go well.

After we changed into bathing suits, conveniently purchased from a store across the street, and after a brief lesson in scuba diving, we jumped in. I was terrified, but I followed him down holding on to the safety line with one hand and a huge flashlight in the other. A few minutes later we were in the underground cave. Although I didn't see the Virgin Mary, I did see a beautiful network of underground cave formations, which were visible only to those few brave individuals who dared swim the grotto. We stayed for about an hour before we returned to the shore above.

Giovanni sped quickly up the sloping hills, to the base of the *Dolomite* mountains. I enjoyed the feel of the wind blowing across my face. The day had warmed considerably, so he let down the top of his convertible. We shared a bottle of cool, sparkling water, neither feeling the need to speak. The simple fact of our being together, enjoying one another's company was enough for us both. I had no idea where we were headed on the mountain, but I knew it involved getting me to overcome another of my fears. I was right.

At the top of the mountain crest, a large group of men and women were gathered, suited up in colorful clothing and rigged to hang gliders. One by one they took a running start and leapt gracefully off the edge of the cliff. Once airborne, they floated momentarily before being picked up by the wind currents.

"Are you serious? No, you cannot be serious! Oh, hell no! There is no way in the world I'm going to jump off a cliff! Diving into a grotto was one thing! But this?! Let's go!" My widely-opened eyes expressed the fear I felt inside. Though technically I may be dreaming, I didn't want to chance it. I remember hearing about people dying in their sleep from falling and hitting the ground. I was not one who wanted to test that theory.

"Remember, you said you would do whatever it is I wanted? I promise you will not get hurt. We will jump together. All you have to do is enjoy the ride down." He parked the car a safe distance away from the hang gliders path.

"Giovanni, I'm scared of heights and I really don't think I can do this." I shook my head refusing to get out of the car. He had no idea how truly terrified I was.

"My dear Lena, I know you are frightened, but trust me. It is the most wonderful feeling in the world to float high above the ground." He knelt to my level. "When I first jumped, I too was terrified that I would crash into the ground below, but ever since I took that first step off the mountain I have never looked back. Whenever I return to my village, I get with my old friends and we spend an entire day doing this. Up and down, up and down, all day long. Look at me, Lena. I will not let you get hurt." He wisely stressed the last sentence.

His touch was enough to bring me around. I nodded my head in agreement and started out of the car. A couple of guys held up two brightly colored jump suits, one for me and one for Giovanni. I pulled the fabric over my still slightly wet swimsuit, and then waited for further instruction. I listened intently as the instructors explained my part of the "jump". In English for me and Italian for Giovanni.

Because we were flying in a tandem hang glider built for two, I was responsible for only half of the flight controls. As long as I was with

Giovanni, I could depend on him to do most of the work, but I needed to be prepared in case something went wrong.

We worked on our coordination, how to steer the hang glider, and finally the techniques for a proper landing – the most important part as far as I was concerned. After a good thirty minutes of practice, I felt I was ready to "take the big step" as he teasingly called it. With the assistance of a few of his friends, we were hooked up in the glider built for two.

"You know what? I feel like I do when I'm on one of the huge roller coasters, like this one called *Titan* in Magic Mountain's amusement park, and it's on its way up the incline before the first big drop. Listening to the clink, clink, clink of the chains, pulling the cars upwards towards the sky, I'd sit there thinking, 'What the hell am I doing on this ride?' All of a sudden, we'd reach the crest and start the free fall down hundreds of feet. I could do nothing at that point. It was too late to get off, so I ended up screaming at the top of my lungs. I didn't open my eyes until I was back at the exit point. That's how I feel right now, like I'm about to step off into nothing and I have no control over anything." I helped Giovanni tighten the straps of his helmet and he helped me with mine.

"I do not want to sound philosophical, but actually hang gliding can be a metaphor for life. If you fail to control the glider, you *will* spiral out of control and crash. The same principle applies to your life, you cannot step blindly out there and expect not to crash, you must plan and prepare. You have to take control of your life so you will not *crash*. And if you have a partner willing to share in the responsibilities, then the two of you working together will do just fine. *Va bene*, enough with this, as you say "deep shit". Let us get this bird flying. Are you ready?"

"No, but let's do it anyway," I replied taking one last deep breath. With practiced precision, we ran in synch and headed for the edge of the cliff.

As we neared the edge, I closed my eyes and felt the ground disappear from under my feet. I subconsciously held my breath. Slowly, I opened my eyes one at a time to take in the magnificent view surrounding us. I began to breathe normally. We assumed the proper position by tucking our legs behind, as if we were lying down. We were actually flying! I felt the currents lifting us away from the mountain we stepped from moments ago. Surprisingly, it was very, very quiet and peaceful. A flock of birds flew by, probably wondering what type of strange, new species we were.

"Are you okay?" asked Giovanni, looking concerned.

"Yeah, so far so good. I can't believe how quiet it is up here. Look how high we are!"

"Yes, it is very peaceful, but not so high – only a few thousand feet." He checked the lines, making any needed adjustments.

"How long can we stay up?" I asked.

"It mostly depends on the wind. On a day like today, when there are lots of wind currents, we can stay up here for possibly ten or fifteen minutes, if you wish," he replied, pleased that I was enjoying myself.

We did indeed remain airborne for what seemed like mere minutes, but was actually closer to twenty, touring the valley laid out below us. It was such an amazing feeling to be really flying that I didn't want it to end. Not wanting to waste the view, Giovanni gave me an overhead tour of some of the older towns hidden deep in the recesses of the valleys.

As all good things must end, we saw the landing zone a few miles away. I did exactly as I was instructed. We landed without incident and located his two friends who waited to take us back to the top. After gathering up the glider and parachute, all four of us piled into the van for the return trip up the mountain. The drive up was much shorter than expected.

"Thank you so much for suggesting we do this. I haven't had that much fun since… Oh, what am I saying, that was the most fun I've ever had!" I unhooked myself from the attached glider, took off my helmet, and finger fluffed my hair that had molded in the shape of the helmet. Helmet hair was not the look I was going for today.

"You are very welcome, my darling. I am happy you enjoyed yourself." He kissed my hand, lingering just a bit too long, looking up at me with those amazing eyes.

His friends chuckled in the background, speaking quietly amongst themselves. They were both amused and intrigued at their friend's reaction to me. Feeling self-conscious, I pulled my hand back and cleared my throat in an attempt to break the mood.

"Hey, where can we get a good meal around here? I'm starving. All that swimming and flying made me feel like I've not eaten in days." My stomach rumbled at the mere thought of food.

Giovanni was still connected to the latches and hooks of the hang glider. As he undid himself, I saw a very familiar person standing off in the distance. It was Simone. She stood alone obviously enjoying the scenery. When she saw me watching her, she merely waved and walked off in the opposite direction. I was puzzled why she was here, but decided not to pursue it. Instead I helped my new friend out of his flight suit. I kept mine on, not wanting to change clothes without the benefit of a shower. Plus I didn't feel comfortable trumping around in only a bikini.

"I know the perfect place to grab something quick and delicious. Just let me get these things back to my friends and we'll be on our way. Okay?" He smiled that brilliant smile, continuing to undress.

Giovanni stood before me stripped down to his swim trunks. I had a chance to check out his magnificent form. Not an ounce of fat was visible anywhere on his well-defined, muscular body. His skin, glistening with perspiration, was the color of golden honey. Thank God he didn't have a hairy back, rather the hair he did have was limited to his chest, arms and legs--just enough to look sexy. He gathered up our equipment and turned to return it to his friends. As he walked away, I couldn't help but to check out his butt. I thought, he is so handsome and sweet, and he has a really nice ass!

"*Mi'amica*, are you ready to put some food in that pretty little stomach of yours? I know a place where we can get very good pizza." He wrapped his arms around my waist, standing nose to nose, facing me. I placed my arms around his neck wanting this moment to last. Forget about the pizza! I inhaled his masculine scent and thought about all the possibilities that existed between us and said, "I'll go wherever you want to take me. Hey, I followed you to an underwater cave and then stepped off a cliff with you. I'm sure I can trust you to find decent pizza."

"I want you to know how proud I am of you. Today, you faced your fears and did absolutely wonderful. You should be very proud of yourself, Lena. Last night, before you fell asleep, you talked about how afraid you have been lately and how you wanted to experience life again. You said you were tired of sleepwalking through life and wanted to regain the excitement of your youth. I asked you to name three things you were most afraid of. Drowning and fear of falling were first and foremost," Giovanni explained. Then he whispered softly, "you are so beautiful, my sweet angel."

The anticipation of his lips on mine was agonizing. He leaned forward and our mouths met, teasing me with his tongue. I responded with a moan of pleasure. He moved his hands from my waist to either side of my face, stroking my neck as we kissed first tenderly and then passionately. I was lost in his embrace and surfaced only when I heard clapping and whistles coming from his group of friends. We reluctantly pulled apart. Slightly embarrassed, I shrank behind Giovanni, who unabashedly took full advantage of the situation and bowed to our audience. I hadn't felt this free in years.

"You said I told you three things I was afraid of. What was the third?"

"You do not remember? Oh, then I will show you later. For now, we will find good food."

"How about we find a shower first?!" After our busy, exciting morning, I was feeling pretty ripe and wanted to shower away the dirt and sweat.

We ended up in a *vitto e allogio* aka an Italian boarding house. Although the rooms were small, they were clean and tastefully decorated to reflect the casual, yet simple elegance of the Italian countryside. His room was across the hallway from mine and we shared a single bathroom with two other guests. I stripped out of the borrowed jump suit and still damp bikini, and wrapped myself in the complimentary robe provided by the lady of the house. I gathered up my toiletries and headed to the bathroom to wash off the crud from this morning's activities.

I was midstream into my shower when I heard a knock at the door.

"*Uno momento, per favore!*" I yelled over the sound of the shower. Unreal! I know they could hear the water running. I hadn't even washed the conditioner from my hair yet.

Instead of leaving, I heard the door open and a voice just above a whisper say, "Lena, it is me, Giovanni. May I come in?"

"Uh, could we talk later? I'm almost finished and then you can have your turn." I was almost in a panic. I had only met him the night before, and wasn't about to get busy with him. Plus, the last thing I wanted was for him to see my softly deflated breasts and my mushy tummy up close and personal. It was one thing to let him see me in a skimpy bikini, but that was only for a little while before I jumped in the water. But for him to see me now – well, it ain't gonna happen!

"I am here to help you face the third fear you mentioned the other evening."

"What fear?" I wondered aloud. So many thoughts raced through my mind. I was half asleep from what he told me and I didn't remember anything about telling him any of my fears - although he had been right on about my fears of drowning and heights.

He came all the way in the bathroom and shut the door behind him. He was wearing nothing but a white terry cloth towel tied loosely around his waist. I wiped the trail of conditioner from my eyes and blinked, hoping the towel would slip.

I didn't have to wait for long because he whipped that towel off – standing in front of my in all his glory. What a sight he was to behold! Lawd, have mercy! His body was perfect from the waves of his hair, to the ripples of his six-pack stomach, to his muscular legs. And seeing his member, standing at full attention, made me want him right there. I had to get a hold of myself. I didn't know this man, yet here I stood in front of him, naked in more ways than one. Yes, I am a grown-assed woman free to make my own decisions, but I didn't want him to think I was that easy. I really liked him and I think he felt the same for me.

"*Permesso*, may I?" he asked, stepping into the spacious shower stall with me. I felt like a fool standing there totally exposed. I wanted to run and hide but he was blocking the exit. I tried to shield myself from his gaze, but he gently moved my arms down to my sides.

"I suppose I told you I'm afraid to let anyone see me naked, huh?" I managed to stammer through my embarrassment. I must have turned the deepest shade of red I was capable of at that moment.

"*Si*, yes, of course you did. *Mi' amica*, you are so breathtakingly beautiful you have nothing to be ashamed of. You look magnificent." He stepped under the water's stream to kiss me on each cheek.

I averted my eyes, not knowing where to look. He raised my chin causing me to focus on his face.

"It is alright. I want you to look at me. *All of me*. See, I am more than my body, just as you are more than your body. Please. Touch me. Wherever you wish – just don't get freaky with me," he added to lighten the mood.

We both laughed at his reference to my statement from earlier in the day. I began with his face and worked my way down, until I touched every inch of his body. When I reached the middle of his back,

I commented on his hook shaped birthmark. "What's this? You have a birthmark in the shape of a Nike swoosh. Did you know that?"

"A Nike swoosh? That is the first time I have heard it called that. Now that you mention it, I suppose it does resemble their symbol.

Please, go on. You have not yet completed your task," he said, looking over his shoulder at me with a mysterious smile.

By the time I finished, I was ready to throw him down on the bathroom floor and ride him like a jockey rides a horse. "You are so strong and muscular. How do you keep in such good shape?" I was no longer self conscious about his seeing me nude. In fact, I was beginning to enjoy myself immensely. I loved running my hands over his body, listening to his moans of pleasure as I touched his sensitive areas. I ended my full body touch by running my lips across his neatly coiffed mustache, watching the corners of his mouth turn up in a smile.

"Oh, that felt so nice. But to answer your question, I stay very active. I cycle as much as I can and I love to dance, but I think my physical condition is mostly due to my Papa's good genes. Now, it is my turn," he replied, leaning in to kiss my shoulders.

While I stood in the warmth of the shower, he worked his way, up down and all around, kissing me all over until I was about to explode-- as was he. "Hey, how about we continue this back in your room?" My voice became low and husky, ready to continue the exploration of his body.

Though he was obviously aroused as I, he responded, "Lena, as much as I would love to take advantage of this situation, I think we should wait until the time is right. I think you are special and you desire much more than a, how do you say, 'casual fling', it is not my intention to have sex with you yet."

Is this man serious? Here we are both ready to get down and no one to stop us and he wants to respect me?! I can't believe what I'm hearing! "Giovanni, are you sure? I mean, I want this just as much as you – probably even more. And wasn't it you who challenged me to be more impulsive?"

"More impulsive. *Si*, but irresponsible? No. You must still use your head. Think what it would mean to become sexually involved. We just met and are only beginning to know each other. Sometimes having sex too soon spoils what may come later. Let us become familiar in other ways first, Okay?" He leaned his head back, allowing the lukewarm water to run down his face.

"All right. I understand what you're saying, but let me tell you, from all that I've heard about Italian men... Well, let me just say for the record, you just dispelled that myth." I grabbed the soap and helped lather his chest.

"What you have heard – I admit, it is mostly true. Italian men are truly magnificent lovers. We are in fact the most skilled lovers in the entire world. However, I choose not to bed you right now, because I want more than sex from you. I want to learn all there is about you. If you were just someone I was casually interested in, I would not have gone to the trouble of bringing you to my family's village and I definitely would not have spent so much of my time with you," he replied, matter of fact, continuing to shower.

"Don't be so modest on my account!" I had to get in at least one jab for his boastfulness. "Thanks for thinking so highly of me. It really makes me feel special to know that you want to know more about me. Hey, I think you're pretty special yourself." I rinsed off the remaining soap and let the warmth of the water wash over me as I watched Giovanni bathe. No longer feeling self conscious, I waited until he was finished to turn off the water and step out onto the cool tile floor. I grabbed a towel for myself and handed him the one he dropped on the floor earlier.

"Now, how about we get dressed and then I will take you to get the best pizza you will ever have?" He dried himself partially and wrapped the damp towel back around his waist.

"That sounds great, but I need another 15 minutes before I'll be ready. I've still got to do some "girly" things first."

"Just don't keep me waiting too long. I shall see you in a few moments. *Sì?*"

I smiled to myself when I heard him break out in a song by Andrea Bocelli, *Il Diavola E L'Angelo*, "*The Devil and The Angel*". How appropriate the words of the song were! I hurried up and quickly dressed, applying the lightest touch of makeup to my still dewy face. Although I was famished, my desire to see Giovanni was more important than feeding my hunger.

Just as I hung my damp bathing suit on a clothesline stretched outside the window, I heard a knock at the door, "Hold on Giovanni, I'll be right there!" I did a quick check of my reflection in the mirror.

"Well, hello Lena," Simone said and stepped in the room.

"Uh, Simone. Hi. What are you doing here?" I felt like a little girl who'd been caught taking the last cookie from the cookie jar.

"I'm just stopping by to see how you're doing. I hadn't heard from you in a few days. How *is* everything going?" she asked, in a purely innocent manner.

"Things are going really good. I am having so much fun and I met a really great guy who's taken me to new extremes. He's helped me face some of my fears and I never imagined I could have such a good time doing some of the things I've done with him."

"Oh? You've met someone new? Whatever happened to that wonderful man you were so fascinated with? Keenan was his name?" Simone questioned me, raising her eyebrow.

"Hey, look. I really appreciate your concern, but I'm doing just fine. And I haven't forgotten about Keenan. How could I? It's just that I had this opportunity to hang out with Giovanni and take a walk on the wild side. It's all part of my getting to know the real me again. Besides, why do I have to explain myself? Why are you following me around? Ain't I here to have a good time and to add a little excitement to my life?" I angrily defended myself.

"Calm down, Lena. I mean you no harm. Of course, I want you to enjoy your time here. But, I also want you to think about the consequences of your actions while you still can. I am not here to judge you. I am simply here to remind you that some times when you choose a path, it's impossible to turn around and retrace your steps because you don't always end up in the same place from which you started. When I said that this time is for you, I meant that this should be your time for reflection. A time to sort out what's important in your life."

Simone continued, "But you are now entering untested waters. You have gone beyond the path of figuring out your current life and have begun doing things you've never done before. I don't want to discourage you from expanding your horizons; I just want to caution you to realize that once you have experienced a life filled with color, it is almost impossible to go back to living a life devoid of it."

"I think I know what you mean. A life filled with color…"

"Remember that woman Carmelita I told you about when we first met? Well, she started her journey out just like you did. She initially planned only on staying a little while, but she ended up having such a good time, she didn't want to go back to the real world and face all the challenges associated with living her life. You do have free will here, but I caution you to think about what it is you really want. That's all. I will leave you for now because I see you are expecting someone. Just think about what I've said. I won't disturb you again during your journey. If you need me, you'll know where to find me. *Buon Viaggio my sistah!*" And with that, she retreated through the door and headed down the hallway.

I became speechless and unable to respond. Before I could digest our conversation, Giovanni came flying through the door to whisk me away.

"Ah, I see you are waiting for me. Come, let us go." He placed my arm through his and led me towards the front entrance.

"Did you pass anyone in the hallway on your way in?"

"*Si*, I passed an older woman just a moment ago. Why?"

"Oh, no particular reason. Let's go eat, I'm starving." I decided to take Simone's words of wisdom with a grain of salt. I finally had the opportunity to have a great time and see things and do things I'd never done before with a gorgeous Italian man. I wasn't about to let a little guilt keep me from enjoying myself.

CHAPTER 8

The town center was filled with locals out shopping, enjoying the springtime weather. Several shops were beginning to close for their daily two hour *reposo*. Women rushed about trying to complete their errands before getting home to start dinner. We ended up at a local pizzeria where I could watch the chefs create their edible masterpieces, finishing by placing the pies in a large brick oven to bake. The aroma made my mouth water and my stomach grumble. After the waitress had taken our orders and brought a carafe of red wine, two bottles of sparkling water, and a basket of breadsticks, we settled back to chat.

"*Alora*, Lena. Tell me about yourself. I know you are not Italian. Where are you from and how long have you been in my wonderful country?" he asked.

"You're right, I'm not Italian. I'm originally from the state of Missouri in the United States. I lived in Italy a few years ago. For now, I'm just visiting." I sipped the wine taking my time to answer. It was very dry, just the way I like it.

"Missouri? Is that anywhere near New York or Los Angeles?" He refilled both glasses and signaled to the waitress for more.

"No, not even close. It's smack dab in the middle of the country. Landlocked on all sides and worlds apart from both LA and New York – both literally and figuratively. It's kind of difficult to describe. Have you ever been to the United States?"

"No. I've never been out of Europe. Why would I want to go anywhere else? Everything I need is right here within a day's trip on the Euro express train or by car. *Alora*, how long do you plan on visiting?"

"That depends on how good of a time I'm having," I replied beginning to feel the calming effects of the wine.

"Good answer. Are there any obligations such as family or work you must return to?" He set his glass down and seemed to look deep into the depths of my soul, awaiting my response.

As I contemplated my response, the waitress brought out two piping hot pizzas, placing one in front of each of us. Her mistake of mixing up our orders was just enough of a distraction to help me avoid answering his question. We both dug into our individual pies, offering and accepting a slice from each other.

"Oh my Lord! This is the best pizza I have ever eaten in my life! This is sooooo good!" I exclaimed, biting into the thin crispy crust.

"Of course, it is the best. Italia is famous for its delicious food. I'll bet you can't find pizza like this in Missouri." He smiled, brimming over with pride for his country.

"I don't think I can find pizza like this anywhere except here. The sauce is so light and this crust has the perfect texture. It tastes so, so fresh! This is really delicious. You know what? I could probably make a million dollars selling this back home!" I plucked a porcini mushroom from the gooey cheese and placed it delicately in my mouth, savoring its texture and flavor.

"I am happy to see that you approve of my choice. Speaking of home... You were about to tell me what is waiting for you when you return to your country..." Giovanni put down his pizza in anticipation of my answer.

I exhaled. What or how much should I reveal about my current situation? If I told him too much, he'd surely put an end to our day of fun. On the other hand, if I lied and didn't tell him the complete truth I'd have to lie to him for the remainder of our time together. I decided to stall.

"Why don't you tell me a little bit about yourself first and then I'll let you in on my life." I offered a sweet smile, encouraging him to play along.

"I see. Lena, are you stalling for time? *Alora.* What do you want to know?" He drained his second glass of wine. Using his thumb and forefinger, he smoothed down his moustache, unconsciously tracing his lips.

"Uh, how old are you? Are you married or in a serious relationship? Have any kids? You know, the usual stuff?" Giovanni's beard, a mere shadow only last night, had now become thick with the stubble of a manicured beard. The wine was affecting both of us, slowing my reflexes down causing me to focus on his every movement.

He signaled for the waitress to refill our wine carafe. We were both on our third glass and I was enjoying how mellow it made me feel. Plus, it was absolutely delicious.

"As for your questions, I am thirty-six years old. I have never been married and I have no children. Up until six months ago, I lived with a woman for almost two years. In the end we decided to go our separate ways. We were simply not meant to be together. I do admit that it was difficult at first to end. I wanted more from her than she was willing to give. Now I focus mostly on me, managing my club and simply enjoying life. Like I told you earlier, I ski, dance and occasionally play soccer during my free time. Although I love to travel throughout Europe, there is no country as wonderful as my own. Now, what about you? Tell me about the mysterious Lena."

"My life is a little more complicated." I decided to give Giovanni a condensed version of the truth rather than going into my "alternate reality, I'm here, but not really" version. "First of all, I want you to know that I really enjoy being with you. You have opened my eyes in more ways than you'll ever know. In the short time I have known you, I've done things I never could have imagined myself doing. You are truly a wonderful, amazing man and I'm so thrilled to have met you." I took a deep breath and blurted out, "I'm married, have been for almost 19 years. I have three sons ranging in age from 17 to 11. I live in a little town in Kansas named Salinas and I work in an army tank assembly factory. I have no interests outside of work, no friends to really speak of, and I came here because I needed a break from the routine." I drank half the glass of wine in one gulp, almost afraid to look at Giovanni, awaiting his reaction. When I finally got the nerve to look, he wasn't smiling, but at least he didn't look too upset.

"Whoa, you really are a long way from home. I do not understand. Why isn't your husband traveling with you? And who was that man I saw you with earlier? Most importantly, why are you with me if you are married?" He still didn't look angry, just confused.

"I needed to get away for a while. I'm traveling by myself. Sort of like a personal vacation. I returned to Italy because I needed time alone to think - to clear my head. I lived here a few years ago and I've always loved the country and its people. What better place to sort out my feelings? My husband is back in Kansas with my children. As for my marriage - remember you said you and your lady friend just weren't meant to be together? Well, I can say the same thing about me and my husband. We've known it for years, but neither one of us is willing to admit defeat first. The man you saw me with was an old friend that I ran into. We hadn't seen each other for ages and we were in the process of getting to know one another again when I bumped into you. Why am I here with you? Mostly because I am extremely attracted to you and I couldn't help myself, but now that I've gotten to know you better, it goes much deeper than that. When I saw your interest in me, I was flattered. It's been years since anyone has reacted to me the way you did. You actually wanted to get to know and spend time with me."

"I see. Explain *por favore*. Why do you not wear a wedding ring? You say you are married with three children? Did you one day decide to come over to *Italia* for a casual fling with an Italian stud before returning to your normal American life. Is that it, Lena!?" Giovanni asked, understandably revealing a hint of anger I had not seen before.

"No. I never intended for anything to develop between us. I was just out having a good time when I happened to meet both you and your brother. And when you invited me to come with you to your village, well, I threw caution to the wind because as you know, you only live once. Right? I stopped wearing a wedding ring when I took that job in the tank factory. I didn't want to risk losing a finger if it got hung up on a piece of equipment. Know what? When I first got here, all I wanted was a nice quiet place to reflect on my life. Giovanni, since I've met you, even though it's only been a short time, I feel like I could know you forever – like I have known you forever. And we're not having a fling – not yet anyway. I feel a real connection to you, almost like a field of energy when you come near. And so far, we've done nothing that can't be turned around." I reached for his hand that now rested on the arm of his chair.

"I feel the same way. Of course, it only figures that you are married. Unfortunately, the news you have given me does not change the way I feel. You say in your heart you know your marriage is over, but does your head also tell you this? Why haven't you left him if you are unhappy?" he accepted my touch and leaned across the table.

"Those are the questions I keep asking myself over and over. But I think I'm much closer to the answer now. Why else would I be here with you and why did I spend so much time with my other friend if I still had those feelings for Mark, my husband? Honestly, I think I've stayed with him all these years because of my children. I know that sounds so cliché, but it's true." I admitted sadly, more to myself than to Giovanni.

"Lena, I think I understand how you are feeling. I want you to decide what is best for you, but I must also look out for me. I told you when we first met that I do not play games. I am now at the age where I am looking for someone very special to share my life with. I was hoping that woman perhaps could be you, but I now see it will not be possible." He leaned back in his chair with a sad look in his eyes.

"Don't take this the wrong way, but I've got to ask. Are you just looking to get with me because I'm... you know...Black? You've got to understand where I'm coming from. In the states there are lots of white guys who get off on the idea of being with a Black woman. They see us as some exotic creature that they can get their game off without really caring how it affects us. For them, we're just a curiosity to be satisfied. Nothing more."

"Is that what you think? I truly hope you do not believe I am that superficial. In my business I meet beautiful women from many countries – in all shapes, sizes and colors. I do not care what color your skin is. Alright, I admit that a woman's physical appearance is somewhat important, but for me, when I show my interest, you must believe that it is for something much deeper. No, I am not only interested in you because you are Black. Besides, you are only a little bit darker than I am. Now, let me ask you the same question. Are you only interested in me because I am Italian?"

"No! That's not it at all. I'm sorry if I have offended you. It's just that I've been in that situation a few times when the guys just wanted to see how it felt to be with someone "different". I like you, not because you are Italian, but because of your personality. Your irresistible charm. Your passion for life... Hey, look at it this way, now the pressure's off and we can really have a good time just being together as friends. What do you say?" I pleaded.

"Okay. We will simply be friends? See what happens? Ah, *mi' amica*," he sighed, "do you know what you are asking of me? I desire you, yet I must restrain my feelings for you?"

"You don't have to totally restrain yourself. I kinda like how things have been going so far."

"I think you are one of those naughty American women, eh? I'm not sure about this. How about we walk off the pizza and wine and then see what develops?" He replied, playfully.

We spent the remainder of the afternoon in town, stopping at several fountains and admiring the beauty of the countryside. People waved and occasionally stopped to have short conversations with us. Springtime flowers were in full bloom, while shiny new leaves sprouted from the trees, offering shade from the hot sun. The village was located very close to a mountain lake, resulting in the need for numerous bridges over the streams.

Giovanni explained that several independent families migrated from the far southern regions of Italy over a thousand years ago and settled the town. While many of his ancestors were Romans, many other families came from poor farmers intent on having a better life than what was offered in the south. The majority of early settlers raised sheep and cattle to sustain themselves and were eventually able to prosper in their own right. The town is now located only a few miles from the *autostrada* and considered as one of the finest ski resorts in all of northern Italy. Every winter, thousands of people from all over Europe, swelled the village's small population overnight.

"It must be wonderful to know so much of your family's history. I get as far as my great grandparents. After that, my history becomes a blur. You see, my people didn't keep detailed records of marriages, births or deaths because so many African-Americans were born into slavery and sold off to different plantations. Dependent upon whom we ended up with determined our last names, causing members of the same family to have several last names. Occasionally, someone in my family tried to do a genealogical search, but it was all so complicated they usually quit before they got anywhere with it. I think that's why I love being in Italy. You all have so much history and pride. I can hear it in your voices whenever you speak about your country. I, on the other hand, sometimes feel like I have no "real" country to call my own. The blood that runs through my veins came from Africa, England, and Native America. I don't consider Africa or Great Britain as home because of the circumstances involving my ancestors and I'm not really Indian either. Maybe that's why I feel lost much of the time. I don't belong to anyone particular group of people. Of course, I'm very proud to be an American. I just wish we were a more connected bunch."

"*Si*, I am immensely proud of my heritage. I can trace my ancestry back for thousands of years and I know that this is my country and I belong here. Unlike you Americans, we are all Italians. And we don't feel the need to hyphenate our nationality. I think that when you do that, you, how do you say, separate yourselves from each other even more." He glanced at his watch, taking note of the time.

"Yeah, I agree with you on that part. I've never been to Africa and neither have any of my other relatives that I know of. I just wish we could all live in harmony together." It was wishful thinking, but perhaps one day we could.

"What lovely brown skin you *do* have." He caressed my arm and said, "I think that may be too much to hope for, at least for the near future, Lena. Now, what would you like to do for the remainder of the evening? I don't have to be in *Gorgazzio* until tomorrow afternoon, so we have the rest of today to do as we wish. However, I just have one request." He pulled me towards him, propping himself up on the ancient, moss-covered stone wall.

"Oh yeah? What is that?" Despite everything I told him about my past, we reverted back to our cuddly, playful, lovable selves. Unable to keep my hands off him, I fingered the hair that peeked under the collar of his shirt.

"Tonight, I want you to only think of me, no one else," he whispered.

We stood so close our noses almost touched. I wanted nothing more than to be with Giovanni basking in the glow of his magnetic presence. He faced the setting sun. The light emphasized the gold flecks throughout his greenish-brown eyes. The sound of gurgling water rushing downstream, reminded me of our surroundings. I felt overwhelmed and in awe. This was almost too much--too much emotion, too much natural beauty, too many new unfamiliar feelings.

I glanced over at the ancient buildings with their modern signs hanging in the windows. It was all so surreal. Amazingly, in the midst of this small Italian village with all its friendly inhabitants, lost in my alternate reality, I suddenly felt I was "home". Finally, for the first time in my life, standing under a weeping willow tree at the side of a stream embraced in Giovanni's arms, I felt like I belonged. I took a deep breath, inhaled the fresh mountain air and slowly began to forget what brought me here in the first place. I wanted to give myself permission to indulge this fantasy, but the old me kept resisting. There were no words to describe how I felt, so I merely said nothing.

"Is that a yes? *Magnifico!* Later, there is something else I want to show you that my town is famous for." His embrace tightened.

He pulled me closer, his manhood stiffening against my leg. I closed my eyes in anticipation of his lips on mine. I was not disappointed. He kissed with the same skill he displayed in every other area of his life. There was such gentleness in his touch, causing me to desire him even more. I kissed him with a passion I didn't know I was capable of. Several minutes passed before we finally released one another. And then, it was only due to hearing the clucking noises of two old ladies throwing stale bread to the ducks swimming in the stream. I didn't know if they were clucking at the ducks or at our overtly display of affection.

"Giovanni, what are you doing to me? Is this what your town is famous for?" I muttered, feeling slightly lightheaded from his intoxicating kiss.

"*Mi dispiace...* You are so beautiful I cannot help myself," he replied in a breathless voice. The stunned look on his face reflected the same feelings I held inside. He laughed. "No, I cannot take credit for making the town famous. But there is something or should I say, somewhere I would like to show you before it gets too late. *Andiamo*, it is not far from here."

The two old women shook their heads in disapproval. We gave them a playful wave goodbye. Knowing the older ladies back home, I imagined I knew what they were thinking. After all, our cultures weren't that different.

We walked until we reached the outskirts of town and approached a sign notifying us were now leaving *Piano Montissimo,* and quite literally ran into a brick wall. A massive stone wall that stood at least 15 feet high and spanned the length of the block towered above us. A huge double wooden door blocked the view of passerbys, adding a layer of privacy to the mysteries that remained out of sight.

Giovanni pushed the buzzer, placed discretely out of view, and answered back in Italian to someone I thought of as the "gatekeeper". We were buzzed in. I thought I had discovered the Garden of Eden. Now this was a villa! It was a feast for the eyes. The thick green lawn was finely manicured. A maze of finely trimmed shrubbery led to what looked like a mansion, set back at least half a mile from the entrance.

The *palazzo* was painted a deep yellow ocher and accented by off-white shutters bordering its dozens of windows. Bright red chrysanthemums overflowed from terracotta planters set deep in the windowsills. Stone water fountains, modeled after Romanesque sculptures, dotted the landscape. Each one spouted out streams of clear flowing water. Roses of every imaginable variety were trellised tightly to hide the entrance wall. Towering oak trees provided shade from the daytime sun.

"You're just a bundle of surprises, aren't you? This place is gorgeous! Is this someone's home? Are they having a private party or something? I feel so underdressed." I was all too aware of my casual look. What felt fine for eating at a pizzeria suddenly seemed a bit out of place here.

"Do not worry, you look fine. Lena, *De La Porcia* is a *palazzo* like none other. It is very exclusive and very difficult to get reservations because there are only 50 rooms in the entire hotel. We can eat at the 5 star restaurants, swim in the pool, soak in the mineral hot springs, walk through winding mountain trails, go horseback riding – or we can simply sit in the gardens and meditate. During the day it is open to tourists, but after 6 only those with reservations may remain. In the village of *Piano Montissimo*, not only do we have fantastic ski runs in the winter for the Europeans to enjoy, but this palazzo attracts almost as many local Italian tourists in the spring." He started towards the front door.

"Hey wait a minute! Don't we need reservations? Giovanni, this place looks *really* expensive. Are you sure about this?" I couldn't help letting a little of my penny pinching "can't afford it" attitude slip out.

"Has anyone ever told you that you are much too full of worry? It is all taken care of, *mi'amica*. I called in a few favors this afternoon. My friend is the co-owner and was able to give me one of his best rooms, at an immense discount of course. Let us try to have a wonderful time. *Si.*"

The lobby was beautiful. The floors were finished in the finest Italian marble. Decorative Egyptian cotton rugs were strategically placed near the overstuffed chairs in the guest seating areas. Large planters filled with palm trees and other native plants were placed throughout the lobby bringing the natural feel of the outdoors inside. A fountain shaped cherub inconspicuously set in a corner surrounded by vegetation, peed an eternal stream of blue water. I smiled, hoping the desired effect was to entertain.

A nice looking, elegantly dressed man who appeared to be in his mid 40's, sat perched on a stool behind a small mahogany counter pecking keys on a keyboard. He stopped to speak into his headphone and checked the surveillance monitor before acknowledging our arrival.

"*Ciao* Giovanni! *Ciao, Signora* Lena! *Arriverderci!*" He hopped off his stool, walked to where we stood and with outstretched arms he grabbed us by our shoulders and enthusiastically planted kisses on both our cheeks. He was a bundle of energy.

"*Ciao* Stefano. *Come va, mi'amico?!* Thanks so much for making room for us. I promised Lena that I would show her a part of *Italia* most American tourists do not have the opportunity to experience. What better place than *Da la Porcia* for a true Italian holiday?" Giovanni explained.

"Ah, no worries my friend. I am happy to help you out. Lena, have you ever seen a palazzo as magnificent as this?" Stefano asked, with well-placed pride.

"*Ciao* Stefano. No, actually this is the first palazzo I've ever seen, and I can't imagine one that even comes close to being this spectacular! I think that being here will be the perfect ending to a perfect day. I can't wait to see the rest!" I exclaimed, excitedly following his lead. His enthusiasm was infectious.

"*Va bene*, I will not hold you up much longer. You two have much to do, as do I. Here are the keys to your room. Giovanni, as you requested, I have put you in one of my best suites. If you need anything, anything at all, please call me on my cell. Now go and have a wonderful time!" He handed us key cards, then made a "shooing" motion as he returned to his work.

"*Grazie*, Stefano. We'll see you later!" I shouted as Giovanni and I headed towards the stairs to find our room.

The day just kept getting better and better. Our suite was located on the top floor at the end of the hallway. Giovanni opened the door. My mouth dropped open. The opulence was overwhelming! Never in my entire life had I expected to ever stay in a room as lavish as this.

The living area was tastefully furnished in the traditional Italian style including ornately detailed overstuffed furniture. Gold-gilded frames with original oil paintings by local artists, reflecting the region's history, graced every wall. A built in "state of the art" sound system with strategically built in speakers played a classic jazzy tune. I excused myself to the bathroom, sat on the edge of the claw-footed bathtub and looked around. Giovanni was in the other room humming one of his favorite tunes, looking for a corkscrew to open a bottle of complimentary champagne. I ran my hand over my short hair, closed my eyes, smiled to myself and exhaled. I felt an overwhelming sense of calm – a feeling I'd become very familiar with over the past few days. I could really get used to living like this.

Minutes later, I heard a knock coming from what I thought was the bathroom closet. A smiling Giovanni stood on the other side holding two wine glasses and an open bottle of champagne. I stepped out unto the balcony reminiscent of Juliet's home in Florence. A padded bench offered a comfortable place to watch the sun set over the mountains.

"This morning we watched the sun rise, now we shall watch it set." We raised our glasses in a toast, sipping it slowly and quietly. We watched the sun dip further down, leaving trails of orange and pink clouds in the wake of an ever darkening twilight sky. Hypnotic music streamed through the open doors. It was a perfect accompaniment to the dramatic scenes of the setting sun.

"This is so wonderful! I can't thank you enough for all you've done for me today. Just look at this place!" I almost pinched myself to see if it was real, but I was afraid if I did I'd wake up and find out that it wasn't.

"You are very welcome, Lena. I have enjoyed myself more than anytime I can remember. So you see it was not just for you. Today was for me as well. How do you feel? Relaxed? I have an idea. How about a massage? The masseuses are professionally trained in China and are guaranteed to smooth away tension."

"I don't know. I've never had a real massage before — at least not from a professional. Anyway, I don't think I'd like having some stranger touch me so intimately." I wrinkled my nose in disgust, imagining all the gynecological exams I'd had in the past.

"That is why I think you should do it. Remember, stepping out of your comfort zone is good." He clicked his wine glass against mine and drank.

After watching the sun set behind the mountain, Giovanni phoned the front desk and scheduled a massage for us both. An opening was available in 45 minutes. We decided to take advantage of the extra time by trying out the suite's Jacuzzi. Cool mountain air wafted through the open doors, causing the hot water to give off curls of steam. The sheer lace curtains floated gently in the breeze. Romantic music filled the air as the light of the moon flooded the suite. Stripping down to nothing, no longer embarrassed about being naked in front of him, we took our champagne and inched into the swirling warm water.

Miles Davis' *Flamenco Sketches* played in the background. The softly muted sounds of the trumpet were perfect to put us in the right mood.

"Lena, come to me," Giovanni breathlessly whispered, taking the glass from my hand. "I need to hold you."

We never made it to the massage....

CHAPTER 9

After a romantic—though tortuous sexless night, we awoke early for our trip back to the town of *Gorgazzio*. As much as we both wanted it last night, we did not give into our sexual urges. Thanks to Giovanni. He wanted me to wait, to be sure of what I wanted—what I needed.

Anyway, Giovanni had to be back for a business meeting that afternoon and I needed time alone to think. After indulging in a sinfully delicious breakfast, we said our goodbyes to Stefano and thanked both he and the staff of *De La Porcia* for making our stay such a memorable and pleasurable experience. I had enjoyed myself immensely and hated to leave the *palazzo's* beauty. Refusing the offer of a ride from the palazzo's limo driver, we preferred to walk the short distance back to the boarding house.

We thanked the owner for her hospitality, even though we barely used the rooms. Giovanni paid for our short stay and I left a small gratuity for the maid. My mother always reminded us to not forget about tipping the people who cleaned the toilets, for it was they who had the nastiest, most thankless job, being almost invisible to hotel guests until something went wrong. The least I could do was leave a "little something extra" to show my appreciation.

Running my hands along the sleek lines of his Z4, I teased, "Hey Giovanni, if you're such a proud Italian, what are you doing driving a BMW?"

"I drive this particular car because it is one of the best built cars on the road and mostly because I like it. Lena, don't get me wrong, Italians do design the best cars, *Fiat, Lamborghini, Masserati...* I've owned Italian cars all my life but wanted to try something different for a change." He shrugged his shoulders, opening the passenger door.

"Oh? Something different for a change? Does that apply to your women as well?" I asked, innocently enough.

"Huh? I never thought of it that way before. I suppose you are correct. You know what they say; variety is the spice of life." He shut the door, leaving me to momentarily contemplate what he'd just said. In that moment, I decided to give Giovanni the benefit of the doubt. It was entirely possible he didn't mean anything malicious with his comment. After all, how many times had I misspoken or used a quote inappropriately? And wouldn't it be presumptuous of me to think he meant otherwise?

"We'd better get going if we're going to get you back in time for your meeting. By the way, what's the meeting about?" I asked, watching him buckle his seat belt and adjust the temperature.

"Lucio and I are considering expanding our club and we are meeting with our attorney and banker. Instead of having just a DJ spin records, we want to have live bands come in a couple times a week. There are so many things to consider. Do we have room? Will we need to upgrade our sound system? We must consider everything from lighting, to advertising, to the final costs. This is something we've wanted to do for a long time. It is very important for me to be there." His cell phone rang. He answered, speaking frantically at first then finally ending his conversation in calm, soothing voice.

"What was that all about? Is everything alright?" I asked, worried.

""That was Lucio. He's very nervous about our meeting. He was calling to make certain I remember. You see, he is very talented fixing technical problems, but I have the mind for business. We, how do you say... take up each other's slack. We complement each other perfectly." He started the car, put it into gear and headed down the mountains. "We should arrive in *Gorgazzio* in about four hours."

"That's ok. I'm in no hurry. You must be so proud of yourself—with your club's success and all. I am pushing 40 and still don't know what I really want to be when I grow up. I call myself a jack of all trades and a master of none," I chuckled inwardly, "I know I lack focus. I just can't seem to find the thing that I was meant to do. There are days when I can't see past tomorrow, much less 5 to 10 years from now."

"Don't be so hard on yourself. When you think about it, most people do not work in careers they love. They settle for any old job, not for fulfillment, but to survive. It just so happened I knew what I wanted to pursue early on. My family encouraged and supported our dream of owning a club. However, only you can decide your path in life. You must let nothing stop you from fulfilling whatever it is you want to do. I believe that is the only way to be happy. Otherwise you live life filled with misery, living day after day, hating the mornings when you should arise with joy. Lena, life is too short to spend your life doing something you dread."

"You're right. Everything you've just said is so true. In my case, life got in the way. I think that if I didn't have so many responsibilities I could pursue my dreams. That's the main reason I came to Italy, I needed time to reassess my life—to focus on what's really important. Well, enough of that. Giovanni, I have had so much fun over the last couple of days. Never in a million years would I have imagined me, a homegirl from the streets of St. Louis, scuba diving in a *grotto*, hang gliding from the Italian Alps, staying in a beautiful *palazzo*, soaking in hot mineral springs—in the nude mind you, dining on great food, drinking fine wine, being treated like a queen by a very handsome, very sweet man. It is just so overwhelming! Thank you so much for inviting me. I just wish there were some way I could repay you." I closed my eyes, leaned my head back and listening to the mellow jazz tunes played especially for me, punctuated by the hypnotic swishing of the windshield wipers.

Giovanni replied, "Thank *you* for coming with *me*. Lena, I've wanted to come back to my village and do all those things for the longest time. You know how it is. For me, the success of my club is my goal. It's also my passion. There's always so much work to be done that I don't have much time to relax. Lucio always says I work too much. He says I should make time to enjoy life. What he fails to realize is I love my work! But he is correct when he tells me success is nothing without someone to share it with. *Grazie, bella*, you've given me precious memories that will last a lifetime. I just pray this won't be the last opportunity I will have to spend with you."

I leaned across the seat and kissed his scratchy cheek, loving the way the stubbly growth felt against my lips. Before I realized it, I once again succumbed to the gentle rocking motion of the car, falling asleep, as if I were deeply drugged. Hours later, I stirred and opened my eyes to the warmth of the sun shining brightly in the cloudless sky.

"Umm," I sighed, "where are we? I'm sorry I went to sleep on you again. It must be something about your driving that relaxes me." "No worries, *mi' amica*. I don't mind driving and watching you sleep. You look like an angel. We are still about an hour away from *Gorgazzio*. How about we stop and get something to drink? Are you thirsty? Need to stretch your legs?"

"Sure, that would be nice. I love your car, but there isn't exactly a lot of legroom to stretch out." I yawned, trying to shake off the grogginess.

He exited the *autostrada* at the next rest stop. I excused myself to the restroom while Giovanni went inside to buy water. Several ladies waiting in line looked at me curiously, probably trying to determine my origins. I remained quiet, used the facilities, paid the attendant and went inside the store in search of my friend. He was in line, holding two bottles of *Pellegrino* water. I added a box of *Baci* candy to his purchase. He laughed because I told him earlier about my weakness for all things chocolate.

Back in the car, I grabbed a chocolate for me and gave one to Giovanni. Each individual *Baci* chocolate is wrapped in foil and enveloped by a sheer strip of paper inscribed with sayings translated in five different languages. I removed the silver foil, retrieved the thin paper and read aloud, 'When you are surrounded by friends you will always have love in your life.' That's a good one. What does yours say?" I asked, placing the chocolate filled hazelnut truffle in my mouth. I moaned out loud.

"Is it that good?" He laughed. "*Alora*, this is what mine says, 'When you live your life for tomorrow, tomorrow never comes'. I like it. It is a good motto to live by." He popped the chocolate in his mouth and in imitation of me and moaned loudly, drawing stares from people walking nearby.

"Stop that!" I shouted, hitting his arm playfully. "People are staring!"

"Oh, so what? Don't let that bother you. Who cares if they look, I say let them look. Maybe then they'll open their eyes and really see!" He leaned towards me.

Still munching on chocolate, we kissed, mingling our passion with the remains of *Baci*. The effect was deliciously exciting. I could feel myself getting tingly all over. I tried very hard to hold back the desires I felt for this man. Even though we hadn't been physically intimate, in spite of how close we came to making love last night, I was emotionally enthralled with Giovanni from the time I first laid eyes on him. I wanted him more than I'd wanted anyone else in a very long time— including Keenan. Reluctantly, we pulled apart. Looking at me with deep sorrow in his eyes, he wiped remnants of our kiss away and started the car for the final leg of our journey.

We rode in solitude for miles, each lost in our own thoughts, until I asked, "Giovanni? Can I ask you a question?"

"*Si?* What is it?" he replied.

"Do you believe in love?" I watched the cars disappear in our wake as we raced down the A-4 *autostrada* going at speeds up to 100 mph.

He hesitated before he answered, "Do I believe in love? But, of course I do. What good is life without *amore*? Why do you ask?" He glanced briefly at me before returning his attention to the road.

"I don't know. Sometimes I think love is overrated. Think about it. You meet someone. You think you're in love only to discover in the end that you don't belong together. In the meantime, you go crazy trying to "work things out". It doesn't last. It only feels good in the beginning. When it's over, it hurts like hell."

"This is not love you speak of, *mi'amica*. *Amore* is a beautiful, wonderful feeling you share with someone special. I believe love begins with a small spark, grows into a raging inferno, finally settling down into smoldering embers that can easily die out if not properly cared for. My Papa says love is like a fine wine that improves with time under the right conditions. If not properly nurtured it turns sour—like vinegar. Maybe it is possible you have not experienced "real love". No? Some say when you are in love, nothing else matters except the happiness of the one you're with. But in my heart, I know love is real and true when it is given as graciously as it is received," he spoke passionately, using his free hand to emphasize how deeply he felt.

"Hmmm, well maybe I've never been in love," I thought aloud, realizing for the first time that it may indeed be true. I looked over at Giovanni. The seed had been planted between us, but it would never – could never grow into anything more. Although we had connected on a very spiritual level, I had not been totally honest with him from the beginning. My whole reason for being here was a farce. I couldn't bear to tell him the truth. Not just yet.

"Lena, if you must ask yourself the question, chances are you probably haven't."

Unsettled by this revelation, I retreated into the hypnotic notes of the music, only managing a shy smile ever so often at my new friend as we drove in silence. Comfortable in our independent thoughts, we didn't feel the need to speak. I felt totally at ease. My normal nervous chatter had all but disappeared. And much too soon, the miles of vineyards that straddled either side of the road gave way to small towns. He exited the *autostrada*, taking back roads known only to the locals wanting to avoid traffic. I was impressed that he remembered how to reach my cottage, considering he'd only been there once.

"Well, thanks for everything. I had an amazingly wonderful time. Would you like to come in for coffee or something?" I asked, not yet ready to say goodbye.

"You are truly welcome. You know I would love to come in, but I really must get back to help Lucio prepare for this afternoon's meeting. We have so much to cover in such a short time." He pulled the trunk release latch, leaving the car running.

Before I realized it, he'd already opened my door, holding his hand out to assist me. "Okay. I guess this is goodbye then," I said, not knowing what else to say. I didn't know if he wanted to see me again or what.

"No, Lena, not goodbye. I would love to see you again, tonight, if you like. You have my number? *Si?* Come here, *bella.*"

"You're gonna drive a woman wild if you keep kissing me like that!" I sighed, pretending to fan myself.

"Ah hah! That is precisely the point!" He retrieved my small bag from his trunk and sat in on the porch. He kissed me again on the cheek. "*Arriverderci, mia bella.* I will see you soon," he said as he drove off.

I hugged myself as I stood in the drive watching Giovanni drive away. I needed time alone for some deep thinking. Some time to reflect. Too much had happened over the past several days. I had to clear my head. A nice hot bath will help me to relax. I noticed Keenan's bike was no longer where he left it.

I stepped into my bedroom and stripped off my clothes in anticipation of sinking into a nice hot relaxing bubble bath. I got as far as the bed when I noticed something was amiss. The bed was now neatly made. The sheets had been changed and all evidence of Keenan and I being together was gone. "Hello, is someone here?" I shouted, half expecting Keenan to appear at any moment. Continuing to call out as I surveyed the cottage, I ended up in the kitchen. On the counter, propped up next to a bottle of *Chianti*, sat an envelope addressed to me. I recognized the handwriting. It was Keenan's. Inside was a short note.

Dearest Lena,

There is so much I want to say, but this is not the right time, nor the right place. I didn't realize the depth of my feelings I still have for you, and seeing you after so many years brought back those good memories. I've decided to return "home" to the realities I know exist in my own life. I know you need time to decide what it is you want – what's important to you. If you want to find me, you will.

You will always have my heart,
K

Interesting… This whole little getaway is becoming more complicated by the moment. Didn't Simone tell me the whole purpose of this "vacation" was for me to enjoy myself? Well, actually I guess I was enjoying myself. This was my one chance to rediscover my uninhibited side. The part of me I lost in the process of becoming my mother and I didn't want to ruin it by committing to be only with Keenan.

I looked at the note and read it over and over again. To my surprise, I wasn't upset about his leaving. On the contrary. Now I can concentrate on me without distraction. Sure it was wonderful being with him after all these years. After all, he was my first love. Funny thing though, as much as I enjoyed hanging out with Keenan, I really didn't know him anymore. We both had changed. I'm not saying I wasn't into him still. It's just that while I'm here, I want to do, go and be with whomever I want. For as long as I can. This is my fantasy. Why blow it being bogged down with all the drama that exists in the real world?

The bath will have to wait. Right now I could sure use a strong cup of espresso. I inhaled the fragrance of fresh coffee beans kept in a small container in the fridge, spooned enough beans for two cups in the grinder, then added the coffee along with water to my stovetop espresso pot and stepped back to watch it brew. I looked outside the window towards the beach. Butterflies flitted from one patch of flowers to another. Butterflies look so pretty from a distance, but give me the creeps up close. Nevertheless, I took my espresso outside to enjoy the beautiful spring morning.

The water was deceptively calm, almost mirror like, reflecting white puffy clouds on its surface. What a perfect backdrop to compliment how I felt inside. I was totally at peace—tired, but still at peace. I sat back and thought about all the men in my life. Keenan Jones was the standard I compared all other guys to. Over the years, I built him up so much in my mind, placing him on a pedestal no man could ever attain – not even he.

When we first started going together, I looked up to Keenan. Admired him. Often envied him. He was only a year older than me, but he was so focused, knowing exactly what he wanted to do with his life. From the time Keenan first spoke with an FBI agent during a school sponsored career day to encourage minority applicants to work for the government, he was hooked. It was all he ever talked about. When that agent told him how important it was for a potential applicant to not only have good grades, but to also be involved in school activities, he joined every club that would have him. And, instead of just focusing on one foreign language, Keenan convinced the guidance counselor into letting him take both Spanish and German. He said the languages were structured so differently from each other, that by taking both, he could increase his aptitude to learn any language he wished. By the time he graduated from college, majoring in International Relations, he was fluent in Arabic as well.

We both attended the same college remaining true to each other, but traveled in different social circles. I don't know how we ended up, or remained together. He was a charismatic academic and I was the shy, quiet type, only getting involved when it was absolutely necessary.

By his senior year, he'd already been accepted in the FBI's Special Agent training program, with a reporting date a month after his graduation. We promised to keep in touch and for a while we did. He visited me when he could during my last year of college. By the time I graduated from college with a business degree, he had completed his first year of training towards becoming a full-fledged agent.

I'll never forget the last time I saw him. It was during his last visit home before he was sent on his first of many overseas assignments. I volunteered to take him to the airport. We both cried, knowing this time when we said goodbye, it would be for good. I spent the entire summer depressed, missing Keenan, waiting for the mailman to bring news of his whereabouts. As the letters dwindled, my sisters encouraged me to return to the world of eligible, single men. Soon after, I met Mark.

I thought being married to Mark would make everything okay, but now I know no one can make you happy. I've often heard women say that you only get one chance for happiness so you'd better do it right the first time. But what is happiness? Family, money, a successful career? How about all three? Why should I place a limit on the amount of happiness I can attain? I do know there is no one definition of happiness. It truly depends on what you're looking for.

When I think of happiness, I picture myself being content in my own healthy body, living in peace and harmony in my surroundings, doing the things I love such as writing, painting and making music. I will be in love with a man who loves me unconditionally and places me first before anything or anyone else. I don't need lots of money. Just enough to live comfortably – not having to worry about the basic necessities of life. I'd open a little bookstore and serve coffee and pastries to my customers. I'd live close enough to ride my bicycle into town. My children will be healthy and have lots of friends to play with. Our lives filled with love and contentment. Yeah, it's a fantasy-filled wish, but what are fantasies but dreams deferred?

Then there's Giovanni Morelli. He's charming, handsome, sexy, smart, funny, adventurous, fascinating, attentive, sensitive, and *molte appassionato*... I can go on and on with his good attributes. What about his bad traits? I'm sure he has some, we all do. But for now, I haven't seen any. I had so much fun with Giovanni. With him I felt alive, willing to try new, different, exciting things. I stepped out of my comfort zone and thrived. I'm a very visual person. I need to see, touch, be surrounded by natural beauty to truly "experience" life. He showed me how to focus on my feelings and concentrate on what I truly want from life without fearing the consequences of my actions. I needed to embrace the fear and use it to my advantage. I could really get used to being with Giovanni.

I drank the rest of my espresso, placing the empty cup on the grass. The coffee cup was made from delicate bone china, something I refused to use at home. After all, the set cost way too much to actually drink coffee from or use for dinner, except special occasions. I laughed aloud. Why do we spend hundreds, sometimes thousands of dollars on dishes we're afraid to use because they might break? Absurd, isn't it?

The noonday sun shone brightly in the sky causing beads of perspiration to trail down the middle of my back. A swim would be refreshing. I looked in all directions. Since I was alone on the beach, I thought to myself, why not? I quickly ran down the rickety stairs removing the rest of my clothing, throwing them in a pile away from the water. I extended my arms and let the wind caress me in places kept hidden from the public eye.

Now I know why people go to nudist colonies. It's the most wonderful feeling in the world to be naked, standing on a beach feeling the warmth of the sun with the wind blowing against unclothed skin. As content as I was to stand there in the buff, I also wanted to experience the feel of the salty cool water on my body.

The surf beckoned me with its gentle lapping against the shore. I answered its call by running happily into the tide. I was never a very strong swimmer, so I was careful to not get too far from the shore. After several minutes of floating lazily on my back, I had enough. It was time to get back to the shore to plan the remainder of my day. I looked towards the beach and saw a lone figure standing waving. It was Simone. *Now* what does she want?

Unknowingly, the gentle currents had carried me out a bit further from the shore than I normally felt comfortable with. I started swimming towards the beach, struggling to get back, but not getting anywhere at all. The harder I swam, the more tired I became. Damn! I've heard about people getting in situations like this. It was an undertow pulling me in. What am I supposed to do? They say swim parallel to the shore until you're out of the riptide. But I am so tired. I continue to swim, but my arms start to feel like lead. I'm not getting anywhere. I go under once, twice. I'm so tired I don't think I can try anymore. I try to float, but the water keeps getting in my mouth. I cough, struggling to clear my throat. I'm so tired. My arms don't work anymore. I tried calling out to Simone for help. She doesn't hear me. I close my eyes. A sense of tranquility overcomes me and I finally succumb to the feeling to just let it all go...

PART TWO

CHAPTER 10

"Lena? Lena? Can you hear me? Open your eyes if you hear me! I think she's coming out of it."

Who is that calling my name? Where am I? I think I'm awake, but everything is so blurry and I'm so tired. A moan escapes my throat. I feel something stick me in the arm. A needle, perhaps? I blink my eyes a few times until my vision clears. A man in a white coat is shining a light in my face. I raise my hand to block the beam, but someone holds it back. "Where am I?" I whisper, surprised by the hoarse unfamiliar sounding voice that escaped from my own throat.

"She's awake! Go find her husband. Now!" The man in the white coat yelled to the younger woman standing beside him. He turned his head back towards me and spoke in a calm soothing voice. "Good morning Lena. My name is Dr. Akbar and you're in the Salinas Valley Regional hospital. You had us pretty worried for a while, but I'm glad you're back." He turned off the light and smiled, revealing unevenly spaced yellowed teeth.

"I'm in the hospital? How did I get here? Who rescued me?" I asked. The last thing I remembered was sinking deep under the water, unable to swim back to shore.

"Rescued you?" The doctor asked in confusion. "Why, no one rescued you my dear. You've been in a coma a little over two weeks."

I slowly realized I was back. I hadn't drowned. Somehow I'd made it back to the "real world". I wasn't ready to come back! I needed more time. I wanted to see Giovanni again! Why had I been forced to come back when I was having such an incredible experience "there"? A lone tear fell from the corner of my eye. I sighed, knowing my fantasy was over.

"Hey, don't cry. Your family will be thrilled to know you're awake. Look! Here's your husband." He stepped back and let Mark through.

"Lena? Hey baby. Are you okay?" asked Mark, stroking my hand, showing the tender side I fell for so many years ago.

"Mark..." I whispered, "Yeah, I'm okay. Sorry to have worried you guys so much. I just needed to get away – to rest for a little while. How are my guys doing?"

"You know your boys…. They knew you'd wake up, eventually. I think I was more worried than anyone. I thought you were sick or something, but the doctors couldn't find anything "wrong" with you. It's so good to see those eyes open again."

I was starting to regain my strength so I sat up in the bed. I ran my hand through my hair. It felt awful. Brittle and dry, like it hadn't been combed for days. Truth be told, it probably hadn't. As I readjusted trying to find a more comfortable position, I caught a whiff of myself and it wasn't pretty.

"Thanks Mark. That's really sweet of you," I replied. "Ooowee! I really need to take a shower. Is it alright doctor?" I looked at the older man's face. He reminded me of those guys from the Middle East minus their turbans.

"Of course. I shall have one of the nurses help you. Wouldn't want you to fall and hurt yourself, now would we?" He wrote something down in my chart, providing verbal instructions to the nurse.

"Mark, do you mind waiting before we talk? I think I'll feel a lot better when I wash some of this funk off of me. Are the boys here?" I sat up, trying to plump the pillow behind my back.

"No, they're in school. I tried to keep things as normal as possible for them since there was really nothing we could do for you. I've been here every day hoping, praying that you'd wake up. Here, let me do that for you." Mark fluffed the pillow and placed it comfortably behind my head. "Are you thirsty? Do you want some water? I could get something else if you prefer," he asked displaying genuine concern.

"Sure, some water would be nice. I am kinda thirsty." I replied loving the new found attention. "So who's staying with the kids while you're here?"

"My Mom flew down for a few days to help out." He poured a cup of water, found a straw, and held it to my lips.

"Oh really? That was nice of her. How long is she staying?" I asked, trying hard to keep my true feelings hidden.

Mark's mother and I never got along. From the time he first brought me home to meet his family, I felt like an outsider. It was only after my first child was born that I discovered what she really thought of me. I'd just brought James home from the hospital. He couldn't have been more than three days old the first time she saw him. I was resting in the bedroom when Mark brought James out to meet his Grandparents.

Anxious to hear her comments about her first grandchild, I admit I was eavesdropping. I remember her words like it was yesterday. She said, "Mark, honey! Look at his color! Lord, I hope he don't end up as dark as Lena and please don't let this child have that same nappy hair. I told you, you should have married "lighter". Now I'm going to have nothing but little niggah babies running around calling me Grandma!" I think what upset me more was Mark's lack of response to his mother's insulting his wife and child. She never let on to my face how she felt about me. Neither did Mark. I hoped and prayed that Mark married me for love and not merely to spite his mother.

"You can rest assured. She was here only for a couple of days. She was going to stay until James' graduation in a couple of weeks, but I convinced her I could handle the house and the boys on my own." Mark looked at his watch and continued, "It's almost 2. Lena, I'm going to pick up the kids from school so they can see you. I'll be back in a couple of hours. Do you need anything while I'm gone?"

"No, I think I'll be alright once I shower. I'm fine. Go get the boys. I can't wait to see them," I replied.

"You sure you're okay?"

"Yes, now go get my boys." I shooed him out the door.

"Okay. We'll be back in a couple." Mark brushed his lips over my forehead and squeezed my arm in one fluid motion.

A nurse who favored Diana Ross in her younger days came in to help. She fluttered around the room doing "nursey" things, never speaking to me directly. Thankfully, Mark had thought ahead to bring in a few of my toiletries. My legs felt like jelly when I finally stood. If it were not for the nurse holding on to me, I surely would've fallen straight on my face. Within moments, the strength returned to my legs and I managed to make it to the bathroom under my own power. "Nurse Ross" took a seat outside the bathroom door, affording me privacy. I turned the hot water on full steam and stepped in.

Lathering my hair with the rich fragrant shampoo, I felt something tangled up in my curls. I picked the item free from my hair, rinsed if off under the water. I gasped. What the hell?! It was a small piece of seaweed! Seaweed? Now how did that get there? It was way too crazy to even consider the ramifications of this little discovery, so I pretended it didn't exist and kept on with my shower.

An orderly brought in a tray of unidentifiable hospital food. Only then did I realize how hungry I truly was. After all, it had been weeks since I had eaten real food. I removed the protective tray covering, turning my nose up in disgust at what was supposed to pass as lunch. Everything on the tray was liquid, white, or both. A cup of broth, soda crackers, some kind of white meat and a small dish of rice pudding threatened to take away my appetite.

I thought back to the delicacies I'd experienced over the last few days in my dream – gourmet meals, decadent deserts and deliciously intoxicating wines. In comparison, I wouldn't feed this crap to my enemy's dog. As hungry as I was, I simply couldn't bear to fill my stomach with hospital food prepared by hairnet clad women slaving away in a cafeteria located one floor above the morgue.

"Chile, you'd better eat something. You gonna need to get your strength back to take care of those boys of yours. I seen 'em when they come by to visit you. They's a handsome bunch of kids. Didn't none of 'em cry though. Not a one! Them's is some strong children – 'specially the little one. He stood there talkin' to ya believin' all the time that you could hear him. He said you just needed a bit of rest and then you'd wake up. All them kids believed you'd wake up. They had faith in their Momma. But that husband of yours… Ooowee! He was a mess! Kept saying he didn't know what he was gonna do without you. Stayed here most nights just holdin' your hand, sittin' in this here cheer. Uh, huh. You got you a *good* family and a *good* man!" Nurse Ross held up her right hand like she'd just testified in front of the Lord. I looked in amazement at the woman whose words betrayed her extraordinary looks. I expected this woman to have the voice of a sensuous, sultry vixen. Instead, images of collard greens, sweet potatoes and fried chicken, seeped in deep southern roots spilled from her mouth.

Shaking off my surprise, I replied, "I'm sorry, but I can't eat this. Look at it! They didn't even try to make it look appetizing. I'll call my husband at home and have him bring me something decent to eat. Have you seen my cell phone?"

"Well, suit yourself. Cain't says I blames you though. They ain't the best cooks in this place. That is why I always brings my own food from home. I don't care what they say, cain't nobody fix no food for hundreds of folks an 'spect it to taste decent. At least drink the apple juice. Kind of hard to mess up juice, huh?" She smiled a toothy grin and handed me the room phone.

"Thank you," I replied. I dialed my home number. No one answered. They must have already left the house. Maybe I can catch Mark on his cell. I quickly dialed the number. When Mark answered, I asked him to stop by the *"Teriyaki Bowl"* to pick me up a bowl of teriyaki chicken, veggies and rice. He agreed and said he and the boys would be by to see me shortly.

Dr. Akbar stepped back into the room. In a heavily accented voice he stated, "I have good news for you, Lena. All your tests have come back normal. We can't find anything wrong with you, but as a precaution, we'd like to keep you another night for observation. After that, I think you can go home tomorrow."

"Thank you, doctor. I'll be able to go home tomorrow? That is good news." I attempted to display an enthusiasm I didn't feel. What was I going home to? My entire world and my perspective on my life had shifted. Nothing about me was the same, nor would it ever be the same again, especially after the past couple of weeks. How was I going to handle stepping back into my old life again? I needed time. Needed to be alone. "I think I'm going to rest now. Will you please let me know when my family arrives?"

"Yes, it is good for you to rest. Although you have been in a coma, your body will feel like it has been through a workout and needs time to recover. I want you to take it easy for a while before you get back into your normal routine." Dr. Akbar wrote additional instructions in my chart as he quietly spoke to the nurse. They both exited the room.

Return to the real world? To a marriage of convenience? Living a life void of passion, returning to a job I absolutely loathe, all the while holding on to the realization that it doesn't have to be this way? I scooted the bedside chair to the window and looked out at the landscape of central Kansas.

As I sat watching strangers go on with their lives, I knew I had to shake up my own life. The only way for things to be different, was for me to do something different.

"Mommy! I knew you'd wake up! I told them you just needed to rest. I told them and I was right! They told me to be quiet because I didn't know what I was talking about. They wouldn't listen to me!" My youngest son Carlos smothered me with hugs and kisses. Neil and James followed suit. Mark stood in the doorway smiling, happy to see his family together again.

"Well, Car, you were absolutely right and they should have listened to you. You guys know I couldn't stay away from you for too long." I touched each of their faces individually. Wiping tears away, hugging all of them, and reassuring them Mommy was back.

Mark eventually joined in our little group, offering me the delicious smelling teriyaki, as my stomach growled loud enough for all us to hear. We laughed. It felt good to be back together as a family. Too bad that feeling wouldn't last.

CHAPTER 11

The next day with Dr. Akbar's blessings and instructions to take it easy, I returned home with my family. Mark and the boys took the day off from work and school to help me get settled in. I wasn't sick and I really didn't need to be waited on, but it made them all feel useful so I accepted their care with patience. The house was in amazingly good shape, though not as meticulous as I normally kept it, but it was clean. Mark had done a good job in my absence. It appeared that the guys could exist quite well without me. I wondered how much of this was Mark's doing and how much was his mother's. Oh well, at this point it really didn't matter.

In spite of everything, I knew it was only a matter of time before things went back to normal, so I had to take full advantage of the current situation. The boys were on their best behavior, diligently trying to not disturb me with their constant bickering. Mark continued to run the house, affording me plenty of time to think. The five of us spent the rest of the day as a family. The boys caught me up on the part of their lives I had missed. I listened to their adventures, smiling happily as they told stories of their antics that made me want to wrap them all in cotton balls and keep them safely in their rooms until they were adults.

Deep down, despite having all the love in the world for them, I knew I had to take care of me first. I couldn't return to the life I temporarily escaped from. I'd gone through too much to simply return to the same old stuff. I had to make a change, but I wasn't sure where to begin. I was still on "sick" days, so thankfully I didn't have to come up with an excuse to take off from work. Over the next several days, I piddled around the house, trying to find things to occupy my time and my mind. I had a couple of weeks before I was supposed to return to work. And because I wasn't sick, I really didn't have anything to "recuperate" from.

Mark, true to fashion, spent his nights in front of the television or on the computer. So, just like every other day before my "journey", I went to bed alone without my husband. Life as I knew it, returned back to normal. Mark and the boys continued on with their routines. During the day, I watched way too many overly dramatic, daytime courtroom television shows. Where did they find these people?

After a week or so, totally out of the blue, thoughts of both Giovanni and Keenan resurfaced. I guess I had suppressed the memories of them both, relegating them to the forgotten dreams that they were. Unexpectedly, memories of both men returned with a vengeance. Time spent with Giovanni came back with a suddenness that overwhelmed me. I remembered it all like it really happened.

Did it? Listening to my husband popping the tab on another can of beer can, I knew what I had to do. I had to know for sure what really happened during those weeks I was laid up in that hospital bed in a coma.

Early the next morning, I heard the front door slam, signaling the last of my brood had finally left. I leapt from my bed, took a quick shower, dressed, stuffed an overnight bag with whatever it could hold, found my passport, grabbed my purse, and headed out the door. Although I was on a mission, the slightest obstacle could stop me dead in my tracks with the pangs of guilt over what I was about to do. I jumped into my little Honda and headed to the nearest branch of my bank.

I withdrew $5,000 from my personal savings account and wrote a check for another two grand from checking. This was my "40th birthday present to me" money. It was an accumulation of all my overtime pay from the past few years. The plan was to take my Mom and one of my sisters on a 7-day, all-inclusive Caribbean cruise to celebrate my milestone. This was much more important than sipping daiquiri's on board the deck of a Princess Cruise Line.

The next stop was the *Day Tour* travel agency. The travel agent didn't seem at all surprised when I asked her to book an open return, round-trip ticket to Florence, Italy. The ticket agent commended my finding such a good fare, especially on the day of the flight. She said same day fares to Europe were usually outrageously expensive; easily triple the amount I paid. I took that tidbit of information as a good sign. I don't remember driving to the airport, nor parking my car. I suppose at the time I didn't think too hard on what I was doing.

I tucked that parking lot ticket in my suitcase and trudged on to the terminal like a trooper; determined and resolved to do what I had to do. I was not about to let anything deter me from my mission. Yet still, as I sat in the cramped confines of the small plane taxing towards the runway, I thought I was either making the biggest mistake of my life or I was in for the adventure of a lifetime. I preferred to think the latter was true.

The flight landed in Detroit. I discovered the connecting flight was slightly delayed. I took this time as an opportunity to call Mark to tell him of my last minute decision to take a well-deserved vacation.

"Hello, may I please speak to Sergeant Delgado?" The young assistant placed me on hold. I listened to elevator music while I waited. I thought companies stopped playing that *Muzak* crap years ago.

"Sergeant Delgado," he answered.

Oh boy! What could I possibly say to explain myself this time? He was bound to think I had lost my mind! Well, come to think of it, even I thought I must've lost my mind. Time to fess up. I settled upon the truth.

"Uh, hey Mark."

"Hi, Lena. I see you finally decided to get of bed this morning. I tried calling home, but no one answered. Anyway, I hope you're well enough to fix dinner tonight. Got a surprise for you. I invited a couple of guys over for a few beers to watch the game. I promised them you'd fix your special gumbo."

Typical. He thinks I'm not feeling well, yet he still invites his friends over and expects me to magically throw together a pot of gumbo while they're watching TV and drinking beer. Thanks Mark, you just helped make telling you this a little easier. "Uh, Mark. I'm not at home. I'm in Detroit."

"Detroit. What the hell are you doing in Detroit?! Woman, have you lost your mind?!" He shouted. I heard a door close in the background.

"No. I haven't lost my mind," I responded calmly. "I'm going to Italy for a little vacation and I'll be there for about a week or so. This is something I need to do for me. I can't be with you or at home right now. I hoped you would understand. Although, I know you don't. Just tell the boys that Mommy loves them very much and I didn't leave because of them."

"Italy! Understand?! Oh, you think you can just up and fly off to Italy any old time you want? What am I supposed to do? Who's going to take care of the boys? What about your job?" He shot off one question after another. Panic, uncharacteristically, entered his voice.

"You'll take care of the boys like you have for the past weeks. It'll be just like I did all those times when you were deployed for months on end. Look, I need some time to think. At this point, I don't give a shit about that job. I hate that job! Why don't you just call them and tell them I'm taking an extended vacation." I heard the boarding announcement for my flight.

"You're running away from home? What are you? A child? Are you leaving me? You going off to be with some man? Lena, I'll tell you what. Since you need so much damn time to yourself, don't bother bringing your ass back home. This way you can have Italy and all the time in the world to think. I'll let the boys know that their mother has abandoned them!"

"Mark, I'm not abandoning my children. And this ain't even about some man either." Well, some of it was about a man, but I wasn't about to admit that to Mark. "After I spent all that time in the hospital, I realized that something was definitely wrong in my life. You know things haven't been all that great between us. If you would only open your eyes, you'd realize it too. Look, I've got to go. My flight is about to board. I'll call you when I get to Florence and let you know where you can reach me. Hey, take care of yourself and I'll give you a call later."

"Yeah, you too," he said sounding defeated, before hanging up the phone.

CHAPTER 12

I slouched down in the window seat of the *Alitalia* flight, nervously biting my nails, barely acknowledging the flight attendant's safety briefing. Thankfully, no other passengers sat in the adjoining seats and I was able to stretch out semi-comfortably for the seven hour flight to Florence. Emotionally drained, I closed my eyes and dozed off.

I awoke with a start. I had been dreaming, but quickly forgot what it was about. I slept for almost the entire flight not realizing the extent of my exhaustion. An older flight attendant, who looked to be rapidly closing in on the mandatory retirement age, nudged me awake to put my chair back to the upright position in preparation for landing. Looking out the window, the magnificent *Firenze* sprawled before me, welcoming all to the splendid glory of *Italia*. Feelings of trepidation overwhelmed my excitement. Suddenly, the regrets of my actions overtook me. Where would I stay? How would I survive?

The plane landed uneventfully and taxied to the terminal where all the passengers quickly deplaned. That is, all except me. I sat there glued to my seat, terrified, contemplating my next move. Several men came aboard, armed with cleaning supplies, and began clearing the debris left by passengers. When they finally reached my row, one young man looked at me and with a huge grin he said, "*Ciao bella. Benvenuto!* Welcome to Italia!"

Those few words were probably all the English that man knew, but they were enough to give me the confidence I needed to get off that plane and get out in the city. I found the train station, bought a one way ticket to *Vivaro* and effortlessly immersed myself back into the culture I lived with for several years.

During the two hour trip on the high speed passenger train to *Vivaro*, I continued to ponder my situation while looking out the window at the welcoming countryside. I knew very well that what I was doing was more than a notion. I was in a very foreign, albeit slightly familiar country. Thankfully, I had plenty of money to survive, if I was very careful. My emotions vacillated between excitement and fear. Too late to turn back now. The train approached the station.

I disembarked, realizing the very first thing I needed to do was find a place to stay. Using my very limited mastery of the Italian language, I searched through the ads posted on the station's billboard. A small card advertising a room for rent on the outskirts of the town of *Gorgazzio* caught my attention. Yeah, *Gorgazzio*. Just like in my dream journey. I thought for sure it must be a typo or either the room was a dump. They wanted a mere 20 euro per day. That's about $18. What a bargain! I phoned the number, attempting to use forgotten bits of a language I was never really fluent in. Luckily the woman replied in English that it was still available. She gave me the address and said the easiest way to find it would be to take a taxi. That's exactly what I did. I gave the address to the driver. He got me there in less than fifteen minutes, despite frequent backward glances, courtesy of the rear view mirror.

He pulled up in front of a beautifully maintained older home. I generously pulled out a few euros for a tip. He smiled a toothless grin and blew me a kiss. What is it with these older guys? I laughed, thanked him and I retrieved my bag from the rear seat. A well-dressed elderly woman came through the entry way and greeted me kindly. She must have been at least seventy, but she had the gait of a much younger woman.

"*Parle inglese?*" I questioned the woman, not wanting to butcher her language anymore than I had to. She nodded. "Oh, wonderful! Hi, my name is Lena Delgado. Thank you for letting me stay in your home. I arrived only today and I wasn't sure where I was going to live." I offered her my hand.

"*Ciao* dear. *Mi chiamo es Signora Malavasi,* but please call me Simona," she replied in a heavily accented English. I closed the heavy wrought iron gate behind us and followed her into the house. A pot of delicious smelling coffee brewed on the stove. She offered me a cup. I accepted.

Simona? What? That's very similar to the name of the woman in my dream only she was Black and younger by several years. Coincidence? Maybe...

"Do you take your coffee with milk and sugar?" asked Simona, as she removed a box of *Parmalat* from the fridge.

"Both please." I looked around the modestly decorated kitchen.

From where I sat, I could see into the living room. The traditional furniture could have been either decades old or merely weeks.

"Lena? What brings you to *Gorgazzio*? From your accent it sounds like you are a long way from home." Simona said, while pouring two cups of steaming coffee. She topped both cups off with warm milk.

"Well, it's kind of a long story and I really don't want to bore you with it. The short version is, I love your country, felt I needed a little vacation, so I decided to take it here. In Italy." I hoped I sounded convincing. After all, it was *mostly* true.

"Are you traveling alone? You are not Italian. I can see that. What brings you to *Gorgazzio* of all places? We are not exactly considered a tourist destination. How long do you think you shall stay?" She eyed me suspiciously.

"Yes, I'm traveling alone. I'm not sure how long I'll be here, though. Probably no longer than a week or two." I sipped the dark, sweet hot liquid, suddenly feeling very unsure of myself.

"Oh. Only a couple of weeks? I was hoping to have someone here longer - at least for a month or more." She looked at me curiously.

"Signora Malavasi, I'll pay you more than what you're asking for the room. I just need a place to stay and I think your house will be perfect," I responded, ignoring her curiosity.

"Ah, I see. *Alora*. Well, whatever it is you are hiding from I hope you will tell me more when you feel it is the proper time. For now, let me show you the room." She stood motioning me to follow.

I picked up my small suitcase and followed her through the house and out the back door. She pointed towards a smaller cottage and said, "My husband and I built this addition for my daughter. She has since gone on to attend university. It has been empty for years. I used it mostly for storage until my daughter suggested I rent it out. My husband passed away earlier this year and the extra money will come in handy. There is one bedroom, a private bath and a small kitchenette. It's fully furnished and there's also a television if you like TV. My only request is that you keep the noise down. I am an old woman and I sleep very lightly. Come, I shall show you the inside."

She opened the door, went inside, pulled open the curtains and raised the windows to let in the fresh afternoon air. It was perfect. It was small, but setup efficiently, maximizing every square inch. "*Signora* this is wonderful! I know you wanted to rent out by the

month, so I'll pay you a full month's rent and if I leave before the month is up, you keep the money."

"Dear, please call me Simona. I think your plan will work out fine. One thing you should know, there is no telephone here. So if you need to use the phone, knock on the back door and someone will let you in. I do not mind you making long distance calls, as long as you pay for them. I do not get out as much as I used to, mostly to mass, but someone will be here. My oldest son lives on the top floor with his wife. I shall introduce you to them later this evening. Well, I will let you get settled. Dinner is served at eight. I always cook plenty of food. You are welcome to join us."

"Thank you so much Simona. I'll keep your invitation in mind. Oh by the way, let me pay you for the room." I started to reach for my purse, but she waved me off.

"You can take care of that later. Why not get cleaned up and go explore? The town is less than a kilometer away. By the time you are dressed, the shops should be open again. You did say you have been here before, right?"

"Yes, ma'am. It's been several years, but I think I still remember where everything is." I couldn't tell her about my "recent travels" to the town. She would think I was crazy if I did.

"Lena, whatever it is you have come here for, I hope you find him. I mean *it*." She smiled and closed the door behind her.

I surveyed the tidy room, which was more like a studio apartment. A full sized bed was pushed to one side of the room, sandwiched between a floor lamp and chest of drawers. Directly off the kitchenette, on the opposite side of the studio was a full bathroom that also functioned as a laundry room with its compact washer and dryer. A small table and chair completed the layout. Obviously, someone with an interest in primary colors had done the decorating because bright yellow, red, and blues – with the requisite green plant thrown in, dominated the color scheme.

Nevertheless, this would suit me just fine. I opened the small refrigerator, took out a large bottle of *frizzante* water and quenched my thirst.

I sat down on the bed and thought about my situation. Either I was crazy, stupid, or both. What was I doing running around Italy, chasing what was probably only a figment of my imagination? I had no proof of what I experienced as being "real". For all I knew, maybe I really was hospitalized in a coma for all those days and dreamt the entire time. Maybe there was no such person as Giovanni. I always did have a vivid imagination and it *was* possible that I imagined the whole thing! But one thing was certain, I had to know for sure.

After walking a few hundred yards from Simona's house, I realized how much I underestimated not only the warmth of the day, but also the distance to the town center. Beads of perspiration trickled down my back into the space between my shoulder blades. I could feel moisture gather in the crotch of my too snug pants. Trying desperately to avoid the cars whizzing by, I had already tripped twice on cracks in the unevenly paved street. As with many small Italian towns, sidewalks didn't exist outside the main business district. So instead of me being a sexy vixen strutting to find her man, I was about to sprain an ankle and end up sitting on the side of the road, waiting for some kind soul to put me out of my misery.

The regret of my actions caused doubt to seep deeply into the depths of my soul. I stopped and turned around heading back to the house to rethink my plan.

Out of nowhere, a car on the opposite side of the road slowed and beeped its horn. It was the same taxi driver who picked me up from the train station. He smiled his toothless grin and waved for me to get in. I eagerly thanked him, ran across the street, and jumped into the front seat of the car. Cool air greeted me as I accepted the man's handkerchief to dab the sweat from my face. He spoke in a steady stream of Italian, grinning at me between perfunctory glances at the road. It was obvious this man felt affection for me, but I couldn't tell if it was fatherly concern or just wishful thinking. After all, the man looked to be in his late sixties. I smiled and asked him to take me to the shopping district.

Within minutes he stopped in front of the entrance to the town center. I looked around at the familiar buildings and this time it really did seem like I never left. I reached inside my purse to pay the old man for his kindness. He waved me off, stroking my face with the back of his heavily veined hand. He looked into my eyes, saying something unintelligible. All I could make out was the word "*angelica*" or angel. Returning his now damp handkerchief, I held his hand tenderly, thanked him for his kindness and reached for the door handle.

I watched the old man drive away, wondering what he could've been thinking. When the taxi was out of sight, I turned and took it all in. The stores were the same as in my "dream". The meat market, the *gelato* café, the *pasticceria,* even the smells — they were all as I'd remembered from just a week ago.

I saw him coming out of the *Banco Populare* carrying a large envelope in his hand! My mouth dropped wide open. He was real! Oh, my God! Giovanni *is* real! It wasn't a dream after all! I didn't know what to do. Before it was all so easy. It wasn't *real*. It was just a distorted version of reality. But there he stood in the flesh, across the street, unaware of me watching him.

"Very *machismo*. Is he the one you have traveled so many miles to see?" The older, Italian version of Simone touched my elbow, startling me with her presence. I jumped, dropping my purse on the sidewalk. Its contents spilled out.

Giovanni looked over and saw me. He called out my name and quickly headed in our direction.

"Oh, Simona. *Ciao!*" I replied nervously, gathering my belongings off the sidewalk. Quietly wishing for her to disappear.

Simona stood her ground watching things unfold before her eyes, anxious to see what truly brought this mysterious Black woman from America to her little village.

Giovanni was even more handsome than I remembered. He appeared more rugged or maybe he was just tired. The shadow of a beard lined his jaw. His eyes were focused squarely on mine. He sauntered across the street and stood before me, taking me in. A hint of a smile teased at his lips before turning into a full blown smile. He reached out his arms for me and I melted into his embrace.

"You are a sight for sore eyes. Where have you been? *Mia bella* I have been looking all over for you." Concern filled his voice with emotion.

"Shhhh. We'll talk later. I'm just so happy to finally be with you again." I felt like I was holding on to him for dear life. The sound of a clearing throat brought me back to my senses. I slowly withdrew from his arms and looked towards Simona and replied, "*Scusa*, Simona. Let me introduce *Signore* Giovanni Morelli, a very good friend of mine. This is Simona Malavasi. I'll be staying at her house for a while." I felt awkward introducing the two, praying that my two worlds wouldn't collide in front of me.

"So, you two know each other well it appears. Morelli, eh? I think I have heard of your family. That's what happens when you become an old woman, Lena. Pretty soon, you know all there is to know about everyone in this town. I shall run along now. I am sure you have lots to catch up on. Lena, that invitation for dinner is still good. Bring Giovanni. Perhaps we can reminisce about the Morelli family." Simona raised her eyebrows questioningly before catching up to her friends waiting a few feet away.

"You're staying with Signora Malavasi? What happened to your cottage? I went back that night to get you, but you were gone. I knocked and knocked, waiting for you. I looked through the windows, but still I see nothing. No lights, no noise, no sign of you at all. I was so worried. I searched the beach and saw the clothes you wore earlier half covered by sand. Lena, I thought something terrible had happened to you." The intensely green of his eyes overshadowed all traces of gold, as sadness overtook his joy.

He cupped my face between his hands and kissed me. Just like magic, everything and everyone on that busy street disappeared right then and there. As far as we were concerned, we were totally alone. If you look up "swoon" in the dictionary, I'm sure my picture was there, because that is exactly what I did. I momentarily swooned in his arms. Thankfully, he caught me before I could hit the ground.

"Oh, Giovanni." I loved saying his name. "That was *magnifico!*" Only then, did I realize how much I was missed.

"Lena, I have so many questions. We must talk," he replied still holding me tenderly.

"Yes, I know. There are so many things I must tell you, but I don't know where to begin. Do you have a free moment now? Is there somewhere private we can go?" I asked, wanting nothing more than to be with him.

"Whatever I was doing can wait. Come, I will take you to my apartment. It is not too far from here."

He led me to a white scooter parked against the curb, handed me a helmet, and helped me climb aboard. I wrapped my arms around his waist and enjoyed the scenery. The town wasn't so bad either.

We pulled into a driveway across the street from the same *pasticceria* Keenan and I had coffee in. That's interesting. I just realized I haven't thought about Keenan. For years, the mere thought of him was never very far from my consciousness, but now he was almost a long lost memory. Giovanni parked the scooter, offering his hand to help me dismount. He punched in a code to unlock the gate and guided me towards the back of the duplex to a flight of stairs. Neither of us spoke, each wondering what the other had to say. He opened the door to a spacious, thoroughly modern bachelor pad.

"Wow! This place is amazing!" And it was. From the outside, his apartment appeared to be an average Italian flat. The exterior was typical nondescript, gray concrete, aged by centuries of grime and grit. Nothing special. However, the outside appearance was deceptive as it thoroughly hid the pleasures waiting behind the locked doors.

The apartment looked like it came straight from the pages of *Metropolitan Home*. Beautiful marble floors greeted me as I stepped through the entryway. The contemporary living room furniture, sleek, simple and stylish, dominated the living space. Natural fiber rugs kept the modern theme going. This is what Italian design is all about-- elegance, simplicity, and functionality. The red leather sofa sat low to the floor and was flanked by two cream chairs on either side. A leopard print throw was casually flung across one of the chairs.

An original Picasso hung behind the sofa, bringing the entire room's look together. Giovanni's style was definitely what I would call minimalist because clutter was nowhere to be seen. There was a place for everything and everything was in its place. He stood back watching me marvel at his exquisite taste. Giovanni continued to watch me explore his personal space.

I opened the last door that led to his spacious bedroom. I expected to find a typical bachelor style bedroom with mirrors on the ceiling and animal print bedspread, but I was pleasantly surprised. A black satin bedspread covered his neatly made bed and the only mirror in sight was a full length one pushed back into a corner. Given that there were no obvious signs of feminine touches to his apartment, I felt confident in the assumption that he lived alone.

French doors opened outwards to a large balcony overlooking a private garden. I stepped outside to admire the alabaster statues surrounded by a variety of plants and flowers in the garden below. Giovanni followed.

"*Alora*, do you approve?" He wrapped his arms around me from behind offering me a wine glass filled with *frizzante* water.

Giovanni held me as I drank. I closed my eyes, enjoying the sound of birds chirping and smelling the sweet scent of flowers from the garden below. "It is wonderful here. I love how you've decorated your place." I tried to snuggle deeper into his arms.

"*Mi' amora*, you must tell me what is going on. Where have you been and why did you leave so quickly?" He removed his shirt.

He just called me "his love". Oh, man! As much as I want to tell him the truth, I still don't know where to begin. It all sounds so farfetched, too unbelievable. This type of thing doesn't happen, can't happen! It is absolutely not possible for me to have met Giovanni in some altered reality! I have such strong feelings for this man. Feelings like I never felt with anyone in my entire life.

I turned slowly around to face him, placed my index finger over his lips, looked at his gorgeous face and kissed him. Our breathing became heavy with anticipation of what we both wanted to occur. I felt his manhood grow hard on my leg and moistness from excitement, not perspiration, soon crept into my crotch. This time, neither of us wanted to hold back our feelings for one another. The bed beckoned us to seal our fate.

Giovanni literally means "*Gift from God*" and God only knows Giovanni had me giving thanks and praise to the highest as he kissed me from head to toe. I know he wanted to take this further and make mad passionate love to me. An acquaintance once told me when a man makes your toes curl, you should stay with him. If he doesn't, it's time to hit the road and find someone who does. Cuz life is too short to have to live with mediocrity. I planned on finding out if this applied to this super sexy man.

A knock at the door cut our passion short. Just as well, because this time, when we made love, it would be for real and not just in my head. I had to tell him the truth—for both our sakes. Giovanni yelled out something in Italian. I heard a man's voice followed by an even louder pounding at the door.

"I apologize, Lena. It is my brother, Lucio. Did I mention we share this house? Actually, I have the top apartment while he has the bottom floor. We were supposed to meet this afternoon to pay the band that performed at my club last night. That's where I was going when I saw you. I totally forgot. I will be right back. I must give him the money." He closed the bedroom door behind him.

I exhaled and quietly laughed, rolling around on the bed, happier than I had been in a long time. Giovanni returned to the bedroom carrying a tray filled with cheeses, bread, grapes, and a carafe of wine. He placed the tray on a table and retreated to the bathroom. I stood, prepared to face the music.

"Now Lena, we shall talk," he replied in a serious tone and patted the empty space besides him.

I couldn't put this conversation off any longer, though I desperately wanted to. After taking a few deep breaths, I sat down, and started to speak, metaphorically "spilling my guts". In between multiple glasses of wine, I told Giovanni the entire story of what happened over the last few weeks. I conveyed Simone's explanation of how I ended up here and the ability to interact with others during my "dream". I revisited meeting him and Lucio, recalling the time we spent together, the places we visited, and how important he was to me.

When he got up and walked away, looking at me like I was a crazy woman, I told him how much he'd come to mean to me in such a short time. Tears flowed freely from my eyes as I expressed my feelings. I admitted that even I didn't believe it was real until I actually returned to *Gorgazzio*, this time by airplane, train, taxi, and finally on my own two feet. I didn't know why it happened, or how it was possible. In fact, I told him until I actually spoke to him on the street and he recognized me I had convinced myself that it *was* just a dream.

Finally when the sun began to set, signifying the end of the day and possibly the end of this relationship, I stopped speaking. During my entire explanation, Giovanni didn't speak a single word, but his facial expressions conveyed volumes. Disbelief, confusion, anger, sadness – all appeared simultaneously. He walked over to the window watching the sun go down, and spoke his first words.

"Lena, please go. I need time to think about what you have told me. *Mama mia!* You understand that it all sounds like you are out of your mind. *Amore mio*, I do have strong feelings for you, but if what you have told me is true… I *know* you were here! We talked, we laughed, I introduced you to my Papa… *Mi dispiace non capisco*, I think you should leave. I need time to think about this. When I am ready to talk to you, I know where to find you." He sighed deeply, shaking his head and went out to the balcony.

Despite the feeling of my heart breaking into a million tiny pieces, I used the bathroom to freshen up. I did not know what to say. The thought of losing him was too much to bear. I straightened my clothes and started to leave, but before I did, I opened the door and said, "Giovanni, I'm so sorry that I hurt you. It was never my intention to deceive you. It all happened so fast. I didn't know how to stop it. We were having such a good time. I didn't know we would become so close so quickly. If you never want to see me again, I'll understand. I came to Italy to find out if it was true, if you were real. I had to know. Now I feel I've hurt you so much... Please forgive me."

He remained standing with his back turned. He spoke not a word, didn't even turn around. On his shoulder blade, a small birthmark shaped like a Nike swoosh, caused me to let out a gasp. I covered my mouth to stifle the surprise trying to escape my throat.

Unable to fix the situation, I quietly collected my shoes from where I left them earlier and locked the front door behind me.

A slight chill was in the air, reminding me how close this town was to the mountains. Stupid me, I didn't even have a sweater. As I went through the front gate, a friendly face greeted me.

"Lena, what are you doing here? Ah, so you are my brother's mystery woman. The one he has kept behind his closed doors. No wonder he tried to get rid of me so quickly." Lucio noticed the pained expression on my face. "Are you alright? Where is Giovanni?"

I couldn't speak. I could only cry, covering my face, shielding myself from his kindness. Finally I said, "We sort of had a little disagreement. Can you give me a ride to my place?"

"But of course, *mi'amica*. Where are you staying?" He guided me to his flashy Ferrari and opened the passenger door.

"Do you know Signora Malavasi? She lives on *via Fabio Filzi*. I'm staying in her guest house for just a little while," I replied accepting a tissue to dry my tears.

"*Si*, I know where she lives. It is only a couple of kilometers from here." Lucio closed the door behind me, glanced at me wearily and sped off.

He pulled in front of Simona's house and I just sat there for a minute. Should I tell Lucio what I told Giovanni? It's probably better that I don't. After all, I don't really know him that well. But, he is Giovanni's brother. On second thought, it's probably better if I keep this information as quiet as possible. You never know what some people will do if they think you're a little wacky.

"Well, thanks for the ride Lucio. I forgot how cool the evenings can be and these shoes aren't exactly made for walking." I attempted a smile.

"My pleasure," he had more to add, "Lena, my brother really does care for you. You should have seen him this past week when he could not find you. He was, how do you say, 'a total wreck'. However, there is something you should know about Giovanni. When he likes a woman, and I mean truly likes her, he spares no emotions. He told me you thought he was only interested in you because you are a Black American. That he was curious about what it would be like to be with you... I know my brother well and nothing can be farther from the truth. Of course, my Papa would love for us to bring home a nice Italian girl, but we were raised to accept love no matter what kind of package it comes wrapped in. Besides, after a week in the sun we are the same color as you." He laughed. "I do not pretend to know anything about you, nor what you have gone through, but just know that Gio is the real thing."

"Thanks, Lucio. I appreciate you telling me that. I'd better go. I need to get cleaned up before dinner." I reached for the car door handle and was stopped by his grasp.

"Whatever has happened between you two, if it is meant to be, then it will be."

I unfolded myself from the confines of the car and watched him drive off.

CHAPTER 13

I stood in front of Simona's house watching cars speed by, contemplating my next move. I sure as hell didn't feel like being alone. I knew in my heart I wouldn't see Giovanni again tonight. He was too upset. It was now 7:43. The grumbling in my belly offset the lightheadedness I felt from drinking too much wine on an empty stomach. I inhaled the fragrant aromas wafting from the kitchen and hurried back to my room to freshen up for dinner.

I showered and changed into a pair of jeans and one of the few light sweaters hanging in my closet. I knocked softly at the back door. A rather unremarkable, casually dressed, plain looking woman answered and invited me in. She spoke exceptional English, introducing herself as Freda, Simona's daughter-in-law. I followed her to the living room and encountered a stout barrel-chested, middle-aged man with a booming voice, approaching me with arms outstretched.

"*Buona sera.* Lena, is it? *Mi chiamo es Vincenzio.* Welcome to our home," he bellowed reaching for me.

I didn't know whether to remain sitting or get up and run, so I stood and accepted his enthusiastic welcome. "Uh, thank you. Pleased to meet you," I replied timidly.

"*Basta*, Vincenzio. Leave her alone. *Ciao*, Lena. I am so happy you decided to come. Where is your friend, Signore Morelli?" she asked, drying her hands on a kitchen towel, looking past me towards the door.

"He couldn't make it tonight. But he said to thank you for the invitation." I lied, not wanting to say more about the situation.

"I see. *Por favore,* make yourself comfortable. Vincenzio, go out and help your brother and his wife bring in the *vino.*" Simona nodded at me and returned to the kitchen.

Freda and I made small talk while the others busied themselves with the preparations for the family dinner. I learned she worked on the American base as a translator. That's why her English was so good. I told her I used to live in the area a few years ago and had returned because I missed Italy so. The sound of a throat clearing drifted from the kitchen, privately chastising me for not telling the entire truth.

Through the front door entered a man as handsome as any movie star. He was dressed fashionably in the typical European style – black blazer over black slacks. A blue silk scarf adorned his jacket. His salt and pepper hair was feathered back from his face.

One look and it was perfectly clear which brother inherited the good looks in this family. Following the man was an energetic young boy who looked to be about 9 or 10. He burst through the door calling for his *Nonna*. Bringing up the rear was a woman I had yet to see, busily giving out instructions in rapid bursts of Italian, not only to her son, but also to Vincenzio. A flurry of colorful fabric appeared through the space in the door.

When the woman finally entered the house she laid eyes on me, covered her mouth in surprise, and gasped. An eerie silence settled upon us all. The woman was Ojuma, the hairdresser I bumped into on my earlier "altered reality" trip.

I stared at Ojuma. I was dumbfounded thinking this can't be happening. This really can't be happening! How am I going to get out of this? Is this just another coincidence or can it be fate?

"Lena, is it really you? What are you doing here?" Ojuma asked softly, confused.
I smiled innocently, once again not knowing what to say. I was getting pretty good at this being speechless thing. All eyes were now on me.

"Ojuma! It is so good to see you again after all these years!" I walked over to her to say hello. We embraced like old friends.

Being the classy woman that she is, Ojuma didn't let on about our previous meeting. She played it off like it had indeed been years since we'd last seen one another--and not a matter of weeks. I appreciated her tact, taking cues off her to put everyone else at ease.

She looked me up and down. Curiosity was written all over her face, but she didn't succumb to the temptation to question me in front of everyone. "Lena, I want you to meet my husband Daniele. Daniele, this is Lena. I've known Lena for many years from her patronage of my salon and I'm pleased to call her my friend."

"It's a pleasure to meet you. I've heard so much about you." I extended my hand towards him, at the same time noticing how the slight graying throughout his hair only served to emphasis his classic good looks.

"No, no, no. Hand shaking is for strangers. If my Ojuma calls you a friend, then you are like family." Daniele embraced me as everyone else looked on.

"Come everyone. The first course is ready to be served." Simona shooed everyone from the living room towards the large dining room table.

We took our seats, and lifted our glasses in a toast. In unison, all shouted, "*Salute!*" We then enjoyed a plate of *antipasto* made up of cheese, fruit and thinly sliced meat. The next course was pasta covered in a deliciously light cream sauce.

As the pasta dish made its rounds around the table, Simona started the conversation. "*Alora*, Lena, tell us a bit about yourself. You are American, *si*? What brings you to our beautiful little village?"

"Well, as I told you before, I used to live near *Gorgazzio* several years ago. My husband was in the Army and stationed at the base a few miles from here. Italy is one of the most beautiful countries in the world. The food, the people, and the culture – I came to love them all. When I used to live here, I felt so alive, so full of passion. It's been a few years and I needed a vacation so I returned to Italy. Let's just say I'm searching for something to make me feel alive again." I tore off a piece of bread, drizzled it with olive oil and enjoyed the full flavored sensation.

"You are married? Does your friend know that?" Simona questioned me as they all looked from her to me.

"Momma, don't be impolite. Lena is our guest. Can you blame her for wanting to return to *bella Italia*? I think she has great courage to travel alone." Daniele replied in my defense.

"I do not mean to be rude, Daniele. I am just saying that if she has a husband at home, she should not be over her frolicking around with one of our young men." She rose to get the main course of roast pork and sautéed porcini mushrooms with rosemary potatoes on the side. Freda followed to help.

"Do not worry about her. She is much too old fashioned. Lena, if you want to get to know a real Italian man, I will be happy to show you around." Vincenzio replied, winking at me.

"Vincenzio, what would your wife think hearing you speak like that?" Ojuma teased.

"So what? I am a man. I still have fires burning even if they do not get stoked as much as they used to," he replied in heavily accented English after gulping his wine.

"Who is this man my Mother refers to? Maybe we know him?" Questioned Daniele.

"He is one of the Morelli boys. The older one I believe. You remember? They own that club in the town center – *Busco's* or something," replied Simona. She returned carrying three plates of steaming hot food, Freda followed with the same.

"He is local?" Ojuma asked, confused. She obviously retained some recollection of the conversation we shared in her beauty salon. At that time, however, I was head over heels for Keenan, although I never mentioned any names. I met Giovanni shortly after we spoke.

"Ah, yes. I know the Morelli's. They are closer to my sister's age, though. From what I understand, one of them is considered to be a real playboy. The other is rumored to be a businessman only concerned with the success of his club. If you ask me, neither lifestyle is healthy. Other than that I do not know much about them. I believe their family is from the north," added Daniele.

"That is enough about Lena's love life. Antonio, tell your *Nonna* about your football game and how you scored the winning goal." Ojuma graciously changed the focus of the conversation from Lena to sports.

The meal was completed with the serving of freshly brewed espresso and plain torte cake. The women retreated to the kitchen for cleanup, while the men relaxed in front of television watching sports.

"Ojuma, why don't you and Lena take a walk? Freda and I can handle this," insisted Simona.

"Are you sure, Momma? You know it goes much faster with many hands."

"*Si, si*. Go. Lena looks like she needs to talk to someone who understands her. Who better than you? We will be fine."

"Thank you for the delicious meal, Simona. It was the best food I've eaten in a very long time," I replied setting a dish on the counter.

Out of the blue, Simona wrapped her arms around me and hugged me like she knew I needed to be hugged. She stepped back nodding her head that she understood more than she let on.

"Come Lena. Let us take a little walk. Do you need a sweater? There is a slight chill in the air." Ojuma reached into the hall closet and pulled out two oversized wool sweaters. One for me, the other for her. She kissed both her men goodbye, telling them she would be back shortly.

I draped the heavy sweater over my shoulders, as did she. We walked for quite a distance before either one of us spoke.

"Alright Lena. Talk. What is going on? Are you *really* here this time, or is this another of your adventures? Although, I must admit it is still quite a stretch of the old imagination to believe what you told me is possible." Ojuma replied with an English-tinged Somalian accent. She kept shaking her head in disbelief.

"Oh, yes. I'm really here this time. I traveled by air on an *Alitalia* flight, took a train from *Firenze* to *Vivaro*, rode in a taxi to *Gorgazzio*, driven by a very talkative old man. Twice. I even have the jet lag to prove it. But, I can't explain to you what's going on because I don't know myself. I had to find out if what I experienced was real, had to know if it really happened. Did it? Did I stop by your hair salon a couple of weeks ago? Did we really sit and drink tea together?" I asked, still wanting confirmation that I was not losing my mind.

"Yes, Lena. It all happened as you remember. You were as real to me then as you are standing before me now." She tried to make sense out of the unexplainable.

"But how can something like this be physically possible? I do believe that spirits walk amongst the living. Some people have been known to see and speak to them. But those spirits are no longer living. I'm still alive. That's the part I don't understand. The part that doesn't make any sense." Our walk took us directly in front of the town's church.

"Lena, look. There are many, many, things on this earth none of us truly understand. Small miracles happen everyday. I know you say that you are not very religious, but think about a child being born. That is a miracle. Watch the sun rise in the morning and then set in the evening sky, night after night. That too is a miracle. My point is we are surrounded by miracles everyday. Maybe this is what happened with you."

"You're exactly right. We are surrounded by miracles," I said.

"The problem is most people are so wrapped up in their busy lives that when something truly special does present itself, their eyes remain closed and they never get the chance to see it unfold. My advice to you is to accept what has happened to you and go on from there. I also advise you to not go telling your story to just anyone. You see, when people do not understand something different they are frightened and often react with fear or anger. Remember what they did to the so-called witches in your country?" Ojuma draped her arm across my shoulder.

127

"Yes, I do remember learning about the Salem witch trials and how they persecuted all those women they suspected of being witches. Believe me, I don't want anything like that happening to me. I understand and agree with what you mean about keeping my story to myself. There's one problem though. I've already told Giovanni everything."

"You did? How did he react?" she asked, eyes wide open in disbelief.

"Well, he didn't have much to say. In fact, he looked at me like I was out of my mind the entire time I spoke."

"This Giovanni… What does he mean to you? Why did you tell him?" Ojuma pointed towards a bench on the church's grounds.

"I met him during my last "trip" here. You know how real it seemed for you to be with me? Well, I ended up spending a great deal of time with him. We really hit it off. He challenged me to do things I never thought I'd ever be able to do. When we were together I felt so alive! I told him about my husband and my life back in the states. He wasn't thrilled about being involved with a married woman, but we just decided to keep things light. You know, only on the surface. Eventually, strong feelings developed between us making everything so complicated. After I returned home to my normal life, I realized what I was missing. I missed me! So I bought an airline ticket to *Italia* before I could talk myself out of it. Ojuma, I had to know if he was real. If what I felt was real…"

"You speak as if you are in love. Is he the man you were going to see after I fixed your hair so nicely?" she joked.

I smiled thinking of Giovanni. "Well, no. To tell you the truth, that was Keenan. He's a very old friend I ran into shortly after I first arrived. I met Giovanni later that day and this man is like no other man I have ever known. Too bad I'll never know how wonderful he really is." I sighed deeply, realizing had badly I had messed everything up.

"Maybe all is not lost. If he is as wonderful and caring as you say, he should be able to get past all this. Give him some time. Trust me when I say your story is a lot for anyone to digest."

"I hope you're right. Now tell me about Daniele. Girl, your man is too fine! He looks like some Roman god. I see why you gave up everything to be with him."

"Yes, he is very handsome. I am very lucky, but so is he. Lena, you must know I did not give up everything to be with him. Being with

Daniele doesn't complete me, but I feel complete when I am with him. Think of me as being a beautiful painting. Stay with me now. Even unframed, the painting is still beautiful. Is it not? Daniele is like the frame to make the beautiful painting stand out even more. We are good together. I love him, he loves me. What more can you ask for?" She replied in a tone that could have been mistaken for arrogance had it come from anyone but her.

"I envy you. You seem to have it all together. Look at me. I have a husband and a family, yet here I am halfway around the world, in love with a man I really know nothing about – in Italy of all places. In my head I know us being together is hopeless, but my heart tells me another story."

"Sometimes you must follow your heart. When you are unhappy and your heart is heavy, it is God's way of telling you to try something else. I am not advising you to totally forsake your family for your own happiness. I am simply saying you have to consider your feelings too. You would be surprised how well life works out when we stop trying to change the course set out for us. Now how about we get some *gelato* before we head back?"

"That sounds perfect. You know I never could resist good *gelato*." I rose from the bench, walking alongside my new confidant.

We came upon the local *gelato* shop. I chose the hazelnut, while Ojuma chose peach and blueberry. She paid the attendant since I didn't bring any money with me. Now why can't American ice cream taste this good? I'd pay a small fortune for this back home. We walked around the small plaza, gazing into windows studying the latest fashions, commenting on our preferences.

"Lena, I do not wish to sound rude, but did you bring any sexy clothes with you? I remember your always being dressed so casually – blue jeans, casual shirt and either sandals or sneakers for your shoes. Look, if you want to win over Giovanni's heart, as well as his forgiveness, you are going to have to look like you mean business and dress the part." Ojuma surveyed me up and down.

Self-consciously, I looked down at my outfit. She was right, as usual. Even if I had taken care to pack my best clothes, I would've ended up with outdated ill-fitting outfits. Since I got married and had kids, I stopped trying to look my best, instead being content to dress in anything that happened to fit at the moment. I needed clothes that made me feel like a woman. "You're right. I do need a few new outfits.

129

In my hurry to get here, I barely packed anything decent." I didn't admit to her that I didn't own anything decent or remotely sexy for that matter.

"It is settled then. You come to my salon tomorrow morning and we will go shopping. I know where you can get fabulous designer outfits at discount prices. That is also a benefit of being married to Daniele. He has contacts in every profession." She spooned the creamy indulgence into her mouth.

"His profession? What exactly does your husband do for a living?" I asked.

"My Daniele is talented in so many ways, but to answer your question, he officially works for the Italia Department of Tourism. He is an architect by trade, but mostly he travels around the country approving new building designs. Usually he travels alone, unless it is to one of the more "exotic" locations. Then, of course, I go with him and we get to have our honeymoon all over again." She smiled demurely.

"Is that how you keep things fresh? He leaves, comes back, then you go away on business trips together?" I was almost finished with my treat.

"Mostly, yes," she said nodding her head, "but I think what has worked and kept us together is the respect we have for each other. With marriage, comes hard work. We never forget that, but our love is solid. Plus we continue to find all sorts of ways to keep the fires burning." She smiled.

"You are so lucky to have a man like Daniele. He's not only very handsome, but it also sounds like he is very smart." I envied my friend.

"Oh, that he is. But he is not without fault. I am going to let you in on a little secret. I discovered he had a secret rendezvous on one of his business trips a few years ago. With who or how I found out isn't important. How I handled it is. I simply told him I would not put up with such foolishness from any man. I told him to either choose me, or face a lifetime of unhappiness without me. He chose me."

"But how do you know he hasn't cheated since or won't be unfaithful again?"

"Because I trust him. It took time. He had to earn my trust again, and believe me, it was a difficult thing for him to do. Although it is in my nature to be very understanding, do not cross me with foolishness more than once."

What she spoke of is exactly what I'm doing. Being unfaithful to my husband and neglecting my children. Why don't I feel guilty though? I think I still love Mark. I mean, I've stayed with him all these years. So, I must love him. Right? For the longest time, I never understood what people meant when they said they loved the person, but wasn't "in love" with them. That's exactly how I feel. My heart is telling me what I need to do. For so many years, I've ignored the whisper. Sense of obligation and responsibility overruled all feelings of being true to myself. I always felt I had to do what's right for everyone but me. Not anymore, now it's time for me. I sighed, looking at people meandering around the plaza.

"I am sorry, Lena. I do not mean to sound judgmental about your situation. It is just that Daniele and I truly do love and are in love with each other. We have survived and overcome so much adversity that only served to bring us much closer. I really do believe when you are meant to be with someone, you should do all you can to make it work. However, just because you married a man, doesn't make him the man you should spend the rest of your life with. We all make mistakes. We would not be human if we did not. Right now, you are not happy with your life. I am. Please do not take what I have said about my marriage and try to apply it to yours. Consider this, if you and your husband were truly meant to be together for the rest of your lives you wouldn't be here now. Would you?"

"I suppose you're right. From the time I was a little girl, I grew up thinking marriage was something sacred. Vows were meant to be taken seriously. I always thought when you married someone, you stayed with them literally until death do you part. I never believed in divorce. I guess I just went on living my life, making myself invisible, convincing myself that I was unattractive to keep men away. Until I met Giovanni, I forgot that I am still a sexually attractive young woman. I let my passion for living die out. Now that it's come alive again, how do I keep it from overtaking me?"

"You do not. Life without passion or love is a life not worth living. Without any passion, you might as well pull the covers over your head and never get out of bed." She immediately appeared mortified at the reference to my having done just that.

I looked at her and smiled. Then she smiled. Then we both ended up laughing at the absurdity of it all. It felt good to be with a friend again.

Ojuma and I said our goodbyes with promises of seeing each other the next day. I thanked Simona once again for the wonderful dinner. Freda and Vincenzio almost persuaded me to stay later, helping them drink their large carafe of wine, but I convinced them I needed to rest. Instead of going back to my room, I walked the short distance to the neighborhood *tabacchi* store to buy a phone card. The nearest public phone booth was only a few feet from the busy street. At this late hour I could have a conversation with very few distractions from traffic. It was just after 11 o'clock, which made it 6 in the morning back in Kansas. I needed to let Mark and the boys know I was all right. I dialed the number. It rang several times before being picked up.

"Hello?" A sleep filled voice answered the phone.

"James, sweetie. It's Mommy," I answered, afraid of my oldest child's reaction to my leaving them.

"Oh, hi Mom. Dad told us you took an unexpected last minute vacation, only he didn't say it so nicely… Why *did* you go back to Italy? Are you in *Gorgazzio*?" he asked sounding more like a man everyday.

"Yeah, I'm in *Gorgazzio*. It's kinda complicated. I really don't want to get into the reasons why I left, but I just wanted you guys to know I made it here safely. James, get a pencil and write down this number where you can reach me. I'm staying with a lady named Simona Malavasi." I read aloud the number from the card I retrieved from the bulletin board earlier. "Just leave a message if I'm not there."

"Okay, I got it. I'll leave it here right next to the phone. So when are you coming home?"

"I'm not sure, but I won't be gone longer than a couple of weeks. There are some things I need to take care of first. James, you're old enough to know that life doesn't always turn out like you expect it to," I replied.

"You mean like me not getting accepted by my first choice in colleges?"

"Yes, something like that. I guess what I'm saying is, sometimes you reach a point in your life where you have to make some really tough choices - decisions that may change the rest of your life. I'm at that point right now. You know how unhappy I was being back in Kansas… Well, let's just say I needed to reevaluate my life. I'm taking this time alone to think about me. I feel really bad about leaving you guys, but I know you'll be all right. I'm not leaving for good, just for a little while. As my oldest child, you probably know me better than anyone else, including your father." Emotion clouded my voice. I sniffed.

"Mom, are you crying?"

"No," I lied. "It's just the night air making me stuffy. You know how my allergies act up when I get in cool night air." I tried to fake a laugh.

"I think I know how you feel. Don't worry. I'll take care of Carlos and Neil. The funny thing is you say I probably know you better than anyone else. I think Carlos knows you even better than I do. When you were in the hospital, he said you would wake up soon. When *you* were ready. He didn't seem worried at all. When you finally came home, he mentioned how sad you looked. The rest of us hadn't seemed to really notice. I guess we were all so wrapped up in ourselves we stopped seeing you. Mom, I'm sorry."

"You don't have anything to be sorry about. You're kids. You're not supposed to notice what's going on with your parents. Not like that anyway. I feel bad because I couldn't hold it all together for you guys. I'm the one who should be apologizing to you."

"Mom, I want you to have a great time and take care of whatever it is you need to. Like I said, I'll watch the boys. And don't worry, Dad's here if we need anything. It's about time he took more interest in us anyway. You've done it all for years. It's no wonder you feel worn out," said James.

"Thanks, sweetie. I can't talk much longer. I'm using one of these calling cards and the time's about to run out. Is your father there?"

"No, he's not here. He left right before you called. I was just about to jump in the shower when I heard the phone ring."

"Okay. Well, tell the boys I said hi and I love them. If you need me, give me a call."

"I will Mom. You take care of yourself and be careful of those crazy Italians," he replied in a mock Italian accent.

I laughed, this time for real. Then in a serious tone added, "James, I promise I will be home in time to see you walk across that stage and get your diploma. You can count on that. I wouldn't miss seeing you graduate for anything in the world. I'm really proud of you, son." The tears returned almost as quickly as they left.

"Thanks, Mom. I don't think I could graduate without you being there. I love you and I'll talk to you soon. Bye-bye," he said.

"Bye James. I love you, too," I replied back, before breaking the long distance connection with my son.

Still jetlagged, my body didn't know if it needed to go to sleep or remain wide-awake. I wasn't tired, but since it was quickly approaching midnight my options weren't exactly unlimited. Despite the late hour, I felt safe walking the streets. I'd done it many times when I lived there in the past. Not much had changed since then, so I still felt safe in my night wanderings. A few cars passed by, filled mostly with late night partygoers too intent on their own revelry to pay much attention to me.

I was almost in front of Simona's house when a car pulled up slowly behind me. Was there someone following me? I continued to walk attempting to ignore the car. Suddenly the fear of walking alone on a dark street overtook me and I quickened my pace. The car continued to follow. I managed to make it to the front gate and quickly turned the key to enter. The car sped off before I had a chance to turn around to see who was inside.

Maybe walking alone at night wasn't such a good idea after all. I decided to return to the safety of my room rather than take foolish chances walking the streets of *Gorgazzio* late at night. After all I was a foreigner, an obvious foreigner at that, in a country filled with mystery and intrigue. Who knows what kind of danger exists on these streets? I certainly did not want to find out.

I relocked the front gate noticing all the lights in Simona's house were off. I rounded the corner to the back of the house heading towards the little cottage. In my haste to get to dinner, I had left a light on and the front door unlocked. I wasn't alarmed. I still felt relatively safe on this property. When I opened the door, I was completely surprised at what I found.

The sweet, unmistakable scent of roses overwhelmed me even before I entered the small space. I counted at least six vases, each filled with a dozen red roses. I stopped and smelled each and every one, imagining Giovanni's face as he agonized over our situation. It could not have been easy for him. On the bed, on top of my pillow, was a heart shaped box of *Baci* candy. Next to it sat a small envelope. I opened it and silently read.

Lena,
Mi dispiace. Please forgive me.
Con amore,
Giovanni
Call me. 099 965 76 54

As much as I wanted to call, I wasn't about to venture back out into the darkness of night and give whoever it was following me another chance to terrorize me. The phone call would have to wait until morning. I smiled, knowing that everything was going to turn out fine.

CHAPTER 14

A knock at the door awakened me from a deep sleep. It was Simona.

"*Buon giorno*, Lena. I was just checking to see if you made it back safely last night."

"Hi, Simona. Yes, I made it back fine," I responded, still half asleep. I pulled myself from the warmth of the bed and peeked through a crack in the door. "What time is it?"

"It is half past nine. I know you are jet lagged, but it is best if you adjust to our time as quickly as possible."

I opened the door the remainder of the way, shielding my eyes from the brightness of the morning sun. She stood holding a tray filled with coffee, fruit and pastries. I stepped aside to let her in. She smiled upon noticing the room filled with roses.

"These are from Signori Morelli, I presume?" She nodded towards the flowers, placing the tray on an empty spot on the small counter.

"Yes. He is a very kind thoughtful man." I smiled at his gesture. "May I use your phone please?" I pulled the jeans I wore last night over my hips.

"*Sì*, yes, of course you may," she replied with an amused look.

I retrieved the card from underneath my pillow. I slept with it so as not to lose the number and dashed past Simona. "Thank you for the coffee. I promise I'll enjoy every last drop just as soon as I make this phone call." I didn't bother to put shoes on.

"Lena, you can use the phone in the back bedroom for privacy. I am going into town to shop, so please close the door behind you," she called out as I reached for the doorknob.

Looking at Simona, I smiled and declared, "It's going to be a beautiful day!"

The phone was on the nightstand in the spare bedroom. I exhaled deeply and nervously dialed the number. It rang four times.

"*Pronto?*" A deep male voice greeted me.

"Giovanni Morelli, *por favore*," I replied.

"*Uno momento.*" I heard the phone being placed down on a hard surface.

I wasn't sure where this number rang. Was it home or work? I waited anxiously for him to pick up the phone, uncharacteristically nervously biting my fingernails. The silence of the house was deafening. Simona had left directly from the cottage on her trip to town. I assumed she either walked or rode her bicycle like so many of the older women did. When I first arrived in Italy, I thought it was amusing to see elderly women in nice dresses riding bicycles into town to do their shopping. After a while, it became a normal everyday occurrence to see someone my grandmother's age riding a bicycle. I wondered why more Americans didn't do the same thing.

"*Pronto?*" His familiar voice answered.

"*Ciao* Giovanni. It's me, Lena," I replied, my voice quivering with emotion.

"Lena! Finally you call. I need to see you. What are you doing this afternoon?" The relief in his voice filtered through the phone line.

"Giovanni, I want to see you again too, but I'm meeting my friend Ojuma later this morning. I'm all yours after that." I really wanted to cancel my plans with Ojuma, but I learned a long time ago that true friends don't dismiss each other over a guy. I know she'd understand if I did, but I didn't want to treat her that way. Anyway, I needed her to help me find some nice, sexy clothes.

"That will be fine, *mi' amora*. Call me when you return and I will stop by for you. I can cook for you, or perhaps, we will go out to dinner. Whatever you desire." His voice conveyed the desperation we both felt.

"I should be back by 4 o'clock. Is that too late?" I wanted to fly into his arms this very moment, but quickly changed my mind when I caught my reflection in the mirror.

"That will be fine. I will await your phone call. And Lena…"

"Yes, Giovanni…"

"I want to apologize for how I acted yesterday. What you told me, well, let me just say that you took me by complete surprise with your incredible story."

"I totally understand. I did lay some pretty heavy stuff on you. Anyway, I can't wait to see you. And thank you for the roses. They are beautiful! I'll call you as soon as I get back. Okay?"

"I am counting the hours."

I replaced the phone and headed back to the cottage. As I was about to open the door, Freda appeared from a small storage building pushing a scooter in my direction.

"*Buon giorno* Lena. *Come va?*"

"*Buon giorno* Freda. I'm still a bit tired. Jet lagged and getting used to the time change. Otherwise I'm fine. Thanks for asking." The chickens in the house behind us started clucking. The large rooster called out cock-a-doodle-do. Twice. Just in case we didn't hear him the first time.

"We thought you would like to use the scooter today instead of walking. It belongs to my Vincenzio. He seldom uses it anymore," she explained, puffing out her cheeks and encircling her arms around her stomach imitating her rotund husband's massive waistline.

"Thank you very much Freda. I'm going to *Pordenone* to visit Ojuma as soon as I get dressed. I didn't know how I was going to get to the train station and I sure didn't feel like walking that far."

"Please feel free to keep it as long as you wish. Here is the key and be certain to park it only in approved spaces at the train station. The *polizia* are notorious for towing away illegally parked vehicles – even scooters." She handed me the key.

"Your family has been so nice to me. I don't know how I will ever repay your kindness. You're treating me like family even though we've only known each other for a few hours."

"It is what we do and who we are. Besides, you are in *Italia* all alone. You must be very brave to travel so far away from home. I could not do what you have done. I have never gone anywhere without my Vincenzio." She blushed.

"Yeah, I'm either brave or stupid. Maybe I'm stupidly brave," I joked. "Well, I'd better get dressed. I don't want to mess with Ojuma's plans. Would you like to come too?" I asked, more out of politeness than sincerity.

"Oh, no I cannot. I have to get to work, but thank you for the invitation. I will see you later. Have a good time." Freda waved as she walked up the driveway to her car.

After hungrily devouring the *brioches* and fruit Simona had so thoughtfully provided, I washed them down with several cups of the still hot coffee. I then showered and dressed, trying desperately not to look like the typical American. This was actually harder than I realized because all I brought with me were jeans and sneakers. Ah, this would have to do for now.

Within an hour of leaving *Gorgazzio*, I waited outside *Somalia's Finest* watching Ojuma lock the door in preparation for our day of shopping. Compared to her, I looked a hot mess.

She stood no taller than me, but her lean frame gave the illusion of added height. Her smooth coffee colored complexion, accented by shiny black hair, now pulled up on the top of her head into a carefree ponytail, made women jealous and men look twice. Her dark brown, almost black, eyes seemed to look right through you. Though she wore very little makeup, her skin appeared flawless. Ojuma walked tall and proud, displaying a self-confidence I had never felt. And when she spoke, rarely raising her voice, you wanted to stop and listen so as to not miss a single word. I loved how she dressed – so fashionably elegant. She wasn't a slave to fashion, but I'll bet a pair of Levi's never touched her thighs. Yes, Ojuma could pull an outfit together and make it look like it cost a million dollars. I wondered how she did it. Hopefully, today I would find out.

"So my friend, are you ready for some serious shopping?" She smiled.

Still on a strict budget, I was glad I brought along my credit cards just in case I needed them. "Sure, I'm ready. But I can't spend a whole lot of money."

"Don't worry. Where we are going, you will barely have to spend anything. You see this shirt I have on? It retailed in the stores for $700, but I paid only €25 for it. Quite a bargain, eh?" She smirked while putting on a pair of designer sunglasses.

"Really?! That shirt is gorgeous! You mean you always shop like this?" I asked, with no attempt to hide my excitement.

"Of course. Why should I pay top dollar when I don't have to? Most of the clothes I buy come directly from *Milano's* top fashion designers. They send their excess clothing to a clearinghouse in a little town not too far from here. I discovered this place through my husband. Daniele was working in *Milano* and was introduced to some people working in the fashion industry. Daniele knows how much I love beautiful clothes, so he arranged for me to meet the owner of this clearinghouse. Now I have first pick before they sell the clothes to various boutiques, usually in the states, for outrageous prices. He and I have an understanding. First we shamelessly flirt, then I buy." She motioned with her hands like it was the most natural thing in the world to pay bottom dollar for designer outfits.

"You are so lucky! I can't wait to get there and see all the beautiful clothes. I just hope they'll fit me. I'm not exactly a size 2."

"Lena, they have clothes in all sizes, although I do believe it gets more difficult to find nicer things in the larger sizes. What size are you anyway? About an 8?"

"I wish. I haven't been able to wear size 8 in years. These days I'm lucky if I can squeeze my butt into a 10." I added, touching my ample behind. I noticed Ojuma's slim frame couldn't have been more than a size 6.

"I'm sure we will find something to fit you perfectly. Follow me. My car is parked around the corner." She nodded her head in the direction of the car.

Since the town was about 20 kilometers away, it was more convenient to drive, although the train could have gotten us there in no time. I settled back as Ojuma maneuvered the car through the city streets finding her way to the *autostrada*.

"Do you think I have any real chance of finding happiness with Giovanni?" I asked, breaking the silence.

"That is a very difficult question considering your situation. If you were single and living in Italy, I would say you definitely have a chance with him. But, how can it be anything more than what it already is?"

"I know. You're right. It's the way I feel about him... I can't just walk away. How would you handle this if you were me?" I turned facing her, waiting for her response.

"I am going to be totally honest with you. Despite what your feelings are for Giovanni, I really cannot see how this will work. First of all, you have a husband and three children waiting for you in the United States. Secondly, you're here only temporarily. Thirdly he is a proud Italian man who owns his own business – his own successful business, and can have almost any woman he wants. Shall I go on? Listen, as your friend, I will tell you the truth. You may not like it, but you need to hear it. Unless you are going to give up your life in the states, divorce your husband, leave your children, move to Italy, and find a way to support yourself, even if Giovanni is willing to forgive you, there is no way this will work. I do not see it."

I faced forward realizing every word she said was true. It isn't fair. Finally, I meet a man who feels as passionately about me as I feel about him, yet it's doomed even before it begins. I can't give up this easily. This is my life and the only life I'll ever have. When will it be my

time for happiness? "Ojuma, what you say may be very true, but I'm not about to give up so easily. I'll play things by ear to see where it takes me. If this only ends up as a couple of fun filled weeks, then so be it. As for my husband, well, he'll do fine on his own. I finally realized we are better off apart. It's the boys I'm concerned about." I looked out the window as a fine mist began to fall. Good, just what I need to match my mood. Clouds and rain.

"Well, you wouldn't be you if you gave up so easily. Anyway, anything worth having doesn't always come so easy. So, when do you plan on seeing the mysterious *Signore* Morelli again?"

"I told him I'd call this afternoon after I returned from visiting you. I didn't tell him we were going shopping. I don't care what country they're from. Men never understand why a woman needs to spend so much money on clothes."

"I'm not so sure about that. I know men who are more concerned with their looks than I am. Look, we're already here. Let's lighten up this mood and go have some fun," she said as she parked in the parking lot of a nondescript building.

I watched Ojuma and a middle-aged man named Paolo, who seemed to have an overabundance of ear and nose hair, flirt incessantly with each other in Italian. They did their double-cheek kiss, hugged like old friends and walked arm-in-arm towards the back. She quickly introduced us then they continued on with the flirtation as if I wasn't there.

I followed them down a long hallway trying unsuccessfully to make myself inconspicuous. Finally, when I didn't think I could take any more of their antics, he opened the door to a huge showroom. I was expecting to see piles of clothing stacked on tabletops like some of the warehouses back home, but his place was organized by designer and size. He provided instructions to one of his workers to assist us if we needed anything then left us to our own devices.

I didn't know where to begin. *Ferragamo, Versace, Dolce & Gabbana, Armani...* and those were just a few of the more popular designer's names I recognized. I decided then and there that I'd never have this opportunity again. I looked to my friend and smiled the biggest smile I could muster, that is, until I looked at the price tag on a nearby dress. This simple dress cost over €4500! I looked at another dress listed at €1200 and another for €2000! There was no way in the world I could afford anything in this place!

"Ojuma?!" I whispered, "Have you looked at how much these damned dresses cost?! I don't have this kind of money, even if he does give me a discount."

"Not to worry Lena. Paolo and I have a special arrangement. He never charges me more than €100 for any item, no matter what it lists for. The only stipulation is I promise not to tell anyone about our agreement and he lets me come as often as I wish. I told him that you were a good friend visiting who needed a few "special" outfits to enchant her man. He is such a romantic and he will not stand in the way of love. Believe me, he more than makes up for my discount from what he charges the Americans." She snickered and held up a beautiful outfit towards me.

I tried on dress after dress. Outfit after outfit, each making me feel more glamorous than I'd ever felt. Now I understood why these designers were so popular. The materials were exquisite, managing to fit like a glove without binding like a girdle. We must have stayed there for hours, each trying on various designers, trying to find the one we liked best. I'd never had so much fun shopping in all my life.

After all was said and done, I left the warehouse with 10 new top designer outfits. Elegant dresses, beautiful pantsuits, funky skirts and blouses. All were made to make me look and feel fantastic. The best part was I spent less than €1000.00 on everything. I don't even want to think about how much this would've cost in a real store. Ojuma also picked up a couple of new outfits. After our purchases were discretely boxed for travel and placed in the trunk of the car, I thanked Paolo profusely for his kindness. He responded with a shyness I hadn't expected. He wished me "good luck" and kissed my hand. We waved goodbye as we pulled away from his building.

I thought we were headed back to town, but Ojuma surprised me by stopping at another nondescript building. "Where are we going now?" I asked aloud, making note of the time. It was now 2 o'clock. The light rain gave way to rays of bright afternoon sunshine. Things were definitely looking up.

"You have the clothes, now you need the shoes to go with them," she said so matter-of-factly.

"I guess you have a point there. I can't go out wearing my sneakers with my designer outfits." I laughed.

"But of course, you can't. Here in this building, works another of my friends, referred to me by Paolo. They are in the export business and work several deals together. Paolo exports clothing and this gentleman exports shoes – fine Italian shoes. He's not as gregarious as

Paolo, but we get along very well." Ojuma parked the car, waited for me, and headed towards the front office.

An hour later, I had managed to find two pairs of shoes, a pair of thigh high leather boots to go with the mini I picked up earlier and a designer handbag. After a bit of bargaining, her friend agreed to accept two hundred euro for €1000 worth of goods.

We headed back to town sailing on a high only achieved by women who've gotten a good bargain. Ojuma offered to drive me back to Simona's rather than my tackling the train with so many packages. I accepted. Although I left the scooter at the train station, I figured I could pick it up another time. By 4 o'clock, we were pulling in front of Simona's house. She helped me carry the packages to the small apartment.

"Thank you so much for everything Ojuma. I had so much fun today. It's been so long since I went out with a girlfriend and treated myself to so many indulgences. I had the best time." I sincerely meant every word of it.

"Perhaps, when you finally decide what is best for you, you will never forget to always treat yourself well. You have to take care of you before you can take care of everyone else. I don't know, but maybe if you had considered your feelings earlier, you never would have ended up in the situation you are in now. Ah, we will never know now, will we? Still, I'm happy you had a fun time. I did too." She looked at her watch. "I must be going. Antonio has an after school football game and I promised to be there to watch him score the winning goal."

"Please tell your family I said hello. And thanks again for everything."

Ojuma got into her car. Before she pulled away from the curve she shouted out, "Have a wonderful time this evening and whatever you decide to do, do it with gusto!" She tooted her horn and waved goodbye.

I returned her wave, noticing Simona peering through the open kitchen window. I really needed a phone because I didn't want to bother Simona every time I wanted to make a phone call. I know they have those temporary cell phones in the states, I wonder if they also have them here? I've got to check into that the next time I go out into town. I unpacked my beautiful clothes. For the first time since this morning, I realized how many hours had passed since I'd last eaten. Nothing remained from this morning's meal, except the tray. I swallowed my pride, picked up the tray and went to Simona's house. I knocked. She invited me in.

"*Ciao* Lena. It appears you and Ojuma were quite busy this afternoon? She does have the most wonderful taste in clothes. I hope she helped you find some of her special bargains." The knowing expression on Simona's face indicated she knew more than she let on about Ojuma's shopping extravaganzas. But I wasn't going to go for the bait.

"I'm returning the tray from this morning. Everything was really delicious. I also need to use your phone again, if you don't mind." I placed the tray on the counter.

"*Por favore*, help yourself. Lena. If you're hungry I made pasta for lunch. Come back when you finish with your call," she said as more of a demand than a request.

I redialed the number I called earlier in the day. It rang only once before a recognizable voice answered.

"*Pronto?*"

"Giovanni, is that you?" I wasn't certain it was he.

"*Si*. You are very prompt, *mi'amica*. How was your visit with your friend?"

I loved to hear his voice. There are some people who have a very distinctive pitch to their voice, making it sound either extremely pleasing or terribly annoying. His voice was particularly nice to listen to. Luckily for me, not only was he easy on the eye, he was also easy on the ear. "I had a very nice time with her," I replied, "We did a few girly things. Nothing special."

"Oh, so you two went shopping?" He laughed.

"How did you know we went shopping?" I joined in his laughter, noting his keen observation.

"What else do women do in the middle of the afternoon?"

"Giovanni! You surprise me. I didn't realize you were so chauvinistic!" I said in mock indignation.

"Once again, I put my feet in my mouth. Let me make it up to you. How about I pick you up and show you a wonderful evening?"

"Oooh, I think I'd like that." I felt myself getting warm. "I'll be ready in about an hour. How's that for you?"

"That will do just fine. How does dinner in *Venezia* sound? I made reservations in a very nice *ristorante*. We can make an entire evening of it, if you wish," he said.

"*Venezia*! I absolutely love Venice. Giovanni, you are something else… I'll be ready when you get here!"

"*Va bene*. I'll see you in one hour and bring a change of clothing. We shall be staying overnight. *Ciao*."

~~~~

Ah, Venice… It is almost impossible to describe how this city first affected me. There are no words, nor pictures that can adequately capture the true essence of the feelings the city invokes in those lucky enough to have visited. It is truly a city like none other.

Pulling into the *stazione de Venezia* is like arrival at any other train station in Italy. Trains bound for destinations far and wide are the norm. Tens of thousands of harried people scurrying off in different directions, rushing past storekeepers hawking their souvenirs to time-strapped tourists is the backdrop for the arrival to one of the most fascinating cities in the world.

One would think Venice's train station would prepare you for something awe inspiring, but it doesn't. The train depot is unremarkable in the true meaning of the word. Purely functional, nothing exceptional. I was totally unprepared for what awaited me during my first visit with my oldest son during the *Carnavale* season.

We exited through one of the numerous glass doors and were greeted by overwhelming hordes of people. Finally, after maneuvering through the crowd and breaking free, I was able to safely look up. The sight before my eyes literally took my breath away and I was immediately spellbound.

The magnificent *Basilica,* with its once bronzed dome now oxidized green over time, loomed across the canal as it had for centuries past. And the canal—the Grand Canal—the main thoroughfare of the city, was fueled with activity. Water taxis brimming with tourists, ferries filled with locals conducting their business, and the ever-present *gondolas* steered by *gondoliers* dressed in black and white striped shirts with red scarves tied around their necks, expertly guided their vessels through the canals. I felt like I had stepped back in time and into a picture postcard.

We walked for miles following the signs to the *San Marco Piazza*. I thought it interesting and a little confusing, how the signs leading to the *piazza* pointed in all different directions, but I suppose all paths eventually led there if you were willing to wander around long enough. I also discovered the only way to truly experience the "real" Venice is to walk through the narrow neighborhood passageways and observe real Venetians in their daily lives.

For what seemed like hours, we followed the massive crowds to get to San Marco square. The maze of alleys eventually gave way to a vast opening filled with thousands of people coexisting with an infinite number of pigeons. At times I thought the pigeons outnumbered the tourists by at least 3 to 1. Most visitors would agree that *Piazza San Marco* is an event unto itself.

I observed the orderly chaos unfolding around me. A massive bell tower towered over the square. For a small entrance fee, you could climb to the top of the tower. Some brave and obviously physically fit individuals took the challenge and climbed to the top for an unobstructed view of Venice.

Bordering one end of the *Piazza San Marco* stood another wondrous attraction. The *San Marco Basilica*. The colorfully glistening façade atop the cathedral adorned by bronzed horses, beckoned tourists to enter and observe the wonders of the ancient mosaics hidden within its recesses.

Back in the plaza square, children amused each other by covering their outstretched arms in birdseed, literally making themselves into pigeon bait. Street vendors shamelessly hawked their wares to unsuspecting tourists expecting to find authentic Venetian souvenirs. Truth be told, many of the items, including *carnivale* hats and masks were stamped incredibly "Made in China".

To truly experience the enchantment hidden off the beaten path, it was suggested to tour the city by boat through the Grand Canal. I have never seen a city as beautiful and wondrous as Venice. Ancient, brightly painted buildings in various shades of ocher, terracotta, yellow, and aqua—even those left in their natural color aged by time, were utterly amazing to see. They stood three or four stories tall, connected to one another like brothers in arms. Marble steps reached down to the water, beckoning visitors to stop by for a cup of espresso. And as an older woman wears makeup to camouflage her flaws, the Venetians used beautiful flowers to conceal the crumbling façade of its ancient architecture.

According to recent studies, probably the most amazing achievement for Venice is how it remains standing. Sadly, scientists now report that the city built upon landfill and old trees so many centuries ago, is slowly sinking and in time will eventually be reclaimed by the sea. If and when it does happen, it will truly be a loss for mankind to lose a treasure such as *Venezia*. And despite the numerous times I've visited Venice in the past, I shall never pass up a chance to return. Some say they left their hearts in San Francisco? Well, I left my heart in *Venezia* – the city by the sea.

CHAPTER 15

I thanked Simona once again for the use of her phone. She offered me a snack. I accepted a small dish of pasta – something to tide me over, and hurried back to my small apartment. I had exactly 50 minutes before Giovanni would be there to pick me up and I wanted everything to be perfect.

A basic black dress, accented by a colorful beaded scarf, was perfect. Ojuma picked a set of matching earrings that complimented the dress and flattered my face. I quickly did my makeup, wearing only enough to enhance my natural beauty. As I was about to strap on a pair of sexy high-heeled shoes, a knock at the door surprised me. I looked at the clock. It was only 5:15. I didn't expect Giovanni to arrive for at least another 10 minutes. I quickly slipped on the shoes, did a quick check in the mirror and opened the door expecting to see his smiling face. It wasn't him. It was Simona.

I'm sorry to disturb you while you're preparing for your date, but you have a phone call. He says his name is Mark… Your husband, I presume? Or perhaps, another suitor?" She furrowed her brow in disapproval.

"Thank you. I'll be right there." I watched her walk back to her house muttering to herself in Italian. Shit, shit, shit! Why is Mark calling me? I hope there's nothing wrong with the boys. I quickly, but carefully folded my new pantsuit, tossed in jeans, a pair of soft Italian loafers that would be comfortable for my long-distance walking in Venice, sexy underwear, toiletries, makeup and stuffed them all into an overnight bag.

I used the phone in the back bedroom again, setting my bags outside the door.

"Hello? Mark?" I heard Simona replace the phone on the hook in the kitchen.

"Hi Lena. How ya doing? So you made it, huh? Is Italy all you remember it to be?" asked Mark casually.

He didn't sound upset at all, just his usual old sarcastic self. "I'm fine and actually it's better than I remember." I wasn't about to fall into the trappings of an argument over the phone.

"If my memory serves me right, you couldn't wait to get back to the United States. Well, how long do you think you'll stay over there?"

148

"I'll be back in a couple of weeks. You don't think I'm going to miss James' graduation, do you? Mark is everything all right back there? Are the boys okay?" I wondered where this was going.

"Yeah, everything's fine. The boys are good. Don't worry about that. I can take care of them. Listen Lena. You know, at first when you left, I was pretty ticked off. I thought how dare you leave me? But after awhile, when I really had time to think about us, I realize you're right. We've become more like brother and sister than husband and wife. Maybe this separation thing is just what we *both* need. I understand you wanting to get away. I just didn't expect you to do something like this."

"Well, I didn't expect me to do something like this either. I'm always the one who goes along to get along. Right? Good ole' reliable Lena. That's who I am. That's what everybody thinks." I looked at my watch. It was 5:25. Giovanni would be here in just a few minutes.

I just wanted to tell you not to worry, the boys will be fine, and they're almost grown men anyway. Do me a favor, will you?" he asked.

"What is that?"

"Just don't forget where you belong?"

"Mark, it's too late for that. I forgot where I belonged a long time ago," I responded.

He was quiet, obviously contemplating what I just said. "Okay, well, take care of yourself and give us a call in a few days."

"Okay. I'll do that. Tell the boys I said 'hi and I love them'. I'll talk to you later. Bye for now."

"Bye Lena." Mark hung up.

Before I could compose myself, I heard Simona calling for me. "Lena, your friend *Signore* Morelli is here for you." I checked my reflection in the mirror, dabbed my eyes and put on a happy face.

I picked up my bags and walked to the kitchen where she had cornered Giovanni with her incessant questions. I stopped, admiring how handsome he was, fashionably dressed in a pinstripe suit, standing there speaking in rapid Italian with a smiling Simona. Obviously, he'd worked his charm on her in a matter of mere moments. Dropping my bags, I went to him offering the traditional Italian greeting. I loved this gesture. It allowed you to get close to those you wanted to get close to, yet it wasn't required in every situation. I inhaled his masculine fragrance and sighed.

"Giovanni, I see you remember *Signora* Malavasi?" I gestured towards a still smiling and on the verge of blushing, Simona.

"Ah, *si*. We were just reminiscing about the beauty of *Gorgazzio*. How are you *mi'amica*?" he asked quietly, gently, gazing intensely into my eyes.

I thought I was going to melt in front of the both of them. Suddenly, I was overcome by a feeling of peace and calmness. All I wanted was him and the only place I wanted to be was in his arms. I reached out. He enveloped me, whispering words I didn't understand. Simone realized how private this moment was so she quietly retreated from the room, busying herself with another project. I accepted his touch, holding onto him as if he were all I needed in this world to live. In this moment nothing else mattered. We stood there, holding onto one another, neither wanting to let go.

"Momma, whose BMW is that parked outside?" Boomed the voice of Vincenzio as he bounded through the front door. "Oh, *scusi*, Lena I thought my Momma was here. *Ciao, mi chiamo es Vincenzio*," he introduced himself to Giovanni. They shook hands and engaged in small talk. I picked up the phrase BMW here and there. I surmised they were discussing his car.

"Are you ready?" Giovanni completed his conversation with Vincenzio.

"More than ready." I smiled at him. "Oh, Vincenzio, I almost forgot. Freda lent me your scooter this morning. I left it at the train station earlier because Ojuma gave me a ride home after we went shopping. Will it be alright there overnight?" I asked.

"*Si, si*. Don't worry about the scooter. I'll send the neighbor's boy for it after dinner. You just go have a good time. And remember what I said if you still need someone to show you around after you're finished with him… I am available" He laughed with Giovanni.

We all said our goodbyes. By this time, Simona had returned to the kitchen, wishing us a fun filled evening. Giovanni picked up my overnight bag.

"You look magnificent in that dress! When I saw you, my eyes almost popped from my head. Wow!" he said when we were finally alone.

"You don't look half bad yourself, Mr. Morelli," I teased.

"Come. Let us go." He brushed my lips lightly with his own. "There is so much I want to share with you tonight."

His pained expression told me he held a million secrets and I wanted to uncover each and every one. We sat in silence until we reached the *autostrada*.

"Lena, we need to discuss the story you told me yesterday. Forgive my hesitation. I am still trying to comprehend – to understand how I could have met you if you were never truly here."

"Do you think we should talk about this while you're driving? I mean, you did get a little emotional when we first discussed it," I replied, glancing at him sideways, looking for any hint of instability.

"I will be okay. Yesterday, it was like you dropped a *bomba* on me with no warning. Since then, I have had some time to think over what you have said. I need to know how it is possible for you to come all the way to *Italia*, meet me, do all the things we did together, yet you say your physical body never left, uh, Kansas?"

"Giovanni, I can't explain it, because I don't understand it myself. Even *I* didn't believe it was real, so I had to discover the truth – one way or the other. I actually thought I dreamt the entire episode with you, but when I saw you and you recognized me… Well, I didn't know whether to laugh or cry. There must be a logical explanation, only I don't have it. Maybe there is someone who can explain to both of us the implications of what has occurred." I observed his hands, noticing for the first time how long and slender his fingers were. I guess some people would say he had hands built to play the piano, but I knew from firsthand experience how truly skilled those hands were.

"Maybe you had some kind of amnesia?" He wondered aloud.

"I suppose that's possible. But that doesn't explain my acute awareness and how I felt while we were together. It all seemed so surreal. I was aware of my surroundings, I controlled my thoughts and actions. It felt as if I were actually here. Not like I was in a dream." I played with the long dangly earrings, not used to having anything hanging so far from my earlobes.

"*Alora*. After you left yesterday, I called an old friend. His name is Claudio Zanus. We first met while attending the University in *Trieste* and became good friends. He is a bit of an anomaly, though. While I concentrated on studying business, he focused more on science, specifically quantum physics. You know—questions about how the universe came into being." He zoomed along in the left lane, flashing his bright lights to those not moving fast enough. In stereotypical fashion, he gestured at the other drivers with his right hand and muttered a few choice Italian phrases as he passed the slower cars.

"Why do you refer to him as an anomaly? Showing interest in science isn't so strange." I made certain my seat belt was snug.

He continued driving as if cursing the other drivers was an everyday occurrence for him. Hmmm, maybe it was. "It is if you are a priest," he replied. "After we both graduated, I knew I wanted to open a nightclub with my brother. As focused as Claudio was on his studies, he had no idea what he wanted to do afterwards, so he applied to graduate school, conducting research for his professors. Eventually, he turned his research skills from science to religion and how one affects the other. The more he delved into religion, the more he felt it was his true calling. Over time, he decided to attend the seminary in hopes of becoming a priest. We still keep in touch, though not as much as we used to."

A priest, huh? I wondered where he was going with this. "What did the two of you talk about?" I frowned.

"I told him about our discussion, not all of it of course, only the part about your out-of-body travel." He glanced quickly in my direction before turning his attention back to the road.

I'd prefer he not look at me at all, considering how fast he was driving. "What did he have to say?"

"He said he knew a bit about the subject and promised to look into it for me. Well, he called me back this morning indicating he wants to meet you. He lives in *Murano*—it's a little island off the coast of Venice."

"*Murano*? Isn't that where they make those beautiful glass sculptures? Why does he want to meet me?"

"*Sì*, the island is known to tourists for its glass blowing. Why does Claudio want to meet you? I do not know. He didn't specifically say. Maybe he's just curious to meet someone who has proclaimed to have done what you have. Perhaps, he simply wants to meet the woman who has captured his friend's heart so quickly."

"I have a question that's been bothering me. If I had told you about my "journey" when we first met, would you have wanted to spend time with me?"

"Maybe yes. Probably no. I knew there was something special about you from the first time we met. But now, *alora*, it is too late to wonder. So what do you say? Will you meet with Padre Claudio?"

"Sure. Why not? Maybe he can help to convince me I'm not crazy," I joked, noticing Giovanni did not join in my laughter.

"I think you will like him. He is very easy to talk to. Oh, you should have seen the disappointed faces on the women of his village when he announced he was becoming a priest. So many of the mothers hoped for their daughters to marry Claudio, for he is not only an educated man, but he is also very handsome."

"How does it feel talking to a friend who also happens to be a priest? Is he at all judgmental about your life? About how you used to "live in sin" with a woman and how you're now spending time with me?"

"No, he is not judgmental at all. It is not his position, nor is it his nature to judge others. He is my friend. We talk as friends, not priest to parishioner, unless I request his guidance. As for me being with you... Well, this is a subject I try not to think about. Not you, of course, but the fact that you are married—with children, and only visiting my country for a short time. I know I should walk away. No, run away from you. But I like you, very much. What more can I say?" He shrugged.

"I'm glad you didn't run from me because I really like you too."

"*Va bene*! It is settled. We both like each other. For now, we will simply try to enjoy the time we have together. The future is left to take care of itself. We will only live in the present. *Sì?*"

"*Sì!*" I enthusiastically responded, hoping to also convince myself.

Changing the subject he said, "I think you will enjoy the *ristorante* I have chosen. And the hotel, the *Palazzo de San Marco*, is top-of-the-line. Five stars," he stated proudly.

"As long as I'm with you, I don't care where we eat or sleep." I meant every word I said. With him, I felt safe.

"Ah, that is sweet of you to say. However, I want to make our trip to *Venezia* extra special, filled with good memories for us both," he hesitated then asked, "Lena, may I ask you a question?"

"Of course. What is it?"

"What do you remember about our time together? Do you remember dancing with me at my club, diving in the *grotto*, hang gliding from a mountain high above my village? How about the *Palazzo* in the mountains? Do you remember the quiet, special moments of us just *being* together, enjoying each other's company?" he asked barely above a whisper.

I considered my response before I spoke, carefully choosing my words. "Yeah, I remember most of it, but the way I remember is kind of how a person remembers a dream. The memories aren't as vivid or intense as when something happens in real life. They're more subdued, kind of muted. You know how you can have a dream, but after a while you forget what you dreamt and only the feelings of how the dream made you feel remain? That's sort of how I feel. I know I felt an extreme attraction to you and we had a wonderful time together, but all the things we did feel more like a distant memory than something that happened only a few weeks ago. You were like some wonderful never-ending fantasy, the kind no one wants to wake up from. When I finally did wake up, I knew that something extraordinary had happened. I just didn't know exactly what. Does that make sense?" I placed my free hand on top of his.

"It makes sense, because for you it was a dream. But for me, the experiences were real. When we were together, every single moment spent with you became seared into my mind for a lifetime of memories. And at the time, I knew you too felt the same way about me. I want you to feel that way again. You probably don't remember, but you remarked that you couldn't remember the last time you had so much fun."

I chuckled softly, "That sure sounds like something I'd say considering my present life is a never ending routine of work, running errands, and taking care of my children. This trip to Italy is the first time I've done anything just for me. Damn if it don't feel good!"

"I want to do something for you. No, for us. Let me recreate the events that led to the memories of when we first met. I'll ask Lucio to run the club for a week. You and I will spend time alone. After spending time together, then we will both know if our meeting is a coincidence or fate. Is it a deal?" The deep green of his eyes mesmerized me as they soaked in the rays of the setting sun.

Was I up to the challenge? It was one thing to take the plunge of adventure in a dream, but I was fully awake now. Did I have the nerves to hang out with this man for an entire week? What happened if we ended up not liking each other? On the other hand, what would we do if we did? Well, this is no time to pull back. I came to Italy for a reason. I wasn't going home without finding out if being with Giovanni was my destiny.

"Okay, dear. You have yourself a deal," I replied. Then looking towards the signs on the *autostrada*, I said, "Wow, we're in *Venezia* already. Where did the time go?"

Giovanni parked in the parking garage located over a kilometer from the actual city. We queued up for the *vaporetti* to take us into Venice.

As the ferry prepared to dock alongside the wooden platform, I pulled Giovanni aside directing his attention to the west. Silently we observed the sun slowly sinking over the city, watching it quietly disappear into what looked like the depths of the sea.

"There is an old superstition that says a kiss at sunrise will bring good luck for the rest of the day, but a kiss at sunset will bring good fortune for the rest of your life."

"Is that so?" He raised his eyebrows. "Well, we don't want to risk missing out on a guarantee of good fortune, do we?" he asked as he gently positioned my face between his hands, pulling me forward to meet his lips. We kissed, smiled, then kissed some more until the boat began filling up with other passengers and the driver waved us off.

As we exited the boat, I threw a kiss at the driver, which was totally out of character for me and yelled, "*Arriverderci!*" He looked at me, smiled and returned the favor. I felt like I did when I was in my early 20s – young, free, with the world at my feet. When I stopped laughing, I noticed Giovanni watching me.

"Do you have any idea how beautiful you look right now?" he asked holding our bags.

I suddenly became very self-conscious about my appearance. The old feelings of being teased as a young girl flooded back. As a child, I imagined I was the strangest looking girl on earth. In fact, my aunt used to call me by saying, "hey funny looking". My childhood nicknames were Cat-Eyes and Black Jap. My full lips only helped to emphasize my prominent cheekbones whenever they dared to curve into a smile. The slant of my eyes made mean spirited children question if one of my parents were Chinese or Japanese. The nose so proudly worn by my Native American ancestors seemed to dominate my other features. And the icing on a cake, was dozens of tiny little freckles dancing across the bride of my nose causing kids to ask if they could play "connect the dots" on my face. I stood tall and skinny with baseball bat shaped legs. I think I cried everyday from the never-ending teasing.

It wasn't until I left the city and went off to college that I realized I wasn't ugly. My looks were unique, that's all. Over time, the boyish body I felt trapped in sprouted breasts and an ample behind. Soon young men who wouldn't give me the time of day began pursuing me.

Strangers stopped me on the streets asking if I were a model or a dancer. While I realize some of those guys only used that line to try to pick me up, others were sincere with their comments. Even women began to comment on my beauty—complimenting my eyes and cheekbones. Although I still felt different, I no longer felt I was ugly.

"Well, thank you for saying that." I absently touched my curly, shortly cropped hair. "I feel so good! Do you know that being with you makes me feel like I'm flying? I think what you see is exactly how I feel." I slipped my arm through his. We strolled towards the *Piazza San Marco*. I did not share my early experiences as a child with him. In time, I probably would, but not now.

"No, I'm very serious. You are very, very pretty. Your hair, your smile and the way your eyes light up when you laugh... I want to sit and watch you always."

"You know what I love about you?"

"I think I already know." He grinned mischievously.

"Yeah, that too! But, I really love how you're not afraid to express yourself. I've known so many men who don't know how to speak their feelings and it drives me crazy. I love the way you say things and how you sound when you say them. So *romantico*! I also think you're beautiful – both inside and out." I watched a smile form on his face.

CHAPTER 16

Darkness descended rapidly upon Venice reminding me that I had never visited this amazing city at night. I looked back towards the canal where the water appeared to be thick as oil. As we walked through the square, making our way to the hotel, I marveled at the peacefulness. St. Mark's square, minus the thousands of day tourists soaking up all its energy, took on an almost mystical quality. All was quiet now, with the exception of an occasional group of tourists returning to their hotels or heading towards the back alleys in search of their next Venetian meal.

Approaching the *Palazzo de San Marco*, we heard familiar soft strains of music drifting from the cafes lining the square. The music was occasionally overshadowed by cooing noises from thousands of pigeons, resting up for tomorrow's performance with visitors from all over the world.

"It's so eerily quiet. Makes me feel like I shouldn't speak above a whisper," I said. I tried desperately to maneuver the cobble-stoned streets in my spike-heeled shoes without tripping.

"Yes, *Venezia* is nothing like it appears during the day when all is loud and vulgar. The nights are magical, filled with mystery and many surprises."

"Ooh, I think I'm going to like Venice at night."

A bellboy rushed forward to open the door as we neared the hotel's entrance. He spoke directly to Giovanni, nodding his head in acknowledgement towards me.

"Would you like to see the room or do you prefer to go directly to the *ristorante*?" he asked, as the desk clerk completed the check in and the bellboy disappeared with our bags.

I was feeling a bit shy about spending the night with him, despite our earlier hook up. Maybe I'd feel more comfortable as the night wore one. I looked around, trying not to reveal how impressed I was. The hotel's lobby was tastefully decorated in brilliant colors of reds and gold. Opulent fabric hung from the ceilings, covering the windows. Similar fabric covered several of the waiting chairs. Original paintings adorned the walls. This place even smelled expensive.

"How about we take a quick look before heading out? I'm anxious to see the mysterious Venice you keep referring to." Not to mention I really had to use the bathroom.

The bellboy reappeared with our bags and we followed him up a flight of stairs to our room. He opened the door, placed the bags on the luggage rack, turned on the lights and opened the windows. Giovanni discretely slipped him a few bills. He silently closed the door and retreated back to the lobby.

We viewed the city's skyline through the open window. He was right. Venice looked totally different at night. Its brightly lit buildings, illuminated by streetlights, stood out against its dark surroundings like stars in the sky. Without the incessant traffic noise usually heard in other cities, it was eerily quiet.

I excused myself to the bathroom, noting the marble floors. Skid resistant mats covered the floor near the vanity and shower. I checked out the toiletries, courtesy of the hotel. It looked like a mini drugstore over there! Shampoo, conditioner, toothpaste, toothbrush, sewing kit, soap, shower cap, even sample bottles of cologne for men and perfume for the ladies were present. After taking care of the important things, I made good use of the toothpaste. After all, I wanted to have minty fresh breath for this evening.

"Is everything all right? Do you like the room?" he asked, handing me a glass of champagne.

I accepted the glass, shutting the bathroom door behind me. "Yes, I'm fine and of course I like the room. It is absolutely exquisite!" I learned that the hotel had recently been renovated. It was hundreds of years old, yet after having been brought up to modern standards, now received a well deserved 5 star rating. The marble floors were polished to a high gloss, and exposed wooden beams adorned the ceiling, adding to its overall charm. The view overlooking the canals was incredible.

"A toast." He raised his glass and said, "To us. May we both find happiness tonight and always." We raised our glasses in a toast to ourselves in anticipation of all that would eventually come.

Giovanni sat near the open window. The cool night air was a welcome relief from the warmth of the room. He motioned for me to join him.

His gesture caused me to pause, for European furniture is by no means built for the fat asses of the rapidly expanding American waistline. The furniture, although very well designed, is more compact than what is typically found in our homes. I could only imagine the chair exploding under our combined weight. Despite my obvious concerns, he was persistent.

"I know you don't think we're both going to fit in that little bitty chair, do you?" A bit of *homegirl* slipped out.

He laughed. "Come here. Trust me. It will hold us both."

I sat on his lap. And you know what? That little chair didn't so much as give up a groan. Giovanni kissed me on my neck, sending shivers throughout my body. I took his glass of champagne and placed it on the table alongside mine. The scarf I wore around my shoulders slowly slipped to the floor. His manhood became hard under my leg. His breathing deepened. Mine matched his.

"So tell me. How did you learn to speak English so well?" I traced the beginnings of a five o'clock shadow with my fingers, kissing each spot where my finger no longer rested.

"It is a requirement in school to learn another language. I choose English, but I am also fluent in French." He nibbled at my ear, planting wet kisses all over my neck.

"Really? Well, call me impressed," I replied. His mustache tickled my neck.

"You like it when I do this?" He traced my ear with his tongue, but thankfully didn't put in inside my ear. That drives me crazy, though not in a good way.

"Oh yes! That feels so good." My breathing became even more labored. "Hey, I have a joke for you. What do you call someone who speaks three languages?"

His hand reached for my breast. "That's easy. Trilingual."

"Well, what do you call someone who speaks two languages?" I moaned.

"Bilingual, of course," he replied, reaching around to unhook my dress. He slipped it down exposing my breasts, fingering my now erect nipples.

"And what do you call a person who only speaks one language?" I helped him out of his jacket. We stood up, carefully undoing each other's buttons and snaps along the way.

He stopped and looked at me curiously. "I don't know what you call someone who only speaks one language. What is the answer?" We stumbled towards the bedroom. "You call them American!" I laughed at my joke and our fumbling. He laughed along with me, helping to remove my dress from over my head.

"Do we have enough time?" he asked, standing there fully exposed and at full attention.

"Oh yeah. But if we didn't we'd make it enough time." I playfully pulled him towards me using his penis as a handle.

Fifteen minutes later, that man had me screaming out his name, silently thanking God for finally bringing me a man who could curl my toes, over and over again. Our lovemaking was something out of a romance novel and I never wanted it to end. Our bodies connected together perfectly, like pieces of a puzzle cut from the same cloth.

"Are you absolutely famished *amore mio*? I feel as if I could eat enough food for the both of us tonight," he asked, resting his hand on my stomach after we both made it to the mountaintop in orgasmic bliss.

We were covered in the perspiration brought on from intense sex. I loved how our scents co-mingled and I absolutely could not get enough of inhaling his natural fragrance.

"Now that you mention it, I am kind of hungry. What time is it anyway?" I turned on my side to face him.

"If we hurry, we can still make our reservation. The *ristorante* is only a short distance from here. It will take no time at all to get there."

"Well, let's go." I sat up much too quickly, feeling the blood rush to my head. "Join me in the shower?"

"This first." He reached for my arm, pulled me on top of him and kissed me deeply, passionately.

"Wow! What was that for?"

"That is for taking a chance to do what in your heart you feel is right. Now, we will shower."

I like to pride myself on being a capable, independent, strong Black woman able to take care of herself in any situation. But I was starting to enjoy how Giovanni took charge of everything. I had no worries when I was with him. I could kick back and enjoy myself, be treated like a lady. I must admit it was rather nice having someone take care of the details expecting nothing from me in return.

Being with a man who knew his way around was a breath of fresh air. I didn't mind him choosing the restaurant or the hotel. In fact, since I was on his turf, I appreciated and trusted his judgment. I knew no matter what his choices were I'd enjoy them.

When you meet someone for the first time, you get an impression of their tastes, their style. Sometimes it compliments your own, other times you realize you're at opposite ends of the social spectrum. However, when I first met Giovanni and saw how he carried himself, his style of dress, the way he spoke... I knew immediately he was someone I wanted to know better. Apparently, he felt the same way about me.

We showered, taking turns washing each other. It wasn't uncomfortable at all. On the contrary, it felt as if we'd known each other all our lives.

"Hey, you'd better stop that if we're going to make our dinner reservations!" I joked as he lathered me up between my legs.

"Okay. I will stop for now. We will have time to finish... Maybe later?" He rinsed the remaining soap from his body, making room for me under the warm spray of the shower.

We retrieved our clothes from where they lay scattered around the room. It was extremely sexy seeing Giovanni wearing a pair of electric blue briefs, rather than the boxers many men seemed to prefer. He sported the athletic physique of a man who worked for a living, in contrast to the muscle bound types who spent most of their waking hours in a gym. I preferred his form much more than the latter. I wiggled back into my dress after spritzing perfume in the air and stepping into the fine mist.

"I like your hair cut like that. It is very sexy. I also like how you don't need to spend hours trying to look beautiful. You know, you are what we Italians call a natural beauty? And I have never known a woman who could get dressed so quickly."

"Thanks. I know you're probably used to women who have hair down to the middle of their backs, but for me, I prefer this short style. And you're right, I don't have to waste precious time dealing with it." I smoothed in a handful of moisturizer followed by a bit of gel, and then finger styled the top. I quickly applied eyeliner, shadow, blush and lipstick, as Giovanni patiently waited for me. "Hey, I just remembered I need to hang my suit when we get back tonight or it'll be too wrinkled to wear tomorrow."

"Tonight I shall remind you. Are you almost ready?"

All he had to do was smooth a hand full of mousse through his hair, work it through his short curls, then finish off with a brush to control his waves. He applied aftershave to his face, dressed, and within minutes was ready to go.

With little time to spare, we left the hotel to walk the short distance to the restaurant. This must've been a very popular place, for lines of people stood patiently waiting their turn to enter.

We strolled to the front of the line, gave our names to the *maitre'd* and was immediately escorted inside. The atmosphere inside was totally different from the noisiness of the crowds waiting to get in. Out there it was loud and chaotic. Once we stepped through the doors, we were greeted by soft background music, providing a sense of serenity in a sea of madness.

We followed the formally dressed waiter upstairs, passing through the dimly lit dining room, to a smaller room on the second floor. He seated us at a table next to a window overlooking the city. The maitre'd pulled the chair facing the skyline from the table. This section of the restaurant provided an intimate romantic setting for couples only. Strategically placed candles and classical music set the tone for romance.

"This *ristorante* has one of the best chefs in all of *Venezia*. Without the proper connections you must book your reservation weeks or perhaps months in advance."

"Don't tell me? You have connections? Now, why does that not surprise me?" I smiled at this man I was rapidly falling for.

"*Por favore,* you must understand. This is how business is done all over *Italia*. I do you a favor; you do me a favor… And so it goes."

The waiter approached the table with a wine list. Giovanni didn't look at it. He knew what he wanted, so ordering the wine for the two of us was effortless.

"I know what you mean… you scratch my back, I scratch yours?"

"*Si,* exactly. I hope you don't mind my ordering for you. I want you to taste this wine and tell me what you think. It is from a local vineyard in *Veneto*."

"No, I don't mind at all. I have no doubt it will be delicious," I replied.

The waiter returned, presented the bottle to Giovanni for his approval, and then uncorked it at the table. He poured a small amount in both our glasses, and then stood back. I wasn't sure what to do, so I took my cues from Giovanni. First he swirled the wine until it thinly coated the glass, tipped it to his nose, and inhaled its bouquet. I did the same. He peered over his glass and discretely smiled at my imitation of him. He raised an eyebrow and subtly nodded at me indicating I should drink. I did, but just a little. I let the dark, red liquid find its way over my tongue to the back of my throat.

It is true what they say about good wine – it engages all your senses. It was dry, which I like, with smoky undertones of raspberry. I nodded my head in approval. Giovanni signaled to the waiter to fill our glasses.

"How do you like it?" he asked, sipping his wine, gazing at me with those intensely emerald green eyes.

"It's delicious. It's delicate, smooth and mellow… I don't think I've ever tasted wine this good before. Yum." I sipped again.

"I'm glad you like it. Now we must decide about the food. Do you have any preferences?"

"I don't know. I don't recognize any of the main courses." I answered, reading the English version of the menu. "I don't know what to choose. What do you recommend?"

"Would you like me to order for you?"

"Yes, if you don't mind. And I eat practically everything so just pick something you think I'd like." I continued to sip the delicious wine, beginning to feel its effects.

A very attractive, big-breasted woman with cleavage pushed up to her eyeballs walked past our table. Her date trailed closely behind. I watched as Giovanni's eyes followed her to her seat. What the hell?!

"Please, don't do that!" I said angrily. The wine made me feel light-headed.

"Don't do what, *amore mio*?" he asked innocently.

"Look at women like that when you're out with me! That's what!" I sat back in my chair feeling disrespected. This was the first time I became upset over something he had done.

"Lena, I am sorry if it upsets you, but all I did was look. When I see a beautiful woman – when most men see a beautiful woman – we cannot help but to notice. It is only natural. I mean you no disrespect. Besides, did you notice how many men's heads turned when you walked by their tables?" he asked.

"That's different," I said, feeling rather childish.

"How is it different?"

"Those guys were only looking at me because I'm Black. They were probably wondering what a man like you was doing with a woman like me." I looked down at my hands trying to hold back the tears that threatened to spring forth.

"Is that what you think? Oh *bella*, you are so wrong! You Americans are so hung up on skin color! Believe me when I say this.

Those men were looking at you because you are beautiful and you are stunning in that dress. Trust me. Would I be out with you if you weren't absolutely breathtaking?" He reached for my hand across the table. "To appreciate a beautiful woman is not a bad thing. It is part of our culture. If you have any doubts, look at our art. Our paintings and sculptures celebrate women's beauty. We love women and we love to look at them. *Va bene*, because I know it upsets you, I will try to use discretion when we are together. Okay?" he asked, touching my chin, with a hint of amusement in his eyes.

I felt really stupid as I replied, "I guess I have a lot to learn about the Italian culture. I'm sorry for being so sensitive. But you are right about one thing. I do look amazing in this dress." I took his hand and smiled.

Over the course of the next three hours, we indulged in a fantastic five course meal, drank two bottles of wine and discussed everything under the sun. How did I, Lena Delgado, get so lucky to meet this wonderful man? He was not only handsome, but was also very intelligent and possessed an amazing sense of humor. He told me about growing up in the village of *Piano Montissimo* with his brother Lucio and his sister. He spoke of his dreams of expanding his nightclub to a tourist destination hot spot. Like Venice.

In turn, I relayed stories about my childhood, focusing on the pits and perils of having four brothers and sisters. We discussed racism and its ugly effects on a person's psyche. Although he didn't totally understand the issues I had to work through, he did empathize with me. I even opened up about my childhood dream of wanting to be a modern dancer, and the latest plan of one day owning my own café, where I would serve exotic coffees and delectable desserts. I soon discovered the more I learned about Giovanni Fuglio Morelli, the more I wanted to know.

"Why haven't you pursued your dream of opening a café? If this is your passion, what keeps you from simply doing it?"

"First of all, it's not that easy to start a business. I don't have a clue about where to begin. I've never known anyone who has owned their own business, so I don't really know if I have what it takes. Plus, family responsibilities got in the way. That, and my moving all over the world, kind of put everything on hold."

"I see. You know if you ever want to get anywhere in life, you have to take a chance and take a leap of faith. It all begins with one small step." He played with his mustache as if in deep thought. "I have an idea. What if I give you a crash course in operating a business? That way you will see if it is really something you wish to pursue."

I thought about it for only a moment. As with every other situation I encountered since arriving in Italy, I decided I might as well go for it. What did I have to lose? "Do you think we can handle spending that much time together? If it's not a problem with you, then I think it's a great idea. After all, you're quite the successful, businessman. Who better to learn from?"

"*Bene*! I will teach you what it takes to run a business. But I must warn you, the Giovanni you see sitting across from you is not the same man you will see running his club. When I am there, I am totally professional." He leaned forward, exposing curly little hairs peeking over the top of his collar.

I wanted to twirl my tongue around each and every one. Instead I replied, "Oh, I think I can handle you. And I can't wait to see you in action." I licked my lips.

"Speaking of action… How do you feel about dancing tonight? I know a great nightclub not too far from here. They play all genres of music; also I want to pick up a few ideas on the crowd and type of atmosphere that works best here."

"So, the teaching begins?" I questioned.

"No, no, no. Tonight is only about having a good time. I want to dance with you again, only this time, for real. Actually, let me rephrase that. Wherever I go, I'm always on the lookout for business ideas. I suppose I always keep my eyes and ears open. You never know when an opportunity will present itself. So consider that lesson number one. Always be prepared to learn from your experiences."

I stretched and loudly yawned. All that good food and wine had slowed me down quite a bit. If I were anywhere else but Venice, I'd have chosen going to bed instead of dancing. But looking at that man sitting across from me, well, how could I resist? "That sounds like a lesson not only for business, but for life as well. Come on. Lead the way. I'm all yours." I accepted his help from my seat and excused myself to the restroom while Giovanni paid for the meal.

"Are you ready?" He met me outside the restroom, extending his arm.

"Yes. And I can't begin to thank you for dinner. I'm having the time of my life." I wiggled my arm around his. We exited from the restaurant and went out into the cool Venetian mist.

I heard the music before I saw the club. The loud boom of the bass from Dr. Dre and Snoop Dogg's collaboration had me bopping in the alley before we reached the door. We entered through a nondescript door into a cloud of smoke illuminated by flickering images, courtesy of strobe lighting. The place was packed. People of all colors, nationalities, and sexual orientation moved to the rhythm of the music, played by an unseen DJ. Waitresses dressed in low cut tops and black biker shorts balanced trays of drinks, without spilling a drop, as they maneuvered through the pulsating crowds. I immediately wanted to head to the dance floor, but Giovanni took my hand, guiding me to the edge of the action. Typical male, he wanted to check things out before diving in.

"Would you like something to drink?" he shouted above the noise.

"No, thanks. I'm okay for now. What do you think about this place?"

"I like it. Lots of energy. Maybe a bit too crowded, but it is good." He nodded his head in time to the beat.

We watched the crowd gyrate through a few more songs before the DJ finally slowed it down. Magically, the crowd thinned.

"Would you like to dance now?" I asked.

He nodded and led the way to the floor. We swayed to the music. I rested my head against his shoulder, enjoying the sensation of his heart beating next to mine. I closed my eyes enjoying the movement of his body. Suddenly we stopped dancing. I opened my eyes as a young brother, sporting a military inspired haircut, tried to cut in. Giovanni looked at me questioning if I wanted to dance with the young man. I shook my head, signifying no. He told the guy no and we proceeded to dance through another slow song. The brother returned. I told him no, once more.

"Looks like you have an admirer," he teased.

I didn't think it was so funny. I thought it was rude and annoying for this brother to keep trying to break in, considering he should have realized we were together. The next song brought the crowd back with a vengeance. It was some EuroTech house music I never heard before, but it was apparently pretty popular. Of course, Giovanni being in the business knew how much of a crowd pleaser this one was. We danced for a few more songs. Well, as much as anyone can dance when you're packed in like sardines being pushed from side to side. Eventually, we gave up and headed back to the sidelines.

"I need a drink. Would you like something?"

"Sure, I'll take a Cosmopolitan. You look hot. You want me to hold your jacket for you?"

"Thank you. It is pretty warm in here. I shall be right back." He shrugged out of his blazer and handed it to me.

I folded it across my arm, watching the crowd continue to pulsate. It had been so long since I had danced. I didn't think I remembered how to move. I watched the partiers, some moving as if they were having sex in public. Come to think of it, probably a few of them were.

"Hey sistah. What cha doing in here with that white boy?" The brotha from the dance floor had unfortunately singled me out of all the other women in the room.

"Uh, excuse me, but do I know you?" I asked, sarcastically.

"No, but if you get rid of that white boy we *can* get to know each other. Damn girl! You is fine!" He slurred his words.

"No, thanks." I replied, trying to ignore him.

"Oh, so it's like that? Huh?"

"Like *what*?" I responded back rudely.

"You all up into that jungle fever shit. Think you too good to be with a brotha? Fuck you bitch! You ain't shit! Girl you need to get you a BLACK man who'll fuck the shit out of you, then let's see who you go home with! What the fuck you lookin' at!" He stared past me.

I looked at him, through him and smirked, not willing to give him the satisfaction of my anger. Suddenly a very tall, dark muscular brother snatched his friend away from me.

"What up G? Why you frontin' on this sistah like that? Dude, she can be with whoever she want to be with. You trippin' man... You shouldn't be sweatin' this fine creature. If I was her, I wouldn't want to talk to your drunk ass either. Sistah, please excuse my partner. He obviously left his manners and common sense back on the south side of Chicago." Tall, dark, and muscular pushed his loud, obnoxious friend away from me.

I mouthed, "Thank you" to the tall one. He nodded in return. I exhaled and turned around to see Giovanni standing a few steps away, looking uncomfortably embarrassed.

"Are you alright? I come back and I see you standing here with these two men. Only one of them did not look so happy." The set of his jaw, the glint of his eyes, all gave indications of an anger he barely managed to suppress.

"Yeah, I'm fine. That guy was an asshole. You know, I thought I'd left all this bullshit behind when I came over here. But you know what they say, 'Wherever you go, there you are'. I get so sick and tired of people trying to live my life for me. Trying to tell me what's right for me. Who I should be with. It's even worse cuz they don't even know me. Hey Giovanni, don't worry about it. I've forgotten about it already. I refuse to let some asshole mess up our evening." I accepted my drink from his outstretched hand.

"What do you say we leave this place? I prefer to have you all to myself rather than share you with these other men. By the way, have you noticed how many have lusted after you this evening? I have," he said replacing feelings of anger with a masculine pride.

"Oh, you are so bad." I playfully punched his chest and handed him his jacket. "You like guys looking at me? Does that make you feel good?"

"*Si.* To be in the company of a beautiful woman is a compliment to any man. Lena, you must start seeing yourself through the eyes of others. You are more special than you seem to realize. Let's get out of here." He reached for my hand with his free one.

I followed the path he made through the club, trying not to get stepped on by an overenthusiastic dancer. We broke free of the crowd and headed for the exit. People continued to push into the crowded club. Finally, we managed to get outside, free from the noise and crowds that continued to grow despite the late hour. From the corner of my eye, I saw a couple so enamored with one another they didn't seem to notice they weren't alone in the alley. I pointed to the couple and shook my head in indignation. It was the young brother who had so rudely chastised me for being with a "white boy" locked in a passionate kiss with a tall model-thin blonde. Hypocritical asshole!

I yawned again. It had been a long day and I was exhausted. "Do you mind if we head back to the hotel? I am so tired, I don't know if I can make it back." I yawned again.

"*Si.* I agree. It has been a long day and we have much to do tomorrow." He wrapped his jacket around me, noticing I had begun to shiver.

A low fog had settled over the city giving it an eerie, surreal appearance. I was reminded of the many "slasher" films I'd watched over the years. You know the ones where the killer comes out of the fog to kill the unsuspecting lovers? When you're in a setting like this, it's easy to let your imagination run wild. Every so often, I heard haunting voices coming from the mist. What made it creepier was I couldn't pinpoint their exact location. Everyone and everything was shrouded in fog like a cloak of fear. All I wanted to do was get back in the hotel, and climb in the warm cozy bed next to my lover.

When we entered our room, it was freezing. In the rush to leave, we inadvertently had left the windows wide open, and despite the evening chill, it was still May, so the hotel's owners had already shut off the heat for the season.

"Let's get these windows closed before we both catch pneumonia." He cranked the windows shut. The time it took for him to close the windows was the amount of time it took for me to strip down to nothing and dive under the covers to get warm.

"Giovanni? Will you come to bed and help warm me up? I'm so cold," I said from beneath the covers.

"Is that your teeth I hear chattering?" He carefully hung his suit in the closet.

"Uh, huh. I'm freezing under here. I didn't bring my night clothes. I didn't think I needed any." Who knew it could get so cool in the middle of May.

"Here, sit up and put this around you." He brought a robe from the bathroom and surrounded me in its warmth.

"How is that?"

"Much better. Thanks. Now how about you come wrap your arms around me too?"

"I would be honored. Come here." He slipped under the covers and pulled me close.

I rested my head on his chest, listening to his breathing, feeling his chest rise and fall. I fingered his chest hairs, moving those that tickled my nose away from my face. I tucked my cold feet between his legs.

"Hey, your feet are cold. Be careful where you put those things. They feel like icicles." He laughed.

"I'm sorry. But you have so much heat coming from between your legs. I couldn't think of a better place to warm my feet."

"*Bene*. As long as you are warm... Do you feel like talking, *mi'amica*? There is something on my mind. I cannot sleep until it is settled."

I sat up in the bed and faced him. This sounded serious. "Sure, what is it? What do you want to talk about?"

"Tonight when those men were bothering you... I overheard only a small portion of the conversation, but what I did hear really troubled me. Is race such an issue in your country that it becomes a problem when other Americans see us together? And to refer to me as a "white boy"! I am not white, nor am I a boy. I am an Italian man whose blood can be traced for centuries back to Roman gladiators." I could feel the anger rising from his pores. "I don't understand such stupidity! Lena, this is all new to me – this race thing. I have dated "black" women before, from other countries, mostly Africa. I have also gone out with European women from other countries, but until now I have never experienced such a problem."

"I understand your frustration and anger. We still have a huge racial problem back in the states. It's getting better, but every now and then I come across someone who has a chip on his shoulder. They refuse to let go of the past wrongs. When I run into these knuckleheads I try to ignore them and just chalk it up to their ignorance. I refuse to let anyone dictate to me how I should conduct my life. I hope this doesn't affect how you feel about me."

"No. It doesn't change how I feel about you. Nothing can change that. I needed to express my anger. This is a new feeling for me." He put his arms above his head, interlocking his fingers as he continued to contemplate our conversation.

"Giovanni. I've dealt with racism in some form or fashion practically every day of my life. Sales clerks who barely make more than minimum wage, have followed me around stores suspecting me of shoplifting. I have been stopped by the police for no reason other than being in the "wrong" neighborhood at the wrong time. I've even had customers refuse my service when I was just a teenager working in a fast food joint. Just because of my skin color. Racism is something you don't ever get used to, but you learn to live around it. Something my parents taught me when I was first starting out in the world was to never ever let someone else's ignorance become your problem. Remember what you told me earlier today?"

"Hmmm, what did I tell you earlier?" He looked at me puzzled.

"You said to always be prepared to learn from our experiences. Both good or bad. Isn't that what you have to learn in order to be successful in business? I think it applies to life as well." I leaned my tired head on his shoulder, stifling back a yawn.

"I suppose you are correct. You are very good at seeing situations for what they are. I believe I can also learn from you, not just you from me. Are you tired? Let us go to sleep. We have a busy day tomorrow. *Buena notte, amore mio.*"

CHAPTER 17

I awoke the next morning to an empty bed. The clock on the nightstand indicated it was only 8:30. Where was Giovanni? I went to the bathroom. I found a damp towel thrown neatly over the towel rack, but still no him.

"Giovanni?" I entered the next room. I looked out the window to see a gloomy, foggy *Venetian* morning. Still wearing the bathrobe from last night, I pulled it taut around me in an attempt to ward off the chill in the air. I wonder where he could be so early in the morning. A knock at the door startled me. I looked through the peephole to find a waiter waiting besides a small cart.

"Breakfast, *signora*." Sang out the voice of the bellhop.

"*Mi dispiace*. I didn't order breakfast," I called out through the closed door.

"*Signore* Morelli ordered for you. He said to bring it to you before nine."

"*Uno momento, por favore*."

That man continued to amaze me at every turn! I ran to the bathroom, splashed some water on my face, and brushed down my hair. I opened the door to an older gentleman who looked like he had seen women in all stages of dress and couldn't care less how any of us looked. His mannerisms and total discretion erased my self-consciousness. He expertly positioned the small table in the middle of the room, borrowed a chair from the desk, and removed the stainless steel lid to expose pastries, fruit, orange juice and coffee. I had a few loose Euros in my purse from last night, which I handed to the man as a tip. He graciously waved me off, tipped his hat, and retreated as quickly as he came. I had just sat down to sip my coffee when the door opened. In strode Giovanni holding my freshly pressed pantsuit.

"*Buon giorno*. I see they brought up breakfast."

"Good morning. What's this?" I rose from my chair to greet him and I took the pantsuit. I was glad I had thought to brush my teeth before sinking into the food.

"With all that happened last night, I forgot to remind you about your outfit. I could not take you to meet my friend in wrinkled clothes. I had the hotel maid press it for you."

"Thank you, thank you, thank you! You are so thoughtful! You realize you are totally spoiling me." I hung the suit in the closet. "Have you eaten yet? This food looks so good." I handed him a croissant and poured a cup of espresso.

"It is no problem." He pulled another chair to the table. "I am used to waking early. You looked so peaceful lying there. I did not want to disturb you, so I dressed and went out for a walk before the city became filled with tourists.

"Mmm, this is good. Just what I needed. What time do you want to go see your friend?" I asked, between sips of the still steaming espresso.

"Check out is 11. We can go then, unless you want to see something else first." He sipped his coffee.

"You know what I would like to see? I'd like to tour the *Palazzo Ducale*." Although I had visited the Doges' Palace several times during previous trips to Venice, the artwork never ceased to impress me. And going over the Bridge of Sighs where prisoners went to receive their final fate was an experience unto itself. I loved touring Venice.

"Okay, we can do that also. We need several hours to properly see the museum. I shall tell Claudio to expect us this afternoon." He picked up his cell phone to call his long time friend.

I took one last bite of my croissant and popped a strawberry in my mouth with the intention of going to the bathroom to clean up. I didn't get very far. Giovanni stood holding the phone to his ear, then loosened the belt to my robe exposing my nudity for his gaze. He spoke softly into his phone, all the while staring at me. After a brief conversation, all in Italian, he hung up and placed the phone on the table. He then began speaking Italian to me. I didn't understand much of what he said, but I got the gist. I loved hearing his voice – smooth and silky as a saxophone played by a master jazz musician. He could have been giving me the weather report, but the way he spoke turned me on.

I helped remove his sweater, unbuttoned his shirt, loosened his belt, undid his pants and pushed him back on the bed. When he was totally nude, I kissed him all over, licked him up and down and fell back in appreciation when he reciprocated my actions. He continued to speak to me alternating between Italian and French. This drove me wild! He pulled me up to look at me, still speaking the language of love and kissed me. We'd kissed passionately before, but this time it was different. Instead of the usual sense of urgency, he kissed me with such gentleness. I became afraid – afraid of the feelings developing between us. This was quickly turning into more than either of us expected. Without breaking our gaze, I mounted him, rocking slowly to his cadence while he continued to speak. Not once during the entire time of our lovemaking did he look away. And that is when it hit me. We were making love, not just having sex, but actually making love.

CHAPTER 18

After an informative three hour tour of the *Palazzo Ducale,* where we alternately commented on the timeless beauty of the *frescoes,* sculptures, and numerous other pieces of artwork displayed throughout the *palazzo.* We made our way to the nearest *ferrovia* to await the *vaporetti* and headed to the small island of *Murano.* The early morning fog had burned off to reveal a bright, beautiful sunny day.

Much sooner than I expected, we arrived at *Murano.* We were about to dock and I noticed a man waving at us. Giovanni waved back. That must be Claudio. I expected him to be decked out in his priest outfit – all black outfit with a white collar. But this man was indistinguishable from those who surrounded him. He was dressed in jeans and a work shirt. Giovanni had mentioned that the man was considered to be handsome, but I was totally taken aback when I first laid eyes on him. He stood a bit over 6 feet tall with a mop of dark brown curly hair. Even from this distance I thought he had the bluest eyes I had ever seen on any individual. They weren't that washed out, pale blue so many people tend to have. No, his eyes were a deep blue. Almost violet and accented even more so by long, dark eyelashes. His Romanesque nose was underscored by full pouting lips. Though not my type, I can understand why the women of his village were upset when he joined the priesthood.

"Is that Claudio?" I asked indicating the man waving his arms. I don't know why I was nervous, but I was.

"*Si.* That is my old friend. Lena, do not be nervous. Relax. Just wait. You will see what a good man he is. He speaks English very well, so you shall have no difficulty conversing with him." He squeezed my hand gently for support.

We were the last passengers to disembark. With bags in tow, we stepped onto the island of *Murano* known the world over for its intricately designed, hand-blown glass sculptures.

"Giovanni, how are you, my old friend?" Claudio asked. They embraced as though they hadn't seen each other for years. Maybe it had been years.

"Ah, this must be Lena?" He encircled me with his strong arms welcoming us to *Murano.*

"*Ciao* Claudio. Giovanni has told me so much about you. I am so happy to finally meet you." I returned his hug.

"My friend dropped off a *Vespa* scooter so you do not have to make the long walk back to my home. Hand me your bags. I will strap them unto my scooter and the two of you can follow me on the other one." He pointed to a bright red scooter parked next to his white one.

"How will your friend get back if we take his scooter?" Giovanni, ever the thoughtful one, asked Claudio.

"Do not worry about him. He is off to do business on the mainland and he does not live far from here, so he will have only a short walk. Come on. Let's get out of here." He started the engine, waited for us to get situated, and then zoomed off.

"Just like Claudio. He is a man of God who drives like a bat out of hell." Giovanni shouted, as we took off after him.

We trailed after Claudio, until we reached a patch of green in the sea of concrete and stucco. His house was the only one on the street with even a semblance of grass, though not much more than a few square feet. He ushered us into the parsonage, motioning for us to take a seat at the kitchen table, while he placed our bags in an unseen room. The men conversed in Italian initially. However after realizing I wasn't following the conversation, they switched easily back to English, catching up on one another's lives over the past few months. I sat quietly, listening, gathering bits and pieces of information about the men I didn't know before.

Claudio's expression unexpectedly clouded over as he returned to the table with drinks. It was fascinating how quickly he went from joking around with Giovanni to being serious with me.

"Lena, tell me, how do you like our beautiful country?" He continued without giving me time to respond. "What I find peculiar is so many of my relatives leave *Italia* for the United States, the supposedly land of the free. They patronizingly refer to *Italia* as the old country. They say we are too traditional. Too stuck in our ways with no desire to progress to the 21st century. Yet, here you are, an obviously modern American woman with a fondness for my country."

"I think your country is wonderful. But the United States does have a lot to offer young people. Maybe that's why they leave. And it's definitely progressive. After all, we are leading the world in a technological revolution. But I think there is something said for being traditional and living a slower paced, more relaxed life. In America, we're so busy working we hardly have any time to enjoy ourselves. It's all hurry, hurry, hurry. Work, work, work..."

"Yes, I know what you mean. This is why I choose to live on *Murano*. We know how to enjoy life. We are not caught up in the tempo of life that happens across the lagoon." He motioned towards Venice.

"Claudio, *mi'amico*, you have slowed down so much, you are living the life of my *nonno*. You need to get out more my friend." He laughed at his reference to his grandfather.

"Ah. I get out all the time, though apparently not as much as you."

"I don't think there is anything wrong with either of your lives. You're both living the lives you've chosen and you both seem content." My observation quickly shifted the light mood back to serious.

"Lena, Giovanni has told me a little bit about your "dream". I would like to hear more, if it is acceptable with you. Why don't you fill me in? And, please take your time. We are in no hurry?" He turned to face Giovanni. "Why don't you go for a walk while Lena and I become more acquainted? I am certain she will be more comfortable by not having to witness the emotions on your face as she speaks to me."

"Perhaps you have a point. My initial reaction was not the most understanding when she told me the first time. Lena, if it is all right with you, I shall leave you in the good hands of my friend." He stood from his chair, came to my side and knelt down until he was at my level. "Do not worry. You will do fine. I shall see you in a short while. *Va bene.*" He patted me on the back before going outside into the garden his good friend spent so much time tending.

"Please." Claudio motioned for me to follow him to the living room. "We will be much more comfortable here."

I sat in an overstuffed chair opposite a well-worn leather recliner where Claudio chose to make himself comfortable. My heart beat so loudly I was sure he could hear, if not see, my shirt rising and falling in a rhythmic pace. I was nervous about speaking to him, exposing my soul to someone I'd only just met. Nervous about opening my heart to this man who dedicated his life to serving God, though at the same time, kept the open liberal mind of a scientist.

"Before we begin, I want you to relax. I hold no prejudice, nor have I formed any judgment about what you proposed to have gone through. My friend asked me to speak with you, so I shall. He also told me how special you have become to him in a very, very short span of time. And as his friend, I only want the best for him, as well as for you. However, as much as I would like to offer insight into your situation, there is the possibility I will have no definite answers to provide you. All I really have to offer is my educated opinion, based on my experience and research, of course." He sat back in the chair, legs wide open, fingers interlaced in his lap.

"Thanks, padre."

"Please, call me Claudio. Think of me as a friend you have not yet gotten to know." He smiled warmly.

"Okay, uh thanks, Claudio." I was still nervous despite his attempts to put me at ease. "Well, I guess I will start at the beginning."

"Giovanni tells me you have a family? Why not start there?" As he reached for his drink, the hair behind his ears sprang loose obstructing his vision. He tucked it back into place. "Excuse me. I know I need a haircut, but it is difficult tearing myself away from my solitude to get to the barber on the mainland." He smiled sheepishly.

"Yes, I do have a family. A husband and three children, well actually two of them are young men – almost grown, but they do keep me busy." I smiled to myself thinking about my boys. "The truth is Claudio, I haven't been truly happy for years. I know when you have children, your life is no longer your own. I have accepted it and lived with this notion up until a few weeks ago. I thought I was the perfect wife, always accommodating my husband, foregoing my own needs. I put my feelings and desires on the backburner trying to be a good mother, but after a while, I forgot who I was. I no longer recognized me. I disappeared, little by little, until only the shell of who I used to be remained. Instead of living, I was merely going through the motions. One day I simply got fed up and decided I didn't want to live like that anymore. The next thing I knew, I was having some kind of out-of-body experience and somehow traveled to a kind of dream world." I stopped speaking to check his reaction. His face was as calm as when I first began. I continued.

"I met a woman. She told me her name was Simone. She informed me she was my spiritual caretaker and that I was "there" because I needed to be there. I was supposedly the one in control and had entered into some kind of "alternate reality". You know, stuck between two worlds. I didn't know what to think. It was like I was there, but I wasn't. When I started seeing people from my past, I actually thought I had died and my spirit was interacting with those who had gone on before me. She said that wasn't the case. I really became confused when I met Giovanni. He was a total stranger, not someone I had known before. After a while, when I really started a relationship with him, I realized I had no control! I knew I was happy. I felt alive for the first time in years. It was wonderful and I didn't want that feeling to ever end."

Claudio continued to listen, making me feel more comfortable in his presence.

"Of course, I felt guilty about leaving my family. I rationalized that they could live without me, at least for a little while. I was intent on fulfilling my own needs. Being with Giovanni was magical, yet so real. Some things I did with him...well, let's just say, in real life, I would have thought twice about doing. Especially the hang gliding. I don't care what anyone says. I was here. I had to be!" The memories of our time together, suddenly returned with amazing intensity.

"Uh, huh. You say that during this dream state was the first time you met Giovanni?" he asked with a puzzled expression.

"Well, yes. I think so... I mean... I've lived in Italy before, many years ago. I suppose it is possible our paths may have crossed at some point during that time. Though, I sincerely doubt it. I really think I would have remembered meeting him." I smiled at the thought.

"I see. Please go on."

"As I was saying, I met Giovanni and we spent an amazing week together. He took me to his village in the mountains and introduced me to his father. I swear Claudio. I felt like I was having the greatest fantasy in the world. It was truly orgasmic!" I blushed, realizing what I had just said and to whom I said it to. "I'm so sorry! I didn't mean to say that in front of you."

"Lena, it is all right. I promise I will not melt if you speak that way in front of me. Trust me, I have heard much worse." He laughed.

I shook my head at my indiscretion and continued. "Anyhow, all was going extremely well between the two of us. On my last day "there", we made plans to get back together later that evening. Only we didn't have the opportunity." I exhaled.

"Why not? What happened?"

"I woke up is what happened. The last thing I remembered prior to waking was almost drowning. Somehow, I ended up in a hospital back in Kansas. They said I had been in a coma like condition for weeks. Understandably, the doctors could not find anything seriously wrong with me." I looked at Claudio for an explanation.

"They are one hundred percent for sure you never left your hospital bed? Is it possible you could have woken up, walked away, and took a weeklong trip without them knowing about it?" he asked, figuratively pulling at straws.

"No, nothing like that happened. In fact, the doctor seemed really excited when I woke up. The thing is, when I woke up realizing where I was, remembering all I had just left, I became depressed. Although I was happy to see my children, I was very sad about returning to the same life I had lived for the past several years. Eventually, the doctor let me return home to my family. Claudio, it was even worse than I remembered. My husband went right back to his old ways of treating me like an old reliable pair of comfortable shoes. Taking me for granted. The last straw was, although I'd just come home from the hospital, within days he expected me to cook dinner for him and his friends while they watched sports on television.

"It sounds like your marriage no longer met your expectations. Is that what pushed you towards Giovanni?"

"You know what? When I first woke up, I managed to convince myself that I had imagined the entire situation, that I had invented this great Italian guy named Giovanni as an object of my fantasy. He was someone who would not disappoint me. He was intelligent, passionate, loving, handsome, sensitive... He possessed all the qualities a woman wants in a man. I thought he was too good to be true. Such a man doesn't exist. Right? After I got home, I couldn't shake the feeling about how real it all seemed. Those images in my mind were much too vivid to have only been a dream. Before I could talk myself out of it, I bought a one-way ticket to Italy and came here in search of that fantasy. Imagine my surprise when I first saw him! I was absolutely stunned when he actually recognized me! Claudio, I don't know how it is possible. You're a priest. How do you explain what has happened to me?" I leaned forward in my chair anticipating his response.

"You say you met a woman who told you her name was Simone? She said she was your spiritual caretaker? Did she tell you anything else?" He also leaned forward in his chair, massaging his temples with his fingers.

"Yes, she was a caretaker of dreams or something similar. She said she was like Mr. Rourke, a character from a television show in the

1980's called *Fantasy Island*. His only purpose on the show was to make sure his guest's fantasy were granted." I waited for his response.

"I see. Is it possible this Simone did only exist in that reality? Nowhere else?" He studied me. "When Giovanni first called telling me your story, it reminded me of a research study on out-of-body experiences conducted by a South American colleague of mine from graduate school. This was well before I became a priest. We were both interested in quantum physics and how it related to paranormal phenomena. After I heard about you, I became curious about the results of his study. I made a few calls and was able to reach him late last night."

"Really! You mean there are others who have experienced what I have gone through?" I asked, excited I was not the only one.

"Not exactly. My colleague has conducted years of study and research on similar phenomena. He studied a group of individuals who claim to have interacted with the spirit world, but on an absolutely physical basis. These people claim to walk amongst the dead in order to help the living. He said they go into trances that can last for mere seconds or entire days. During this metaphysical state, they claim to meet with dead ancestors in an attempt to gain knowledge about their life or someone else close to them. They also claim they can project not only their spirit, but also their physical presence into situations to protect or help the lives of the living. Vaguely reminiscent to the theory of a parallel universe."

He continued, "There are numerous accounts of people observing peculiar strangers warning them away from danger. And based on the results of his studies, my colleague truly believes this phenomenon does exist. Usually the people who claim to be able to project themselves come from ancient civilizations that still practice rituals and ceremonies to honor their deceased ancestors. They are indigenous to the land, mostly Indian tribes from both North and South America, although Australian aborigines also allege to possess these powers. They call themselves *Shamans*. What you have stated sounds similar to these occurrences, albeit with profound differences."

"*Shamans*?" I tried the new word in my mouth for the first time. "You say these people have walked amongst the dead? They interact with the spirits of their dead ancestors? As far as I know, my journey only exposed me to the living. Although Simone did say some people end up in this alternate reality when they are close to death, like being in a coma."

"That's interesting, but I do not see how that applies to your situation," he continued, "*Shamans'* beliefs are based on myths and legends. Their stories are passed down for centuries from generation to generation. I don't claim to understand how these people are able to have visions and interact with their deceased elders, but my colleague seems to feel it is possible."

"But do you think this is what I have experienced? I wasn't only "here" spiritually, I was also here physically." My brain had started to hurt, attempting to figure out the situation.

"On the surface there are many similarities to *shamanism*, though there is one important difference. What you seemed to have experienced is actual out-of-body travel where you were free to interact with others, just as easily as you sit talking to me now. Lena, there is a small group of scientists who only focus on paranormal phenomena who would be extremely interested in what it is you have to say. However, I must warn you, they are not taken seriously by their fellow scientists. But keep in mind, due to the nature of research, scientists are often considered to be a "bit off".

He smiled and continued. "You must realize there is much that remains unexplained, mysteries that are never solved. What you have told me is fascinating because there are no documented cases of anyone who was capable of projecting their spiritual being to another location only to have their physical body also materialize during the process. At least no one who was credible. My colleague is very interested in interviewing you to share your experience and have it documented as part of his scientific research. *If* you are interested." A strange, excited look overshadowed his face. I suppose the curiosity of the scientist temporarily overtook the civility of the priest.

"I'm sorry Claudio. Right now, I'm not interested in becoming part of any study. I just want to understand how I was able to do what I did. Most importantly, will I be able to do it again?" I wondered aloud.

"I did not mean to insinuate that you should become involved in his research. And I cannot say for certain if it will happen again. Of course, you are only concerned with gaining answers to your dilemma."

He held up his hands to back off. "My advice for you is to simply accept this unique opportunity, this precious gift, you have been given.

There are many mysteries in this world that are destined to remain so. For instance, scientists know human bodies are made up of organic matter. This they can prove in the laboratory. However, we still cannot define what makes us uniquely us. Why we have souls. These are the mysteries of life, my dear. If I were you, I would stop wondering *how* it happened and start asking yourself *why*."

"What do you mean, start asking why?" I asked, so wanting to push the curly hair away from his eyes.

"There is obviously something missing in your life – something that drew you here. To *Italia*. To my friend, Giovanni. You need to focus on why you chose to travel all this way in search of what may only have been a dream, a fantasy. Why you left your family? Why you have chosen to remain and explore this relationship with Giovanni?" He explained, now sounding more like a priest than a scientist.

"You're saying I should just accept what has happened and move on?"

"That is precisely what I am saying. Listen to me. Sometimes when we look too closely for imperfections, we tend to overlook the beauty. Right now, I would say your immediate concern should be the situation with your family and deciding what you truly want from my friend. I am certain you are a good woman, but I worry about Giovanni. His feelings for you are unlike any I have ever seen in him before. I do not wish to see him get hurt."

I knew he was right on with his observations. Instead of putting my energy into how it happened, I needed to focus on what I was going to do. It isn't possible to lead two separate lives on two different continents. Recent events notwithstanding.

I had to face the facts. Now that I had met Giovanni, face to face and spent "real" time with him, I knew he wasn't some fantasy I conjured up. Maybe my Native American ancestors worked a little of their magic for their modern day descendant? Was Simone a *Shaman* from a previous life? Or perhaps she really did exist in an alternate reality, allowing me to experience a bit of happiness for a change. Or quite possibly, she was merely a figment of my imagination. Well, whatever she was and whatever it was that led me to this point, there was no turning back. I had to meet this challenge head on if I wanted to have even the slimmest chance of fulfilling my destiny.

"You're right. All this time I have been focusing on the wrong stuff. Giovanni has come to mean so much to me. I don't intend to hurt him. Look, I've come all this way to find this man I believe to be my soul mate. I don't want to lose him, Claudio. I just wish I knew what to do." I held back the emotions threatening to come out. "There's one more question I'd like to ask before we finish?"

"Please…"

"Do you believe me? Do you think I actually experienced out-of-body travel to Italy?" I waited for his response.

"I believe something miraculous and wonderful has happened to you. In the eyes of both a scientist and a priest, I know all possibilities exist in this world. As far as what I feel? I do not know. There are many questions which remain, yet no answers. Perhaps when I know more, I can answer you." He shrugged.

"Thanks for your honesty. It really means a lot to me that you don't think I'm crazy on top of everything else."

"For now, I suggest you continue with your vacation. Get to know more about Giovanni. He does have his bad points, though none you cannot live with. Most importantly, I believe you should take care of your situation back in the states. Decide what it is you want. When you do ultimately make up your mind, nothing will stand in your way of finding happiness. Okay? Anything else?" He rose from the chair, stretching to his full height. "Follow me. I will take you to Giovanni."

I got up from the comfort of the chair and followed him to the backyard. I know this man is a priest, but I couldn't resist wondering if he missed living a "normal" life. As if reading my mind, he stopped and turned around.

"Lena, I need to make a few phone calls. Giovanni is in the garden. Just follow the stone path. It will lead you straight back to him. I will be back in a moment," he replied in English, with just a hint of an Italian lilt at the end.

"I don't mind waiting for you…"

"No, no, please go see the garden. It is a very tranquil place. And he is waiting for you. I will be with you two in just a *momento*."

"Okay. Follow the path back there?" I asked, pointing towards an ancient looking brick wall in the back of the yard.

"*Si*, it is impossible to get lost." He nodded, putting his hands on his waist.

I stopped at the foot of the stairs. His yard was small, yet charming. Terracotta pots filled with ornamental plants and flowers, turned what could have been a harsh sterile environment, into a comfortable retreat. The stone paved walkway, leading to an opening in the wall, was bordered by creeping ivy on either side. As I made my way through the entrance to the garden, I saw Giovanni sitting on a stone bench, next to a gurgling fountain, surrounded by plants and flowers planted in the same type of pots displayed in the back yard.

An intricately designed mosaic of a panoramic view of *Venezia's* skyline gleamed from the wall behind the bench. It was at least six feet wide and must have taken years to complete. The spacious courtyard garden was filled with trees sprouting blossoms in shades of white and pink, giving no clue as to the type of fruit they would eventually bear. I silently watched Giovanni read the newspaper, aided by a pair of glasses, while simultaneously tossing breadcrumbs to the birds that happened by. I called out to him. Hmmm, I didn't know he wore glasses.

"Giovanni?" He turned and looked.

I noticed how his face seemed to light up when he saw me. He stood, removed his glasses, stowed them in his inner jacket pocket and came to me.

"Lena? How did it go? Are you all right?" he asked, grasping me gently by the shoulders.

"It went quite well. You were right about Claudio. He was very easy to talk to. He told me I should concentrate on what's in front of me, rather than the past. And right now, you are what's most important to me." I put my arms around him, this time with a much lighter heart.

Claudio ducked under the entrance into the courtyard. "I see you have found him," he said, brushing unruly hair from his eyes.

"Claudio, you have had time to discuss with Lena these strange dreams. What do you think?" he asked.

"Giovanni Morelli! You never cease to amaze me! How is it you have found such a magnificent woman, who came halfway around the world to meet you, yet you leave her alone with a priest?" He joked. "Seriously, all kidding aside, I think Lena has experienced a truly miraculous episode in her life. As I have told her, the phenomenon shall most likely always remain a mystery. Unfortunately, I have not encountered such a story, so I am completely bewildered! Therefore, for your own sakes, I think you both should simply accept this for what it is – an unexplained bump on the road to your future happiness. Now that you two have found one another, take the time to really get to know each other. No man can provide the answer you are searching for with one hundred percent certainty, but you must realize not all life's mysterious are meant to be solved." He shrugged again. Apparently this was one of his favorite expressions.

"I agree with you *mi'amico*. I too feel it is time to stop looking back and start looking forward. Now, how about you give me a quick tour of this place? I want to see how my dear friend spends his days," he said to Claudio.

"Lena? Would you like to come with us or do you prefer to remain in garden? My surroundings are not much to see, but you are most welcome to join us."

"No, I'll be fine. Why don't the two of you go on? I'm sure you have some catching up to do. Anyway, I like it here. It's so peaceful." I caressed Giovanni's arm.

"We will not be gone very long." He replied and kissed me lightly on the cheek.

I observed the two friends speaking in rapid Italian punctuated by bursts of hearty laughter, disappear from my view. I casually strolled through the Venetian garden, touching flowers, inhaling their perfumed fragrance. The garden was filled with bees moving from one flower to the next getting drunk on the flower's nectar. Hummingbirds zipped in between tree branches in pursuit of their food. And birds filled with song called out to one another, coordinating their future flight plans. I watched the wonderfulness of nature unfold before my eyes. In the distance, a soft braying noise came from beyond the garden fence. Curiosity got the best of me. I walked towards the direction of the noise. On the other side of the fence, stood an old wood building. I stepped inside.

It was a barn. I watched in amusement as animals chased each other. Sheep, goats, and chickens were cordoned off into their own little separate areas. I laughed when I saw one sheep aggressively trying to mount another. I'd never seen anything like that before. I saw dogs go at it, but never sheep. I couldn't help but to keep watching. Would he succeed or would he fail? Only time would tell. Eventually, the female sheep acquiesced, permitting the male to mount and fill her with his fluid. They continued to "baa" during the entire time they were stuck together. After awhile I felt like a voyeur. This was so bizarre to see, I could not make myself look away until I heard someone clearing his throat.

"I see you have discovered my farm animals. I also used to stand here for hours watching them play. They can be like children sometimes."

"Yes, especially the sheep." I pointed to the two sheep stuck together in the corner "baa-ing" away to their heart's content.

"Oh, no. He is at it again. Before I started tending sheep, I did not realize that something like homosexuality could also occur in animals." He grinned.

"What do you mean?" I asked confused.

"I keep the females in another part of the barn. They only come together during mating season. Those two are male. I suppose it doesn't hurt them, though," he stated so matter-of-factly.

"You mean those sheep are g-g-gay?" I laughed at the absurdity of it all.

"Quite gay. At least one of them is anyway." He joined in my laughter.

"Hey, where's Giovanni? Are you two finished with your tour?"

"Yes and he is in the house arranging a special tour to the glass making factory. You cannot leave the island of *Murano* without seeing how authentic *Murano* glass is developed. Come on. Let's go back to the house." He guided the way, placing his hand on the small of my back.

I followed Claudio out of the barn, through the courtyard and back to the house. Giovanni stood speaking on the phone. When he completed his conversation he turned to me and asked, "I have just arranged a special tour for us before we leave. How would you like to see *Murano* glass being made?"

"I'd love to go. I've seen the glass being sold in shops all over Italy, but I've never had the opportunity to actually see it being made. That's a great idea!"

"*Bene. Molte bene.* After all, no one who visits *Murano* should leave the island without first visiting one of the glass factories. It is something to see." He looked at his watch. "We should go. They will close in just under an hour, which gives us plenty of time to see the process. Okay?"

"I'm ready. Let's go. Uh, Claudio, would you like to join us?" I asked the tall, curly haired handsome priest.

"No, but thank you for inviting me. As you can imagine, I have visited the factories many times. You two go have a good time. I shall be here when you return."

On the way to the glass factory, I reflected upon Claudio's wisdom. He was an extremely intelligent, perceptive man. He advised me to change my focus, accept what had happened and move on. Because he is a priest, I knew I had his complete confidence. This was my choice to put the past behind and move forward, but I owed it to Giovanni to include him in my decision.

"Giovanni, Claudio tried to explain to me the possibility of out-of-body travel. He said before he became a priest, he and a colleague studied quantum physics and paranormal phenomena. As part of their dissertation, they researched theories of alternate realities and even *shamanism*." I explained.

"I have heard of those subjects before, but never put much thought into their possibilities. Science was never an interest of mine, so I can't put much faith or credence into their findings. Does he still believe in those possibilities now that he is a priest?" he asked, as we passed groups of tourists heading in the opposite direction.

"He didn't really indicate if he still believes in it or not, though I think he remains interested. It must be very difficult for him to stop seeing the world from a scientist's perspective, especially now that he's a priest. He also said his friend, the paranormal research scientist, really wants to interview me if I'm interested in telling my story."

"Are you?" he asked point blank.

"I don't know if that's such a good idea. Think of all the publicity I'd get. People from all over the place, nuts included, will want me to tell my story over and over again. I don't want that kind of chaos in my life. If I start telling people I have traveled to another dimension by means of an out-of-body experience, someone will want to throw me into a mental institution." I became flustered.

"Lena, you do not have to do anything you do not wish to. This is your life. I do not profess to know the secrets behind my earlier time with you. I only know how much you have come to mean to me now. What do you want to do?" He stopped walking.

"I want to put all this paranormal crap out of my life and into the past. I want to forget the circumstances of how we met and concentrate only on the good time we had together. I want to be with you. I want to be happy. I don't want to make my life a spectacle just to add some excitement to it." I looked into those eyes, knowing my secret would be safe with him.

"It is done. Your secret is safe with me. As far as I am concerned, we met while you were here on business. Or maybe pleasure would be more appropriate? Lena, I do not pretend to understand your life, but I respect your wishes," he replied sincerely, sealing the promise with a kiss.

"Thank you, Giovanni," I whispered. I was grateful for his acceptance and his understanding.

With Giovanni serving as my translator, we spent over an hour touring the factory watching skilled artisans craft their magic, spinning and blowing silica into works of art. They moved with careful precision, expertly handling the red hot molten glass, forming it into colorful masterpieces ranging from small glass candies, to fish shaped paperweights, to beautifully designed intricate figurines. At the end of the tour I bought 3 elaborate pieces, albeit at a huge discount, to remind me of my time spent in *Murano*. I profusely thanked the owner of the factory, as well as the glass blowers for their time.

"That was really interesting! I'll bet it took those guys years to learn how to work with that liquid glass without burning themselves. How on earth do they keep from burning the place down? One little mistake and poof! The entire building seems like it could go up in flames." I marveled.

"It is funny that you should mention the building burning down. In fact, it is believed centuries ago, when the first glassmakers came to *Venezia* from all over Europe, it was decided to locate the glassmaking factories only on the island of *Murano*, far away from the city and separated by the lagoon. Therefore, if a fire were to occur, as it often happened in the past, the city of Venezia would not be in danger of burning down. Because of their forward thinking and proper planning, *Murano* is now famous the world over for its intricate glass art designs and the threat of fire in Venezia's has been lowered considerably," he explained, reaching for my heavy reinforced shopping bag filled with *Murano* glass.

"Thanks for the history lesson. You know, it makes perfect sense for all the glass making factories to be located here, especially with all the priceless art and historical relics that reside in Venice. It would be a shame if such an accident went down. I'm not saying it wouldn't be a shame if *Murano* were to burn to the ground, but to think of Venice being destroyed… Well, that would really be a tragedy," I said trying not to imagine what the outcome would be.

"*Si*, you are very correct in your observations." He glanced at his watch. "It is getting late. We should probably return, say our good-byes to Claudio and head back to *Venezia* for our return trip."

We retraced our steps from whence we came, meandering through narrow ancient cobble-stoned streets, lined with souvenir stores selling the famous glass. Green and rust colored awnings shaded entrances of the stores now closed to customers. I peered through windows at the colorful glass knick-knacks displayed. As the main source of revenue for the island, I imagined if the glass factories ever did shut down, the town of *Murano* would quickly disappear.

He looked up towards the rapidly darkening sky. "Oh, no! It is beginning to rain. We should hurry!"

Suddenly the sky broke open, releasing a major downpour. Unable to escape the torrential rain, I picked up a discarded copy of the *La Repubblica* and held it over our heads as we tried to dodge the sheets of water cascading down upon our bodies. And despite our coordinated maneuvering of quickly filling puddles, we both ended up thoroughly soaked by the time we reached Claudio's house. Giovanni knocked at the door.

"You two look like a couple of wet noodles. Come on in and dry off." He left us to get a couple of towels.

"Oh no! My new shoes! They'll never be the same!" I looked down at my sopping *Ferragamo* shoes and gently removed the squishy delicate leather exposing wrinkled feet. My new *Versace* pantsuit was a soggy, wet, uncomfortable mess. I accepted the towel Claudio offered and attempted to soak up as much water as possible. I laughed when Giovanni removed his jacket and streams of water drained to the floor. He looked so pitiful. I'm sure I didn't look much better.

"Claudio! We are dripping water all over your floor! We need more towels!" Giovanni yelled out to his friend, frantically searching for more dry towels. He tried in vain to wring his pants out while still wearing them.

"Hey, I know a quick way we can both dry off. All we have to do is generate enough heat between the two of us and before you know it…" I whispered as I leaned in, taking him by his shirt lapels.

"Lena, *amore mio*. Claudio is my friend, but I never forget he is still a priest. We must be totally respectful of him while we are in his house.

Capisce?"

"I'm sorry. You're right. It's just that I tend to lose my mind when I get too close to you. We'll just have to keep that thought in mind for later then."

We managed to dry most of the water before splitting up to use the separate bathrooms to change clothes. It was getting late and we wanted to get back to Venice before the heavy rains started again. I don't know about most people, but I am never thrilled about being out in a boat during a heavy downpour. I imagined they would delay the trip across the lagoon, but this being Italy, I couldn't be certain of anything. Thoughts of capsizing always seemed to creep into my mind whenever I was in a boat. Courtesy of the rain and non-waterproof mascara, I'd managed to go from having bedroom eyes to sporting an unattractive raccoon look in mere seconds. After I checked my reflection in the mirror, making sure I was once again presentable, I slipped back into the living room where Claudio sat tending a roaring fire.

"Where's Giovanni?" I asked feeling the warmth of the flames.

"He is still in *il bagno*." He poked at the flames. "You two are about to head back, eh? Listen, I want you to know I have really enjoyed meeting you. And I hope everything works out for you – either way."

"Thank you. I feel so much better since I've had an opportunity to share my experience with someone like you – a scientifically inspired man of God." I laughed and he joined in.

"There you are." Giovanni said to me as he entered the room. "Lena, I think we should be going now. There is a break in the rainstorm. Hopefully, it will last until we reach the parking garage. Claudio, *mi'amico*, it is time to say good-bye. Thank you for agreeing to meet with Lena. Let's not allow so much time to pass between our next visit."

He was casually dressed in slightly faded jeans and a black sweater. His hair, still wet, glistened as the light of the fire danced across his face. I watched the men's affection for one another shine through as they embraced in a farewell hug. I knew men back home who would never ever hug another man, unless it was a very close relative. Then it was only for a brief moment. Each man secure in his own masculinity, continued to laugh, sharing a private joke as I looked on. We gathered our bags in preparation for leaving.

"*Espeta.* We will use the scooters again. It is much faster than walking," said Claudio heading for the door.

"You know, he is a really good man. I can see why you two are good friends. And I'll bet he's one helluva priest too." I held on to the sides of his waist.

"*Si.* He likes you too. Now hold on!" He revved the engine before taking off.

By the time we arrived at the station, Claudio had moved the bags under the overhang and was patiently waiting for us. The ferry was already there waiting. It looked as if it were about to pull back at any moment. I believe Claudio somehow convinced the driver to wait for us.

"Thank you again for everything. Your hospitality, your kindness, your understanding... I really do hope I see you again someday soon. Do you mind if I keep in touch?" I asked Claudio as I adjusted my jacket.

"You are very welcome. It was also nice to meet and speak with you. And I would be delighted to keep in touch with you. After all, any friend of Giovanni's is a friend of mine." He kissed me good-bye in the traditionally Italian manner and embraced his friend once again. The *vaporetti's* driver tooted his horn, signaling his patience had come to an end.

"Claudio. *Arriverderci!* I will see you soon, *mi'amico.*" He waved to his friend while helping me into the boat.

"Ciao Claudio! *Arriverderci!*" I also waved good-bye to my new friend, watching him wave his arms from the dock until I could no longer distinguish him from the others. We found seats inside the boat this time, noticing the outside ones were still wet from the earlier rain.

"See how beautiful the city is viewed from the water? The rain washes away all the grit and grime leaving *Venezia* as fresh as a baby after a bath." He indicated the skyline in the distance and continued. "I would have liked to spend much more time with you there, but because we have only a short time together we must make the most of each day."

He pointed out the clock tower as the *vaporetti* passed by *San Marcos Piazza* on the way to the parking garage. We now had a totally unobstructed view of the Venetian skyline. Despite the gloominess caused by the cloud filled sky and the darkness descending upon the city, seeing it from the canal, illuminated against the impending darkness, provided an entirely new perspective. It almost seemed ethereal, like a heavenly galaxy in an infinite sea of black.

"How beautiful!" I exclaimed. "I've never seen a city that looks so magical from a distance. It looks like an illusion."

"Just think. If you lived in *Italia*, you could visit *Venezia* most anytime you choose." The look in his eye was as far away as home felt.

I sighed. No matter how much I would love to drop everything in my life, move to Italy, and spend the rest of my life getting to know this man, right now it was all too complicated to ponder.

CHAPTER 19

We arrived back to the parking garage finding his Z4 in the same condition as we'd left it.

"How about we stop and get something to eat before we head back? I'm starving." I asked. We hadn't eaten since this morning.

"For you, anything. What do you feel like? Pasta, seafood, something more substantial?" He steered his car towards the outskirts of Venice where dozens of restaurants offered up delicious inexpensive food, mostly for the locals.

"Um, nothing too heavy. I don't want to fall asleep on the way back to *Gorgazzio*. How about some *zuppa* or a *panini*?"

"That sounds fine. I know a small *trattoria* nearby that makes excellent minestrone." He drove the few short blocks, pulling in front of a restaurant off a narrow alleyway.

Within minutes, the waitress brought us two big bowls of thick, hearty soup brimming over with beans, pasta and vegetables. We sprinkled freshly shaved *parmigiano-reggiano* on top and dug in. The soup was complemented perfectly with a loaf of crusty Italian bread. Giovanni limited himself to one glass of wine, while I splurged and had two. After all, I was only the passenger, not the driver.

"Mmm, this is so good! I haven't had a bad meal since I've been here. Does everyone in Italy know how to cook this well?" I asked in jest.

"No, not everyone. Some wish to believe they are masters in the kitchen. I know of plenty bad *ristorantes*. Unfortunately, most are concentrated near the large tourist attractions. Perhaps it is because tourists cannot distinguish good Italian food from the mediocre?"

"Hey, believe me, when you grow up eating Chef Boyardee, frozen Jeno's pizza, or having the local Olive Garden as examples of Italian food, everything else is an improvement. What you consider mediocre is probably even delicious to me. Would you believe I did not like Italian food when I was a child? I thought pizza came from a box in the freezer. And the only spaghetti I ate was from a can. Talk about being sheltered?! If you ever come to the United States and try some of the food in these chain restaurants that claims to serve authentic Italian cuisine… Well, let's just say you would never eat Italian again. Every now and then you may run across a traditional family restaurant that makes a good meal, but I recommend you stay as far away from the chains as possible." I continued to eat, savoring the complexity of the flavors.

"It sounds like you have disdain for American food. What foods did you enjoy most as a child?"

"I wouldn't call it disdain. It's just that when you think of American food, you think of hamburgers, hot dogs, and fries. Mostly unhealthy, fattening stuff. Our really good food comes from other cultures. Mexican, Chinese, Thai, French, Jamaican, and of course, Italy. We don't really have a food that specifically shouts out 'I'm American'. But I suppose that says a lot for us. Our country is like this minestrone soup. Lots of very different ingredients, simmered over a low heat for a long time, eventually coming together to make a fabulous tasting meal."

"You are delightful with your comparisons. Someday, I would like to visit your country to see what all the fuss is about." He sopped the remaining soup from his bowl using a piece of the bread and finished with a sip of wine.

"Maybe one day I'll be able to show you around." At least I hoped I could.

"What would you show me? Where would you begin? I know. What do you think are the major differences between our countries, not counting language?" He sat back in his chair, relaxing the way you do after you've eaten a good meal.

"I think the most obvious difference is the age of your country. Everything here, the buildings, the land, even some of the people, seem like they have been here for an eternity. For instance, you can trace your family's history centuries back. You have customs and traditions as old as time – maybe even older than time. In the states, our oldest city is St. Augustine, Florida, and it's barely 500 years old! You have pottery older than that! In America, our cities look so new, fresh, and modern, but they have no character and no center. There's not much to distinguish one from any other city in the country. But when I visit a village or city in Europe, I know where to find the pulse. Churches, stores, restaurants, parks, schools... It's as if European cities have a heart that holds the town together."

Seeing his interest I continued. "There are no true Americans. With the exception of Native Americans who were there long before Christopher Columbus ever set foot on the land. You see the thanks they got for welcoming foreigners. The government banished them to live on reservations where now too many of them exist solely on government assistance. Yeah, most of the population of the United States immigrated from elsewhere. Of course, when you have so many people from so many different cultures, there's bound to be problems. For the most part, we are learning to get along and coexist with one another. One good thing I can say about Americans is we are a very tolerant people who respect your right to choose your religion and will accept your lifestyle, as long as it doesn't interfere with our own. When I see people in other countries fighting over religion, I am appalled. I don't understand it." I finished my soup, drained my second glass of wine and suppressed a satisfying burp.

"It must be difficult living with so many different cultures. In *Italia*, we also have foreigners moving here to begin a new life. Unlike your country, those who come only for a visit must leave when their Visa expires. My government can be very generous, but we refuse to support anyone who comes here with no intent or means to support themselves or their family. Is it true, I heard this after the terrible tragedy in New York, that thousands of tourists who visit the United States never leave? They remain indefinitely for years and in come cases even receive benefits from your government?"

"Yes. It's pretty messed up. Our system is broken in so many ways. Did you know those assholes who turned out to be the terrorists from September 11th lived amongst us for years, went to school with us, ate and drank with us, probably even slept with our women... Some of them had expired Visa's and were being tracked by the government, yet they were still able to remain. The frustrating and sad thing is, many people in our government knew about them, but did nothing." I shook my head at the irony of the situation.

"I do not intend to criticize your government, but for your country to claim to be the world's greatest superpower, you certainly have a lot to learn." He pulled out his wallet, signaling for the waitress.

"Amen to that! And I won't even begin to touch on the problem of having two Bush's for president! Well, enough about politics. Are you ready to head back?" I insisted on paying for the inexpensive meal, it was the least I could do after all he'd done for me.

The melodramatic Italian blues music, I didn't realize there was such a thing—played from the radio. Actually, the group was pretty good, though hearing the blues sung in Italian took a little getting used to. Kind of like hearing rap in Italian, it's an entirely new experience. The world had truly gotten smaller, with music leading the way, helping to bridge the gap. I nodded off every now and then, waking up occasionally to keep Giovanni company on our two hour trip home. I loved seeing his silhouette highlighted by headlights of passing cars. I felt a strong desire for him to stop, providing me with the occasion to show him how I felt. I was never this passionate with any other man before, not even in the beginning of a relationship when all is new and fresh. It was like I couldn't get enough of him. I had to touch him all the time, even if it simply meant brushing my hand against his. I reached out and laid my hand on his forearm. He smiled, turning my insides to jelly. I dozed off again.

Much too quickly, he pulled in front of Simona's house. It was well after midnight and all was quiet. I didn't want him to leave, but time apart would make our time together even sweeter. He opened the door for me, retrieved my clothes and the *Murano* glass from the trunk, and escorted me through the gate to the little cottage. I opened the door and turned on the light. It was a mess, just like I'd left it. Bags and boxes filled with the evidence of my shopping trip with Ojuma were everywhere.

"Please excuse the mess. I guess I was in a hurry. I usually never leave my place this disorganized." I was embarrassed, hoping he wasn't forming an opinion of my domestic skills.

"Do not worry. I understand. *Alora,* I shall see you tomorrow? And you will be ready to begin Lesson Number One on running a business?" He stood with his arms around my waist. Mine rested on his shoulders.

"Most definitely. What time?" I wanted him to spend the night.

"Let me see. I have many things to do tomorrow morning, but I will be at my club by 4 p.m. Would you like for me to stop by and pick you up?"

"No, that's all right. I think I can manage on my own. Besides, I have a few things I need to get in town before I come to see you. Hey, you're more than welcome to stay here tonight."

"Oh, you make this so difficult. As much as I would like to stay with you, I need to get home. I have an early morning planned. You make sure you are well rested because we will be busy tomorrow. Friday is my busiest day of the week." He reluctantly let go.

"Okay. But if you change your mind, just knock three times." I watched him walk back towards his car, get in and slowly pull off into the darkness of the night.

I closed the door and exhaled. What a man! Oh, I can't wait until I see him tomorrow! I looked around the room at the mess I'd made and decided to straighten up before I went to bed. I managed to fill two trash bags, then took them to the dumpster across the street. This was one facet of Italian life I never did get accustomed to. The community trash cans. Anyway, as I went to open the door, I stepped on a folded sheet of white stationary. I had obviously overlooked it earlier. I picked up the note and unfolded the paper exposing carefully written words.

Your son, James phoned. He says they are all well and they miss you. Not to worry. The reason he called is you received a phone call from your cousin Keenan who says he has not seen you in many, many years. He wants you to call him immediately. This is his number in California (415) 557-4412
    Freda

I stood outside the cottage reading the note over and over again, barely able to make out the words in the dim light. It finally registered. Keenan called? Keenan in California? My Keenan? I went inside and sat down. I felt faint. If my travels to Italy really did happen, then that means I also saw Keenan, spoke to him, held him in my arms. I interacted with him. Were we both here in a metaphysical state, like Claudio alluded? Or was he part of a shared alternate dimension fantasy of mine? Maybe it was just a coincidence – his calling me now. But why lie and say he was my cousin? And why the urgency to speak to me?

I didn't know what do. I needed to talk to someone, but it was after midnight. The only others who knew about my dream were Giovanni and Ojuma. Speaking to Giovanni about Keenan was out of the question. I couldn't call Ojuma at this time of night. Anyway, I didn't even have a phone. Oh hell! There was no way I was going to be able to sleep tonight if I didn't get this over with. Though I wasn't thrilled with the idea of going out in the middle of the night to use the pay phone, what choice did I have?

I rummaged through my purse trying to locate the calling card I purchased prior to my trip to Venice. I changed into a pair of sneakers and pulled on an extra sweater. It may be late spring, but the air remained surprisingly chilly. I headed up the street to the co-op store where the pay phone was located. I tried imagining what I was going to say to him. I couldn't get past 'hello'. I didn't know what time it was in California. Let's see, half past midnight here, and California is nine hours behind, so that makes it a little after 3 in the afternoon. Guess I'll take my chances on his being home.

The darkness was absolute in the moonless night. Most Italians do not leave outside lights on, preferring to let the public streetlights offer relief from the dark. I always try to remain aware of my surroundings, and scouted the area for any hidden dangers, feeling like a spy on a mission. As I walked the quiet street, a snarling dog leapt forwards, separated only by a chain-linked fence. I jumped back in surprise and gasped. Maybe it wasn't such a good idea to be out by myself. The last time I decided to take a night walk, some creep in a car nearly scared me half to death.

I was almost there. Thankfully the outside of the store was well-lit exposing anyone or anything that didn't want to be seen. On the other hand, I would be just as visible standing out in the open, in the middle of the night, using a pay phone. I took a deep breath. Here goes… I picked up the phone, entered the calling card numbers, dialed the number on the note and waited.

The phone rang five times before finally being answered. I was just about to hang up when I heard a faint voice on the other end.

"Hello?" answered a woman's voice.

"Uh, hi. May I please speak to Keenan?" I asked, uncertain as to whom I was speaking to. For all I knew this could be his wife or girlfriend. After all, I didn't really know him anymore.

"Who's calling?"

"Uh, my name is Lena. I'm an old friend of his from St. Louis," I replied.

"Lena McAllister? Is that you?" asked the woman, this time with more excitement in her voice.

"Why, uh yes," I replied, though my last name hadn't been McAllister for quite some time. "Do I know you?"

"Honey, this is Keenan's mother. I came out here to help him until he can take care of himself again. I am so glad you called. All he's been talking about for the past few days is Lena this and Lena that. Kept telling everyone who'd listen how he had let you get away. How have you been doing?"

"Oh, hi Mrs. Jones. I'm doing fine. It's good to hear your voice. Uh, what do you mean about helping him out? Is he all right? What happened?" I asked, fully aware of his situation.

"You remember how he was with his bicycling? Well, maybe you don't, but he's been into this bike racing thing for the past couple of years. A few weeks back, there was a big race through the hills of Yosemite. An old white man, who should not have been driving in the first place, pulled out of nowhere and hit him. We thought we lost him. He was in the hospital in a coma for days. It was touch and go for a while. He kept fading in and out of consciousness. When he finally did come to, all he could talk about was you. It was the strangest thing," she said more to herself than to me.

"Is he all right now? Is he there? Can I speak to him?" I enjoyed talking to her, but I really needed to speak to Keenan, especially now.

"Oh, he's fine now. He came home from the hospital a few days ago. Lena, it sure was good hearing your voice again. Hold on, I'll go get him."

"Thanks, Mrs. Jones," I answered, feeling my heart beating in my throat. I heard her put the phone down, followed by the click-clack of heels against a hardwood floor.

An apprehensive sounding male voice picked up and asked, "Lena? Is it really you?"

"Yes, it's me. Keenan, how have you been?" I responded in a gentle voice, unsure what his state of mind was. The last thing I wanted to do was upset him.

"Well, I see you received my message. Guess it's been a few years, huh?" I felt his warm smile come through the phone. "As far as how I'm doing? I could be worse. I guess my Mom told you about my little accident. Other than a few fractured ribs, a broken leg, a minor concussion, lots of scrapes and bruises, I think I'm doing fairly well." He attempted to laugh.

"Oh, Keenan. I am so sorry to hear about your accident. Are you going to be okay?" I asked, wondering when he'd get around to the reason for his call.

"Sure, I'll be fine. I was in pretty good physical condition before the accident, so I'll bounce back in no time at all," he said, clearing his throat.

"Good. It's really good to hear that." I wasn't sure what I should say, nor how much I would say. I decided to let him speak.

"I know it has been a long time since we last spoke, but I had to get in touch with you. I couldn't wait any longer. And it's not just because of my accident."

"It's good to hear your voice again too, but what is so important that you had to call me now? I haven't heard a word from you in years, yet you made this sound so urgent." I looked around the parking lot, checking to make sure I was still alone.

"Lena, something very strange happened to me when I was in the hospital. In that coma. I had a dream, but it was like no dream I have ever had before. I was "there", inside the dream and it seemed more real than life itself. The strange part is you were right there with me. There is no way possible I could have imagined something this real." He explained, clearing stressed about the experience.

If I confirmed his suspicions, both our lives as we currently knew them, would be drastically changed. Keenan was an FBI agent, and they weren't exactly known for their progressive thinking. I recalled the television show, *X-files* and how they treated Fox Mulder. He had absolutely no credibility with either his colleagues or his superiors. Although he was a fictional character, I could just imagine how Keenan would be received walking around telling people he had an out-of-body experience and traveled to an alternate reality in another dimension. It still sounds crazy, even to me!

"Well, isn't it normal to dream when you're in a coma? Isn't it possible your brain was working overtime trying to keep itself occupied? I've often heard accounts of people coming out of comas relate very vivid dreams. Why do you feel yours was different?" I asked, realizing how I intended to play this out.

"It was the circumstances surrounding the dream. In this dream, you and I were in Italy. We were both older and we had some very personal conversations. You told me about your husband and children. You filled me in on your life over the past decade. You said you weren't happy. I could not have imagined such intimate details. I haven't spoken to you in years, so how do you explain how I have tracked you down so quickly?" His argument would have caused the most skeptical of people to think twice, but I didn't take the bait.

"Well, you might have heard from someone in my family. Or maybe your mother provided you with updates about me from time to time. You know how it is with gossip. Remember our families only lived a few miles apart back in the 'hood?" I tried to ease his mind, noting he provided no specifics of his encounter with me and I wasn't going to ask for them.

"I suppose that could be why I know so much about you. I could have stored away little tidbits of information about you in my subconscious. But why Italy? I have never been to Italy. Don't even have a desire to go there. Also, how do you explain our detailed conversations?"

"Remember how I always talked about wanting to travel to Italy when we were together? I used to show you pictures of all the places I wanted to visit. Maybe you just retrieved those memories. Keenan, the mind plays tricks on us all the time. How many times have you thought you remembered being somewhere only to confuse it with a movie or a book you've read? Those are called false memories. It is possible your brain went into overdrive in an attempt to keep busy while your body healed itself. Hey, I confuse real memories with false ones all the time. It's a danger of being an avid reader and a seasoned world traveler."

"So you're saying you think it *was* just a dream?" Relief flooded through his voice.

"I can't imagine it being anything else," I replied, confident I'd done the right thing.

"I know it sounds strange, but it is a relief for me to have confirmation that you feel it was only a dream. Not to change the subject, but what have you been up to? And where are you anyway? I am sorry I lied to your family, but I really didn't think they'd understand or appreciate having an ex-boyfriend calling you after so many years. I spoke with your son, James. He sounds like a very intelligent young man – all grown up. Anyway, he said you were away on vacation. What's up? You taking solo breaks now?" He inquired in a much lighter voice, sounding like himself again.

What to tell? I couldn't admit to being in Italy. That would be too coincidental. I had to stretch the truth. "I'm just taking a little break away from the family, away from the grind. You know, spending time with an old friend. And you are certainly correct about James. He is turning into a fine young man." I raised that boy well. He knew not to give away too much of my private business to someone he never heard of claiming to be a long-lost relative. I'd have to high five him when I got back home.

"Well, it was really good hearing from you again, especially after all these years. I'll let you get back to your vacation. And thanks again for calling me back so quickly."

"You're welcome. I hope you feel better soon. And, uh, Keenan?"

"What's up, Lena?"

"That must have been some kinda dream you had about me to bring you back from the depths of a coma," I added.

"Woman, you don't even know the half of it! But like I said, it was good hearing from you. Let's keep in touch. Okay?" He cut the call short apparently getting what he needed from me to comfort himself; never truly considering the consequences his calling may have had on my life.

"All right. You take care of yourself and watch out for those little old men who can barely see above their steering wheels." I laughed, knowing this conversation was a way to say farewell.

"You too. Be cool and take care. Bye now." He hung up the phone sounding more relieved than I could have ever imagined.

I replaced the phone on its hook, positive I had done the right thing. There was no sense in burdening him with this physiological mumbo jumbo. It actually felt good to give him back his peace of mind. And at that moment, I knew I had heard the last from Keenan Jones. He had been a good friend to me, back in the day. However, after our most recent encounter, I knew I had built him up to be more than he deserved. The feelings I kept in my heart all those years were for a fantasy man who didn't exist. I still thought he was a good man who would make some woman extremely happy, only it wouldn't be me. We had both changed throughout the course of our lives. Sometimes you realize you just have to let go and move on. This is one of those times.

Upon returning to the cottage, I needed to feel the sensation of hot water beating down on my body, chasing away the shivers brought on by the chilly night air.

As I stood under the faucet with the water caressing my skin, I closed my eyes to reflect on the day's events. I feel so good! I finally found my own peace of mind when I accepted the fact I have been given a special gift, a second chance at finding this ever-elusive thing called happiness. On top of everything else, I discovered the man I secretly lusted after for so many years, was just a fantasy. And what I thought was fantasy wasn't.

Strange how you can live your life believing there is only one path to follow. One day you wake up to discover the path you've been traveling on is riddled with many, many other paths leading to missed opportunities. You didn't see them because you were walking along with blinders on. My world has expanded off the hook and I'll be damned if I don't take advantage of all the blessings I've been given.

After my shower, I huddled under the warmth of the thick blankets. This time when I slept, images of diving into a grotto, hang gliding from a cliff, and enjoying a romantic meal with a wonderful man became more than just a wishful dream. Content in the realization that anything is possible, I settled down into the most relaxing sleep I had in a very long time.

CHAPTER 20

The annoyingly loud noise coming from a crowing rooster awakened me. Remnants of last night's phone call remained in my thoughts. I smiled at the gift I unselfishly offered to Keenan. He had months of getting his body back into shape to deal with. He did not need the added burden of deciphering his nighttime memories only to discover what he thought was a dream wasn't a dream at all. Maybe one day I would contact him and let him know my version of the truth, or maybe not.

By 9:30 I was fully dressed and on my way into town. The sun shone brightly in a crisp blue sky, reflecting my present mood. I was in search of a cell phone and I would not rest until I found one to purchase. I was tired of bothering Simona every time I needed to make a call and the thought of another night stroll wasn't exactly something I looked forward to. Couldn't nobody tell me that I didn't look good! I wore a purple silk shirt, a short form fitting skirt and a pair of sandals that made my legs appear long and sexy.

I walked to town to get breakfast. I bought *foccacia* bread covered with a thin layer of soft cheese and a container of orange juice from a local *trattoria* to tide over my appetite until I was able to have a real meal later. I took a seat on an empty bench underneath a tree, watching people while I ate. The electronics store where I stood my best chance of finding a temporary phone, displayed a sign in the window indicating the owner would be back at 10. I had a few minutes to wait so I bought a sturdy notebook for my session with Giovanni.

I was about to leave the stationary store when to my surprise I saw Giovanni's car parked only a few stores down. I wonder what he's doing there? With my hand on the door handle and thoughts of surprising him swirling in my head, I noticed he wasn't alone. The woman I saw Lucio with so many nights ago, I forget her name, walked alongside him. As he had done for me so many times before, ever the gentleman, he opened the door and let her in. She folded her lean gorgeous body in the same seat I had sat in mere hours ago. And flashed a perfect smile while flinging her long, thick, shiny black hair from her face.

Watching the two of them, I imagined an attractive couple on their way to some secluded, romantic hideaway. He hopped in the car and sped away, never noticing me standing at the door looking like some pitiful, homeless puppy dog.

He told me he was going to be busy this morning. There were unlimited reasons for them to be together, though he never mentioned anything about her to me the entire time we were in Venice.

It could be innocent. Maybe he was just giving her a ride. Or maybe he went by her place after he dropped me off last night and had a night of uninhibited wild sex! It was possible he was doing her a favor by taking her out shopping. C'mon Lena! Get a hold of yourself! After all, I've only just met the man. I know he must have had a life before I came along. I will not make myself crazy just because I saw him with another woman, even an extremely attractive woman. I will not blow this out of proportion. After all, he tells me how special I am all the time. But who am I to talk? I have a husband, three children, and I live in the United States. What claim do I have on him? What right do I have to say he can't date other women? I am so messed up in the head! I have got to calm down. Okay, I feel better now. I can handle this.

Whatever the hell is going on, I still needed to buy a damn phone. I spent almost an hour in the electronics store talking to the salesman who didn't speak much English. In spite of my very limited Italian, his nonexistent English, and numerous universal gestures, I finally purchased a prepaid cellular phone.

Before leaving, I made certain I could use the phone correctly and had purchased enough minutes to see me through the next couple of weeks. When I returned home, it would only be a souvenir. Anyway, when I finally left the store, I had the ability to call anyone at anytime. No need to disturb Simona and her family to use their phone again. I thought about calling him. Stupid me! The only number I have of his is at the club. Why didn't I make sure I had his cell phone number? All I could do now was wait until we got together later.

Still upset and distracted about seeing Giovanni with another woman, I realized there was absolutely nothing I could do about it now. I had to let it go until we got together later that afternoon. It wasn't even noon yet. I decided to buy some fruit and snack foods from the co-op store to have something to munch on back in the cottage. While in the store, my eyes got bigger than my stomach. I ended up putting half of what I'd chosen back on the shelves, forgetting I'd have to carry the bags for almost a kilometer.

Halfway back to the cottage, a car blew its horn, causing me to jump away from the road. I hated when people did that. Nearly scared the crap out of me.

"*Ciao Bella*," Lucio sang out. "Do you need a ride?"

I looked over to see a familiar face smiling back at me from a cherry red *Ferrari*. "*Ciao* Lucio. What's up? How's it going?"

"Hop in. I'll take you home." He leaned over to unlock the passenger door.

"Thanks. It's just right up the street."

"I remember. Well, you look extremely pretty today. Going somewhere special?"

"Thanks, I was just headed back to the cottage to put my food away. I'll probably just hang out there for a few hours. I'm meeting up with Giovanni later today. By the way, have you seen him this morning?" I thought I'd do a bit of snooping to figure things out.

"No. I have not seen him since you left on your trip. He did call me this morning to ask if I could pick up stock for the bar. That is where I am headed now – to *Paglia*. There is a discount liquor store we do business with. Usually they deliver, but because we only need a few bottles, it is better if I go. Would you like to ride with me since you have free time?" He pulled in front of Simona's house.

"Sure. That sounds like fun. Just let me put this away and I'll be right back." I opened the door and got out. I back looked at Lucio who reminded me so of his brother, only Lucio wore his hair longer and freer and his eyes were dark where Giovanni's were light. Each brother was charming in his own right, though Lucio seemed less inhibited and more willing to take chances than his sibling.

"*Molte bene*! I will wait for you." He watched me go through the gate, lighting up a cigarette to pass the time.

Freda was in the backyard tending to the garden. I approached the spot where she toiled away, tangled up in tomato and green bean vines. Instead of the typical smooth wooden stakes I'd always seen vines tied to, she secured the climbing plants to crooked tree branches removed from trees in the yard. Very economical of her! In the same patch of space, at least a dozen rows of strawberry and zucchini plants graced the ground. Along the fence in the southern portion of the yard, several grape vines appearing to be decades old, climbed up and over a rustic trellis, displaying buds that would eventually spring into plump juicy grapes. Freda's hair was held back from her face by a colorful scarf. I noticed she looked younger, more feminine and almost pretty.

"*Ciao* Freda. Thanks for taking the message for me yesterday," I said letting her know how appreciative I was.

"Ciao Lena. It was no problem. How was your trip?" She stood up, wiping perspiration from her brow, managing to smear dirt where sweat no longer was.

"My trip to Venice was wonderful, magical, indescribable! I had such a good time I cannot wait to return!" I gushed.

"*Bene, bene. Venezia* is also one of my favorite cities, though it has been a while since I was last there." She looked at me forlornly then recovered. "What are you up to now? I have another pair of gloves if you would like to work with me in the garden?" She teased.

"Oh, no. Sorry. I was just returning to put away my groceries. I'm on my way to *Paglia* with a friend. It's business. He's picking up some things for his club." I shifted the bag in my arms, conscious of Lucio waiting in the car.

"Too bad. Well you have a good time. I am trying to complete this before Simona returns. She has been at me all week to take care of the weeds. 'Freda, when are you going to work in the garden? Freda, the strawberries are being strangled by weeds. Freda, there are more weeds than vegetables' and on and on and on... So, while you are running off to *Paglia* please think of me covered in dirt on my day off. The things I do for that woman." She shrugged it off in good-natured defeat.

"Freda, you are too much!" I joked.

She stopped laughing and looked at me confused. "What do you mean, I am too much? Too much of what?" she asked defensively.

I stopped laughing, not wanting her to think I was making fun at her expense. "I'm sorry. It's just an expression we use back home. Nothing bad. It means what you said is very funny. It makes me laugh," I explained.

"Oh, I get it. I am too much. I often hear the Black women on the base say that, but I never knew what they meant. You Americans and your expressions... It is a wonder any of us can learn your language." She laughed. "Who did you say you are going to *Paglia* with?" She bent over to take a sip from a bottle of water.

"His name is Lucio. Lucio Morelli," I replied uneasily.

"Ah, Lucio. Is he the brother of Giovanni?" Her interest was piqued.

"Yeah, yes they're brothers." I wanted to leave it at that. "Well, I'll let you get back to your gardening. I'll see you later. *Ciao*."

"*Ciao* Lena." She waved good-bye and knelt down returning to her work.

I put the food away and rushed back to the car where Lucio waited patiently. Just as we were about to pull off, Simona crossed the street in front of us riding her bicycle. She saw me in the passenger seat and scowled, shaking her head in disapproval. I could only imagine the indecent thoughts dancing through her mind about me.

"*Ciao* Simona!" I yelled out as Lucio drove away. She must think I am a first class 'ho. Every time she sees me I'm going out with someone new, or getting a call from my husband back in the states. I wanted to jump from the car, throw myself at her feet, and convince her I am not as bad as she thinks. Oh well, guess that will have to wait. For now, I fastened my seatbelt and hung on for dear life as Lucio punched his *Ferrari* to the extreme. I don't know if he was trying to impress me with his driving ability or if he drove this way all the time.

I had no idea where *Paglia* was. Nor, I realized, did I know anything at all about Lucio. This was as good a time as any to hear his story. I sank back into the soft leather seats feeling the power of the engine come alive as he shifted gears. The way that car hugged those curves was a miracle unto itself. While we zipped along the curvy mountain highway, memories of being on this road resurfaced. Only the last time, I was with Keenan. Now why did I have to think about him?

"Tell me Lucio. Do you have a girlfriend?" I didn't know how else to open our conversation. Discussing *his* personal life seemed a safe subject.

"A *ragazza?* No, no *ragazza*. You see Lena, I am like the wind. No one woman can capture me and hold me down. Of course, there are a few girls I prefer over others, but so far none of them are able to keep me interested for long. I get bored after a few months and move on. I am what you would call a confirmed bachelor," he spoke, saving most of his concentration for the road.

"What does hold your interest? Is there anything special you like to do?" I asked curiously trying to get to know this man so unlike his brother.

"There are so many interests. Take for instance this car. I know everything there is to know about *Ferrari*. Ask me anything you would like to know." He motioned with his hand to encourage my questions.

"Sorry. I don't know enough about a *Ferrari* to ask an intelligent question."

"That is fair. Another of my interests is music. I play the guitar, sometimes when it is slow in the club, I will perform for the audience. Someday, I shall perform for you." He smiled a million dollar smile.

I almost blurted out about my son James being a guitar player. I wasn't ready to open up that part of my life to him yet. Too many questions would surface if I did. "I like the guitar, too. I have tried playing a bit on the acoustic, but haven't quite mastered it yet. I do know it's extremely relaxing. And I'll take you up on hearing you play."

"How was your trip to *Venezia?* Did you two do anything special? What do you think about my brother? How are you two getting along?" I didn't know if he was being nosey, or merely showing brotherly concern.

I didn't know what if anything Giovanni had told his brother. "Oh, we're good. Still getting to know each other. You know how it is… Taking things one day at a time." I added, intentionally being vague.

"If you are worried about my brother being like me, do not bother. He and I are nothing alike. My brother is strictly a one-woman man. He is very focused and knows what he wants. Listen when I tell you, if he likes you, you have nothing to worry about. If he doesn't like you, he does not waste his time pretending that he does. In all our years, I have never known my brother to be with more than one woman at a time." He looked at me with those intense almost black eyes.

Hearing him say those words helped to alleviate my worries, though jealousy still nibbled at my heart. I so much wanted to bring up the subject about Giovanni and the woman I had seen him with earlier, but thought better. "If you say so. You are his brother. You probably know him better than anyone else. You have any advice for me?"

"Always be honest with Gio. While he can and will forgive you for lying, he never forgets. Other than that, follow your heart. I should not say this, but he was extremely hurt by his last girlfriend. I always told him she was not good for him. But you know love can be blind. She was only after his money and what he could buy for her. She would spend, spend, spend… Did not want to work. She was very traditional, wanted Gio to take care of her. They were total opposites. She had no ambition, no drive. He thought he loved her, so he put up with her for years and treated this woman like a queen. When he tried to encourage her to learn about our business, she left him. Never looked back, just packed up her things and walked out. Do you mind if I smoke?" He lit another cigarette, rolling down the window.

It felt strange listening to stories about Giovanni's life with another woman. Lucio didn't seem bothered by it at all. He puffed on his cigarette, tossing it out the window when he finished. I thought about what he'd just revealed. Now I know why Giovanni was so excited when I agreed to learn about his business. Maybe it was just a test. He knew I wasn't a traditional woman. That I worked to help support my family. He encouraged me to pursue my dreams of opening up my own coffee shop. In fact, he seemed enthusiastic about it. We were more alike than different, despite our cultures and upbringing.

"Did you know I agreed to let Giovanni teach me about running a business? He invited me to hang around and watch you guys in action while I'm here?" I asked smiling, simultaneously seeing the sign for the village of *Paglia*.

"No. He did not mention it to me. You are actually coming to the club to take lessons from my brother? Club Operations 101? When?" He laughed to himself.

"Yeah, starting this afternoon. We discussed it while we were in Venice. I just didn't want you to think the only reason I was interested in your business was because of the story you just told me. It's not like that at all. I didn't know anything about him and this other woman. We shared our dreams of the future. I told him about my interest in one day opening a coffee shop and he just offered his assistance. Totally out of the blue." I shook my head in wonder at the irony of this revelation.

"It is good you tell me now, otherwise, that thought might have crossed my mind. Look, we are here already. *Alora*, Lena. Because my brother will teach you how to operate a business, I will teach you about ordering supplies. Follow me, *bella.*" He hopped out and opened my door. The car was so low to the ground I appreciated his assistance helping me out.

The liquor store was in an old warehouse with an indiscrete sign hanging above the door indicating as much. In an attempt to soften the harshness of the building, someone had thought to paint amusing murals of men and women indulging in bubbly drinks on the outside walls. Huge green glass bottles, traditionally filled with wine, lined the entrance way. I followed Lucio inside.

There was liquor from literally all four corners of the globe in this place. Each section was arranged by country of origin, and then further separated by the type of liquor.

While Lucio found a cart to carry his selections, I wandered through the narrow aisles reading labels from exotic, foreign drinks. Because most labels were written in their native language, I couldn't decipher exactly what was inside some of the bottles. I handled the sturdy glass bottles that came in all shapes, colors, and sizes. I was utterly amazed such an assortment existed in one place. *Sake* from Japan, *Ouzo* from Greece, and *Cachaca* from Brazil, all coexisted peacefully on the shelves with one another. When I reached the United States section, I suddenly became homesick, well, maybe just a little. I touched the shelves filled with whiskey and smiled. Though I never drank whiskey, I couldn't stand the taste of the stuff, the familiar names of Jim Beam, Jack Daniels, and Southern Comfort were a beacon of familiarity in a sea of strangeness.

"Do you see something you like?" Lucio snuck up on me. In his cart were three boxes, filled with various bottles of liquor.

"No. I was just noticing the variety. Who'd have thought there were so many different kinds of alcohol in this world? I haven't heard of even a tenth of these brands." I exclaimed at the enormity of the selection.

"*Sì.* There are hundreds of variations. But for now, this is all we need."

He looked at me with those piercing eyes I couldn't read. I'm still not sure what to make of Lucio. Is he being friendly or does he want something more from me?

"No. I'll stick to whatever it is you all have. I usually don't drink mixed drinks unless I'm out partying. When I'm with friends I prefer wine or a good beer." I stated, "I'm ready if you are."

"*Bene.* Follow me."

He pushed the cart to a counter where a harried looking man wrote feverishly in a well-worn notebook. He reminded me of the nutty professor because of his thick glasses and nervous mannerisms. I watched Lucio and the man patiently review his accounts, totaling up each order, making sure the numbers were correct. Ten minutes passed since we stepped to the counter and after much dialogue, numerous gestures, and raised voices, the man gave him a white piece of paper waving Lucio off. I opened the door as he pushed the cart through the door.

"What was that all about?" I asked, curious as to what I'd just witnessed.

"In *Italia*, all business is done like this. A businessman attempts to make more profit by raising his prices by a percentage. This is a practice understood by all. In this business, prices constantly fluctuate day to day because the majority of his merchandise is imported. I resist by telling him we are one of his best customers. We argue back and forth. Nothing is very serious. We finally agree on the prices, he adds it to my account, and this order will show on my next month's billing statement." He placed the boxes in his small trunk.

"Everything here is negotiable?"

"*Si.* Most everything in *Italia* is negotiable. Only the very foolish and tourists accept the first price quoted. You will learn. It is our way of doing business. I have one more stop before I take you back. Do you mind? Usually Giovanni takes care of this, but since I am out this way, I will do it for him."

I leaned back in the seat wondering where the brother of the man I was falling for was taking me. I didn't really care as long as I was back in town by 4. "Where are we going now?" I asked.

"To a friend's home. It is only a few kilometers away. Do not worry. I will have you back in time to see my brother." He glanced at me sideways, like he was up to something.

The Italian countryside has always filled me with such peace and serenity. Lucio drove towards the majestic mountains, passing fields of corn as high as my shoulders. They would reach well above my head before the time came for harvesting. Row after row of corn, planted in straight lines, stretched for miles in all directions. I sneezed as the pollen made its way through the car's air filter into my sensitive nose. Lucio offered me a small package of tissues he kept in a hidden compartment of his car door.

He turned left and ended up in a driveway that one would have easily passed by if they didn't know it was there. Kicking up dust, we continued for about half a kilometer before reaching a small clearing. He stopped. A rather modest house, with a similarly styled smaller building loomed in the distance. It was completely surrounded by a wall of very high hedges that served as filters keeping out the blowing dust from the fields. Clothes hanging from a clothesline in the backyard, flapped gently in the breeze. I looked more closely at the house, then at the cars parked in front. Sitting next to an older model *Fiat* was a black BMW Z4. Giovanni's car. I positioned myself so I could see Lucio's face more clearly. He continued to look in the direction I no longer wanted to see, then reached for another cigarette, lighting it with the car's lighter.

"Is that Giovanni's car?" I asked—confused as to why he would be here.

He nodded, blowing smoke through his nostrils. He looked like a bull. Lucio didn't drive any closer to the house. Instead, he put the car in neutral and proceeded to calmly smoke his cigarette, planning his next move. I turned towards the house letting all kinds of thoughts enter my head. Imagining the worst, praying for the best. Lucio was no help at all. He didn't say a word, nor did he look at me.

"Lucio? What's going on? Why did you bring me here? Is Giovanni inside? Why haven't you pulled any closer? Are we going in?" Questions shot from my mouth one after another.

He turned and finally faced me. "Lena, I am truly sorry. I suspected they would be here together. My friend Maria lives there with her mother. You met her a few weeks ago. Remember, in the parking lot of my uncle's *ristorante*? You were with your American friend."

He looked at me with an expression I had not seen before. If I didn't know better, I could have sworn I saw the green-eyed monster of jealousy appear on his face. Giovanni's inside the house with that woman from this morning? What is he doing with her? Why did Lucio bring me here if he suspected his brother being with Maria?

"Lucio, I trust Giovanni and I don't believe he's doing anything he shouldn't be doing. Hey, since we're here, let's go say hello. If she is your friend, I'm sure she'll be more than happy to see you." I sincerely wanted to believe what I said was true, but the threads of doubt hung long.

"Are you sure you want to do this, *mi'amica*? What if you discover my brother isn't as dedicated to you as you seem to think? We can always leave and pretend we were never here. The choice is yours." He tossed his cigarette out the open window.

"Yes. I am sure. Aren't you curious? Isn't that why you came here in the first place? And who are you trying to catch in the wrong, Maria or Giovanni? Come on, I'm going with or without you." I said it, but it wasn't true. I wasn't that confident to go marching up to a stranger's door. I waited for him to follow. He turned off the ignition and trailed behind.

We followed the short path to the front door. I moved aside to let him do the honors. He knocked. We waited. A short time later, an elderly woman answered the door. Her back was hunched so far over I could barely see her heavily wrinkled face. A colorful silken scarf covered what remained of a once luxurious head of hair. When she spoke, she had to look up revealing a mouth devoid of teeth. I didn't understand her at all. Lucio took over. He spoke to her in a dialect I'd never heard before. She apparently recognized him and welcomed us both inside the house. She looked intensely at me, concentrating on my every feature as if she were trying to decide if she knew me. She took my arm and softly stroked the skin on my forearm. She murmured something, turned to Lucio and laughed hysterically.

"What did she say?" I asked, feeling like a recently discovered species.

"She says you have beautiful soft skin. Like a baby's bottom. This is Sofia, Maria's grandmother. She is old and feeble, harmless really. I told her we came to see Maria. She says she and Giovanni are in the back yard."

At least I felt better knowing they weren't in the house alone. How much mischief could they get into with this ancient woman wandering around? We followed her through the house, decorated obviously in furniture from another era, to the back door leading to a patio in the backyard. Maria and Giovanni sat opposite one another at a small wrought iron table, both with heads bent looking at a sheet of paper.

An older gentleman dressed in a suit, much too formal for the warm weather, sat on a concrete bench only a few feet away. He was speaking to them. An attaché case stuffed with papers, rested at his feet. They looked up when we made our entrance.

Giovanni spoke first, "Lucio! Lena! What are you two doing here?" He seemed more surprised than annoyed.

Suddenly the urge to turn and run almost made it to my feet. I looked at Lucio, exasperated at his suspicions. I opened my mouth to speak, but the words refused to come out. I looked first at the bespectacled Giovanni, then at Maria. They did not look like two people enthralled in a passionate love affair. Not knowing what to say, I crossed my arms, tapped my foot and turned to Lucio for an explanation.

They all began to speak at once in rapid bursts of Italian, each trying to over speak the other. The grandmother heard the commotion and came out giggling like a little girl let in on the adult's conversation. I couldn't make out exactly who did what, but I caught my name being thrown around a few times.

Maria looked hurt and started to cry. She rose from her chair facing Lucio yelling and gesturing wildly, first at him, then at Giovanni. The look on her face when she noticed me was filled with the sorrow of a woman carrying too many of life's burdens. She no longer looked like the carefree woman I first saw sitting in Lucio's car, head bopping to the music. Maria ran inside the house. Lucio followed.

I stood back letting the dust settle. The man in the suit sat back with an amused look on his face. This was probably the most excitement he'd seen in years. Not sure what had just transpired, I remained silent. Giovanni watched the couple's retreat then approached me.

"Lena, I am sorry you had to be involved in this. My brother has confused the situation. He saw me this morning with Maria in my car and jumped to awful conclusions. He thought we were involved in romance, but nothing can be further from the truth. She asked me to meet with this nice gentleman from the bank. Her family is considering selling off some of the familial estate. I have some experience in this matter, so I said I would look at the documents." He explained as he removed his glasses, placing them in a case on the table.

"I'm sorry too. I had no idea we were coming here – to this house. I saw Lucio on the way home, he offered me a ride. He asked me to accompany him to *Paglia* to pickup supplies for your club. When I saw your car, I admit I didn't know what to think. Lucio suggested leaving. Maybe we should have." I felt terrible. This situation wasn't my fault, but I could have put a stop to it before it reached this point.

"No need to blame yourself. What is done, is done." He turned to face the banker and said, "Maybe another day would be better?"

We watched the banker gather his papers, then leave through the back yard. He remained amused by the scene of misguided love played out for his entertainment. The old woman's rheumy eyes looked glum when she realized the excitement was over. She said something to crack herself up then ambled off to the cornfields using an old tree branch as a walking stick.

Giovanni sighed heavily, rubbing his neck trying to ease away the tension.

"Here, let me do that. Sit down." I stood behind him as he sat in the chair. Mark always did say I had the magic touch and could work kinks out of even the most knotted muscles. Sometimes the person you want to think about least is always forefront in your thoughts. I wonder why? I rubbed and kneaded his neck until I felt the muscles relax. It was really peaceful back here. No traffic, no airplanes, no screaming kids... The only sounds came from the wind blowing across fields of corn. Unfortunately, the prevailing winds also brought with it the disgusting stench of pig manure. It was the manure preferred by the local farmers for its fertilizing properties. I continued to massage his neck until he dropped his chin, pulling my arms downwards until my face was near his.

"*Grazie, amore mio.* You are exactly what I needed this morning. I am sorry I did not keep you around last night. Perhaps, this situation may have never occurred had you stayed with me." He kissed each of my fingers, one by one.

"See. I told you. You should have spent the night." I buried my chin in his thick black hair, noticing for the first time how a few silver stragglers blended themselves in. "What do you say we leave these two to straighten their situation out? I guess Lucio cares more about Maria than he was willing to admit – even to himself."

He smiled at my observation. "My brother is very stubborn with women. He will proceed only so far, then he pulls back when the relationship becomes serious. Maria is a very nice girl. Is she the one for him? I do not know. That is not for me to say. Perhaps what you say about him is correct. Come on, I will drive you back to town." He stood from the table and took me by the hand. I loved the way our hands fit together. Just right.

I didn't tell Giovanni about my earlier suspicions. He had given me no reason to suspect him being with another woman. Besides, he had every right to date other people, whether I agreed with the idea or not. Before we pulled off from Maria's house, he leaned over and kissed me. He had received an answer to an unspoken private question he kept hidden deep inside his heart.

217

CHAPTER 21

Instead of returning to the cottage, we went to his place. With over an hour remaining before he had to be at the club, Giovanni just wanted to relax. I surely didn't mind.

"Please, make yourself at home. I will be in my office. I have a few emails I need to answer and a couple of business calls to make. You can watch television or listen to music. Whichever you prefer." He pointed to the remotes for the TV and stereo.

I wandered around the apartment making mental notes about his taste in furniture, music, books and food. From this vantage point, I could see our tastes were very similar. I picked up a jazz CD featuring a Brazilian group and put it in the CD player. The notes flowing from the speakers picked me up, sending me on a natural high. I swayed to the music, unaware I was being watched. When the music ended, I heard soft clapping.

"I see you also enjoy this music. I have not played this CD in quite a while. I cannot say it had the same effect for me, but I am happy you like it. May I?"

We slow danced in perfect harmony to another three songs. It was nice. When the music ended, we gazed lovingly into each other's eyes. Neither wanted to break the bond forming between us. He felt it. So did I. We were falling dangerously, foolishly, deeply in love.

"Now don't start something you can't finish Signori Morelli." I teased, feeling his heart beat strongly against my own.

"Never. I always see my beginnings through to the very end. For now, I must get you back to your place to change. You do remember our date this afternoon? Can you be ready to go in an hour? Do not worry about eating dinner. We have excellent food at the club."

"Oh, I haven't forgotten. I'll be ready. How should I dress? What will I be doing?" I asked, all too aware how our relationship would proceed to another level once we switched from romance to business.

"For tonight, you will want to dress comfortably, but not too casual. No jeans or sneakers. Definitely no tee shirts. I really liked that pantsuit you wore to *Venezia*. Something along those lines. Of course, wear comfortable shoes and leave the high heels at home—at least for the first few days. I am sure whatever you select will look fine," he said.

I checked out my wardrobe, courtesy of my recent shopping trip. I settled on a two-piece outfit made of some kind of slinky material that never wrinkled. Spaghetti straps held up the sleeveless top. The pants fit my butt and thighs perfectly and flared out slightly at the bottom. I completed my ensemble with a pair of silver, fan shaped earrings and checked out my reflection in the mirror. I had to admit I looked positively gorgeous. A bit of makeup around the eyes, some blush on the cheeks, a little lipstick. I was ready to go.

Giovanni knocked. He was decked out in a long sleeved black shirt with the sleeves pushed up, black slacks, and black leather shoes. A single diamond stud resting in his left earlobe caught my attention. A simple, elegant watch enveloped his wrist. He smelled good and looked even better. He was too fine!

"*Mama mia!*" He whistled. "You look beautiful! You ready?"

"Thanks. You don't look half bad yourself. Let me grab a jacket and my notebook." I picked out a small clutch for my keys, phone and lipstick. "Look, I bought a cell phone. It's a prepaid one, but it's all I need for now."

"Let me see that. I will program my numbers for you." He took the phone and began punching buttons. "I see the roses I sent are still in bloom. The florist guaranteed they would last at least a week. You know Lena, if you belonged to me – lived with me, you would have roses in your life everyday for the rest of your life."

My heart ached for both of us. I tried not to think about it, but eventually the day would come when I would have to leave.

"You have no idea how tempting that sounds. Every moment I spend with you, I can imagine living the rest of my life with you. All I can ask for is your patience. I know how difficult this situation is. Trust me, I am just as confused. How about we get going? I have a lot to learn and not much time to learn it in." I kissed him on one cheek then the other, finishing off with his soft lips.

We arrived at the club at a time when most people were leaving work. The surrounding stores bustled with business, probably the most business they'd seen all day. *Busco's* opened for drinks at five and the disc jockey started playing music at seven for the early crowd, encouraging them to stick around for the excitement later. The real partiers usually didn't arrive until well after 10. He closed the doors at 3 in the morning on weekends.

The staff was already there, making preparations for the busy night. Giovanni took me around introducing me to his curious employees. I met the bartender, Nicky, who remembered me from my previous visit. Guess I made quite an impression. I was also introduced to a few waitresses who looked to be of barely legal age, and two very muscular guys who worked the door as bouncers. All greeted me kindly, silently wondering who I was.

Giovanni explained that the DJ usually showed around 6 leaving just enough time to do a thorough sound check. I admired the club's décor. It was a cross between an old English pub and a modern discotheque.

Nicky kept a towel in his hand wiping down any surface needing it. A smoky mirror lined the wall behind the bar, partially obscured by two shelves of liquor with caps replaced by spigots ready for quick pouring. The very top shelf displayed at least a hundred beers from all around the world. Lucio had delivered the liquor purchased earlier in *Paglia* because the empty boxes were pushed to the side. The dance floor was at least 50 by 60 feet. An older woman was hard at work using a dust mop to shine the floor. She sprayed a liquid that gave off a strong lemony fragrance on the floor then continued to mop. The waitresses cleaned the tables with cleaning liquid and wiped them down with a dry towel. The lights flickered, went bright, back to dim, followed by strobes in colors of red, green, and yellow.

"Do you all go through this every day?" I watched the diligent workers, each focused on their particular tasks.

"*Si*. Every day we perform the same routine. If you think this is something, wait until you see what happens when we close. Follow me, I want to introduce you to my friend and chef, Roberto."

I followed him past the bar into a surprisingly spacious kitchen. Immaculate stainless steel countertops lined the room. The Sub Zero refrigerator took up half of one side of the wall. A grill and walled-in brick oven were on the opposite side. A sink, large enough to give a small child a bath, was filled with hot water and stainless steel pans. A short, stout middle-aged woman, dressed all in white stood with her back turned to us busily working at the sink. She was up to her elbows in soapsuds, loudly singing songs to help pass the time.

"*Ciao* Rosalita. I want you to meet Lena, my friend. She will be assisting me for the next week or so," he said to the woman who stopped singing when she realized she was not alone. She turned and eyed us both.

"Giovanni! *Come va!*" She reached out to hug him, but had the presence of mind to wipe her hands dry on her apron first. She spoke to him in Italian, nodding her head at me.

The overly excited Rosalita reached out to shake my hand, still speaking in Italian. I understood only that she was pleased to meet me. I nodded my head as a signal of understanding. I looked at Giovanni. "What is she saying?"

"She says it is so nice to finally meet the woman who has mellowed out her employer. And for you to always take care of me," he replied, loosely interpreting her words.

Through the open back door, I heard men's voices, laughing and joking as they so often do. Lucio came in, followed by who I assumed was Roberto. Both men carried boxes. They quickly fell quiet. Lucio most likely from the embarrassment he suffered this afternoon. Roberto placed his box of vegetables down on the counter and nodded for Lucio to do the same. He stood back with a hangdog look on his face.

"*Ciao* Lucio. *Ciao* Roberto. Roberto I want you to meet my friend Lena. She will be here for about a week or so observing us – how we operate this club. She is a good friend of mine, so be nice!"

Roberto took my hand and gave it a good shake. "I am pleased to know you *signora*. You need anything, anything at all, food, drinks, *un amico* to speak to, *por favore* come to Roberto. *Si, sono,* I am the one to operate *Busco's,*" he said in broken English. He let go of my hand and released a deep robust laugh. The others joined in.

Giovanni spoke to both Roberto and Rosalita. Both nodded their heads in agreement to whatever it was he said. Lucio looked at me then dropped his gaze. I wanted to tell him I didn't hold any bad feelings towards him about this morning, but before I could, Giovanni guided me to a room off of the kitchen. This was a matter for them to straighten out. I had no place in their personal affairs.

He unlocked the door. It led to an office furnished with a large mahogany desk, paired with a leather chair. A flat screen monitor sat on top of the desk next to a multi-line telephone. Two chairs sitting opposite the desk, a file cabinet and a floor lamp completed the furnishings. Two long, narrow windows on either side of the room offered just enough light to keep his potted fern alive. A lone calendar from the *Banco Populare* graced the bright blue walls.

I sat down in the chair closest to Giovanni. He motioned for me to come closer. He unlocked the desk, pulling out a thick ledger filled with small neat writing. I watched him pull eyeglasses from his jacket pocket and place the stylish frames on his face. He appeared more distinguished, more knowledgeable, and definitely more powerful. Interesting how plastic frames and two small circles of glass can change one's appearance so quickly. Either way, I was hooked.

A knock at the door caused us both to look up. Lucio stuck his head in and asked, "Giovanni, do you have a minute? There are a few issues I need to discuss with you." Distress was evident on his face and in his voice.

"Give me just a moment, Lucio. I will be right with you," he sighed, "*Scusi*, Lena. It is time my brother and I cleared the air. Do you mind waiting here until I return or do you prefer to sit at the bar?" His expression told me the tension between the two was not a usual occurrence.

"How about I sit at the bar while you two talk. I think I'll be more comfortable waiting out there. Besides, I can get to know Nicky. I really do hope you two get this straightened out. Stay there, I think I can find my way." I rose from my chair, bent down to kiss his cheek and started for the door. I returned to the kitchen, seeing Lucio pace the floor.

"Lena, I wish to apologize for my behavior this afternoon. It is not in my character to be jealous, especially when it concerns my own brother. I am sorry to pull you into this."

His eyes showed more emotion that I'd ever witnessed from him. He usually appeared so cool and distant.

"Hey Lucio, don't stress over it. These things happen." I put my hand on his shoulder. He surprised me by giving me a quick hug.

"*Grazie*, Lena. If you need anything tonight or any other time you are here, please contact me. Oh, I forgot to tell you how lovely you look tonight." Finally he smiled, showing a bit of his old charming self again. He went into the office and quietly shut the door.

Roberto and Rosalita looked on, curious to what was going on. I smiled and took a seat on one of the bar stools.

"Something for you?" asked Nicky.

"Um, I think I'll just have a Coke. I'm going to need to be alert for this evening," I replied.

He looked at me for a moment too long and flashed a quick smile. "One Coca Cola for the pretty lady coming right up."

Charm. That's what these Italian men have so much of. They are full of glowing, outrageous compliments and aren't afraid to give them out freely. I don't care if the guy is short, fat, and bald with no teeth. If he can come up with a way to make a woman feel special, she will always forgive his physical deficiencies.

Take for instance this Nicky guy. He's not exactly what I would consider as handsome, but he is good looking in an average sort of way. He wears his long hair in a ponytail. His teeth aren't perfect, but at least they're still his. He has an okay body, no obvious beer belly, but he could stand to lift a few weights to bulk up his skinny arms. Incredibly, he possessed a way of looking at a woman that made her want to spend time with him. His gaze had an intensity that conveyed 'I am interested in learning all there is to know about you'. Apparently he had also mastered the 5-second rule for staring into a woman's eyes, in an attempt to look into her soul. If he could lock eyes for at least 5 seconds, he would be assured of having someone on his arm at closing. I shook my head and quietly laughed to myself.

"For you." He placed the soda and a napkin imprinted with *Busco's*, on the counter. "What is so funny? A private joke?" He leaned over, holding onto the drying towel.

"No. Well, yeah. I was just thinking how charismatic you Italian guys are. I haven't met one yet, who wasn't up to something. Always flirting with the women…"

"It is true *signora*, we can be very charming. Also very passionate." He gave me a look as he wiped an imaginary spot from the bar. "*Signora* Lena. What brings you here? Are you a special friend of the Morelli's?"

"Yeah. They are my friends. Both of them," I replied, sipping my drink.

"Didn't I see you here with someone else? A tall Black American? What happened to him?" He was all up in my business.

"You know you ask a lot of questions. For your information, I was with an old friend. But now I'm here with Giovanni. I'm surprised you noticed."

"Oh. I see. *Va bene*. Will you be working for Giovanni now?" he asked while straightening the glasses, arranging the liquor for better access.

I considered my response, not wanting to supply gossip fodder for the employees. "No, I'm not working for him. I'm more like an intern trying to learn the business. You know, find out what it takes to successfully operate a club."

"Learn the business? Are you considering owning your own business?" He seemed genuinely interested.

"One day I'd like to." I changed the subject. "Nicky, how do you like working here?" I finished my drink.

"I have been here from the very beginning – over ten years when they first opened. It is a good job. Giovanni and Lucio are very good employers. They treat their employees like family. So we, I guess you can say, we remain extremely loyal. *Busco's* started out first as a restaurant serving light bar food and drinks. Business was excellent, they wanted to expand, so they added the dance floor and a premium sound system a few years ago to attract a different crowd, a younger crowd. They started bringing in some good local bands, sponsored a few contests, and it took off from there. You shall see. Tonight it will be standing room only."

He refilled my soda, this time topping it off with a maraschino cherry. "Thanks." I spun around on the stool for another view. The two bouncers looked like they stepped off some movie set. Stereotypical thugs with long dark hair, bulging biceps tattooed with who knows what, and earrings in both ears. One looked as if he had a bad case of acne as a child, for pockmarks marred what otherwise would have been an attractive face. Perhaps that's why he sported a neatly shaved beard. The other muscle bound maverick was clean shaven. They sat in one of the booths near the front door going over what looked like very important papers. "Hey Nicky? What's up with those two?"

"Who? Them?" He indicated the bouncers. "They work as a team to keep our customers who have had a bit too much to drink under control. They both have black belts in *tae kwon do* and work as personal trainers during the day. You will not meet a nicer pair of guys. Can you believe they are homosexual?" He added in a conspiratorial whisper.

"Really? Good for them." I wasn't homophobic, just surprised that such masculine looking men weren't into women. "Is it some big secret that they're gay?" I asked.

"No. They are very open about it. No one seems to have a problem with their sexuality. Some of our customers attempt to flirt with them – both men and women – but they remain professional at all times. They do their jobs well, that is all that matters. I just thought I should mention it, in case you had any ideas." He left to attend a customer.

A hand rested gently on my shoulder. I turned around. "Hey you!" I spoke softly. "Did you two get everything straightened out? Are you all right?" I looked into his deep green eyes.

"*Sì.* Lucio and I had a very good talk. It was just a misunderstanding, but we have cleared the air. All is well again." He sighed then smiled. He reached for my hand, but thought better of it considering the audience discretely watching us. "I think it is better if we spoke in my office."

"I think you're right!" I added, noticing how everyone looked up when he came out to speak to me. I got up from my stool and followed him to the back room.

He closed the door behind us. "I see you have become acquainted with Nicky. He is a good bartender, however, he likes to gossip. Did you tell him anything about us?" He asked in a husky, inquisitive voice. His nose was mere inches from mine.

"I told him we were madly in love and involved in a passionate love affair." I teased, running my finger over the surface of his pouting lips resting comfortably under his neatly trimmed moustache. "I said we were going to run away to a deserted island and live the rest of our lives screwing each other's brains out." His nose brushed against mine. I closed my eyes in anticipation for the kiss that never disappointed me. He teased my tongue with his, exploring my mouth as I explored his. Our breath deepened, our hearts raced, yet we both realized this wasn't the time nor place to display our feelings.

"Oh, *amore mio.*" He exhaled and pulled away. "With you I feel so alive. Everyone has commented on the differences they notice in me. But while we are in *Busco's*, I must display only professionalism. For now, this office is the only place I shall display my feelings for you. *Capisce?*"

His eyes mirrored the way I felt. "Of course I understand. This is your business and these people are your employees. They don't need to know what goes on in your personal life. As far as they're concerned, I'm an intern from the United States working in a foreign exchange program you support. How does that sound?" I tilted my head, speaking in a quiet tone. Though we were alone, I was ever cognizant of peering eyes and perky ears.

"You are a very special lady. You know that? Now, let me show you a few things you need to know to operate a business this size. Come sit with me at my desk." He guided me around the large desk to the chair I occupied earlier.

He rebooted the computer. "I usually leave my door open unless I am in a meeting or working with money. You see that door? It is reinforced steel, as is my safe I had built when this part of the building was constructed. Although we do not have a large crime problem in *Gorgazzio*, one can never be too careful. *Bene*. Lena to begin, I must tell you the secret of my success. Lucio and I treat all we meet with respect. This we learned from our parents. That includes everyone from the deliveryman, to the bank officer who handles our account, to all our employees--especially our employees, because without them, all we would have is an empty building. Most of them have been here since the beginning. We are a team who look out for one another. When they step through those doors, they become part of *Busco's* family." He picked up his glasses, placed them on his face and reached for the ledger on the desk.

"I think that is an excellent policy. Let me tell you, I have worked for people who treat their employees like shit, like they're dispensable. In the end, the employees either quit or do as little work as possible. They have no loyalty because they don't feel anyone cares. On the other hand, I have had some great bosses I would have done anything for, because they showed they cared. And it wasn't always some grand gesture. Sometimes it was little things, like asking how our kids were doing or how I did in a tough class."

"Then you understand what I mean?" He seemed pleased. "As co-owners of this club, Lucio and I must know something about every position, because you never know when we will need to fill in at the last moment. I studied business at university and received what is equivalent to an MBA in your country. Therefore I take care of all the business functions. I am the accountant, supply person, secretary, billing clerk, you name it, if it has to do with finances, I am the one to come to," he explained, "sometimes I have also taken over as the chef, the bartender, the disc jockey, even bused tables and swept floors. Lucio is more of the technical guy. When he was younger, he worked side by side with my Papa, who was an electrician. That guy can rewire an entire building if necessary. He is also a very good plumber. That he learned by trial and error. We work well together, each taking up the slack the other leaves behind."

"You guys seem to have it all together. Did you learn how to run a business at the university or did someone mentor you?" I was impressed by his vast knowledge.

He typed in his password. "In *Italia* families have operated their own businesses for generations. Sometimes it is expected to start your own business rather than work for someone else, especially for men. What you sell is not important, the fact that you have tried is. I guess you can say it is expected to at least attempt a business before going out into the corporate world. To answer your question, most of what I learned I picked up from watching my family members operate their own businesses. I learned other aspects like finance and supply-side economics from the university. They taught me how to be more efficient, in addition to several other considerations as a small business owner."

I reflected upon his words. As a child, he'd been exposed to operating a business as naturally as going to school. "How lucky you must have been to grow up with a family who not only had the confidence, but also the ability to start their own businesses. For that, I envy you."

He began to protest, not wanting to acknowledge an advantage.

"No, let me finish. When I was a child, I didn't know anyone who ran their own business. I grew up in a small, economically disadvantaged town amongst people whose thoughts focused on their daily survival. And going to college was never discussed as an option for me or the other kids in my neighborhood. Most of us were lucky if we managed to graduate from high school. Giovanni, the only "career people" I knew were teachers, because the majority of adults in my community were blue collar, unskilled laborers or they worked in factories. I didn't know any real "professional business people". Of course, there were a few entrepreneurs who ran small businesses from their homes, mostly selling food, liquor, or performing hair care services, but I didn't know anyone who was truly successful running their own business. I couldn't fathom owning a business, let alone know where to begin."

He looked away, momentarily embarrassed by his good fortune. "Lena, please do not envy me. Just because you did not grow up in a family of business owners does not mean you had less. You had many wonderful experiences that shaped you into the person you have become today. Look at you! You are a very intelligent, beautiful, brave woman. You traveled thousands of miles on your own, managed to find a place to live, and now you're sitting here asking questions about starting your own business. When you consider your abilities, not many others would have, or even could come close to being where you are."

"Well, when you put it that way, I guess I have lived a pretty good life. And I am a very confident person. I didn't mean to put you on the defense. It's just that life seems to have been so much easier for you. You know, being raised in a country with a long proud history and all. Growing up surrounded by a very loving extended family…"

"Perhaps. But we each have our individual burdens to bear." He looked at his watch. "Time is getting short. Look at this. I want to show you the importance of keeping good financial records. I use both a detailed computerized financial spreadsheet, as well as this written ledger for a general idea of where we are. And I always keep at least two backup disks for all my files locked away in a safe place."

For the next hour, I watched and listened as he carefully explained his accounting procedures, trying to remember the days of my undergraduate accounting courses. I was able to follow his every explanation, as he was an extremely good teacher. I was distracted by the soothing tone of his voice, or his thoughtful expressions, feeling an uncontrollable need to touch him, but I did not surrender to my own desires. Instead I paid attention to my private lessons realizing this incredible opportunity he was offering me.

He went over the different accounts, each set up to automatically record deductions for utilities, supplies, and employee payroll. Each financial transaction required two coded signatures, Giovanni's and Lucio's, before the transaction could be approved for payment. It was all done electronically. The only time money exchanged hands was when the nightly deposit was made in the bank the next morning. Numerous safeguards were built into the system. Even the cash register was hooked into a computer program that tracked each transaction as it occurred. The inventory system was coded to track supplies before they ran out. Each employee received extensive training to insure it was used to its maximum potential.

A knock at the door signified the night was about to begin. Showtime. "Whew! I see why you have to be so committed and enthusiastic about your work. If you were to let the ball drop, there's no one else to really pick it up. Is there?"

"Why do you speak in sporting euphemisms? Are Americans so fixated on sports you speak about it even when you do not intend to?"

"See. There you go teasing me about my Yankee expressions. I wish I understood your language well enough to know the silly things you all say." I feigned hurt feelings.

"I mean no disrespect. Besides, if you stay around here long enough, you will pick up my language *rapido*." He removed his glasses and ran his hands over his face. "*Va bene*. It is time for me to go out to meet the crowds. Are you ready?"

"You know, I've been meaning to tell you how sexy I think you look wearing those glasses." I had to touch him one more time before we left the room. My hand rested on his arm. "You are so irresistible."

"Oh. You think so? Come here. I will show you irresistible," he replied, helping me from my chair and backing me against the wall. "Tonight, I will not have much time to spend with you, but later... We shall see?"

I stood with my back against the wall feeling his hot breath on my face. Wanting his mouth all over my body, I had to settle for my neck. His hands cupped my behind bringing me closer to him, his masculinity rising as fast as my temperature. A devilish smile lit up his eyes, once again bringing out those golden flecks, as he kissed me gently. I wrapped my arms around his neck trying to hold on to this feeling for as long as I could. I felt like I had been starving and he was the food I needed to survive. I couldn't get enough of him.

"Giovanni! Time to get the show on the road. *Andiamo!*" Lucio knocked on the door putting an end to our torturous session.

"I don't know how I'm going to make it through the rest of the night without being able to touch you." I exhaled into his ear.

He backed away slowly. "Nor do I. Are you all right?" He attempted to pull himself together to portray the role of the boss.

"Yeah, I'm okay. It's just that I...never mind, we'll talk about it later. C'mon let's go." I smoothed my hair and reapplied my lipstick before following him out the door.

The aroma of pizza made my stomach growl loudly for all within earshot to hear. How embarrassing!

"*Fame, Signori?*"

"*Si*, Rosalita. *Grazie.*" I nodded my head to let her know I was indeed hungry.

"I am sorry, Lena. In all the excitement, I forgot you had not eaten. Please order anything you wish from the menu. I must go out to the floor and make my rounds. If you have any questions, most of the staff speaks at least some English. Also everyone here will be more than happy to assist you. Roberto?" He shouted at the chef. "*Por favore* take care of Lena for me? *Molte grazie.*"

"I'll be fine. You go on and do what you need to do. I'll find a seat, have a bite to eat, and wander around. This place is spacious, but I'm sure we'll see each other again tonight. Go on." I fought the urge to kiss him. When he finally left the kitchen to get to work, I asked Roberto for a small pizza with *porcini* mushrooms and a small anti-pasta salad.

The DJ had finally arrived. The club previously filled with quiet employee energy, now reverberated with a deep heart-thumping drum beat from a popular song.

The club was filled with dozens of people in varying stages of dress. Young women, mostly in their mid to upper 20s, were clothed in outfits running the gamut from tiny tops and even tinier bottoms, exposing the once popular thong, to the other end of the spectrum wearing almost elegant evening wear. The men were almost always dressed in black from top to bottom. An occasional brave soul wove color into the act breaking up the monotony. I marveled at how Italian men could dress so effeminate, yet still display masculinity. An openly gay couple hung all over one another, vying for Nicky's attention. I found an empty stool closest to the kitchen and watched the show.

"*Come va, Lena?* Are you enjoying yourself yet? Can I get you something?" Nicky asked during a lull in the crowd. He was obviously used to the attention from both women and men. A young man emptied boxes of beer into the bar fridge below. I assumed it was his assistant.

"Nicky, thanks. I'll just have a *frizzante* for now. I see you have a couple of admirers." I tilted my head in the direction of the joy boys. I hadn't been in a club in such a long time I felt self-conscious and out of place amongst the youthful partygoers. Thankfully, Lucio stopped by to keep me company.

"*Come va?*" He positioned himself between me and the guy on the stool next to me who kept throwing sideways glances in my direction.

"Hi Lucio, I'm doing fine. This place is wild! Do you ever get used to all the excitement?" I yelled above the noise. And it was only around 8 o'clock.

"It is not so bad and yes you do get used to it. After time, it becomes just like any other job. What are you doing now? Has my brother given you some thrilling assignment?" He sipped from a bottle of water.

"Right now, I'm waiting on my pizza. What's going on with you?"

"Just making rounds, making sure all is working correctly. How long ago did you place your order?"

"Not too long. Just a few minutes."

He touched my arm and said, "*Andiamo*. I will seat you where you can eat without being disturbed. A lovely lady such as yourself sitting at the bar alone will have to fight off the wolves. Follow me." He led me to a table away from the crowd. A reserved sign sat squarely in the middle. "I will return shortly with your food."

As promised, Lucio quickly returned with a tray filled with pizza, salad, and silverware. "*Buon Appetito*," he replied as he put the tray away to the side. He pulled up a chair. "May I?"

"Anybody who brings me delicious food is more than welcome to share my table. Have a seat." I dug into the salad first. Better to let the pizza cool down. I'd managed to burn the roof of my mouth by biting into too hot pizza enough times to last a lifetime.

"Once again, please accept my sincere apologies for this afternoon. I do not know what came over me." He popped a cigarette into his mouth.

Unlike Americans, Europeans do not consider smoking while someone else is eating to be rude. I decided to just deal with it, especially since practically everyone in the club was lighting up.

"Don't worry about this afternoon. Know what? I absolutely love *porcinis*. They are so good. By the way, is Maria okay?" I recalled her overly dramatic exit.

"No, Maria is not well. She told me part of the reason she asked Giovanni to read over her papers was to make me jealous. He thought he was doing a friend a favor. Women. A man will never figure them out entirely. My brother is a shrewd businessman, but he does not have time to spend wondering about a woman's motives. He is very intelligent. However, Giovanni can be naïve about women. I, on the other hand, consider myself to know you all fairly well. Take you for instance. I do not know much about you, but I can see you like my brother very much. But I am confused. You come out of nowhere, supposedly here on holiday, only weeks since your first visit. Are you some rich American woman who can afford to travel back and forth to *Italia*? Lena, what is it you really want?" He eyed me suspiciously.

"Nothing! And I am not rich. In fact, I work extremely hard for a living. I just happened to have some extra money that I've been saving. I decided to use it for a vacation. I mean for a second visit." I didn't like the direction this conversation was headed.

"I see... Tell me. What happens to my brother when you must return to America? You cannot keep returning to *Italia* every few weeks. What are your intentions? How much longer do you intend to remain?"

My appetite was rapidly disappearing. I picked at the pizza. "Look. I don't like discussing my personal business with you, but I'm telling you like I told Giovanni. I never expected for this to happen. The feelings I have for your brother are more real than any I've ever had. I think I'm falling in love with him. At this point in my life, I am more confused than you may believe. I don't have any ulterior motives for Giovanni. And if I could drop everything, move over here, and start my life anew I'd be the happiest woman alive. Please don't judge me or think I'm after your brother for anything other than his love."

His tone and demeanor softened. "*Mi dispiace*, Lena. You have to remember he is the only brother I have. We are family and we look out for each other. Always. I believe you when you declare your feelings for him, but you are not from here. What will happen when you must return to your home? Have you considered that? Okay. I will leave it alone. For now. Maybe this is only a holiday romance that will go no further? He is my older brother, *si*, but like I said he does not have much experience with what motivates women." He snubbed his cigarette out in the ashtray and then sat back in his chair. "*Por favore*, eat before it gets cold."

I separated a piece of the pizza, placed it on a napkin and held it to him as a peace offering. "Look, I can appreciate everything you've said, because I've said the same to myself a thousand times. I have considered just walking away. Ending this before it becomes more serious, but I can't. The pull, the attraction to him, is too strong. If you think this will be difficult for him when I leave, imagine what it is like for me. My entire life is turned upside down right now."

He accepted the pizza, folding it in half before biting in. "I would not like to be in your shoes, Lena. I do not know what kind of life you have back in America, but I wish to propose an alternative. You do realize that you can move here – to *Italia*? Locating a job will not be difficult. You know me and my brother. That is half the battle. We can help you find a more suitable place to live. Just say the word, it shall be done." He took another bite of pizza.

We both turned around when he heard a commotion coming from the front of the club. He replaced the half eaten slice on the table. "I am sorry, but I must go see what trouble there is. Just think about what I said. *Sì?*"

Up until that moment, the thought of moving to Italy was nothing more than a passing notion. He made the offer and I believe it was with the utmost sincerity. I felt so much better after speaking with Lucio. He kept it real and I liked that. He said he'd let me and Giovanni handle our own affairs and I was grateful for his acceptance.

I watched the continual progression of performers in this mini drama unfolding before my eyes. Observing people was better than watching any movie, especially after they started drinking. All the liquid I drank eventually caught up with me and sent me searching for the nearest ladies restroom.

While I was in the stall, I overheard a couple of girls conversing in English. Their comments were all about the handsome brothers who owned the place. The plan was to flirt shamelessly and encourage the guys to take them home that night for some good old-fashioned group sex.

While washing my hands, I got a good look. They were both in their early 20s, bleached blonde, both average height and slightly chunky. Both wore too much makeup. One was dressed in a low cut mini dress and thigh-high black boots. The other wore a halter top and hip hugger jeans that showed her crack when she bent over to adjust her clunky shoes. They turned their noses up at me without saying a word, then laughed their way out of the door.

I exhaled. I knew I'd have to be strong being around Giovanni in his club. Damn! Those girls were trying to plot to get my men into bed. Ha! I just referred to them as "my men". How possessive one could so quickly become. I knew what women did in clubs, because years ago, I would have tried the same thing. Well, maybe not the group sex, but I definitely would have set my sites on the Morelli brothers. They were both fine as hell! I dried my hands and rechecked my face. I hadn't done any major sweating, so I still looked fairly decent. Those girls couldn't hold a candle to my flame.

The only employee I had yet to meet was the disc jockey. I skirted the dance floor until I was at the booth and was pleasantly surprised to see a handsome young black man standing behind the plexiglass. The DJ booth was filled with CDs and vinyl albums. I waited until he changed songs before I introduced myself. He noticed me standing there and pulled his headphones from his ears.

"Hi. I'm Lena, Giovanni's friend. I think I've met everyone except you." I extended my hand.

He replied with a very proper British accent, "Hello Lena. My name is Jeremy. Jeremy Miles. I am so pleased to meet you. Lucio told me we had another friendly face around here somewhere. I must say I am quite surprised to see it is you." He reacted as if he'd just met some long lost relative.

"The pleasure's all mine. Well, I must admit I was also surprised to see you up here. Are you from England?" He wore his curly hair in shoulder length dreadlocks.

"Yes. I grew up in Manchester. Do you know the area?" He pointed his finger indicating I should wait. He pulled the microphone towards his mouth and spoke in perfect Italian. The crowd responded enthusiastically. He said something else to pump them up even more. I felt the heavy beat of the bass deep inside my chest. The dizzying strobe lights flickered in time to the music as the crowd cheered in appreciation while pumping their arms into the air.

"What was that you asked me?" I yelled above the music.

"I was asking if you were familiar with Manchester?" He shouted in return.

I shook my head signifying no.

"That's okay. You're American, right?" he asked, standing very close so I could hear him above the roar of the crowd.

"Yeah, I'm American. Well, I'll let you get back to work. I just wanted to come up and introduce myself. Oh, by the way. You have really got this place jumpin'! I'll talk to you later."

"Good meeting you, Lena. Do you have any special requests?"

"No, but if I do, I know where to come. Bye-bye."

Jeremy replaced the headphones and went back to work, grinning like I'd let him in on some big secret.

I found an empty spot on the wall, simply content to watch. Several guys asked me to dance, but I declined them all. I still hadn't seen Giovanni. I was relieved to know I wasn't the oldest person out there. In fact, the closer I looked at the women, the more I noticed that half were around my age. The major difference between them and me was they seemed completely comfortable with their bodies and dressed in a style much younger than I typically preferred. They danced not only with confidence, but also sensuality. I could take a few lessons from these women and proud of what I've got and not worry that my body isn't perfect.

I spotted him probably the same time he saw me, cornered by the two girls from the restroom. The look on his face said he needed rescuing. I smiled, making my way across the floor, all too happy to oblige. When I got closer, I heard the one in the dress make a rude comment to her friend about me being a Nigerian prostitute and that I had a lot of nerve being up in there.

"Giovanni, where have you been? I've been looking all over for you." I looked at the girls who simultaneously turned three shades of red.

He reached for me, kissed me on both cheeks and said to the girls, "I believe you owe my friend an apology. She is neither Nigerian, nor a prostitute. Although for you, I cannot say the latter is not true."

Obviously the last part flew right over their heads. The one in the dress said, "Uh, I'm sorry about saying that stuff. We thought you were someone else. I was only playing."

I couldn't let this go without adding my two cents. "In the future, let me suggest that you keep your stupid little comments to yourself because you never know who is listening to your senseless conversations. Did you really think you could get Giovanni and Lucio to take you two home? Ha! I don't think so!" I didn't shout, nor did I raise my voice.

Giovanni laughed before he could catch himself. The girls slunk away, defeated at their own game. I heard one of them comment that they didn't know I spoke English. I rolled my eyes at their ignorance.

"*Grazie*, Lena. Those two followed me everywhere. I could not get rid of them. Were they really trying to get me in bed? I thought they were being a bit too friendly." He laughed out loud and continued, "Enough about them. Where have you been? You been staying busy?"

"Uh, yeah, right! Do you go through this every night? Women throwing themselves at you?" I was surprised I wasn't more upset. Trust can be a powerful motivator for any situation.

"Mostly, yes. As I told you when we first met. I meet beautiful and occasionally not so beautiful women all the time. It is a hazard of my profession. However, I look at them the same way you may look at a bin of machine parts. It is business and they are my customers. I try to keep my private life and professional life separate. Now what else have you been up to besides spying on women in the *bagno*?" He caressed my hand.

"That is not funny! For your information, I have been checking out your customers. Oh yeah, I also met Jeremy. He seems like a nice guy."

"Yes. He is. In fact, all my employees are good people. It took years to put together this team, finding the right personalities to fit well together. Now, I believe I have the perfect mix."

"You have done an absolutely wonderful job with this club. No matter where I went, no matter who I spoke with, I felt totally comfortable and safe. Let me tell you, for a single woman to be able to come into a club and feel safe is an accomplishment unto itself. Oh, and the food was delicious. I'll have to personally thank Roberto."

"It really means a lot that you enjoy being here." He checked his watch. "I must finish up a few items in the office. You may join me, but I will be extremely busy writing letters to my suppliers."

"Why don't I help? I'm a very good typist," I replied enthusiastically.

He cleared his throat, "I appreciate your offer, but I must decline."

"Why?" I asked, feeling hurt at his refusal of my offer to help.

"Lena, I am certain you are a great typist. But you do not speak Italian well enough to compose the letters."

"What was I thinking? Of course, your letters are in Italian." I laughed, in spite of myself.

"It is no big thing. I know what you mean about forgetting about our differences. So often I want to speak to you in my native language, but then I remember you only know a few phrases," he said this with no intended malice.

"Giovanni, you are teaching me so much, exposing me to new challenges and opportunities, including me in your life. I just want you to know that I appreciate your patience with me and I wish I had something more to offer you."

He took me by the hand and guided me to the front door through the crowds of people. When we were outside, away from the crowds standing alone on the side of a building he spoke, "Lena, you think you have given me nothing. I see it another way. You have made me feel alive again. For the past couple of years, all I wanted to do was work, work, work... Nothing else. My life revolved around this club because I had no one special to share it with. As you can see, meeting women is not a problem. But meeting the right one? Well, I truly believe that only happens maybe once in a lifetime. I do not know what the future holds, and to tell you the truth, I do not want to know. Since I met you, I have shared my thoughts, my dreams, and my passions. Please believe me when I say I have never, ever fallen this fast for any woman. You are unlike anyone I have had the pleasure of knowing. *Amore mio* we will get through this. I have faith." He leaned in, barely brushing his lips against mine.

I listened to his words spoken in heavily accented Italian. Please don't say it. Please don't say it. Please don't say it. I kept repeating those words over and over in my mind like a mantra, because if he were to tell me he loved me, I would have lost it right then and there. Instead I wrapped my arms around him and held on for dear life. I did not want to let him go, I could not let him go. I was already too far gone. He witnessed my internal struggle play out in my facial expression. The words "I love you" were on the tip of my tongue, but I held back.

"How about I take you home now – to my apartment? I must return to the club, but you may wait for me there. You can spend the night. If you wish."

I shook my head. Too afraid to speak, unsure of the words that might spill forth. "Um, no. That's okay. I mean I'm all right. I'm sorry Giovanni." I regained my composure. "Let's go back inside and have fun. Well, at least I'll have fun while you work."

"Are you sure you are okay?"

"Yeah, I'll be fine. Anyway, I don't really feel like hanging out on my own. You trust me enough to leave me in your apartment? Alone?" I had to ask.

"Of course, is there any reason I should not trust you? Considering what we have gone through in such a short time, I can see no reason not to. Let's go back inside." He replied matter-of-factly.

He placed his hand on the small of my back and guided me towards the club. The two big, burly bouncers opened the doors, greeting us as they did. The loud thumping of techno music had everyone who could move up on the dance floor. I looked at Giovanni and smiled. "Dance with me?" I tried my best to look coy.

"Oh Lena, I have so much work to do." He sighed. "All right. Just one dance, then I must go." He led me to the floor.

I loved the way he moved. No wild booty shaking would ever come from Giovanni. We kept our movements small and controlled. He kept his eyes focused on mine. Mine were on his. And wouldn't you know it? Jeremy came through for us and slowed the music way down. Almost like a hidden courtesy to the romantics in the room, the dance floor cleared by half. I reluctantly attempted to leave, but he pulled me back. I didn't care. I wanted to dance with him all night. He wrapped one arm around my waist and took my free hand in his. We danced cheek to cheek. In the midst of the crowded *Busco's*, I felt as if we were the only ones there and nothing else mattered.

Jeremy got back on the microphone and in a blend of English and Italian, he called out to the crowd. They responded in kind. It was almost ritualistic to hear. Most of the newbies like me just kind of stood back and listened, surprised by the response. Jeremy was really good at this. He knew precisely when to pump up the music, when to mellow it out, then get the crowd back into the groove. It was almost like watching him make love to hundreds of people all at once.

We left the dance floor as the dancers were coming back from their breaks. I said to Giovanni, "Jeremy is very good at what he does. I see why you keep him around. How did you find him?"

"Actually he found us. This is the story as he tells it. One day he and a few friends met here for drinks. They decided to stay late to check out the girls. Well, eventually the DJ began playing music. He noticed how few people were dancing, but even more upsetting was watching customers leaving within a few minutes of arrival. He was a disc jockey in his hometown of Manchester, but was looking to get out of Britain to travel Europe. He proposed how he could increase the numbers of our customers simply by playing better music. More popular, hipper music. He did not have his equipment or music with him at the time, so we agreed to listen to a demo tape he always carried. Lucio and I listened. We liked what we heard. We were always on the lookout for ways to increase business, so we decided to give him a try. I introduced him to the others, who all gave their approval. I tell you, we are like family. To hire someone who does not fit in would be a mistake. Anyway, we hired him on the spot for a one month trial period. He went back to England, packed up all his equipment and drove here. He has been with us for over five years now."

"That's a great story. He just packed up his stuff and moved here, huh?" I marveled at his bravado.

"*Sì*. Of course, this is not his only job. We pay well, but not enough to support him and his wife. He does construction during the day and works with us on the weekend. You will have the opportunity to speak with him later tonight, if you wish. *Basta!* Lena, if I wish to leave at all this evening, I must go to do my work. I will see you later. If you need me, I will be in my office."

"I understand. I've distracted you long enough. You go do what you have to. I'll be around and I promise to stay out of trouble." I swayed to the music.

"Before I go there is something I want you to do. While you are hanging out, try to pay close attention to what is going on around you. Notice how the waitresses serve the customers and their reactions when they receive their drinks. Watch who stays on the dance floor and who hangs back. Observe what food is being ordered, who is ordering it, and if any remains on the plate when it is returned to the kitchen. Take a walk outside, listen to the crowd. You won't need to interact. Just listen. Keep your eyes and ears open. You will be surprised at how much you can learn through observation."

I did just as Giovanni suggested. I hung back and watched the crowd. I saw couples hook up for the first time and relationships on the verge of ending.

Several young men sat at the bar banging down shots of liquor lined up in rows six deep. Those not participating in the revelry stood back cheering the others on to victory. Nicky and his assistant were much too busy to notice me now. I watched as they poured drinks and popped beer caps with practiced precision. The bar remained surprisingly clean. When they weren't passing out drinks or ringing up orders, they had a towel in their hands wiping up spills. Nicky gave me a wink and a smile, indicating he'd seen me watching.

Roberto and Rosalita were busy at the stove and the oven. Delicious smells circulated throughout the room. They acknowledged me, but kept right on doing what they were doing. I looked at the stack of trays the waitresses returned to the kitchen. Most were empty – no visible signs of food remained on the plates.

I walked the length of the room managing to stay out of their way. As busy as they seemed to be, the kitchen was void of stacks of dirty dishes I expected to see. For sure, if I had to cook so many meals in record time, there would be piles of dishes in the sink and all kinds of food scraps on the floor. Apparently, they were much better at this than I could ever hope to be.

I watched customers coming and going. Of those entering, most were ready to party. You could tell by their raucous laughter and loud talking. Still others entered hesitantly, as if they were just a bit unsure about this place. I'll bet this was their first time. From personal experience I knew they'd feel at home in mere minutes.

One of my favorite songs came through the incredible sound system. I bopped my head up and down to the beat. I observed how Jeremy could stir the crowd into a frenzy then effortlessly bring them back down using only his voice and music. The dancers moved in every way imaginable. Young and old alike shook what their mama gave them to the deep thumping bass of the drumbeat.

The guys at the door seemed to be having a good time flirting with the ladies, despite their rumored sexual orientation, and keeping the hardheads in order. Occasionally someone grabbed my arm to get my attention. Some simply wanted to dance. More often than not, I became the object of drunken obsession. This one guy in particular, who was not my type – way too young, became fixated with me. He slurred phrases of love in a language no one but he understood. He touched his fist to his chest whenever he saw me walk by. I thought he was hilarious. I went outside to breathe in air unadulterated by smoke and to take Giovanni's advice to listen in on a few conversations. The youngster followed me outside.

I found a seat on a bench facing *Busco's*. The club was housed in a really nice building, now that I had time to look at it clearly. *Busco's* was neighbored by a fine department store that specialized in men's clothing. A jeweler, a few nondescript businesses, and a realty office were located on either side. The façade blended in nicely with the other buildings. The only indication that this was a club was the name scripted in bright red paint on the front window and a large 'B' engraved on the brass door handle.

No one paid me any attention. I blended in and became one of them – a woman from the club taking a much needed break. For the most part, they spoke loudly in Italian while they smoked clove scented cigarettes. I picked up on a few people speaking English, although none of the conversations seemed significant. All revolved around the girls being hot, or who was going home with what guy. Comments were made about the employees, especially the guys at the door or Nicky. Way too many of the girls wanted Jeremy. They thought he was really hot. Typical club speak.

A tap on my shoulder got my attention. I turned around to find that annoying guy from earlier. He obviously had too many drinks, because his eyes couldn't remain focused for more than a few seconds. Thankfully, he lacked the drunken swagger.

I checked him out. Okay, he wasn't that bad. He looked like he was all of 22. Maybe 23. Layers of shaggy brown hair hid big brown puppy dog eyes. He had so little hair on his face he couldn't possibly need to shave more than once a week. His lips were surprisingly plump, just the right size to make some girl happy. I checked out his clothes. If he were in the states, I might wonder if he were gay. He wore a skintight yellow and blue striped nylon shirt and a pair of tight fitting jeans that managed to show every bump and bulge. His shoes looked like work boots with a slight heel. Overall, not too bad, but he was such a little boy. I'll bet he had no clue as to my real age.

"*Scusi, signora. Parla italiana?*" he asked.

"*No, non capisco,*" I replied, hoping to get rid of him before he made a scene.

"*Parla inglese?*" Maybe he wasn't as drunk as he appeared.

"*Si, parlo inglese.* What do you want?" I didn't want to be rude, but also didn't want to be bothered with a slobbering drunk. Okay, he was kind of cute, young but cute.

"You are so beautiful. I think I am in love." He returned to doing that stupid gesture of holding his hands to his heart.

People near us stopped talking, instead focusing their attention on the scene unfolding before their eyes. Damn! This is the last thing I wanted—to draw attention to myself.

"Why don't you sit down next to me?" I asked trying to put an end to this spectacle.

He sat and rested his head on my shoulder. "Do you know I fell in love the first moment I laid eyes on you tonight? You are like a bright shining star in a moonless night. What is your name?" He sat up still speaking just a little too loudly for my tastes.

"My name is Lena. And that is very nice of you. What's yours?"

"*Mi chiamo es Angelo.*" Suddenly he jumped up, grabbed my hands and yelled out, "Lena the beautiful! Dance with me!"

"But there's no music, Angelo. Why don't you sit back down and talk to me instead? Sit down!" I whispered loudly through clenched teeth, suddenly conscious of the snickering coming from the growing crowd.

"*Por favore*, please!" He dropped to his knees pretending to beg.

Oh what the hell?! This couldn't get any worse. All of a sudden, some helpful soul in the crowd cranked up a boom box playing some sappy Italian love song. The crowd surrounded us. I looked around at the smiling faces. "Okay, I'll dance." I stood up.

"*Grazie*! You will dance with me!" He clapped his hands and returned to his feet. He looked towards where the music came from and nodded his head as a signal.

I followed his gaze feeling like I'd been set up. A group of similarly dressed guys huddled around one another, egging him on. I had no idea what this kid was up to. I decided to go with the flow.

He guided my left hand to his shoulder, placed his arm around my waist and took my right hand in his free one, just as Giovanni had done earlier. The music played in the background. I followed his lead and he expertly guided me around our makeshift dance floor to the haunting melody. He twirled me around and dipped me backwards, never missing a beat. I think we were dancing the rumba or something close to it. Whatever it was, I was really feeling it! Our faces were so close I breathed in the breath he exhaled. It wasn't as heavily laced with alcohol as I initially thought it was. At times, he held me so tight it was like we were one.

This guy can really dance! And I don't mean "ass shaking dancing". He moves like he's classically trained! I was so engrossed in our dance, I didn't notice the growing crowd until the music died down, only to be replaced by applause.

"*Grazie, Signora* Lena. You dance beautifully. I knew you were the right one for dancing when I saw you glide across the floor instead of walking. Now my night is complete." His soft lips pressed against my cheek in a sweet kiss. He let me go and bowed to his audience, encouraging me to do the same. Any hint of drunkenness had all but vanished.

The crowd dispersed leaving none other than Lucio standing there, smiling and applauding our performance. I couldn't tell if he was pleased or being his cynical self.

"Lena? Why am I not surprised? Who other than you could have drawn a crowd such as this?" He referred to me then looked at Angelo. "That was a very good performance. Where do you study?"

"I am in my final year at the University of Genoa, Department of Music and Performing Arts Section. I am a theatre major," he answered proudly.

"Angelo, this is Lucio. He's a friend of mine and he owns *Busco's*." They shook hands. "How did you know he studied dance?"

"Well, Lena. Not many young men are capable of dancing in such a classical form. You were very good," and to me, "you followed him extremely well. Have you also studied dance?" asked Lucio.

"Not classical, but I have done some modern dance – mostly just for fun when I was younger. The secret to dancing is to be in synch with your partner and try to anticipate their next move. Angelo was easy and fun to dance with. Thanks!" I replied back.

Angelo took my hand in his and kissed the back of it, lingering. "*Molte grazie* Lena. You are very beautiful and very nice. Thank you for dancing with me. Until I see you again…"

He threw me a kiss, touched his fist to his heart, and backed away slowly to where his friends waited. We watched Angelo get into a car full of his friends and drive away. They tooted the horn until they were out of sight.

"He seems very nice. Perhaps a bit overly dramatic…" Lucio rolled his eyes.

"He wasn't so bad. What can you expect from a theatre major? He probably lives his entire life being overly dramatic. But he sure could dance." I was certainly impressed.

"Come back inside before you have half the young men in *Gorgazzio* chasing after you," said Lucio.

"Oh. Is present company included?" I teased.

"You are involved with my brother, so there is no need for me to answer that question. Is there? And you might wish to mention your little performance to him before someone else does. He does tend to fall on the jealous side, but as we are brothers that is to be expected. *Passione* always invokes strong feelings," replied Lucio.

I avoided answering his question with a question of my own because the last thing I wanted to talk about with Lucio was passion. "You ever thought about modeling?' I asked admiring his profile.

"No. Never. Modeling is for girls and men who wish to be girls. It is much too feminine for me to consider. How about you? Have you thought about it? With your *esotico* looks, you could easily make lots of money in my country."

I laughed at his ridiculous question. "Oh, you have got to be kidding? Right? First of all, I do not look like a model. I'm about 30 pounds heavier than any model I have ever seen. Secondly, I'm not pretty enough to model and I'm way too old for it." I knew what I saw in the mirror.

"But you are mistaken. I see many models who are not half as beautiful as you. Also, it is not good to be so skinny. You are a good size." He smiled, genuinely.

"Thanks for the compliment, but I still don't see myself that way. I think I'm popular over here because I'm different. You all don't see too many Black women running around in Italy unless they're from Africa. I think I'm more of an oddity at the moment. C'mon let's go back inside. I'm starting to get kind of cold." It was getting late and I wanted to see if Giovanni was finished with his work.

"Ah, Lena, you do not give yourself the credit you deserve. Have you ever considered that we see more than just your skin color?"

He paused, "While you are here in *Italia*, I think you should forget your American prejudices because we view life in an entirely different way."

"You know what Lucio? I think you're alright." I playfully bumped into him as we made our way back inside. It was around 1:30 a.m. and much of the crowd had thinned out. I spotted Giovanni sitting at the bar holding an almost full glass of beer talking to Nicky. We headed towards him. A few diehard partiers remained on the dance floor grooving to Jeremy's music. The waitresses relaxed at a booth, kicking off their shoes, taking a much needed break. It was probably the first they'd taken the entire night.

Giovanni looked in our direction and placed his glass on the bar. "There you two are. I looked all over for you Lena." He looked first at me then at Lucio.

"Do not worry, Gio. I was only keeping her company while she was out getting a breath of fresh air," he said to Giovanni, and then looked at the bartender. "Nicky, *una birra por favore. Grazie.* "

"Giovanni, you won't believe what just happened!" I had his full attention. "I was just walking around checking out the club like you suggested – people watching, you know? Well, I went outside to get away from all this smoke." I looked towards Lucio who was in the midst of lighting another cigarette and continued, "when this very persistent, pain-in-the-ass boy asked me to dance with him."

"He was not exactly *un ragazzo* Lena. I would say he was more like a virile young man." Lucio added with a smirk.

"Oh be quiet! Will you please let me tell him?" I said in mock anger at Lucio and then returned my focus back to Giovanni. "I saw him inside earlier, giving me the eye. Anyway, I thought he was drunk, so I tried to get rid of him. He was so persistent he actually went down to his knees, pleading with me – almost begging! All at once the crowd started cheering me on. You get the picture. I agreed to dance with him before I realized he had set me up." I explained, using my hands for exaggeration.

"What do you mean he set you up?" asked Giovanni, looking very interested.

"He was with a group of guys who had a boom box all ready to go. They turned it up playing some music I'd never heard before. He said he saw me inside earlier and decided I was the one he wanted for his dance partner. We started dancing and he was actually very good. And he wasn't so drunk after all. I think it was all part of his act."

"Giovanni, you should have seen the two of them. They performed like they were on stage. As if they had danced together many times before. I tell you, even I was impressed." He accepted the beer from Nicky, tipping his glass in appreciation.

"Thanks Lucio." I turned to his older brother. "His name was Angelo and he's a theatre major studying dance. I believe that's why he was so good. You know what? I enjoyed dancing with him." I leaned over and whispered low enough only for Giovanni to hear, "but he wasn't half as good as you."

"I am happy you are enjoying yourself. And I know of this Angelo person. I have seen him dance before and I do agree he is very good. You should feel honored he chose you. I only wish I was there to see the dance with my own eyes." He sipped his beer and motioned for me to sit on the empty stool next to his.

"Something for you *Signora*?" asked Nicky displaying pure professionalism.

He must be showing off for the boss. "Why not? It seems like everyone else is having a drink. I'll take a *rossa birra* please." I joined Giovanni at the bar. "Well, did you get all your work completed?" I wanted so much to wrap my arms around his neck and plant a big, wet kiss directly on his lips.

"For you." Nicky placed the amber beer on the counter.

"*Mi'amica*, you seem to be the popular one here tonight. Remember what I told you when we were in *Venezia* about Italian men and their love of all things beautiful? It is in our blood." Giovanni whispered so quietly only I could hear.

I could get used to this attention. These men were a real boost to my fragile ego, especially after endless years of receiving little or no compliments from my husband. Why did I have to think about Mark? Here I am having such a good time, soaking up all this admiration when all of a sudden my real life intrudes. In truth, I didn't think of myself as especially pretty, or sexy, or worth drooling over at all. I'm simply me. My self-esteem was in the red zone for so long. I'm almost ashamed to admit I had let myself go. But no more, it's my time now! Lena time! Time for me to get my groove back, much like Stella did in that movie, back in the day. First, I had to take care of business back home then I could really begin living the life destined for me. I felt a plan brewing.

"Are you alright? You seem to be a million miles away," asked Giovanni.

"Yeah, I was just thinking how much I enjoy being here – with you, and of course all the others." The lights dimmed once, twice, three times, then came back bright. "I guess that's Jeremy's signal that *Busco's* is about to close?"

"*Si*. In about fifteen more minutes. All in all, I think tonight was a good night. Now if we can just get rid of those few stragglers over there, we can all prepare to close and go home." He made reference to a booth filled with four women and two men. "You stay here. I know them. I will be right back." He stepped down from his stool and went to talk to his last customers of the night. He spoke to them as if they were old friends.

"How do you like your beer?" Nicky leaned across the bar. A few stray hairs managed to come loose from his ponytail, ending up in his face. He removed the band freeing the rest of his mane.

"I like it. It's good beer. Nicky, you know you have really nice hair? It's so thick and shiny." I commented on his shoulder length locks while I sipped my beer, wondering where Lucio disappeared.

He ran his fingers through his long hair gathering it all back together. He replaced the hair band and revealed, "The secret to beautiful hair is using lots of olive oil. I will also tell you another secret of mine. When I wore my hair short, I met only a few women. Now that my hair is longer, so many girls want to run their fingers through it I cannot keep up with them. But tonight, there was no one who interested me. Maybe tomorrow night will be different?" He shrugged indifferently.

"Well, here's to tomorrow." I raised my glass towards him.

"*Si. Ecco domani.* Perhaps, *you* would like to run *your* fingers through my hair? Hmmm?" He teased. At least I think he was teasing.

I let his comment go without responding. No need to. I spun around on my stool and looked at the now empty club. It was amazingly quiet. And Giovanni did manage to get his last customers to leave after all, with minor protests. He locked the doors behind them and turned off the front lights. The guys who watched the doors left when the last customers did.

"*Busco's* is officially closed!" He yelled out to his employees. "Thanks to you all, it was another successful night!"

His announcement was met with whoops and yells from the staff. Jeremy had already begun to pack up his music and shut down his equipment for the night. As if on cue, all the dance floor lights went off one by one. Sounds of pots and pans being put away came from the kitchen, clearly audible now that the music was gone. The waitresses were sitting down in one of the booths busily tallying their tips, making sure all received an even split. Nicky quickly forgot about me and was now busy ringing out his register, quickly stuffing tonight's money and receipt tape into a large moneybag to be counted later in the office. His assistant was busily washing down the countertops, putting empty glasses into the dishwasher, and simultaneously sweeping up the floor behind the bar.

Lena turned to Giovanni and asked, "Is there anything I can do? I feel so useless just sitting here."

He accepted the moneybag from Nicky and said, "Lena, follow me."

I followed him to the kitchen where Roberto and Rosalita were just finishing up. He checked that the backdoor was securely locked. *Busco's* policy was to have all employees leave through the front door after closing, thus insuring the back door wasn't left open by mistake as happened one time in the past. Luckily, it was discovered by the *polizia* making their nightly rounds rather than some unscrupulous person intent on doing damage.

Lucio sat in the office at a small table with money spread out before him like food at a banquet. An adding machine with a small roll of paper was set off to the side. He looked up apparently not surprised to find me there.

"Lena, sit here next to me. You can help separate the bills and coins. After all is separated, then we count."

Giovanni locked the door behind us and handed Lucio the moneybag. His focus was intense as he pulled up the files showing tonight's numbers. I sat next to Lucio and did as he did, separating the euro by denomination. I put the coins in a different bucket, because their coin counter not only counted coins, but wrapped them as well. "This went much faster when the currency was still *lira*. We arranged quickly by size. When the new euro went into circulation, we were accepting both types of currency, but we all had to be educated on how to spot counterfeit bills. We had two deposits, one for the *lira*, and the other for the euro. It was very confusing. Many criminals took advantage during that time when so many were confused about the authenticity. We took extreme care to not accept counterfeit money. Now, I can separate the bills as quickly as Giovanni can pull up all the different computer programs."

"What's he doing over there?" I whispered, sneaking a peek at him thoroughly engrossed in whatever he was doing. He resembled more of a shrewd businessman, than my lovable Giovanni.

"He is capturing the data from the cash register. You see, whenever Nicky or his assistant made a sale, they entered that information, including the type of drink, number purchased and the method of payment. Anything that is sold or given away, such as your complimentary drinks, is entered into the computerized cash register that is linked into one big system. The totals from the computer should match the total amount of euro's we have in front of us."

"That's a very good system. Does it work?" I dropped coin after coin from the bag into the bucket on the floor.

"*Si*, it works extremely well. Better than we expected. Our inventory is also tied into the system, which can notify us when we need to place an order." His nimble fingers quickly arranged the bills into perfect piles.

I placed the colourful bills into different stacks separated by denominations of €5, €10, €20, €50 and an occasional €100. Then we inserted each stack into a mechanized bill counter and wrote the individual sums down on the bank deposit sheet. When all was tallied, rolled, and banded together, *Busco's* final take for the night was €5,063.78. The total was off by only €1. That was a lot of money spent for liquor and food! Both brothers signed the deposit slip and put the bag into the safe where it would remain until the bank deposit on Monday morning.

Nicky and Jeremy waited at the bar. They followed the same routine every night. It was their way of looking out for the brothers, their friends, as well as employer—who remained locked away in the back room. Giovanni and Lucio did their final walk through, checking closets, restrooms and underneath benches for those unfortunate enough to have been left behind. Tonight they found no one lurking where they shouldn't have been. With the flick of a switch and the turn of a key, *Busco's* once again stood quiet in anticipation of the next night's extravaganza.

CHAPTER 22

"*Ciao* Jeremy. *Ciao* Nicky. See you tomorrow." I waved good-bye to Busco's staff. I caught up with Giovanni and Lucio walking towards their respective cars, parked next to each other across the street. I stood between Lucio's cherry red *Ferrari* parked on my right and Giovanni's black BMW Z4 Roadster to my left. Their choice of cars spoke volumes about the brothers.

"*Va bene.* It is time to go. Lena, I will see you tomorrow?" Lucio broke the awkward silence.

"Yes Lucio. I will see you tomorrow and I had a good time tonight. It was fun hanging out with you guys." I felt Giovanni's eyes on me. "Well, *buona notte.*" I kissed him on both cheeks. He returned the favor.

Giovanni reached for his brother. They embraced and said good night to one another. Lucio got in his *Ferrari* and drove off.

"Have you decided what you wish to do tonight? The offer to stay with me is still open. I would love your company."

He looked at me with those gorgeous eyes and there was no way I could turn him down. I didn't even consider it.

"Alright, let's do it. I've got to stop by my room and pick up a few things. And I might as well get an outfit for tomorrow night." I couldn't wait to wrap my arms around him, so I did the next best thing and held his hand.

"As you wish." He eased his car onto the eerily quiet street and turned towards the direction of Simona's house.

The little cottage was bathed in the kind of darkness that only comes in the wee hours of the night. Subtle light from the full moon provided only enough illumination for us to find our way. This time when I opened the door and turned on the light, I made sure to look for any messages that may have fallen to the floor. There were none. I quickly chose an outfit. As an afterthought, I grabbed the suit that needed to be taken to the cleaners, and my entire lot of toiletries, which wasn't very much. I surveyed the room for anything else I needed. I couldn't think of anything else.

Minutes later we entered Giovanni's home carrying an overly stuffed suitcase. I kicked off my shoes, leaving them by the front door.

The events of the day suddenly overwhelmed me. It was well past 4 in the morning and I was totally whipped.

"Lena, you may put your clothing in my closet and your bath items in *il bagno* off my bedroom." Giovanni pointed to the hallway bathroom. He looked tired.

I opened the doors of his massive mahogany armoire and was not at all surprised to find his clothing hanging neatly from satin clothes hangers. The shirts were arranged by sleeve length and color, all facing in the same direction. His pants were neatly arranged and all sweaters were folded and put away on the shelves. I didn't know where to put my clothes. I didn't want to mess up his things. And I wasn't sure how much of a neat freak he really was.

He saw my dilemma. "Here let me help you with that," he said and casually pushed his clothing aside, making room. He placed my clothes right in the middle for easy access.

"Thank you. I wasn't sure if I should move anything. Your closet is so tidy." I turned around to see his smiling face.

"Now that you have seen my closet, you know all there is to know about me. The way I keep my home, the way I run my business – it is all how I live my life. I like to know where everything is at all times. Nice, neat, and simple. However, I also have a wildly passionate side, a side I have become reacquainted with since I have met you." He backed me against his clothes.

"Careful now! We don't want to mess up this closet of yours." I playfully ducked under his arms and went into the bathroom. I motioned for him to follow. I turned on the *jacuzzi* and ran the water very warm. From my toiletry bag, I retrieved a bottle of scented bubble bath and poured it into the running water. The room immediately filled with the scent of jasmine. He stood in the doorway watching. Amazed and pleased at my boldness in making myself right at home. I placed the vanilla scented candles around the bathroom and turned off all the bathroom lights. "Hey Giovanni? Will you play your *Sogno* CD by Andrea Bocelli for me? Whenever I hear that music, I just...." I shuttered and exhaled.

"Of course. I will be back in just a moment."

While he was gone, I tested the water. It was the perfect temperature. I moved the candles around until the light and mood was perfect for romance. The music came through the speakers set deep within the walls. I loved listening to the deep, rich voice of Bocelli. Giovanni returned to the bathroom, shutting the door behind him.

"Ah. *Amore mio*. Are you attempting to seduce me?" He slipped the strap of my blouse from my shoulder, replacing it with an erotic kiss.

"I, uh, yeah. That was my plan," I replied, in between deep breaths. "Giovanni, I've got to turn off the water before it overflows." I tried to pull away, but he stopped me.

"Stay here. I will do it for you." He reached for the faucets, turning both to the off position. He freed the other strap and pulled my top over my head. Within moments we both stood totally nude. I loved how the candle light bounced off his body, strategically shading some places, while highlighting others. I could stand here looking at him and listening to this haunting music for the rest of my life. And I was no longer self-conscious of my body not being perfect. He made it known how he accepted me no matter what I looked like. We kissed, slowly, tenderly, passionately…ending up on the cold tile floor making love, exploring one another's body, enjoying wave after wave of orgasmic bliss.

Giovanni, calculating and methodical in his business, was quite the opposite making love. He combined tenderness and passion with some good old fashioned bumping and grinding making me yell for more. When we made love, I wanted him in me, on me, around me… My toes curled over and over again! I can honestly proclaim to the world that out of all the lovers I've had in my life he was the absolute best!

After round two, we were absolutely spent. He pulled the drain from the tub of now cool water and we both decided a hot shower would be quicker, although a bath would've been extremely nice. The shower stall was cramped with the two of us inside, but that didn't matter. We stood under the steaming water, wrapped in each other's arms, enjoying the sensation of having our bodies so close together.

"Lena, we must get some rest or we will both be worthless later today. Here let me help you dry off." He took the towel and gently dried my back.

"Yeah, you're right. The sun is going to be coming up soon. What time does *Busco's* open today."

"On *sabato* the doors open at 4 p.m. and we close at 2 in the morning. For *dominica* we are closed. What do you think about driving up to see my village again? We can leave directly — like we did before?" His eyes clouded over at the reference to "before".

"Listen, how about we not make my previous trip a big deal anymore? As far as everyone else is concerned, I was really here. Who knows? Maybe I actually did have some kind of amnesia, flew over here, met you then returned home a couple of weeks later." I touched his still wet face. I reached for a clean towel hanging from a bar and began drying him, as he'd done for me. Apparently I wasn't doing a good enough job, so he took the towel and proceeded to towel the water from his body.

"I hate to bring this up, but *when are you* returning home?" he asked, avoiding my eyes.

I had thought about it, but kept pushing the issue to the back of my mind. When was I going to return to my old life and leave this man I had quickly fallen in love with? I hadn't spent much money, not counting my rent to Simona and the clothes I bought. But it would soon run out. And although I didn't dwell on it, I really missed my children. They were the only reason to leave Giovanni behind and return to my prior life. Mark, well, I didn't miss him at all. And in my heart of hearts, I didn't want to go back.

"Well, I have an open ticket. But my son's high school graduation is next week. Sunday." I looked at his face, seeing the hurt I brought to him.

"*Va bene. Capisco.* You shall return to your home in a week to see your son graduate. I would not be so selfish as to insist on your staying with me causing you to miss such an important event. However, until the time you get on that airplane, you will be mine, *amore mio. Sì?*"

I hated seeing him in such agony — a misery that lay squarely at my feet. "Giovanni, if I could change everything, I would. All I want is to be with you, but I have to also be there for my boys. You understand, don't you?" I pleaded.

"Lena, yes I do understand, but life is too short for such complications," he replied looking in the mirror, studying his day's growth of beard. "I need to rest, are you coming to bed?"

"Yes, but first I have a few personal things to do." I applied lotion as he stood watching from the door. When I pulled out night cream for my face and foot cream for my feet, he sighed and went to the bedroom. I heard the bed creak under his weight and the rustle of sheets. Within minutes I heard light snoring. I smiled.

I sat on the toilet thinking about how I was going to get myself out of this mess. In the past when things got really bad, there was only one person I could talk to who'd help me figure things out.

Though we weren't as close as we used to be, she was there when I needed her. She was there when I thought I was having a miscarriage with my last child. She talked me out of leaving Mark when I told her about his creepin' around. She advised me to think about the children. If I could provide them with a better life, then leave. If not, I should stay until I could. She encouraged me to take that job at the factory whether I liked the work or not, because it brought in some badly needed cash.

Yes, my mother always came through for me. However, this time it was different. This time I wasn't so sure. One thing I did know, I couldn't wait a week to speak to her. I did have my cell phone. One short phone call to the states could eat up my minutes in no time flat. Oh, well. I'd just have to buy more time tomorrow.

I wrapped myself in Giovanni's terry cloth robe hanging on the back of the bathroom door. I quietly opened the top drawer of his dresser, noticing he'd placed his wallet and keys in a decorative box on top, and borrowed a pair of athletic socks. I slipped them on my feet, found my purse, retrieved my cell phone, and quietly opened the French doors to the balcony. It was cold. Thank goodness the robe was long enough to cover my legs. I didn't have any idea what time it was back home, but it didn't matter. If my Mom was there, she'd take the call.

"Hello?" answered a male voice I didn't recognize.

"Hi. Is my mother there?" I asked.

"Who 'dis?" asked the voice on the other end.

"This is Lena. Who is this?"

"Hey Auntie Lena. This is Ramone. Whassup Auntie? You still living in flat assed Kansas?" asked my nephew, sounding like he had just a little too much of whatever it was he was into these days.

"Yeah, I'm still living there. How ya doing? You still making them babies?"

At 24 years old, Ramone had seven kids by three different women and hadn't shown any intentions of slowing down.

"Naw, Auntie. I ain't down with that no more. Too many mouths to feed."

"I heard that. Hey it's good talking to you. Is Momma there?" My time was slowly ticking away.

"Hold on Auntie, I'll go get her." The phone probably fell on the floor because I actually heard it bounce a couple of times.

"Hello Lena. Well it's about time you called. The boys told me you went out of town. Where'd you go this time?" She yelled something undistinguishable to someone in the background.

"Momma, I need to talk to you. This is serious." I didn't have time to waste with small talk.

"What is it Lena? Is something wrong with the kids? With you?" She sounded worried.

"No, nothing like that. We're all fine. In fact, James is graduating next week. You are coming right?" I had to put her mind at ease before I continued.

"Of course, I'm coming. I wouldn't miss seeing that child walk across that stage for nothing in the world. Now, what's so important?"

"Momma, I'm going to file for divorce from Mark as soon as I get home." I said the words aloud for the first time, marvelling at how good it felt to actually say them.

"You're going to do what?! And what do you mean when you get home? Where are you, Lena?" She sounded desperate.

"I'm filing for divorce. I've told you about our problems before. Well, it's been the same old thing year after year and I'm tired of going through it. No amount of work on either of our parts is going to change anything. We've gone to counselling for couples, tried talking to a minister, and even tried separating a few times. Nothing worked. I'm just ready to move on. Now don't try to talk me out of it. I need your support not your judgment. I'm not in love with him and haven't been for years. Momma, I'm tired of being in an unhappy marriage. I am tired of being unhappy period. My mind is made up. It's over." Hot tears of anger, mixed with hopelessness rolled down my face. I used the sleeve of the robe that smelled like Giovanni to dry them away.

"Girl, I do believe you have lost your mind. Where are you?" She demanded.

"I'm in Italy – staying with a friend." I heard nothing but silence on the other end.

"In Italy? Staying with a friend?" She repeated after letting the reality of my words sink in. For the first time in my mother's life, I think she was speechless.

"Lena, this friend you're with... Is he why you're leaving your husband?" Her voice was soft, gentle, almost understanding.

"No, Mom. He's not the reason. He has nothing to do with my decision to divorce Mark. This is something that is a long time coming.

It's been so many years since we were happy. I can't even remember the last time we spoke about anything substantial. I've stayed with him all these years only because of the boys." I sniffed.

"You know how I feel about Mark. I love him like he's my own son. I sure would hate to see the two of you break up. I hoped at least you two would make it work, not like your sisters. What are you going to tell the children?"

"I'll tell them that we grew apart. They are not stupid. They've seen how we've acted towards each other over the years. Hell, we don't even sleep in the same bed anymore." I ignored her comparison to both my sister's marriages ending.

"Who is this man you're staying with? And how did you end up in Italy? Is he Italian or what?" Her curiosity peaked again.

Now I don't like lying to my mother, but sometimes a daughter has to stretch the truth.

"Yes Mom, he's Italian. His name is Giovanni Morelli. You remember we used to live here before? Well, I met him back then and we stayed in touch. It wasn't anything serious, we were just email friends. I decided to come over for a visit and it just happened." Thoughts of Giovanni made me feel giddy just talking about him.

"Baby, does he make you happy? Does he treat you right?" Her voice sounded farther away than the distance created by miles.

"Yes Mom, he makes me very happy. I am crazy about him. When we're together, nothing else matters. I love looking at him. l love the way he speaks, the way he holds a pen, how he walks. The way he smells. How he eats soup without slurping. I love his strength and his gentleness. I love how caring he is. How attentive he is. He listens and values my opinion. He's very intelligent and teaches me things – with patience. Mom, he knows how to dance and can even carry a tune better than most of today's so-called singers. He's the most thoughtful, caring, honest, sweetest man I have ever known. I've never felt this way before. Not with Keenan, not with Mark, not with anyone." Upon realizing how loudly I spoke, I purposely lowered my voice.

"Honey, you know I don't like interfering in your marriage. If this man can make you feel like this and the feelings last and only get stronger, then it's probably the real thing. I understand you wanting to leave your husband. I've wanted to leave your Daddy many a times. But the truth is I love him. Always have, always will. I'm sure the boys will handle it just fine. James will be on his own in a couple of months. Neil will be a senior next year and will be on his way soon. That only leaves Carlos. He's the one you have to worry about. I'm not too sure how he'll react to having his parents split up."

"I know. I'm not sure how I'll handle Carlos. He's such a sensitive child," I hesitated. "Mom, there's one more thing."

"What is it Lena?"

"I'm seriously thinking about moving to Italy." Just then the operator came on with a one minute warning that my time was about to end.

"Who was that? Sounded like a foreign language. It sounded like you said something about moving to Italy!" She laughed.

"Yeah, Mom that was the operator. I'm using a cellular phone I bought to use over here." I didn't tell her about Giovanni being fast asleep inside. "Listen, I can't talk anymore, my time is about to run out. I'll be home for James's graduation next weekend. We'll talk more then. Thanks for listening Mom. You've helped more than you know. I love you." I dabbed at my eyes.

"I love you too, Lena. You be careful over there and don't pick up nothing you can't get rid of. I'll see you when you get home." We were cut off just as she got out her last words.

It was quiet and peaceful out here. I walked to the edge of the balcony to get a better look at the beginnings of the sunrise. I smelled cigarette smoke. I looked down barely making out a male figure with a bright orange glow where his mouth should've been. It was Lucio.

I leaned over the railing. He walked from underneath wearing only a skimpy pair of briefs that left nothing to the imagination. Oh my!

"Uh, hi Lucio. What are you doing up so early?" I questioned. I wondered how much of my conversation he heard.

"*Ciao* Lena, I see you are spending the night. Where is Giovanni? Is he asleep?" He snubbed the cigarette into a potted plant.

"Yeah, he's asleep." I had to ask. I couldn't go to bed until I knew the answer. "Lucio, did you hear any of my conversation with my mother?"

He stalled, possibly weighing the advantages against the disadvantages of being an eavesdropper versus a liar.

"*Si, si* Lena. I heard your entire conversation. I was standing here enjoying the sounds of the night, having a cigarette before going to bed, when I heard you. *Mi dispiace*. I could not help but to listen," he answered. His face was more distinguishable with the approaching light of the day.

I exhaled out all the remaining air inside my lungs. I looked up at the colors becoming more visible in the morning sky. I had nothing to say. I shook my head and lowered my chin.

"Lena?" he asked, "does Giovanni know?"

I nodded. "Most of it. Not everything," I answered, feeling the tears fall freely.

"Do not worry. Your secret will remain safe with me. Tell him in your time. On your terms." He smiled a smile that reached all the way up to me.

"Thank you Lucio. That means so much to me. Thank you so, so much." I touched my hands to my heart.

"*Prego*. Now, I must get some rest. I will see you later. Okay?" He waved his hand disappearing from my view.

I returned inside and closed the doors behind me making certain the heavy curtains were drawn to keep out the light of the rising sun. The music of Bocelli continued to play in the background. I quietly tiptoed to the living room and turned off the stereo. When I got into the warm bed, Giovanni wrapped his arms around me. I snuggled back towards him and sank into the welcoming warmth of his body. Happy and content, I quickly fell fast asleep.

I awoke to the sound of Giovanni singing some new popular song I recognized from last night. He actually sounded pretty good. I felt more groggy than refreshed when I saw it was already a little after noon. I dragged my sleepy butt out of bed, used the bathroom, brushed my teeth, and tried to make myself slightly presentable. I borrowed one of his oversized T-shirts before padding out to the kitchen in his socks. Giovanni was casually dressed in khaki pants and a pink silk t-shirt looking fine as wine. Does he own any jeans? He was stooped over the oven pulling out a delicious smelling dish.

"*Buon giorno, bella donna*." He sat the pan on the countertop and planted a huge kiss on me. "Sit here. I have cooked for you. We have *frittata*, croissants, and fresh strawberries. Would you like a *cappuccino* to begin?" He led me to a stool at the counter where all the food was laid out. It looked and smelled delicious.

"*Buon giorno*. Yes, a *cappuccino* sounds great." I returned the kiss tasting traces of coffee. "Mmmm. That smells really wonderful! What is it?" I inhaled the aroma of the spread laid out before me.

"This is a *frittata*--eggs, onions, vegetables and cheese. It is similar to an omelette, but is cooked in the oven. I was just about to wake you. You have perfect timing. I hope you are hungry."

He looked so cute standing there with oven mitts on his hands.

"Oh. You are so sweet. Thank you so much for cooking breakfast! Let me help you. I have been known to make a pretty mean cup of *cappuccino* myself." I noticed an envelope laying on the counter with my name on it. "Giovanni, what's this?"

"Lucio dropped that off this morning. He said you would understand." He shrugged and poured fresh coffee beans into the grinder.

"I wonder what it could be..." I said aloud, turning it over in my hands. I pulled the envelope flaps apart and pulled out a simple white card. The card contained a phone card, with more time than I would possibly use to recharge my cell phone. The white card contained no words only Lucio's stylish signature.

"What is it?" he asked while pouring water into the bottom of the coffeepot. He added the freshly ground coffee and placed the pot on the stove over a low flame.

"Well, this was sure nice of him. It's a phone card for my cellular phone. After you went to sleep, I went out on the balcony to call my mother. He must have overheard me when I told her I was running out of minutes and had to hang up. I didn't know he was there until I told her goodbye." I appreciated his thoughtfulness.

"Lena, you could have used my phone to call your mama. *Amore mio*, whatever I have is for your use. Next time, okay?" He glanced towards the stove, waiting for the coffee to boil. He shook his head in mock frustration and said, "My brother behaves so strangely at times. He should not have been listening to your conversation. I shall have a talk with him." He warmed the milk in a separate pan in preparation for the frothing.

"It's okay. He apologized for eavesdropping. Actually, he was already out there smoking before I made the phone call. No harm done. You know, you really wore me out last night. I had such fun with you. I can't wait to do it again."

I placed a strawberry in his mouth and sealed it with a kiss. The coffeepot began to gurgle. I slipped a mitten off his hand and used it to remove the pot. After carefully frothing the milk, trying not to make much of a mess, I poured the espresso into two cups. I noticed the Italian cups are smaller than the average American sized coffee cup and nowhere near as huge as those bowls we like to call *cappuccino* cups.

I topped off the hot liquid with a healthy head of foamy milk and set the two cups side by side. The perfect prelude to our meal. We ate, fed each other, laughed about the previous evening, and all in all had a great afternoon meal.

After brunch, I got dressed while he straightened up the kitchen. We took a casual stroll through the town, as was his custom after eating a large meal. Quite possibly this was one of the reasons he stayed in such good physical shape. It was early Saturday and the streets were filled with shoppers scurrying from store to store.

"Lena, I have been thinking. And I want you to carefully consider what I am about to say." He cleared his throat, looking towards the sky as if some huge answer was going to materialize from the air.

I stopped, anxious to hear his next words. "What is it?" I turned to face him wondering what could be so serious.

"Um, uh, I would like for you to move in with me – for the remainder of your time here. You are with me all the time as it is. It makes no sense to keep a room for your clothes only. Stay with me."

"Yes! Yes! Of course I will stay with you! I'd like nothing more! The only problem may be Simona. I hope she doesn't give me too difficult of a time about moving early. I told her I'd pay a month's rent if she let me stay for a couple of weeks." If staying with Giovanni was the alternative, I didn't really mind paying her for the entire month.

"*Fantastico*! And do not worry about Signora Malavasi. Trust me. I have dealt with these women before. I will speak to her if you wish, but I believe she will treat you fairly." He smiled as if a weight had been lifted from his shoulders. "Come. Let us go get your things now. We have another busy night tonight. After closing, we leave for *Piano Montissimo*." We returned to the house to get his car.

Lucio was coming through the front gate pushing a bicycle just as we made it to the car. He was decked out in a fluorescent yellow bike riding outfit carrying a helmet and goggles. "*Ciao* Giovanni. *Ciao* Lena. I am going for a ride. Would you care to join me?" he asked more towards his brother than me.

"No. Not today, Lucio. We have a few errands to take care of before work. Hey, just so you know, Lena will be spending more time here. I have invited her to stay with me for the remainder of her vacation. *Capisce?*" He nodded, letting him know he meant business.

I added, "*Ciao* Lucio. Thanks for the phone card. You really didn't have to do that." I wanted to go over and give him a big hug, but thought better of it.

Lucio held up his hands in surrender. "Gio, no need for you to clear your plans with me. I like Lena. I think she is good for you and I hope one day she will make *bella Italia* her home *permanente. Ciao!*" He said before hopping on his bicycle.

"Now what did he mean by that?" asked Giovanni.

I decided then and there I wasn't going to keep any more secrets from him. During the short drive to Simona's house, I clued him in on my conversation with my mother. I included the part about Lucio overhearing it all and swearing himself to secrecy. I told him about my decision to divorce Mark and how it really wasn't because of him or even about him. I didn't want him to feel he was breaking up my family. And I even decided to tell him about my considering moving to Italy. If he had any problems or concerns with this idea, now would be a good time to find out, rather than waiting until later.

He slowly took in my explanation. "Are you sure you want to do this, Lena?" He parked the car in front of Simona's and turned off the engine.

"Yeah, it'll only take a few minutes to pack all my things. Probably less than that to talk to Simona." I looked at his expression, immediately knowing we were referring to two different subjects. "Oh, you mean about moving here? Well, I've been thinking about it. I'm kind of confused, but I think it will be a good thing – the right thing for me. Since moving back to the United States all I've thought about is returning to Italy. I love your simplicity of life and zest for living. Living in Italy has been my dream for years. Of course, first I'd have to find a job and a place to live."

He paused for a moment and said, "If you decide to live here, you could work with me. And you may stay with me in my home for as long as you wish."

I shook my head in protest. "No, no thanks, Giovanni. Look, if I'm going to move here, I'm going to have to maintain some kind of independence. I'll need my own space. As much as I enjoy being with you, I don't want you to get tired of me because I'm in your face all day and *all night*. For now, it's different because we know I'll be leaving soon. If I were to move into your place *and* work for you, well, we just might get sick and tired of seeing each other. What we have is still new and fresh. I want to keep it like this as long as possible." I also had to consider the possibility of my youngest son coming along with me. However, now was not the time to discuss that one very important detail.

"I understand. But how will you find work without speaking the language? And you must know it is extremely difficult for foreigners to move here without having a job. You will initially receive a 60 day tourist visa. If you do not find a job within that time to obtain a working visa, you must leave the country. Unlike your country, we enforce our immigration laws." He stared ahead, considering the possibilities.

"I've been thinking about that. Remember I told you I lived here a few years ago when my husband was stationed with the military? Well, they, the United States government, hire people all the time, bringing them overseas to work. I think I'll stop by the human resources department on the post when I return and ask a few questions. You know, see if there's anything available. Maybe I can make a few connections and get my foot in the door. There's no guarantee they'll have any openings, but for now it's a possibility." I was both afraid and excited about the notion of moving all the way to Italy – by myself.

"*Va bene*. Whatever you decide, either way, remember I will be here for you, as your friend before anything else. And the offer I made was sincere. From *mi cuore*. Now let us go get your things."

Fifteen minutes and three hundred euros later, we were on our way back to unload my clothing in his apartment. Simona had been very understanding, although a bit skeptical at my abrupt change of living arrangements. In the end, she knew that love won out over common sense every time.

Giovanni made room in the guestroom for my things. I had the choice of using his bathroom or the guest bathroom. I chose the latter. His was so organized, plus I felt funny about moving his stuff around to make room for mine. I didn't mind. It was just a place to keep my things, nothing more. He told me to make myself at home. I did. All the discomfort we felt initially was gone, and was replaced with the familiarity and comfort of being long time friends, as well as lovers.

CHAPTER 23

Busco's was filled with diners enjoying the delicious spoils from the kitchen. The succulent aroma of onions and garlic wafted from the back and permeated the air. Nicky was behind the bar joking around with a young couple indulging in shots. Subtle background music played from the in house speakers as the television behind the bar broadcast the latest soccer match between *Lazio* and *Perugia*. The occasional overzealous fan yelled out loudly when his team of favor scored. Even so, the noise level was nothing compared to the night before.

Jeremy had yet to arrive. He still had a couple of hours to go before changing the atmosphere from the casual *ristorante* to a "get your groove on" discotheque. Giovanni made his rounds greeting each employee like they were part of the family before finally retreating into his office. I decided to wait for him at the bar.

"*Ciao* Lena. I see you are brave enough for a second night of this madness? *Bene.* What can I get for you?" I noticed Nicky had gotten a haircut, cleaning up the extra hairs around his hairline. He also trimmed back his moustache.

"*Ciao* Nicky. How could I resist another night of *dancing and partying*? I'll just have water for now please. Thanks."

"Lena, there is a rumour of Giovanni being more than your mentor. Is it true? Do you and he have something more going on the side?" he whispered conspiratorially so only I could hear.

I looked deeply into his eyes in search for an ulterior motive. I didn't see any malice, only curiosity. Yet I still wasn't about to put our business out there. "Nicky. You know how rumours spread. I don't know why you should say such a thing about your friend and *employer*." This time *I* raised *my* eyebrows.

He backed away returning to his side of the counter. "Okay. Okay. I will let it rest for now. But I will be watching you. Just so you know, nothing goes on in this club without me knowing about it. And if the rumour does turn out to be true… I say, good for you. Sorry for me, but good for you." He poured a beer from the tap and placed it in front of me. "I remember you like *rossa birra*. It is only half a litre, not enough to do you any harm."

I accepted the beer and raised it in a toast. "To Nicky. May you always remain observant with your eyes and discrete in your voice." This was my way of confirming his present suspicions about our relationship without coming right out and saying it.

"*Capisco.*" His tone of voice conveyed his understanding, "My lips are sealed." He made a zipping motion across his mouth. Soon more customers bellied up to the bar taking his attention away from me.

The young waitresses stopped by to pick up their drinks, apparently aware of the passing rumour of my relationship with Giovanni. Their response was unexpected. I anticipated a hostile reaction dripping with jealousy, resentment, and mistrust. Instead what I received was filled with nothing but warmth and affection. They began treating me like I was part of their large family. It felt good.

Much too quickly, the night passed and closing time arrived promptly at 2. After Lucio locked the doors after the last customers, Giovanni and I retreated to the office to count the money. I followed the procedures exactly like Lucio showed me the previous night. Giovanni's fingers worked the keyboard, pulling up databases and spreadsheets to track their business. I separated the bills from the coins, put each in the counter, annotated the amount on the deposit slips and patiently waited for Giovanni to complete his online transactions.

We both looked up when we heard a key turning in the lock. It was Lucio coming to help finish up so they all could go home.

"Lena, you have finished so quickly. We may just have to put you on the payroll if you stay with us. What did you get for your total?" He pulled up a chair and sat down besides me.

"See, I did exactly as you showed me yesterday. I only had to bother Giovanni a few times, but he really didn't mind. Did you?" I looked back at him busily making his keyboard work overtime.

"Did you say something Lena?" He looked up distracted, his glasses rested on the tip of his nose.

"No. I was just joking around with Lucio." I looked at Lucio as if we shared a special connection, "Okay, you asked about the total. I counted out €5,989.07. How close are we?"

He retrieved the printout from Giovanni's desk and said, "We are right on the money. To the last coin. Amazing! There are not many days when all is this perfect. This is a good sign, Lena." He looked at each stack, verified the totals against the deposit sheet, and then stuffed the cash into the bag. He gave the bag and sheet to Giovanni who also verified and initialled the totals. Giovanni fastened the bag with the attached lock and placed it into the safe. A final spin of the dial insured it was securely locked.

He turned to face his brother and said, "Lena and I will be driving to *Piano Montissimo* tonight. I need you to make the bank deposits tomorrow. We only plan to be there for the day. If we decide to remain longer, I will call you. Okay?" With the push of a button, the computer screen flickered off.

"*Si*, I can take the deposit to the bank. Do not worry. I want you to go and have fun. Why not stay for two days instead of one? I can handle the club's business without you for a couple of days. Show Lena the magnificent waterfalls. I am certain she will enjoy seeing them." He stepped towards Giovanni and put his arm around his shoulder. "Leave it all to me, big brother. I will take care of everything. I want you to go, get to know this *bella donna* better and come back refreshed and ready to go. Oh, I forgot to tell you I have a race coming up and I need you to cover for me at the end of the week." Both men laughed.

"*Grazie*, Lucio. And I will cover for you at the end of the week. It will not be a problem." He opened the door and flicked off the light switch. We were finished with the business for the night. "Lena, are you ready?"

Standing in the mostly dark room, the pupils of his eyes expanded so rapidly the green iris was almost nonexistent. I was mesmerized at how quickly it happened.

I nodded, admiring how much the two of them actually seemed to like one another. Too often siblings let rivalry get in the way of their mutual success. And to look at the Morelli brothers, you would think they were conceited and full of themselves. They were handsome to a fault, owned their own successful business, and could probably have any woman of their choosing. Yet, once you got to know them, they were the most caring, down-to-earth people you could ever hope to meet. I followed them out the door to the bar to where Jeremy and Nicky waited.

While the other three were busily going over the night's events, I talked to Jeremy. He only worked Thursday, Friday, and Saturday. I wouldn't see him again for several days.

"Hi Lena, I hoped to be able to catch up with you, but it's been so busy. How are you enjoying yourself? Seen any interesting sights since you've been here?" asked Jeremy.

He fastened the straps of a huge suitcase-like container that held all his music His dreadlocks hung well past the middle of his back. I so much wanted to touch them. He noticed me focusing on his hair.

"You like my hair? I must say it is somewhat of a conversation starter whenever I travel this country." He fingered a thick rope of hair hanging in his face.

"I'm sorry. I didn't mean to stare. I know how rude it is to have people stare at you because you look different. But I think your hair is cool." I nodded my head in approval. "As far as my getting out seeing the sights… Well, I've travelled some since I've been here. I used to live here a few years back so I'm not really into the tourist mode, if you know what I mean."

"Yes, I do. In fact, when we first moved to the continent, my wife and I travelled every spare moment we could. One weekend was spent in Germany, another in Spain, one in Greece, you get the picture… Coming from England, this part of the world was a totally new experience for us. In the short span of a few hours, we could travel to an entirely different country. It was simply wonderful! Now we are much too busy and we seldom travel out of *Italia*. So what brings you here to this part of the world? You have family? Friends?" He sipped from a bottle of dark German ale.

I looked from Jeremy to the guys. The others were all still engaged in shoptalk. "Uh, I'm here visiting. Like I said, I used to live in Italy a few years ago. I had an opportunity to visit and I jumped on it." I wanted to change the course of this conversation from me to him. "So Jeremy you have a wife? What does she do to keep herself busy?" I envisioned a pasty-white, overweight Brit sitting at home with a houseful of beige children running around.

"My wife, Paige, found a job working as a translator for a major telecommunications company. She speaks Italian, German, as well as the Queen's English – all fluently. It was not difficult for her to find a job. In fact, she was recently promoted department manager for her section. That may not appear very significant to an American woman, but it is an amazing accomplishment for a Black woman in *Italia*." He paused when he noticed the guys breaking up their impromptu meeting.

"Ah, I see they are finally finished. Well Lena, I shall see you on Thursday, perhaps. Please do enjoy your stay." He drained the bottle empty and reached out to shake my hand.

I was so wrong about him and even more so about his wife. I was so used to seeing Black men with white women; I automatically assumed he was the same. I felt ashamed and guilty of the stereotypical assumptions I chastised others for. I wanted to apologize, but of course Jeremy was not privy to the thoughts that swirled inside my head. Instead I extended my hand.

"It was really good talking to you. Maybe one day I can meet your wife. She sounds like a really interesting lady."

After the final walk through, Lucio checked to make sure the doors were securely locked. Nicky and Jeremy went their ways. The three of us walked the short distance to the parking lot

"Drive safely Giovanni and tell Mama and Papa I will visit in a couple of weeks. They always say I should come home more. Now with you going there…" He held his head pretending he had a headache and sighed, "Lena, my Papa told me he thought you were extremely gracious. He said he liked you. Coming from my Papa, that is a compliment. When you meet my Mama, do not let her upset you. She does not like any girl we bring home. 'No one is good enough for her boys'." He hit the remote lock for his car. It responded with a shrill beep, beep.

"Don't worry. We'll be fine." I reached out and gave him a nice big hug. I whispered softly in his ear, *"Molte grazie Lucio, per tutto."* I kissed his scruffy cheek as I pulled away.

He squeezed my hands and genuinely smiled, looking slightly embarrassed.

The early morning three-hour drive was thoroughly relaxing. We filled the time with music and small talk about the days of our youth. Strange how much you can learn about a person by discovering his childhood and the events that shaped him into the person he is today.

Take Giovanni for instance. He was the oldest child, often times burdened with the responsibility of being head of the family when his father travelled to find work. His family went through some very tough times. He helped his family out by finding odd jobs around the village to bring in extra money. He was a responsible child who turned into a responsible adult.

On the other hand, Lucio was the youngest. He was used to doing what he wanted, getting away with almost everything and making his mother crazy with his antics. His sister, the middle child, was virtually ignored by his parents. They were either too busy trying to survive or trying to take care of the sons. Eventually his sister moved away to attend university, got married, and had a few kids. She seldom came home at all. In some respects, our families were more similar than not.

Once we exited the *autostrada,* the roads to the town became steeper, narrower and more winding. They were probably barely drivable during the winter months, if at all. Giovanni drove with care and practiced precision. By the time we reached the outskirts of *Piano Montissimo*, the sun was beginning to rise above the terrain. I had the sudden feeling of *déjà vu* upon reaching the top. Of course, it wasn't *déjà vu* because I'd been there just a few weeks ago. all the same, the feeling was slightly disconcerting. In the distance, I spotted a field of tall grass and wildflowers swaying gently in the ever-present wind.

"Do you mind pulling over?" I observed his bloodshot eyes.

"Why? Is something wrong?" He looked alarmed.

"No. Nothing is wrong. It's just that beautiful meadow over there… I've always wanted to run through a field of grass. You know, like they do in the movies. Does that sound silly?" I felt foolish, but wanted to do it anyway.

"Why do you want to run through a field of grass? It *is* only grass. You are serious about this? Okay. I shall pull over to let you run through the grass." He parked his car in the gravel off the side of the road and turned off the engine.

"Thank you. I know it sounds childish, but I just have this overwhelming urge to run in the meadow. You want to come with me? It'll be fun."

"No, thank you. I will wait in the car. Besides, I am not dressed properly for frolicking in the grass. And for that matter, neither are you," he replied with a look of amusement.

"Okay. I'll be right back. Sure you don't want to come with me?" I pecked him on his cheek, got out of the car and closed the door.

Almost immediately I was toppled by the strong winds, which appeared deceptively calm while still in the car. At this high elevation the force of the wind was fierce – close to knocking me off my feet.

Maybe this wasn't such a good idea after all. I looked back at Giovanni sitting in the safety of the car smiling. Or was he smirking? He waved. I returned the smirk and headed for the meadow. I stepped gingerly in the grass. It came up to my knees. I opened my arms, threw my head back towards the sky and let the wind have its way. It felt heavenly standing in that vast meadow all by myself. I glanced backwards when I heard a car door slam. Giovanni decided to join me after all.

I stepped timidly at first, unsure how steady the ground was below my feet. When I was certain the ground was firm and would not swallow me up, I took off in a full stride towards the openness ahead. I turned to see Giovanni following the path I made. It made me laugh to see him trotting behind me. In fact, I was laughing so hard at him I didn't see the small rocks hidden underneath the long blades of grass. Suddenly, I tripped and went flying face first into the vegetation.

"Lena?! Lena, are you alright?!" He called, quickening his pace until he reached me laying face down in the grass.

I sat up, looked at him and laughed at my own clumsiness. "I'm okay. Just covered in dirt is all." I spit a blade of grass from my mouth.

He stooped down to my level. "Are you hurt? Can you walk?" His concern was endearing as he examined my outstretched limbs. "I'm all right. Very, very embarrassed, but I'm ok. I think I lost one of my shoes." I searched the grass on my hands and knees until I found it.

"Well, since you are not injured how about I join you in your little romp in the grass?" He brushed flecks of dirt from my face.

"This isn't exactly what I had in mind when I saw this meadow, but I must admit it's a whole lot better having you here with me." I returned his kiss, feeling all those ancient feelings rise deep within my body.

"You are truly amazing. Do you realize that? I have never known a woman who wanted to frolic in a meadow." He looked around. "It is not so bad here. Not bad at all," he replied sitting down next to me on the meadow floor. "Actually, it is very peaceful and calming."

He put his arm around me, I leaned my head on his shoulder. We remained that way without feeling the need to speak for a good fifteen minutes.

"Hey, you ready to get out of here? Where are we going to stay anyway? The boarding house?" I asked. Giovanni appeared ready to fall asleep at any moment. Truthfully, I was almost at that same point myself.

"I am ready. Do you remember my friend Stefano? The villa he owns? We shall stay there again. *Va bene. Andiamo!*" He stood offering his hand to help me up.

After brushing off as much grass and dirt as we possibly could, we returned to the car for our drive down into the village. Because it was still early – not quite 7 yet, the streets remained relatively quiet. In no time at all we arrived at the villa. We parked across the street.

Approaching the villa, once again I experienced that feeling of wonderment seeing the grounds leading up to the amazing architectural feat. The massive building loomed before us, surrounded by vegetation covered in a fine layer of early morning dew. The ornamental fountains were operational, spilling water forth through their various orifices. Not many guests were out this early, but I did see one hearty soul doing a *tai ichi* routine on the lawn. He appeared to be in his late 60s, though his fluid movements belied his age.

We continued on the stone walkway leading up to the entrance. It was as beautiful as I remembered. Opulent marble floors, traditional Italian furniture, and beautiful works of art, framed in gold gilding decorated the foyer. The clerk checked us in and offered assistance with our luggage. We declined. As tired as we were, all we wanted to do was to get to the room, snuggle up in the large comfortable bed and fall fast asleep. Once again, I felt I was at home. Even in this far away place, I was home.

CHAPTER 24

As usual Giovanni was up first, singing songs of love while he showered. It was almost 2. At this rate, my body clock would never be right again. Even though I was nowhere near a mirror, I knew I looked a hot mess because I hadn't bothered to wash my face last night. I imagined rings of mascara circling my bloodshot eyes.

From my hair, I removed blades of grass that remained from my romp in the meadow! I sat up in the bed thinking how I could sneak past Giovanni to straighten up before he saw me. I heard the water shut off. I lay back down, pulled the sheet over my head and pretended to be asleep. He returned to the bedroom. I snuck a peek through an opening in the covers. He had a towel wrapped around his waist, his hair was dripping wet, and his back was covered with beads of moisture. I watched him quietly get dressed, trying desperately not to make noise to disturb me. He returned to the bathroom to put away the wet towel before combing his hair.

Prior to leaving, he stood at the foot of the bed and sighed. "Such a beautiful angel... How can a man be so lucky, yet unlucky at the same time?" he asked himself.

He's probably going out for his stroll. Or maybe coffee. I threw the covers off, jumped out of bed and ran to the bathroom mirror. Good Lord! Even I wouldn't want to take myself out looking like this. I looked exactly as I imagined. Forget this! I've got to get myself together before he comes back.

I must have been in the shower for at least 20 minutes before I heard Giovanni call out my name.

"Lena? Lena, I have returned. Where are you?"

I turned off the steaming water. "I'm just finishing up my shower. I'll be right out."

He stuck his head through the door. "You want company?" he asked with a grin on his cleanly shaven face. The glasses he wore mostly for reading quickly fogged over. He removed them.

"Sure. C'mon in." I stepped from the shower stall, dripping wet. He handed me a towel. "Thanks. What have you been up to?"

"I took a walk around the grounds. Went to say *ciao* to Stefano, picked up today's paper... I am happy to see you are awake. Now we can begin our day, or what's left of it."

He was dressed in casual blue slacks and a light blue silk pullover shirt. It was the closest thing you could get to a tee-shirt without actually wearing one. On his feet, he wore designer leather loafers. He was stylishly dressed even when he was casual.

"You look nice. I especially like the glasses. They make you look intellectual." I touched his face. "What do you have planned for us today?" I squeezed a dollop of lotion in my hands then rubbed it on my body.

"Let me help you with that." He took the bottle, squirted some of the rich cream into his hands and applied the lotion to my back, rubbing in circular motions, using a very gentle touch and said, "I thought perhaps we might go horseback riding. That is, if you are comfortable with the idea. Stefano has a stable of horses he makes available for guests to ride. They are very gentle and very safe. What do you think?"

"Horseback riding? I haven't been on a horse in almost twenty years. I don't know if I can still ride. What about you? Are you comfortable around horses?" I applied an extra layer of deodorant.

"Ah, Lena, you forget I grew up in this village. Being around horses for me is as natural as having dogs are to others. As long as you are not afraid of them, you will be fine. We will take it one step at a time. Okay? Trust me, I will not let you get hurt, *amore mio.*"

What in the world was I going to wear to ride horses? Oh, yeah. I almost forgot my good ole' American jeans. I know I brought at least one pair with me. And if I top it off with a really cute top and some nice shoes, I may just blend in with the locals. Because honestly, I can probably count on one hand the number of Italian women over 30 years old I've seen wearing blue jeans. I quickly dressed, checked my reflection in the mirror and was out the door within 15 minutes.

I grabbed a croissant and a cup of coffee in a take-out cup from the guest service counter in the lobby. Though the sun shone brightly in the sky, there was a slight chill to the mountain air.

We walked the short distance through a forested trail to the stables. A stable hand guided two saddled horses from the barn, holding them tightly by their reins. One was massive, standing at least 7 feet tall at its shoulder. He was obviously a male and his coat was a brilliant shade of black. The other horse was smaller, female and the color of chestnuts. She appeared bored and slightly perturbed at the idea of having someone ride on her back simply for fun. But we were going to do it anyway whether she liked it or not. I watched Giovanni gently stroke the black horse's enormous head, speaking to him in quiet tones. He motioned for me to do the same with my horse.

"You want me to talk to the horse?" I asked incredulously.

"*Si*. The horse's name is *Bella*. Your voice helps to put her at ease. Talking makes both of you comfortable so you will be relaxed while riding her. And it is only proper to first get to know the animal you will become so intimate with." He grinned slyly.

"Intimate? I don't plan on becoming intimate with this horse."

"Lena, of course you will. Look at it this way. The most intimate part of your body will be in contact with this horse in a very open, some would say sexual manner for most of the afternoon. Would you conduct this type of behaviour with a stranger? Someone you have never met before today?" He arched his eyebrows in amusement.

"No! I suppose I wouldn't. Okay, I see your point. But a horse is just an animal. They don't really count in the feelings department. I mean, they don't consider my being on their back in a sexual way. It's not like I'm giving them an invitation for sex or anything." I rubbed the horse's neck. She turned her head looking at me with those huge eyes. It was almost as if she understood what we were talking about.

Giovanni laughed at my comments. "Never consider an animal you are about to entrust your life with as insignificant. Horses are amazing, intelligent creatures and deserve to be treated with reverence." He kissed his horse on the side of its neck.

"I am not kissing this horse no matter what you say." I jumped back as the horse brayed, baring her teeth. "See, she doesn't like me whether I stroke her or not." I pretended to walk away.

"Come back. She is just behaving like any temperamental female acts when her feelings are hurt." He pulled me back towards the horse and guided my hand in making loving tender strokes. The horse began to purr. "See, she just needs to be shown a little affection. Now are you ready to mount her?"

I laughed and couldn't resist. "No, but I'm ready for you to mount me!"

"That, *amore mio*, will come later. For now, grab on to the saddle, put your foot in the stirrup and throw your leg over the side."

I handed my empty cup to the stable hand and went to the horse.

Because she now appeared much calmer, I was able to mount the saddle on the first try. "See, I'm a pro at this already!" I grinned down at Giovanni.

I watched him expertly mount *Fulmine,* which loosely translates as lightning bolt. My goodness! Was there anything this man couldn't do? He called out to an idle stable hand that stood back in the shade of the barn, watching our antics. In an instance, the man appeared at our sides handing each of us a straw hat.

"The sun is deceptively strong at this elevation and the hats will keep us from becoming overheated. Are you ready to ride?" He pulled his horse alongside mine. "Just hold the reins loosely in your hands. Like this...yeah, you got it. *Bella* is a good old girl. She is very safe and extremely gentle."

"Alright. I'm ready. Let's go for it!" I held the reins loosely in my hands, just as Giovanni instructed. *Bella* took off in a steady trot. "Just don't leave me!" I shouted out as we exited the *palazzo's* grounds.

The horses climbed gingerly up the side of a mountain on a rocky trail meant only for four-legged beasts. And despite my nervous demeanor, *Bella* did amazingly well. Giovanni made sure I kept up with them by making frequent stops along the tree lined path. After a few miles, Giovanni stopped at a clearing up ahead. I caught up with them.

"Are you doing alright?" he asked when I pulled up alongside him. By this time, I controlled the reins rather well – starting and stopping at will.

"Yes. But I am kind of thirsty. Did you bring any water?" I asked, feeling like I had been sucking on cotton balls all day.

"No, but I know where there's plenty." He removed his hat and wiped his brow with a handkerchief from his pants pocket. He dismounted the horse, holding the reins.

"Is the ride over already? I was just getting used to ole' *Bella* here." I patted her on the head, causing her to wildly toss her mane.

"Yes, for now. I wish to show you something up ahead. Let me help you down." He held the horse steady while I jumped down.

"Oww! My ass really hurts. I didn't notice until I got out of that saddle." I rubbed my sore behind and massaged my inner thighs.

"Would you like me to kiss it for you and make it all better?" He teased, patting my behind.

"You want to 'kiss my ass'?" I almost fell to the ground laughing at the course our conversation was going. Maybe it was the thin mountain air, but something was definitely making me behave extremely silly.

He realized what he said and joined in my laughter. "For you my dear, anything." He managed to say between fits of laugher. The horses looked at each other, then at us, then back at each other, probably wondering what our problem was.

When we finally got our bearings back, the sound of gurgling water caught our attention and drew us in that direction. On the other side of the clearing, several weather worn picnic tables shaded by tall trees sat near the side of a rushing stream of clear mountain water. We tied the horses to a trough filled with fresh water and continued on the narrow trail by foot.

"Giovanni, this place takes my breath away." I marvelled at the serene scenes of nature unfolding in front of my eyes. I forgot all about my thirst when we happened upon another truly wondrous sight. We stood at the base of a towering waterfall. Streams of water cascaded down the surface of a magnificent red wall of rock. The normally jagged surface was made smooth by the constant flow of water. I knelt at the pond and trailed my hands through the clear water. I wanted to take a drink, but knew better from watching the *Discovery Channel's* survivor series about the hazards of drinking fresh water. That series taught me to never drink from any fresh source of water because the possibility of invisible microscopic parasites, that could wreak havoc with your intestines, existed in every sip.

"*Si. Es molte bellisimo.* This is one of my most favorite places in all of *Italia.*" He tossed a pebble into the pond. We watched the ripple come back to shore. "My brother and I would come here everyday in the summer to spend hours swimming in the cool water. Come. There is more I want to show you."

Ever the mischievous one, he took me by the hand and led me towards the entrance of what appeared to be a cave.

"What are you up to?" I looked at him suspiciously.

"Follow me. But be careful, the rocks are very slippery." He winked, obviously avoiding my question.

He guided me through the mouth of the cave using a flashlight retrieved from a crevice, strategically hidden from view. The midday light somehow made its way through tiny openings in the cave's walls, guiding our path in what otherwise would have been total darkness.

The flashlight came in handy when daylight couldn't find its way through. I was beginning to feel a little claustrophobic. This journey reminded me of all the caves I visited all over the world and how they all somehow managed to give me the feeling of being buried alive. The thought of walking through an underground maze has never appealed to my sense of well-being. I imagined the sooner I got out of there, the better off we both would be.

The temperature inside the cave dropped several degrees from the outside air, hovering around 70. We walked a few minutes through the narrow passageways until we came upon a large cavernous "room". The cool air chilled my skin.

"Stay here my love and do not move. I have a surprise for you." Giovanni dropped my hand and used the flashlight to locate a lantern hanging from a large hook on the side wall.

I could barely make out his silhouette as stepped away. There was just enough light to make out shadows that appeared to move, courtesy of my overactive imagination. I hugged myself tightly to keep the slight chill at bay. I heard a barely audible clicking noise. Within moments, a soft warm glow filled the room illuminating cavernous formations hanging from the ceiling and simultaneously reaching up from the cave floor. Giovanni stood in the middle of a crystal garden holding a lantern in his hand. Each formation changed the light from the lamp into a dozen different dazzling colors. And each reflective color danced as if it were alive.

"Oh my goodness! How beautiful! What is all of this? Is this a diamond mine or some kind of precious stones?" I exclaimed, never imagining how spectacular cavern formations could be. I carefully walked to where Giovanni stood, hesitant to step on the fragile looking objects laying all over the ground.

"No, no precious stones here. This is nothing but crystallized salt and it is more durable than it appears to be." He pushed his foot against a mound the size of a boulder. It didn't budge. "I can only imagine these formations have been this way for millions of years. As a child, I often came here to escape from the heat of summer and also from my parents when there was work to be done." He laughed at memories of his childhood.

"I'll bet you were always up to something when you were young. Weren't you?" I asked, wanting to learn as much about him as possible. I picked up a bit of the salt. It broke apart in my hand. It was strong when it was part of a larger mass, but in small pieces it was very fragile. Contradictory, as is so much of life.

"No, being the oldest, I was always expected to be the responsible one. Lucio was the one who caused my parents, especially my Mama, the most worry. From the time he started school until the time he graduated, he was always finding ways to keep them in the school headmaster's office. I was very surprised he was accepted to go to university—even more so when he finally completed it. His grades were what kept him in his teacher's good graces, but his behavior was what kept him in trouble." He led us back from whence we came.

"I can see a bit of that mischief remaining in Lucio, but he seems to have turned out all right. What about your sister? Where does she live?" I asked, following him out of the cave. I was no longer hot, but the thirst still existed, especially after being around so much salt.

"She lives in a small village near *Firenze*. Her husband is a manager of a food store. With the business and all, I do not have very much time to see them. We mostly get together with the rest of the family during the holidays."

"I know how a parent's expectations and actions can really mess up a kid. It seems like you give them too much attention or not enough. I haven't met anyone yet who seems to get it right all the time. We all just do the best we can and hope and pray our children turn out okay. And really, I believe family can be a blessing or a curse dependent upon how you look at things." I replied, more in response to my own memories than his.

Giovanni replaced the lantern in a vestibule near the opening of the cave for others who wanted to explore. We returned to where the horses patiently awaited our return. A small cooler sat on the ground near the trough. Don't know how I missed seeing that before. He reached in and took out two bottles of ice cold water, uncapped one and handed it to me.

"Lena, we have much to learn about one another and no time to waste. I will ask many, many questions about you and your life. All I want is for you to be totally honest with me. *Va bene?*" He looked me squarely in the eye, then drank half the water in one gulp.

"Okay. But I expect you will do the same for me. And you are correct. We don't have much time to really get to know each other, so let's get started now. But before we begin, can we find some food? I'm starving!" I quickly drank my water, not realizing how absolutely thirsty I was.

We mounted the horses and rode back in silence to the stables. We had been gone for hours and the afternoon had turned into early evening. After a quick shower and change of clothes, we decided to have our meal in the dining room. Italians normally have late dinners, as such, the dining room was almost empty. We sat at a secluded table near the window to watch the sun set while we ate.

A waitress described the house specials, took our orders, feeling no need to write them down, and retreated into the kitchen as quickly as she came. A young man placed a basket of breadsticks and a carafe of wine on the table. We made small talk about the restaurant's décor and how much fun we had earlier in the day before we treaded deeply into the territory neither one of us wanted to go.

"After your visit with Claudio, we did agree to never speak again of "that time". However, I still have questions that need to be answered. Not about how you got here, but what was in your heart that brought you here in the first place. Our conversations were very intimate and detailed. And I am only going over this again because I want to make sure I am speaking to the same Lena that I met and fell in love with. You said you did not remember specifics, but I must know what it is you are looking for. What do you want from me?" he asked. He was not angry, just very curious.

I kinda let the part about him falling in love with me slide, but it was the first time he said it and it had not gone unnoticed.

"What am I looking for? Well, for about the past few years, I have asked myself that same question over and over again. I told you about Mark. Well, it stopped feeling like a marriage many, many years ago. He became more like my roommate and less like a husband. I knew there were things about him that I didn't particularly like or even care for when we were married, but I accepted those imperfections and hoped I could continue to live with him the way he was. I mean, I'm not perfect either. No one is. But, it soon felt like everything I did with him was out of step with who I was. He wanted me to act a certain way, to speak a certain way, to dress how he wanted me to. My husband was what we Americans call a "control freak". If things did not go his way or I did not do what he wanted, my life became intolerable. I could not be myself around him."

"To keep my sanity, I started doing more and more outside activities to keep me out of the house and away from him. My life revolved around my boys and things we could do together apart from their father. The boys didn't seem to mind and as long as they stayed out of Mark's way, he seemed perfectly content."

I continued, "Somewhere along the way I stopped living my life and started living his. Funny thing was, he never seemed to notice anything was wrong. As far as he was concerned, all was well. He was focused mostly on getting ahead in his Army career. There was no one and nothing that was going to get in his way. He seemed to forget about "us" and only focused on himself. The only time attention was poured on me was when he needed something from me, like having me accompany him to official functions. When he introduced me to his co-workers and peers, he lavished me with attention and referred to me as the "power behind the force". As soon as we were alone at home, he went back to his corner of the house and I went to mine. We shared no affection and I felt no affection for him. When it was displayed it was perfunctory. So, to answer your question. What I am looking for? I'm looking for me. I want the fun loving, spontaneous, passion-filled, happy, gregarious, upbeat, optimistic Lena back. I don't want to compromise who I am for anyone. Ever! And if I cannot be the person I'm supposed to be with my own husband, who can I be it with? As painful as it is to admit, I had to escape from that part of my life to return to who I used to be. That's where you came in."

He leaned back in his chair and sighed. The waitress refilled our carafe with wine and the waiter brought out the first course.

"I see. Yes, you have explained this to me before, but I had to hear it again. I am sorry for bringing back bad memories for you, *mi amora*. I cannot imagine you having to stifle yourself in order to keep your husband lifted. The woman I see in front of me is all the things you describe yourself as and more. Your husband sounds like a man with very little confidence, especially when he treats such a special person as yourself as if she has no value. You should be celebrated and encouraged to develop to your fullest potential."

He continued, "When I first saw you with your friend, I was immediately attracted. I remarked to Lucio, "What a beautiful woman she is!" The way you danced and laughed out loud, you were a force to be reckoned with. You appeared so confident and poised. You walked with your head held high and your back straight. Then I rephrased it and told him that you did not walk, but you glided. You were like royalty—like a queen. I had to find out who you were, so I convinced Lucio into cutting into your dance and taking you away from your friend." He too was intrigued, so it did not take much persuasion from me.

I smiled at the reference to Keenan. "I must admit, since I've been back to *Italia*—both times—I have been more of myself over the past few weeks than I have in a lifetime married to Mark. I learned quite a bit about myself during my "vacation". I learned that I cannot return to the life I once lived and be content. I have experienced a life filled with color and it is impossible to go back to one devoid of it."

"Giovanni, during the short time we were together, you helped to bring out the real me. I don't have to compromise who I am with you at all. For the first time in years I am able to be myself. You accept me just as I am. You ask what do I want from you? Well, you have given me everything that I could possibly ask for. You have given me myself back. You have encouraged and embraced "the real" me without so much as blinking an eye. You lavish me with attention and affection expecting nothing in return. You have reminded me that I am special and I deserve to be treated as such—that I don't have to compromise myself and live a life filled with mediocrity. You have shown me how powerful authentic love can be and the possibilities that exist when you have it in your life. I discovered something about myself with you and I cannot go back to a loveless marriage. I just can't." My head was beginning to ache.

"As much as I do not want to discuss this, what *will* you do when you return to your life in America? My feelings for you are undeniable, but I am just a man. You say your life has changed. So has mine. I want to get to know you more and I want to spend more time with you. The thought of finding you only to lose you again. Well.... It does not seem fair."

"I don't know what I'm going to do when I go back. As much as I want to stay here with you, I have to return because my children are there. Look. I'm not trying to hurt you, but sometimes I wish I left well enough alone and just gone back to my old life. It only complicated things when I came over here to find you. You asked what I want from you... What do you want from me? I'm an American, a Black-American. I'm married and I already have three children. Seems to me like you should be running away from me, as fast as you can. In the opposite direction."

"On the surface, I suppose you are correct. To expect anything more than what we currently have does appear to be pointless and a painful exercise in futility. Not because you are an American, or Black. It's because you are married with a family. I do not presume to think the outcome of our meeting is for you to divorce your husband and leave your children to come to be with me. I will tell you this though, during those times we first spent together, I developed a deep respect for you. You put your fears behind and you took a leap of faith with me. We do have something special here. What I feel for you is unlike anything I have felt for any other woman. I feel alive again, as if I can do anything. I, I, uh…" He ran his hand over his head and exhaled.

He continued, "I also want to let you in on a little secret. Shortly after I realized I had developed feelings for you, I had to know who you really are and what your true story was. Please understand when I tell you that I am a businessman first *mi'amora*. I had a criminal background check run on you. I apologize for the mistrust, but in my country, one must know who they are dealing with at all times. I could not let you into my life without knowing anything about you. That said, the point I want to make is, I intend to explore all the possibilities that exist between us and it will not be possible with you in one country and me in another."

"You're right. It'll never work with us living in different countries. But listen to me, whatever happens between me and my husband has nothing to do with you. I decided I was going to divorce Mark the day I embarked on this journey to Italia. I even told my Mother as much. So, when I do divorce my husband it is a totally separate action from us being together. If I still loved Mark, I would not have done what I have. *Capisce?* Well, well, well… You had my background checked out? I can't really blame you for doing that. I would probably do the same thing if I were in your position. I suppose I checked you out also, although my information came from *Signora* Malavasi and her family. I appreciate your honesty."

Ain't that a trip?! Background checks on prospective lovers aren't just an American phenomenon after all? I was slightly taken aback by this revelation, but quickly got over it.

"Lena, you have traveled all the way to *Italia* because you had to know if I was real—if what we experienced was true. You sought me out not knowing if I really existed. Obviously, you felt something for me that was very intense. I believe it was more than mere curiosity. One can satisfy their curiosity and have nothing to lose by doing it. This is more than that. You said it yourself. You simply cannot go back to your old life and be content living a life devoid of love and passion."

"Yeah, I know. There is no way I can do that, not now. Not ever!" He had said a mouthful, summing up my dilemma up in a few sentences.

The remainder of the dinner was served. We both ate, but for the life of me I couldn't begin to tell you what I had. The conversation continued along the same lines with both sides discovering more about the other.

"You told me that you were involved with a woman, but it ended because the two of you wanted different things. So far, you and I get along great. But we haven't been together long enough to know the really important things. The things that can make or break a relationship." I sipped on a cup of freshly made cappuccino.

"What is it you would like to know? Because, I believe we already know the most important things about each other," he replied matter-of-factly.

"Oh, you think so, huh? Well, what religion are you? Do you want to have children? Are you a spender or a saver? Morning or night person? Cats or dogs?" I shot question after question. He smiled and listened attentively.

"I was raised Catholic, but currently not practicing. Yes, I would eventually like to have children. I am a "saver". Umm, a night person, of course. And if I had to choose, I'd say dogs. Anything else? What about you?" He was enjoying the game.

"I'm currently not attending church, though I am very spiritual. I do believe in God and at some point I want to get back into religion. You already know I have children, but I also want a baby girl. I'm actually more of a spender than a saver, but we can work with that. I love the early morning and I also prefer dogs. Still think we know the really important things?"

"I know I love you, Lena and I believe you also love me. That is what I do know." He responded, all kidding aside.

Okay. He finally said it. He loves me. How do I respond to this? Do I really love him? Can I trust my feelings at this point? I only know that when I am with Giovanni, nothing and no one else matters.

Nothing exists except the two of us and when we make love, we are in this world alone. He makes me feel like jumping up and down with joy. I feel pure happiness whenever he is near me and sadness when he is away. He is on my mind every moment of the day and in my dreams at night. Everything I do is done with him in mind. He cares about me and doesn't hesitate to express how he feels. He doesn't hold back on any of his emotions. He is open, honest and loving. I see his love for me shining brightly in his eyes. The passion that lives between us is so big, it overtakes all our senses. The thought of sharing my life with him makes my heart beat a little faster. He is the yin to my yang. The butter to my bread. My inspiration and motivation to excel. Do I love him? Yeah, I do.

"Sweetheart, I love you too." I finally admitted it to more to myself than to him.

CHAPTER 25

It was if time stood still. The rest of the world and all its problems no longer mattered. Giovanni took the rest of the week off so we'd have more time together. We spent the next few days in our room talking for hours about everything under the sun. We made love like it was the end of time and simply enjoyed one another. Not only were we lovers, but we soon became best friends sharing all our secrets. We only came out to take early morning strolls or an occasional meal in the dining room. Other than that, if it weren't for my screams of pure bliss during our love fest, no one would have known anyone was in the room.

When we finally came up for air and were almost ready to face the realities of the real world, it was time for us to leave *Piano Montissimo* and quite possibly whatever was left of our newly developed relationship. The Friday before I was due to return to the United States snuck upon us much too quickly. If I was going to make it to James' graduation on time, I had to fly out the next day. Giovanni had almost forgotten one of the primary reasons he had brought me to his village. We had been so caught up in being together, we had all but forgotten about visiting his parents.

"*Si, si, si,* Papa. I will come for a visit before returning to *Gorgazzio. Si,* Lena is with me and I shall bring her along." He covered the phone's receiver, shaking his head, feigning impatience. "*Va bene.* We will have lunch with you and Mama today. *Alora,* see you soon." He snapped the cell phone shut, sat down on the edge of the bed and hung his head.

"Is everything all right?"

"*Si,*" he sighed. "No, it is not. You must leave tomorrow and I forgot I promised my Papa that I would visit. I do not want to share you with anyone. *Amore mio,* I want to have you all to myself for as long as I can."

"Hey, it's okay. I want to be with you every moment too and at this point I wished I didn't have to leave—not yet. I am not finished with you. But you did promise your father that we would stop by. You can't leave the village without seeing them. We'll just stop in and say a quick hello and then we'll leave. Don't worry." I massaged his back and kissed his neck.

He took my face in his hands and kissed me, then pulled back so I could see him clearly. His eyes glistened as he uttered, "I love you and I do not know if I can ever live without you. Must you go?"

"Giovanni? Don't. Please don't do this to me. Not now. You know I have to go back. I can't *not go* to my son's graduation. I don't want to leave you either, but I don't have a choice. I have to go." The tears threatened to come. Somehow I held them back. "Let's go see your parents, then head back to town for our last night together. Okay? Okay?" I had to have him onboard or I would break down right then and there.

"*Si*, my little angel. I apologize. Please forgive my selfishness. But of course, you must go back. I will be fine. Let us get ready for a visit with my parents. I must warn you about my Mama. She, uh, is not as pleasant as my Papa."

"Yeah, I remember Lucio saying as much. I'll be fine. You're with me. Anyway, we won't stay long."

Giovanni let out an uncharacteristically nervous laugh and replied, "When I visit my Mama, there is no such thing as a short visit. She somehow finds a way to bring up everything I have not taken care of since I moved out. Gio, when are you going to get married and give me grandchildren? Who is going to carry on the family name? You are the oldest boy and should have a wife to take care of you. Why does so much time have to pass between my visits? Am I taking care of Lucio and watching out for him? And on and on and on...." He sighed again and held his head between both hands.

"Thanks for warning me. She sounds very, uh, familiar." I thought about Mark's mother and almost immediately began to dread the upcoming family visit.

After we dressed, we packed up the car with our things and walked the short distance to his parent's house. His family home was a fairly large two story house. Modest by American standards, but quite spacious for an Italian home. The yellow stucco exterior was accented by green trim on the storm shutters and window sills. I could tell the house had been recently painted, not by the freshness of the paint, but by looking at the collection of empty paint cans gathered in a corner of the yard.

The yard was fenced all the way around to either keep someone out or something in. When we opened the heavy wrought iron gate to climb the short flight of stairs to the front door, I soon discovered the purpose of the strong fence.

Two humongous brown dogs ran up to Giovanni and stood up on their hind legs, putting their huge paws on his shoulders and proceeded to give him doggie-breath laced kisses. I thought they were going to knock him down and lick him to death. I backed up as far as I could to get out of their way. Giovanni responded to the dog's greetings by rubbing each one vigorously behind the ears of their enormous heads. I think they were bull mastiffs and looked to weigh around 200 pounds each. If I wasn't with him, I would never have had the nerve to go through those gates after seeing those beasts.

The front door opened suddenly and a middle-aged woman with an apron tied around her waist burst through the door. She shooed the dogs away and replaced their massive paws with her arms around Giovanni's neck.

"Gio! Mi figlio! Bentornato! Papa, es Giovanni e tu amica!" She kissed Giovanni all over, put her arm around his waist and led him into the *casa*.

"Giovanni! Lena! Bentornato!" Papa repeated, also enthusiastically kissing us both.

"Ciao Mama e Papa. Come va? Mama, questa mi'amica Lena Delgado." He introduced me to his mother and reacquainted me with his father.

"Prego. It is very nice to see you again Papa. I am pleased to meet you *Signore Morelli."* I offered my hand to greet them. I was unsure what the custom was for kissing his parents hello.

"Santo cielo! Vieni qui!" She exclaimed and pulled me towards her in a motherly embrace.

"Lena non capiscono l'italiana. Por favore parlare inglese, Mama." Giovanni quietly whispered in his mother's ear.

How do I describe his mother? Well, to begin with, she is not at all what I expected. I thought she would be a frumpy, dumpy, boring housewife. You know, the stereotypical Italian grandmotherly type. I could not have been more wrong. Mama Morelli, Mama M, must have been near 60 and was absolutely stunning! She was about 5'3", very petite and stylishly dressed in a cream colored cashmere sweater and matching slacks. Silky, thick black hair grazed her shoulders and framed what could have been the face of a model whose time had come and gone. Her deep brown eyes were set off by her smooth, olive complexion which was accented by the slightest hint of makeup. Her movements displayed an energy that belied her age, yet she was poised and graceful at the same time.

When I looked at her, I saw traces of both sons, although Lucio seemed to have more of her genes in him than did Giovanni. I watched how Gio reacted to his mother. His father took a momentary backseat to his wife's affection as his oldest child reclaimed the love uniquely reserved for a son from his mother.

We were led into the living room, tastefully decorated in a classic *italiante* neo-classical style. Mama M. sat next to Giovanni on the sofa. I sat in a stiff upright arm chair and Papa Morelli sat opposite me.

After Mama M had adequately insured her child was aware of how much he was missed, she then put her focus on me.

"*Va bene*, Giovanni. For you, I will try to speak English. Lena, you have already met Papa? Do you live in *Gorgazzio*?" Her full attention passed from Giovanni to me. She smiled a much too sweet smile, as she looked me over from head to toe. Instinctively my guard went up. She was a mother protecting her son, much like I would do someday for my own. I had to be careful.

"Uh, no, I'm just visiting for a little while." My voice cracked and I cleared my throat. Guess I was a bit nervous.

"*Pardone*. Where are my good hostess manners? Would anyone like something to drink before we have lunch? Coffee, water, soda, perhaps something stronger?" she asked, still holding on to that smile.

"I'll take a glass of water please." I smiled back, hoping to at least get in her good graces.

Mama M started to get up from the sofa to get drinks for all. Giovanni beat her to the punch and offered to get the drinks himself. Thank you for being so thoughtful, my love, I thought sarcastically to myself. You are going to leave me alone here in the lion's den? I could handle his Papa because all he wanted to do was look at me, but his mother was a different story altogether.

"Visiting? Oh, so you are taking a holiday? How lovely! Do you have friends or relatives in *Italia*?" The forced smile remained.

"Um, no, not really. I came over on my own." Where was that man? I looked towards the kitchen hoping he would come back soon and rescue me.

"Oh? You are taking a holiday alone? In *Gorgazzio*? How strange. *Gorgazzio* is a lovely town, but to vacation there... I cannot imagine anyone doing such a thing. You sound American? Are you an

American?" she asked. The smile faded slightly as her suspicions began to grow.

Where are you Giovanni? Get your ass back in here! I thought to myself, hoping he would pick up on the telepathic waves I was sending out in droves.

"Yes, I am an American. I used to live in *Gorgazzio* many years ago and I just wanted to come back and visit your beautiful country. I love it here!" I hoped my enthusiasm about her country would throw her off my trail.

"You mean you used to live here, so obviously you must have held a job, yet you cannot speak the language? How did you manage to get by without speaking any Italian? Who was your employer?" A puzzled expression crossed her face.

"I, uh, well, I used to work on the American military base. I really didn't need to know much Italian. I did manage to learn enough to get by though. I could speak to my landlord, my neighbors, the shopkeepers in the market, and of course I learned enough to ask directions when we got lost." I felt myself trying too hard.

"The military base? *Alora.* You did not live here alone then?" She zeroed in on her prey.

"Uh, what do you mean? Why do you ask me that?" Beads of perspiration roll down my back.

"You said we. Who is 'we'?" She had found her mark.

Just then Giovanni returned to the living room carrying a tray of coffee and a glass of water for me. I was never so happy to see him.

"Mama, leave her alone. You ask too many questions. Lena is my guest and because she is my guest, that makes her your guest as well. Now stop being an investigator for once in your life and just enjoy our company while we are here." Giovanni stooped over to kiss me on the cheek as he handed me a glass of water.

I mouthed "thank you" and nervously sipped from my glass of water. As I drank the cool liquid, I looked over the glass to see Papa sitting in the chair with his head drooped back and his mouth hanging open. He was sound asleep. I laughed inwardly at the entire scene. Here Mama M was asking me all sorts of questions to find out my story and get up in my business, yet Papa could not have cared less. He was probably bored by our conversation and found sleep much more intriguing than the story of how I met his son.

"Papa, wake up! We have guests! Mama walked over to Papa Morelli and shook his shoulder. "Wake up and come to the table. I have fixed a feast for us. Look at my poor boy. You are much too thin. He is too thin! Right, Lena?" She winked a conspiratorial eye at me.

"I like him just the way he is. I think he is a very good size." I smiled at Giovanni, who also got the unintended double-entendre. Come to think of it, his mother probably got it as well because she didn't so much as crack a smile at my comment.

The four of us relocated to the dining room. His mother really had gone all out with the meal and it showed by the spread laid out on the table. There was freshly baked bread, an *antipasti* platter filled with all kinds of meat and cheeses, and lots of wine to drink. While Mama and Papa Morelli went to the kitchen for the main course, the two of us had a little chat.

"Lena, my mother used to work for the Italian government as an investigator. Her job was to conduct background checks on tourists who applied for work visas. She did this job for over twenty years and was extremely good at what she did. She has only been retired from it for five or six years, but as you can see, she still has a suspicious nature." He attempted to explain his mother's behavior.

"I understand. But I think her questions didn't come so much from being an investigator as it had to do with being a mother. She asked all the right questions and would have continued if you hadn't rescued me. Did you use her to check up on me?" I asked, admiring the woman who had given birth to my new found love.

"No, of course not! My mother would not understand our current situation. For now, it is better for her to know you through your involvement with me. But to answer your question, I did not go to my mother, but I know many people who were more than willing to help me out and do a favor. They did not know why I wanted information about you. They were too professional to ask personal questions. I told them you were a potential employee who required a criminal background search. It was not so unusual because I have done it before. So, you see. I am my mother's son."

"Well, if you want to know something about me you can just ask. You do not need to go running background checks on me." Even though I could understand his need to know, I was hurt that he didn't come to me first.

"I am sorry, *amore mio*. Please forgive me. When you suddenly disappeared, I had to know something about you. You were a mystery. You were here one day and gone the next. When I could not locate you, I thought misfortune had happened. I even wondered if you were running from legal problems. When I could not find you, that is when I requested a background check. You will be pleased to know that you have never been arrested and you have no criminal background."

"Well, I could have told you that. Anyway, I forgive you. But now that you know what you know, please don't ever do something like that again. Okay?"

"*Va bene*. Okay."

For the next two hours, we ate wonderful food and I heard many interesting, funny, sometimes embarrassing stories about the Morelli family. To my delight, his mother finally gave up on cross examining me. I suppose she figured out that if Giovanni liked me, I could not have been all bad.

"Mama, the food was *delicioso*. I would like to stay and visit some more, but we both have to get back to town before it gets too late." He looked at his watch and shrugged his shoulders in a defeated gesture.

"But you have only just arrived. Must you leave so soon? I was just getting to know your Lena."

"I am sorry Mama, but we must go. I promise you the next time I visit I will allow more time to spend with you." He made a "cross-my-heart" motion as a promise. It was a gesture retrieved from his childhood.

Giovanni stood and I followed his lead. He walked over to his mother, kissed her on top of her head and reached across the table to shake hands with his father.

"*Signore and Signora Morelli*, thank you for your graciousness and allowing me into your home. The meal was absolutely wonderful. Giovanni said you were the best cook and I wholeheartedly must agree. You must give me the recipe for your *tagliatelle*."

"*Si*, I will send the recipe to my son and he can give it to you. How much longer do you plan on being in *Italia*? she asked, displaying a genuinely puzzled expression.

"Actually, ma'am I'm scheduled to fly out tomorrow evening." I felt sad at the thought of leaving all this behind.

"Oh, so soon? That is too bad. I would have liked to get to know you better. After all, my Gio seems to be so taken with you. You do know that you are only the second woman he has ever brought home? You must be very important and also very special to capture his attention. Lucio said I would like you once I got to know you and he was right." She stood from her chair and hugged me tight.

"I would also like to get to know you better as well. Perhaps, when I return we can get together again and go out for lunch."

"So you do intend to come back soon?"

"Yes, I do plan on returning. I'm just not sure when yet," I said more for Giovanni's benefit than hers.

"Very well then. Just know that any friend of Gio and Lucio are welcome in our home anytime. *Buon viaggio, mi amica!*"

"*Ciao* Papa. I will call you soon."

We looked back and waved at the two standing in the door, looking like the happy couple I wanted to resemble in my later years. We walked the short distance to the hotel parking lot.

"And that my dear Lena is my fabulous Mama. She is my number one fan and supporter. There is no trouble too big for Mama Morelli. She is the force behind my Papa. She may have appeared to be wary of you, but that is only because she wants the best for me."

"Hey, I understand. I will probably be the same way when my boys bring girls home for the first time. No matter how my boys feel about a girl, none will ever be good enough in my eyes. That's just what it is to be a mother." I replied matter-of-factly and slipped my arm through his.

The drive back went by too fast. We told jokes that were sometimes lost in translation between our two languages, listened to music, reminisced about our time together, and took solace in the fact that "this" could not possibly be the end of "us". One day we would be together again. We both realized that a whole lot of life stood between us and that day, but if it was meant to be, it would be. And no one or nothing—not even time or distance—could keep us apart.

The rest of the evening passed quickly. Neither one of us got any sleep that night. We made love and he held me close as I cried tears of sorrow at the thought of our impending separation. I was usually meticulous when it came to packing my clothes, but that morning I carelessly shoved a tangled heap of shoes, clothes, and toiletries into a bulging suitcase. Giovanna took me to the airport and made sure I was well taken care of at the counter. Despite my objections, he convinced the ticket agent to upgrade my coach fare ticket to first class. At the security gate, I kissed this man who had so quickly won over my heart. We had no words that could capture the profound feelings that had developed so quickly between us.

"Lena, please call when you make it home. I will not rest until I know you are safe," he said with a concerned look.

"I'll call as soon as the plane touches down on American soil. Giovanni?"

"Yes, I know. *Ti amo tu.*" He wiped the tears from my face.

"I, uh, I… I love you." I kissed him, tasting the saltiness from my own tears.

I hurried towards the security checkpoint before I changed my mind and decided never to leave. I thought I was strong, but it turns out this man was my kryptonite. My weakness. An internal battle took place between my heart and my head. The overwhelming urge to run back into his arms threatened to keep my feet firmly planted in Italy. I only looked back after I passed the metal detector. I waved and he did the same in return. I did not want to leave, but I also could not stay. Not now. Not yet. Not like this.

PART THREE

CHAPTER 26

On the long flight back to the states, I watched a low budget B movie starring a couple of actors whose days of fame and fortune had long come and gone. Can't begin to tell you the plot or if it even had one. I ate a couple of inflight meals, including a light lunch and later something that vaguely resembled brunch. I was surprised that the airlines still served food at all. I suppose they really didn't have a choice on long continental flights. I must have dozed off because before I knew it, the flight attendant was coming through the cabin with an open trash bag collecting empty cups and passenger's garbage. I checked the time. We would be landing in about 30 minutes. I would make my connection flight. Funny. I almost didn't want to.

"Ladies and Gentleman, on behalf of *Alitalia*, the crew and I would like to thank you for choosing to fly with us today. The temperature in Detroit is in the mid 70's with partly cloudy skies. The winds are calm and it's supposed to be a gorgeous spring day. We should be on the ground in about 20 minutes. Once again, thank you for choosing to fly *Alitalia*." The voice of the captain was calm, yet authoritative. He sounded just like the kind of man I wanted to be in the cockpit in case of an emergency.

I replayed the events from the past couple of weeks over and over in my mind. This time it was real and not a dream. This time there were consequences involved as a result of my actions. This time I could not come home from the hospital and pick up from where I left off. This time I had come too far to turn around, both literally and figuratively. This time, I had to make a decision—a choice that would forever change my life and all the lives of those most precious to me. This time, I had to choose wisely.

Because I was returning from an international flight, I had to pick up all my bags and process through customs before checking in for the domestic portion of my flight. I felt totally weighed down and not just by luggage.

"Welcome back, ma'am. You have anything to declare?" asked the bored looking customs agent, barely glancing my way after reviewing my passport.

Yeah. I declare that I must have been out of my mind to take this trip in the first place. What did I hope to accomplish by chasing down a man who could have existed only in my mind? And now that I know he does exist, I was hopelessly head-over-heels in love with him and wanted to spend the rest of eternity with him.

"No, I don't have anything to declare." I sighed and waited for the man to stamp my passport.

"Here ya go. Have a good day. Next". He handed back my passport and motioned for the next passenger to step up to the counter.

I maneuvered my luggage towards the Delta ticket counter, checked my bags, picked up my boarding pass and got directions to the departure gate. I had a two hour layover to get through.

The cell phone weighed heavily in my purse and on my mind. I told Giovanni I would call as soon as I touched down on American soil, but I wasn't ready to talk to him. It was too soon. In my current state of mind, just hearing his voice may have caused me to seek out the *Alitalia* counter and book a return flight right back to his loving embrace. No, I had to wait until it was no longer possible to jump on a plane. I had to put a few more miles between us, so I decided to wait until I arrived in Kansas. Kansas was a world apart from Italy in every way imaginable. Once I was in Kansas, it would take more than a notion to get me back to Italy.

Finally, after I thought I couldn't bear to watch another plane board, the gate agent announced. "Flight 117 for Kansas City now boarding at Gate 28. Please have your boarding passes ready at the gate. Thank you."

The announcement was welcomed with a sigh of relief. Time to get this show on the road.

CHAPTER 27

An ominous looking thunderstorm loomed far away in the distance. Cloud-to-cloud lightning lit up the afternoon sky. It was eerily quiet as the turbulence tossed the small airplane around, despite being near to the impending storm. Either altitude or the aircraft design prevented the sound of thunder from making the situation appear worse than what it was.

Between breaks in the clouds, I looked out the window at the patchwork designs carved in the farmland below. My restless mind wandered aimlessly. How in the world do those farmers get those lines in their fields so straight? And forget about how they make crop circles in corn fields. Maybe those people who insisted on aliens having a hand in them weren't too far off the mark. As long as those aliens weren't like the ones in M. Night Shamalayan's, movie "*Signs*", they could keep making crop circles to their heart's content. That was some freaky shit that happened in that movie!

The captain's voice interrupted the random thoughts running through my mind. He announced over the airplane's intercom that due to bad weather we would be circling until we were cleared to land. His estimation was about 30 minutes. A collective groan reverberated throughout the cabin.

I played out the scenario of telling Mark I wanted a divorce. No matter how I approached it, it was going to be painful—for all of us. I knew I had to do it. I could not continue to live with him holding on to the fact that I no longer loved him. I had declared my love to another, now there was no going back to the way things were.

My marriage was over long before I took this trip. I was just too busy existing to do anything about it. Somewhere along the way, I had convinced myself that life with Mark wasn't so bad. So what if we didn't have love, passion, intimacy, or romance in our marriage? We had more than most couples did. We lived comfortably and provided a safe environment for our sons. After all, isn't that what marriage was about? Being comfortable?

For a very brief moment, I considered staying with him for the sake of my boys, but in my heart I knew that should never be an option. What kind of a mother would I be if I continued living out my life pretending to be happy with their father? My sons were way too smart for that—they'd see right through me. In retrospect, I suppose they already knew Mommy wasn't happy. What kind of an example was I showing them about life and love? I was basically telling them to accept mediocrity. Instead of giving them an example of holding out for the love of their life, I was telling them that merely existing was "good enough".

Well, one thing was for certain. I wasn't going to tell him right away. James's graduation was tomorrow and I absolutely was not going to let anything ruin it. It was bad enough that I wasn't there to help him arrange his graduation party. I figured all I needed to do was pick up a few buckets of chicken, order a couple of pizzas, grill up some of my world famous ribs, and fix a few side dishes.

Everyone who was coming from out of town had already arrived and checked into their hotel. Ironically, I was probably the only one left who hadn't arrived. When I talked to James before leaving Italy, I assured him, come hell or high water, I was going to see him walk across that stage. Incredibly, as I looked out at that storm preventing me from landing I wondered if that premonition was going to come true.

I awoke with a start when I felt the plane touchdown. I both welcomed and dreaded returning "home". Overhearing other passenger's conversations about mundane topics as we taxied to the gate only managed to elevate my anxiety.

Didn't these people know I was about to embark upon a heart-wrenching journey? Why did they have to be so damn happy? Chattering about Kimberly's fabulous new house or Bob's presentation to the department heads. I really didn't want to know that Grandma was about to see her newborn grandson for the first time. I wanted them all to shut the hell up! I had some serious thinking to do and I didn't care, nor want to hear about their perfect little insignificant lives!

Now where did I park my car? I was in such a hurry to catch my flight that I didn't consider writing down the parking spot location. After walking around for a good ten minutes dragging my luggage behind me, I began to panic. I must have had that "desperate look of a woman on the verge of snapping" look about me because a kind parking lot attendant driving one of those carts took pity on me.

"Ma'am? Are you okay? Do you need help finding your car?" asked the young woman driving the little mini cart.

She must have done this many times a day. She looked like one of those "around the way" ghetto fabulous sistahs who only kept a day job to keep their hair and nails done. Her hair was plastered to her head and a fake ponytail bobbed whenever she moved. Two inch acrylic nails displayed beautiful artwork on each tiny tip, causing me to wonder if she could actually do any other work involving her hands. Although she wore an airport attendant's uniform, she had a way about her that screamed "put me in your next ass-shaking video".

"Yeah, actually I do. I know I parked my car somewhere around here, but I was in such a hurry that I can't remember where I left it!" I exclaimed.

"C'mon. Get in. I'll help you find it." She put the cart in park and helped me load up my luggage on the back. For such a petite woman, she picked up my heaviest bag with little effort and her nails didn't get in the way at all. "Ma'am what kind of car do you drive and how long has it been here?"

"Uh, it's a late model Honda Accord. Dark blue. I parked it here almost two weeks ago?" I suddenly felt so weary I could barely keep my eyes open.

She got on her walkie-talkie speaking parking lot attendant lingo to someone on the other end.

"What's your license plate number Ma'am?" she asked, popping her gum at the same time.

I provided her with the license plate number. She got back on that walkie-talkie and within a few minutes she pulled up in front of my car.

"Is this it, ma'am?" She turned towards me, popping her gum, looking indifferently towards my situation.

"Yeah, this is it. Thank you so much 'cause I would have been here all day trying to find this car. How much do I owe you?" I asked, reaching into my purse.

"You're welcome and you don't owe me anything Ma'am. It's my job." She threw the cart in neutral, set the brake and helped unload my luggage.

I pulled out a twenty and handed it to her. "Girl, you helped me out more than you know. Here take it. Please." I insisted.

"Well, we're not supposed to take tips, but I need all the money I can get to help pay for my college tuition and books. Thank you ma'am and God bless you." She stuffed the cash in her pants pocket and waved goodbye as she drove off—ponytail bobbing and smacking on that gum.

Tuition and books? She's a student? I shook my head at my own judgmental ass. Okay, when was I going to learn that perception is flawed? Without knowledge of the entire situation you really don't know a damned thing about someone else's life. Just because you see something you believe to be true, doesn't necessarily mean that it is. Lord have mercy!

I found the parking ticket and paid the booth operator $120 to get my car out of hock. Salinas was about 30 minutes away. I wasn't quite ready to go home yet, so I drove to the nearest park and took out my cell phone. My first call was to the house.

The phone rang several times before someone picked up. It was Neil, my middle child.

"Hello?" he answered.

Wow, his voice had deepened! When did that happen? "Hello son." I tried my best to sound happy. I said, "Just wanted to let you all know that I'm back in Kansas and should be home in about an hour. Did you miss me?" I faked a smile to push back all the conflicting emotions inside me. Of course I missed my children, but what kind of life was I going back to?

"Hey, Mom! Hurry home! I can't wait to see you. How was your trip?" My child's excitement helped calm me.

"Oh it was okay. I can't wait to see you too!" Which was 100% true.

"Yeah, it's been crazy around here. Everyone's been asking where are you and when will you be back. Grandma Delgado came a few days ago and has been driving all of us crazy. You know how she is..." He sighed and laughed at the same time.

"Yes, I do know. But everything will be okay. Tell your brothers and your Dad that I'm on my way home. I'm kind of jet lagged but I'll take over when I get there. I love you."

"Love you too, Mom. Can't wait to see you."

Damn! Not only do I have to deal with James' graduation, but Mark's mother was there also. That woman could smell deception a mile away. I had to do my best to be cool and act like a version of my old self until this weekend was over. If I pulled this off, someone should nominate me for an academy award.

The second call would be much more difficult. I had to call Giovanni and let him know I made it back safely. I started to dial, but couldn't finish the number.

What was I going to say? That I was in Kansas and was headed back home to my husband and children? That he didn't have to worry about me anymore because I was *home*? "Home" implied family and family included my husband. And I don't care how secure a man is about his woman's love for him…if there is another man living under the same roof, especially if she was married to him for any length of time, he had reason to be worried because a married couple has history, shared memories, raised children together—commitments and obligations to one another. These were the tangible things that the two of them did not share. And when it came down to it, the family would win out every time. History dictates that people simply do not leave their significant others for their lovers no matter how much love and affection they hold for them.

Too often that old adage, "it's cheaper to keep her" reigned supreme. It was not economically, nor emotionally feasible to end a long term marriage only to start over with someone new. Lena knew this and so did Giovanni. It was one thing to dream and fantasize about falling in love with someone new and fresh. But it was an entirely different situation when you realize life isn't some fantasy or a dream—it's genuine and hard and painful. However, to discover that person you've waited your entire life for—your soul mate—is real and you know they do exist, changes everything.

Giovanni was that man for me. I had absolutely no doubt in my mind. I was at this juncture now of having to make a life changing decision and didn't know what to do. I dialed his number.

"*Pronto?*" he answered after five or six rings.

"Hey baby. It's me. I'm back in Kansas." I tried to sound cheerful even though I missed him like mad already.

"Thank goodness you made it back safely. I was out of my mind with worry. I expected to hear from you hours ago." Relief was evident in his every word.

"I apologize. I wanted to call you when I landed in Detroit. I didn't trust myself not to get back on a return flight to Italy. I had to wait until there were a few more miles between us. Baby, I miss you already." How in God's name am I going to do this, I thought to myself?

"*Capisco.* I miss you as well. Are you alright *amore mio*?" he asked with concern.

"No. Yes. Hell, I don't know. My mind is spinning in a hundred different directions right now. I'm tired. I'm hungry. I want to be there with you. But I've got to go home and make sure my son's graduation goes well, deal with out of town relatives, and try to do it all with a smile on my face while I have this heaviness in my heart from missing you. I don't know how I'm going to do it. I don't know what I'm going to do." I did not want to cry—again.

"You *will* do this. You have no choice. You cannot break down and fall apart. You must be strong. You will make sure your son's day is memorable. You will entertain your out of town guests and keep a smile on your face while doing it. I will not try to convince you to not think about me, because I know that is not possible. My love, this weekend is not about us. It isn't even about you and your, uh, uh, husband. It is about your son and his future. For the next few days, do not make any decisions about anything not related to your son's graduation. *Capisce?* I will be right here awaiting your phone call when you need to speak to me."

"I love you. You do know that. Right?" I needed to tell him.

"I have never doubted your love. From the moment we laid eyes on each other, there has never been a question of it being anything else. For now, you need to take care of yourself. Have a light meal and get some rest. Call me when you need me."

"Giovanni?"

"*Si?*" he answered.

"I need you." I smiled as I said it.

"Okay, *amore mio*. I understand. I will talk to you in a few days. Be strong my Lena. *Ciao bella.*"

"*Ciao,*" I replied back as I hit the call end button. Time to get moving. Time to get this show on the road. Couldn't put it off any longer.

Before I realized where I was or how long I had been driving, I found myself pulling into the driveway.

I tooted my horn to get the boys to come out and help bring my bags in. Much to my chagrin, Mark was the first one out the door.

"Oh, I see you made it back. How was your little "vacation? Have a good time?" he asked, sarcastically.

"Mark. Let's not do this now. I promise we will talk, but not now. We have a house full of people and James' graduation to get through. I know you want answers and I intend to give them to you. Let's just get through these next couple of days first. Okay?" I felt like turning around and running away—again.

"Alright baby girl. We will play by your rules. For now. But don't be coming back here thinking everything is okay. You walked out on me without even bothering to talk this situation over. You left me and the kids to run off to Italy for who the hell knows what, leaving me to explain to everybody where you were and why you left. Shit! I didn't even know myself, so I made up whatever came to mind. Don't for a minute think you're gonna come back and pick up where you left off!" He pulled my luggage out of the trunk and stomped back inside. I heard the faint slam of a door.

I looked towards the house and saw his mother peeking through the curtains. Why did she have to be here? I wonder where she left her hen-pecked husband. He was probably hiding out in the bar down the street to get away from her overbearing ways. I always felt sorry for Mark's father. He was such a sweet man. I wondered how he could stand to be married to that woman for all these years. She didn't even let him speak. Most of the time, she answered for him—like what he had to say didn't matter. When she did talk to him, she talked down to him like he was one of her children. He even referred to her as "Mother". How did such a strong man get to be so damned compliant? How he could stand to be around her was a mystery to me.

Mark's mother was sitting in the living room in my favorite overstuffed chair. "Hi Ruth. How are you?" I asked, attempting to be cordial.

"Hello Lena. I see you're feeling much better. The last time I saw you, you were laid up in the hospital. How in the world did you make such a fast recovery that allowed you to fly off to Italy for two weeks? What made you go all the way over there anyway?" she asked, eyeing me suspiciously.

If I hadn't known Mrs. Ruth Delgado so well, I would have sworn she was genuinely concerned for my well-being. However, being as I did know her, I was not going to fall into the trap of trying to defend my behavior to her. "I guess all I needed was a vacation. You know how it is? Sometimes you just need to get away and take a little time for yourself." I smiled sweetly, put my purse down on the counter and went to look for the boys. I was not going to get into a conversation with her about why I did what I did.

"Well, if you ask me, you were being very selfish just leaving like you did. Flying off like that on the spur of the moment... You should be ashamed of yourself for leaving these kids alone."

"You know what? I didn't ask you. Sometimes a woman has to do what a woman has to do. And the boys weren't alone. They were with their father!"

"Humph! You women today just don't know how to take care of your families. Always thinking about yourselves first. At the first sign of trouble, you walk out. No wonder Mark's been talking about leaving you for the past few years. If it weren't for me, your marriage would have been over years ago!" She appeared pleased with the shocked expression she helped place on my face.

That tidbit of information stopped me dead in my tracks. "What did you say?"

"I said if it were not for me, Mark would have divorced you years ago. He's only stayed with you because of the boys. I'm the one who convinced him to stick it out." With a smirk on her face, she picked a piece of lint off her sweater and looked up at me.

"And how do you know that?" I didn't attempt to conceal my surprise.

"He said as much to me—many times. I told him to hold on until the boys were older and out on their own. He could do it. Told him to be a man and stand up to his commitment to the marriage. His daddy did. Look at us. Over forty years and we're still together." She added that last comment like it was a badge of honor.

I didn't say anything else. Instead of walking out of the living room to find my boys, I plopped down on the sofa. She had totally managed to knock me off center. All these years Mark has wanted to leave me? Is that why he acted towards me like he did? The only reason he hadn't divorced me was because his mother told him to "stick it out" until the boys were grown? I watched her walk out of the room without saying anything else. She didn't even look at me. I wondered if she regretted telling me what I needed to hear. No, it wasn't her place, nor was it the time to say what she had, but now it was out and eventually had to be addressed.

"Mommy! You're home!" Neil and Carlos yelled in unison as they ran towards me. Though Neil was almost seventeen and bound by the strict laws of teenage boys not showing emotions, neither son bothered to hold back their excitement of having their mother back within arm's reach.

"Hey guys. I missed you both so much!" I peppered their faces with kisses and held on to both of them for as long as they would let me. Despite my most recent piece of news, I had to shake it off and be there for my boys. This thing with Mark would have to wait.

"Mommy, why didn't you tell us you were taking a vacation? I came home from school and Dad told us you were flying over to Italy. You should have seen his face. He was really, really pissed off! I thought he was going to explode! He kept telling us that you were sick and must have lost your mind while you were in the hospital. Mom, you had us all worried about you." Neil looked at me with a pained expression on his face.

"I'm so sorry son. It was a spur of the moment trip and I left without thinking. I had all that time off and I just needed to get away. I know if I told your Dad, he would have tried to talk me out of it. And if I told you guys, you would not have understood. So, I made the decision on my own to just do it and face the consequences later. The last thing I ever wanted to do was hurt any of you. And what did I tell you about saying "pissed off!" I caressed each son on his cheek.

"Sorry, Mom. Well, I guess you're right about that part. Dad would not have wanted you to fly all the way to Italy by yourself. Weren't you scared to travel that far on your own? Where did you stay? What did you do with all your time?" Neil was more curious than upset.

"Know what? I wasn't scared at all. After living over there for so many years, it kinda felt like going back to visit relatives in another city. I had a really nice time and I'll tell you all about it someday. But for now guys, I need to clean up, get some rest and start making arrangements for tomorrow. Have you seen James today?" I didn't want this discussion to go any further than it already had. In my current state of mind and operating on such little sleep, there's no telling what secrets I would unintentionally reveal.

"He's out shopping with Grandma and Grandpa McAllister. They took him to get some new shoes for his graduation. He wanted to wear his old dirty ripped up sneakers, but Grandma said no way!" Neil laughed at his brother James, who obviously lacked his younger brother's concern for fashion.

"And Grandpa told him he needed a haircut!" Added Carlos, wanting to be part of this grown up conversation.

"Oh yeah?! Grandpa told him that? Well, good for him!" Both my parents stepped in and took over where each was needed. "Where are they staying anyway?" I hadn't noticed any traces of them in the house.

"They're staying at the hotel down the street. She said it was too crowded in the house with Dad's family already here."

Shoot. I heard that. It was my own house, yet it already felt too crowded with them here. And now that there is this added dimension of knowing that my husband has wanted to leave, the house became even smaller. So what if I had just spent two weeks with Giovanni? That didn't diminish the fact that Mark had been keeping up this façade for years. If what his mother told me was correct, he was just been playing a role and doing only enough to keep me here until the kids were older. I guess he was going to leave me when Carlos graduated from high school. We had both lived engrossed in our own lies for years. Now ain't that a trip?

"Okay. I'll give them a call later to catch up." I stood up and stretched. "By the way, where's Pops? Where's he off hiding?" I started towards my bedroom, and then stopped.

"Oh, he's outside in the gazebo reading the newspaper. You want me to go get him?" Carlos offered.

"No, that's okay. I think I'll go out and say hello before I settle in." I had no idea where Mark had gone. He was probably in the study on the computer where he typically was if he wasn't sitting in front of the television. I went to the fridge and picked up two beers and walked out the back door.

CHAPTER 28

"Hey Pops! How are you?" I found Mario out in the gazebo, sitting there quietly watching the birds pluck birdseed from the feeder. As usual, he sat staring wistfully off in the distance. Thankfully, for both our sakes, Ruth was nowhere to be seen.

"Lena, how's my favorite daughter-in-law?" He was genuinely pleased to see me. He stood up and gave me a fatherly hug.

I had always liked Mario. He was the total opposite of Ruth. Maybe that's why we got along so well. "I'm fine. Here ya go. I brought you a cold one." I handed him the beer.

"You bad woman! Now you know Mother doesn't like for me to drink. But if you don't tell her, neither will I." He liked sharing our own little secret.

I wanted to know, but was afraid to ask. What the hell? If the next few days went as I imagined, it could be a while before I got another chance to speak to Mario like this. "Pops, can I ask you a question?"

"Sure Lena. What's on your mind?" He smoothed out the newspaper on the bench and invited me to sit next to him.

I sat. "Well, if I'm being too personal, please tell me to mind my own business. Uh, well, hmmm," I exhaled, not knowing how to pry into my father-in-laws personal life.

"C'mon dear. Whatever it is, it can't be all that bad. What is it that's troubling you child?"

"Okay. Well, I've known you and Ruth for the entire time I've been married to Mark and I can't help but wonder why you let her treat you the way she does. Why is she so unkind to you?" I sipped the beer, hoping he wouldn't tell me to mind my own damn business.

Mario sat back on the bench and closed his eyes for a moment. If I hadn't been paying close enough attention, I might have missed witnessing him momentarily deflate. My heart broke for him in that moment. Had I crossed the line? I was about to get up and let him regroup. He opened his eyes, turned to me and began to speak.

"Lena, I'm not going to lie… This has been a long, hard road for me and Ruth. We have been through some terrible, terrible days. You asked, so I am going to tell you. After high school, I joined the Army because I wanted to get out of my hometown and see the world. Well, during those days, the Army was still "unofficially" segregated and the colored troops were hardly sent anywhere, 'cept down South. Anyhow, I had my fair share of girlfriends during the few years I was stationed away from home, but me and Ruth always kept in touch. She was a good friend who kept writing me letters, telling me what was going on in the old neighborhood, asking how things were going with me. One time, I went home on leave and was feeling a little lonely. I was sick and tired of the continuous stream of women coming and going in and out of my life. None of them meant anything—nothing at all. I was ready to settle down with one girl and raise a family.

On the spur of the moment, I stopped by the local jeweler, picked out a nice little engagement ring and asked Ruth to marry me. Just like that, she accepted. Funny thing was, I knew very early on that I'd made a mistake in marrying Ruth. I say I made a mistake because I was never in love with her, but she was a sweet, nice girl from a good family. She was my high school sweetheart and that's what you did back in those days. You got married and started a family. It was expected. It's what you did. And for a colored Army sergeant, I had it pretty good. My life was on track. I had a beautiful wife, two fine sons, a stable career, and lived in a nice neighborhood. We were comfortable. But you know what Lena? There was something missing in our marriage. No, not something, everything—well everything that mattered anyway. There were no sparks between us, no passion, no romance, no longing for the other when we were apart. We were simply just kind of "there". Our conversations had no enthusiasm. And I soon discovered how different Ruth and I were from one another. Total and complete opposites is what we were." He stopped long enough to take a sip of beer, as he reminisced about the past.

"Well, to make a very long story short, about five years into the marriage, I met this amazing woman named Viola. Now, I want you to know that I never intended to stray. I wasn't looking for another woman. I didn't really need anything more than what I already had. I had accepted that my life with Ruth was what it was. It wasn't a bad life and I was okay living it. But from the moment I laid eyes on Viola, my entire world shifted. It was like the sky opened up and placed her in front of me. It all began innocently enough. We started out as friends. I met her in the mess hall where she worked clearing tables. She was beautiful and had a smile that could light up a room. She wasn't your classical beauty, but she was very pretty. And she was noticeably elegant in a way that made even the most jaded men take notice. So many of the fellows wanted to get to know her, but she wouldn't have any of it. Said she was strictly about putting her life together and didn't have time for the foolishness that being with a man would bring. Matter of fact Lena, you kind of remind me of her." He chuckled and continued speaking.

"I was so smitten that I got to the point where I swapped my lunch break with the other sergeants, just for a chance to see her. I found out that she was a widow. Her husband was killed in some freak accident working in a coal mine. We got to talking and before you know it, we discovered how much we had in common. Over time, our lunch conversations turned into cocktails at the club. We began meeting over in the next town to see a movie or go out to dinner. Before either of us realized what was happening, it was too late. We were hopelessly, foolishly, sadly in love. I say sadly because I was married to Ruth and had two young boys at home. We tried to break it off, several times in fact, because we both knew it couldn't work. There was no way we could ever be together."

I interrupted "Did you ever think about divorcing your wife, divorcing Ruth?" I asked.

"Oh, no, no, no. The only people who got divorced back then were those movie stars out there in Hollywood. Us regular folks couldn't even consider it. And with me being in the Army and having those two boys...there was no way I could ever leave Ruth. So I did what most of the fellows I knew did—I kept her on the side. Viola and I had "an arrangement". We kept it going for about three years before she finally had enough and broke it off. I was heartbroken." He wiped the corner of his eye.

"Whew!" I blew out a small sigh imaging the life he led back then and continued to live now. "Okay, I understand why you had to stay back then, but why did you stay after the boys were grown?"

"Oh child, that ain't the end of the story. Turns out that Ruth found out 'bout me and Viola a few months before she broke it off. I found this out after the fact. Anyway, one day me and Ruth got to talking about how strange life and love is when she asked me if I loved her. I said the right thing and told her of course I loved her. Then she blurted out that there was no way I could love her and have a three year love affair with another woman. I was floored. Didn't know what to say. Couldn't deny it, nor did I want to. I wanted to see what she was going to do because it was one thing for me to want to divorce her, but an altogether different thing for her to leave me. A little piece of me hoped for the latter, 'cause if she left me then maybe there was a chance I could find Viola and start over."

He continued, "Well, Ruth quietly informed me that she had met my "mistress"! I hated that word and never thought of Viola like that. Anyway, Ruth told me that she went to Viola's job and warned her, in front of all her coworkers, that if she didn't stay away from me, she would not only spread the word that Viola was a whore, but would ruin my career and me in the process. Of course, Viola refused to acknowledge that she was involved with me. She accused Ruth of being a jealous housewife and said half the men on base fantasized about her. But Ruth was no fool, Viola may have convinced her coworkers that Ruth was out of her mind, but she got the message nonetheless. That's why she broke it off so quickly. She wanted to protect me. Even the hint of infidelity back in those days was enough to ruin a service man. She told me that if I even so much as breathed the same air as Viola, she would do everything she could to ruin my career, have me locked up in jail, and make for damned sure I would never see either one of my boys again. I believed her and the very next day, I put in for a transfer to another post." He exhaled.

"Haven't seen, nor heard from Viola ever since. But Lena, I know that woman was the love of my life! She was the one I was supposed to be married to. And if only I had waited a few more years before marrying Ruth, I would have been living a life with my queen, rather than being locked in this prison of a marriage with someone I was never in love with. You asked me why I never left? After awhile, Ruth and I got back into the routine of our so called "marriage". We continued to raise the boys and build a comfortable life together. I did twenty-two years in the Army and must've had a dozen brief casual affairs. And that's all what they were--flings. I didn't care about any of those other woman. They were just a physical release. After all, I am still a man. Ruth looked the other way. As long as I came home at night and kept her accustomed to her lifestyle, she looked the other way. I stayed with her because I couldn't have a life with my one true love and after awhile it was just easier to stay with her than it was to leave. I have tried to look for Viola many times over the years, but I figure she eventually moved on, remarried and changed her name. Just as well though...Ruth would never have given me a divorce. She seems to be at her happiest seeing me miserable. She has even told me that she will never forgive me for disrespecting her, but I should make it my priority in life to do everything possible to earn her forgiveness. Guilt is a powerful motivator and I guess that's what I've been doing all these years—repaying my debt." He drained his beer and wiped at the other corner of his eye.

I didn't know what to say. I put my hand over Mario's and we both sat in silence contemplating all that he had just revealed.

"Lena, my dear. I don't know where you have been, nor do I want to know what you were doing while you were away... Something in you has changed. I don't know if it is due to your sickness or what, but there is an obvious change. You know I love you, my son, and my grandsons with all my heart, don't you? I'll bet you're wondering why I told you this story I've held so close to my heart all these years. I have never told anyone. Well, I want you to realize that some of us only get one chance to find our true love. For the majority of folks, love is elusive. It doesn't come around too often, so when it is within your grasp, fight to hang on to it. I've seen the way you and Mark are together and it makes me sad. You two are like apples and oranges trying to raise pears. I don't want either one of you to end up the way me and his mother have. I'm not saying that you two don't belong together, but if you have an opportunity to be truly happy, then you'd better think twice about letting it slip away."

"Thanks for sharing your story with me Mario. I know it took a lot of trust and courage for you to open up like that to me. I want you to know that I heard every word you said and I will keep your story in strictest confidence."

For the first time, I understood why Mark was the way he is. He was raised in a family filled with deceit, empty of love, and void of any obvious display of affection. What a messed up way to raise a child. Looking at Mario was like looking at a gorgeous home that was trashed on the inside. He was a shell of his former self. I pitied my father-in-law. I think he saw it in my eyes, but was too indifferent to care.

"There you two are. I've been looking all over for you. It's time for supper. Mario! I know you haven't been drinking! You know you can't handle your liquor!" Ruth had broken the spell and Mario once again retreated back into himself.

"I'm sorry Mother. It's alright. Lena and I just had the one." He apologized.

"Tsk, tsk, tsk…" She looked first at him, then me. Ruth shook her head again in disgust and went back inside.

"Mario, it was just the one and why can't you have a beer if you want one? Mark told me that the only reason you don't drink is because Ruth doesn't want you to. Not because you can't. Is that true?" If there was another reason, I wanted to know.

"No, there's no real reason why I shouldn't drink. It's just easier to do what she wants. Life tends to be more peaceful when Ruth gets her way." Mario gathered up the newspaper, squeezed my shoulder and went inside like a dutiful husband should.

CHAPTER 29

"James, hurry up! You're going to be late for your own graduation!" I screamed at my oldest child who seemed to possess only one speed – slow!

"I'm coming. I can't find my cap!" He yelled back from his room.

"You can't find it because I'm holding it in my hand. Remember, you didn't want to risk crushing it. You asked me to hang on to it for you?"

I walked down the hall towards his room and stopped at the scene unfolding before me. His grandfather stood behind him as they both faced the mirror. Mario was very patiently showing James how to correctly tie his necktie. I took my digital camera out to permanently capture this "Kodak moment". The pride was evident in his grandfather's eyes. My own eyes misted over when James draped the graduation gown over his Sunday best clothes. He looked so grown up. When the moment became just a bit too serious for him, he loosened everyone up with a silly pose for the camera. That's my boy! What a ham!

Mark's voice boomed over the house's intercom system, "Come on people. Let's go! Everybody who's going needs to form up in the hallway. Right now!" He ordered.

The boys, their cousins, aunts and uncles, gathered up and broke off into smaller groups to ride together. A procession of six cars followed me and Mark in the lead. My mother and father were going to meet us at the downtown convention center where the ceremony was going to take place in less than two hours. Thank goodness it was only a fifteen minute drive from the house. I don't think I could have ridden any longer in the car with Mark.

We all arrived at approximately the same time. Both sides of the family. It was a mini family reunion between the Delgado's and the McAllister's and we filled three rows of seats. There must have been over 500 graduating students and each one had at least fifteen to twenty people there supporting them. It was a mad house filled by the buzz of excitement electrifying the air.

The promise of a bright future was on every parents mind and the anticipation of a fun-filled evening was on every students. When James's name was called and he walked across that stage to pick up his diploma, our entire section went wild. We blew into noise makers. Everyone who could whistle did, and others just screamed out his name. The support everyone showed for my baby's milestone overtook me. I sat quietly and smiled at my firstborn's achievement. He did it! Though there was never a doubt he would graduate from high school, to see him finally make it was a wondrous event.

Mark took my hand in his and gave it a gentle squeeze. "We did it. One down, two to go…" He exclaimed, displaying a proud grin.

Any other time I wouldn't have thought twice about such an innocent remark, but Ruth's words were still fresh in my mind. He was going to leave me when all the kids were finished with school. Asshole!

"Yeah!" I agreed, "Only another few years and it'll be just the two of us!" I admit I said it just to get a reaction out of him. He didn't take the bait. Just sat there and nodded his head in agreement. I looked over at Mario and Ruth. Their body language said it all. Get out before it's too late! Then I looked back at my parents. They were holding hands, giddy with excitement and were laughing their heads off. Whatever problems they had in the past, they must have fixed them. As much as I tried, I could not remember their ever holding hands in public. I had to have a long talk with that woman.

I felt something vibrate in my blazer pocket. In my haste, I'd forgotten to leave my Italian cell phone at home. It vibrated again, and then rang two times. The only reason I heard it at all was because of a lull in the ceremony, as the valedictorian prepared to speak. I put my hand in my pocket and hit the button to quiet it. That worked for a moment, then the phone vibrated and rang again. Mark looked at me trying to quiet the phone. There was only one person who called me on that cell and I wasn't about to answer it.

"What's that?" asked Mark, obviously not recognizing the distinctive ring tone.

"Oh, it's just my cell. I forgot to turn it off." I wanted him to think it was my old phone. I couldn't very well justify having bought a new one.

"Give it here. I'll turn it off. And where did you find that ring tone? It's annoying as hell." He held his hand out for it.

I wasn't about to pull out that funny looking little phone that I would not be able to explain. I turned around as if I were looking for something.

"Hey, I'll be right back. I'm going to the ladies room before the mad rush out of here. Just give me a minute." I stood up and excused myself as I scooted past the relatives.

Mark looked at me with a puzzled expression on his face before turning back to the program. Apparently Mario and Ruth had overheard part of the conversation and had focused their full attention on me. The phone rang again as I reached the end of the aisle.

"Lena, why don't you just answer your phone and tell whoever that is to stop calling." Ruth seemed annoyed.

Oh shut the hell up old woman, is what I really wanted to say. But I gave her my best Mona Lisa smile and kept going. Upon reaching the exit, I pulled out the phone. Just as I expected, it was Giovanni calling. What could he possibly want right now? And why has he continued to call over and over again.

"Hello?" I answered, putting my hand over my other ear so I could hear.

"Lena, *ciao bella*."

"Giovanni, it is so good to hear your voice. Baby, I wish I could talk, but I'm right in the middle of James' graduation. Is everything alright? Are you okay?"

"*Si, si*, all is well. I am well. Lena, I apologize, I forgot about the time difference and of course, I was not thinking that you were with your family when I called. I hope my calls have not caused you troubles."

He didn't know the half of it. Why should he expect me to *not* take his calls? I had been his and his alone since we'd know one another. There had been no one to shield his calls from. That is, not until now. "No, it's okay. What's going in?" I only had a few minutes to talk before people began pouring out of the auditorium.

"I just found out I have the opportunity to come to the United States for my first visit. There is an international convention for those in the Nightclub and Entertainment business and it is being held in Dallas, Texas. I will be there next week and I was hoping you could meet me." He sounded excited.

"You're coming to Dallas next week? For real?" I couldn't hide my enthusiasm. Well, not until the reality of the situation walked out of the auditorium looking for me. Mark looked to his left, then his right. He walked towards the ladies restroom and stood outside like a guard at a prison gate. I scooted further behind the pillar out of his view.

"*Si, amore mio*. I would very much like to see you. My heart has been aching for you ever since you left. As luck would have it, I received this invitation in the mail just this morning. I looked on a map and see Kansas is not too far from Texas. *Alora,* I want to mix business with pleasure by attending the convention, but mostly I want to see you again. Do you think you will be able to come?" His voice was hopeful. He sounded so far away.

"Oh baby. I'll see what I can do. There is so I have to take care of. I haven't even had time to think straight. And as much as I want to, I really can't talk about it right now. I'm sorry. I'll try to call you later and give you more of an answer. Okay? Baby I've got to go. The ceremony is almost over and I have a million things to do." I felt awful having to hang up, but I had no choice.

"Lena, of course you cannot just drop everything to be with me. What was I thinking? *Si,* please call me when you have more time to talk. I miss you." The disappointment in his voice was evident by his tone.

"I miss you, too. Baby, I've got to go…*ciao.*"

"*Ciao* Lena. Talk to you soon." He hung up reluctantly.

I clicked the end call button, turned the phone off and stowed it in a hidden compartment of my purse. Mark was still standing by the ladies room. Luckily he was looking in the opposite direction from where I stood. I pulled myself together and hurried towards him calling out his name.

"Mark, what are you doing out here? I told you I'd be right back." I tried to act normal, whatever normal was for me nowadays.

"You were acting so strangely. I thought I'd come out and check on you. Where were you? I thought you were going to the ladies room?" he asked, looking me up and down suspiciously.

"I did go to the ladies room. This one was being cleaned, so I went to the one down the hallway. What's with the sudden concern anyway? I can't remember the last time you came to check on me when I've gone to the restroom?" I was not going to get into this right now. Yes, we both had a lot of questions, but now was not the time, nor was it the place.

"Let's see. Well…. You've been in the hospital, lying there in a coma for a couple of weeks. Scaring me and the kids half to death, I might add! Then before you've had time to fully recover, you jump on a plane and run off to Italy without telling anyone. Now, during our son's graduation, I hear the ringing of a cell phone I don't recognize and all of a sudden you have to use the restroom?! Now, I am not the sharpest tool in the shed, but given your behavior, don't you think I should be concerned?" He restrained his growing anger, barely.

"Okay. You have made your point. Look, let's just get through tonight and then we can talk. I know you have a lot of questions you want answered. So do I. However, we have a graduation party to host and a whole lot of folks to entertain. Let's do that first. Then we'll talk. All right?" I knew above all how Mark hated to be put on the spot. The last place he wanted to be was the center of family gossip. Considering both sides of the family were in town and closely watching everything that went on in our house, this may have been asking for too much.

"C'mon. Let's go back inside. The graduation ceremony is almost over." He guided me by the elbow leading me back to my seat.

Ruth glared as I sat down. I smiled in return. We listened to a few more key speakers, heard a couple of unrecognizable songs sang by the youth chorus, then watched as the graduates tossed their caps in the air signifying the end of high school and their youth, as they knew it. I was so proud of my son and in that moment nothing else mattered, only his happiness.

The house was filled with teenagers stuffing their faces with too much food. James was extremely popular and convinced a few of his friends to combine their graduation parties into one location—this house. There were kids coming and going, disturbing the peace as only teenagers can.

Thankfully, Mark had the foresight to warn all the neighbors of the party and apologized in advance for the noise and inconvenience they would surely encounter this evening. The last thing we wanted was some ticked off neighbor calling the police and disrupting the celebration. Music blared from the speakers and kids danced wherever there was open space. There was plenty of liquor flowing among the adults for whoever wanted to partake. The men had a game of cards going and the ladies jumped in to lend a hand wherever they were needed. The party was a success. Now, I could finally think.

I picked up a bottle of wine someone left on the counter, took it outside and found a nice quiet spot in the yard. Oh no! Here comes Mom. I was wondering when she would finally make her way over. I didn't feel like talking to her about my problems, but the discussion was inevitable.

"How you doing Lena?" asked my mother, recognizing I wasn't as upbeat as usual.

"I'm okay, I guess. Today went well. Look. Everyone's having a great time." I responded looking towards the house and listening to the laughter coming from inside.

"Yes, I know today went well. But how are *you* doing? The last time we talked, you were in Italy or somewhere. What's going on?" she asked with motherly concern.

"Where to begin? I don't know, Mom. I'm really, really stressed out and confused about so many things. I'm at a crossroads. I am not happy or fulfilled with how my life is going. I feel like I've been going through the motions of living. I've been existing. Not living. When I was in the hospital, I had something like a spiritual awakening. I haven't been the same since." I turned the bottle upwards drinking St. Louie style.

"What do you mean, "a spiritual awakening"? Are you saying you saw God?" She was the one who now appeared confused.

"No, nothing like that. Well, maybe…. But something happened to make me "wake up" and realize I am not living the life I'm supposed to be living. Mom, we have one life to live and if we don't take full advantage of each moment, we are not living the life God intended for us. When I was over there in Italy, I felt alive. You know I love my children and they are most precious to me…it's just that being a mother is not enough. Do you understand what I mean?" I felt the wine beginning to work.

"Of course, I know what you mean. But most of us aren't able to jump on airplanes and fly off to another country on a whim. So what do you think is missing in *your* life?" She chuckled to herself.

"Love for one thing. I think I have been sharing my life with someone who doesn't *really* love me. Most of the time, I think he doesn't even like me. Yeah, he does care about me, but big whoop. I'm just kinda here, like furniture, ya know? When Mark looks at me, he might as well be looking at the dishwasher. We both get about the same attention. Do you know we haven't been intimate in so many months I can't remember when the last time was? And you know what the worst part is? I really don't mind. In fact, I prefer it that way." The wine was loosening up the connection from my brain to my mouth.

"Lena, all marriages go through this. Child, it's impossible to keep that romantic, giddy feeling forever. That only happens in the beginning. After a few years, you settle down and become companions. You get used to each other and stop paying so much attention to one another. That's just the way life works. Comfort settles in and romance walks out. Can't expect to be lovey-dovey all the time." Mom was resigned to her way of life.

"Mom, I believe some of what you're saying, but what if you were never really in love to begin with? What if what you believed was love wasn't? What if you met someone who had such a profound effect on you that you'd do anything and everything to be with him? Someone who invoked feelings you didn't know you had? What would you do if you met a man who felt more like your husband in a few days than your real husband had in twenty years? What if your heart did flip-flops whenever you thought about him? What if just the sound of his voice made you sigh? What if having him near made you feel more like you than you've ever felt? What would you do?" The wine bottle was rapidly approaching empty.

"I don't know. Me and your Daddy have been together for so long I have never considered any of what you described. Now don't get me wrong. We have a good thing going, but I don't believe I've ever felt that way about anyone, even him. Lena, you have always been such a romantic. You are one of the rare people who must feel passionately about their mate. Most of us can take or leave the romance. But you, you always felt things so much deeper than anyone I have ever known. You always were the passionate, sensitive child, the one who both gave and craved affection. Always so touchy-feely..." She eyed the bottle in my hand, but thought better of mentioning it.

"I guess you're right. I do need to have that intensity in my life. I crave those intense emotions, the need to really feel something deeply. What Mark and I have is so shallow. It only exists on the surface. What you see is what you get. Its only enough to keep us living in the same house, raising the kids, and doing what's necessary to maintain a comfortable standard of living."

"Lena, oh my goodness!" The proverbial light bulb flickered above her head as she finally made the connection. "Is that man you were visiting the reason you ran off to Italy? When you called me that night, you sounded so unlike yourself. It was like I was speaking to the Lena from years ago. You sounded happy that night, truly happy. Baby, you're thinking about running off with him? Umh, umh, umh...." My mother seemed genuinely surprised.

I looked towards my mother and turned up the wine bottle until it was empty. The velvety smooth liquid warmed my insides as it coursed down my throat. There was no need to answer her questions. My silence confirmed her suspicions. I hung my head in shame. Guilt washed over me.

"I just found out that Mark told Ruth as soon as the boys are all grown and out of the house, he's going to leave me. The only reason he's stayed around this long is because he made a commitment to raise the children. Can you believe that shit? Here I was for all these years, thinking that he was perfectly content to live in a loveless marriage. I thought I was the only one unhappily married. Turns out neither one of us want to be in this marriage." I laughed quietly at the irony.

"How do you know that? What are you talking about? Who told you that mess?"

"Ruth did. I guess she was pissed off at me for leaving Mark and the boys. When I came home today, she just blurted out that Mark has wanted to leave me for years. She said she was the one who convinced him to stay so the boys would have a daddy in the house. So now my boys have a drunk for a daddy and a mommy who cries all the time. Some happy family, huh?"

"That woman had no business telling you something like that even if it were true. Some people just don't know how to keep their noses out of other folks business! I'm gonna have a talk with her and tell her to butt out. You two are both grown and don't need your parents in the middle of your marriage." My mother was annoyed with Ruth and her constant meddling.

"Mom, none of this is Ruth's fault. Actually, she did me a favor by telling me the truth. Now I know how Mark really feels and what he's felt about me for years. It wasn't just in my head and it wasn't just me feeling like this. It's both of us. Yeah, it was too bad I had to find out his plans from his mother, but at least now I know the deal." I slurred the last sentence, but what the hell. I was drunk. I tried to stand, but my legs wouldn't cooperate.

The wine had accomplished its intended effect. I was numb and only wanted to lie down in my bed. It was late and people were slowly started to leave. My mother helped me inside. I found all three of my children and hugged them goodnight. They found it amusing that Mom had just a little too much celebration and needed to lie down. Normally, Mom was the sober one who always made sure nothing got out of hand. Not tonight. Tonight, Mommy was just another drunken adult. I pulled the covers back on the bed, kicked off my shoes, and climbed in fully dressed.

The last thing I remember was my mother closing the door and turning off the light. I welcomed sleep. I welcomed the escape.

~~~~

I felt really strange. Like I was actually dreaming. I stood outside looking into the window of the now familiar cottage. It was that part of the day, just before daylight turns into dusk—when the grays and blues of the waning sunlight suddenly morph into darkness. *The Golden Time of Day*, as Frankie Beverly of *Maze* described it.

Did I go back to that "place" again? I couldn't have. There were so many things I still had to accomplish back home. Wait a minute…there is something different. Where's Simone? Why isn't she waiting for me? I looked back to the cottage. A folded piece of paper was stuffed in the door jamb. Wonder what that is? I climbed the rickety stairs and felt like I was moving in slow motion. Just as if I were in a dream. I pulled the paper free and saw that my name was written on the outside. I opened it and read:

Dearest Lena,

You may be wondering why I wasn't here to greet you when you arrived… Remember when we first met, I told you that you've been here many times before? The only difference about that visit was your ability to see me. Although I am always able to see you, this time, you will not see me. That is why I have written you this letter. It is the only way I can interact with you. You see, you are actually dreaming right now.

Your heart wants desperately to escape and bring you back here. However, your mind is in direct conflict with that action, so any attempt to remain will be thwarted. Deep down you know that there is unfinished business you must take care of and until you do, you will not be able to rest comfortably.

Precious one, you cannot run away from your problems. Face them head on and deal with your life in the real world. You do not need to live within the confines of your mind. There is an entire world out there awaiting you and what you can add to it.

This place is not long term for you, which is why you couldn't stay then, or now. You possess a zest for life that can only be satisfied by living it. Do not shortchange yourself and do not deprive your loved ones the opportunity to have you in their lives. Go back to your world and try your best to live each day as if it were your last. I will always be with you to watch over you and keep you safe, but do not expect to see me again for a very, very long time.

Simone

I stayed in the rocking chair on the porch until all the stars shone brightly in the sky. I was alone. Positively alone. There were no children playing, no partygoers on the beach. No Giovanni and no Simone. No distractions.

The gentle sound of the waves breaking against the shore and seagulls calling out to one another soothed me. Much too soon, I felt it was time to go back to the real world and live the life I was supposed to be living. No more fantasy escapes, no more alternate realities where I run to avoid my problems. It was time to grow up. Time to make conscious decisions and deal with whatever consequences that arose from those decisions. I closed my eyes and let the sounds of the night take me back to where I was supposed to be.

CHAPTER 30

"Hey Mom, wake up!" James was sitting on the side of the bed gently nudging my shoulder. "We're about to leave."

He was riding back with my Mom and Dad to St. Louis. He had been accepted at Washington University and wanted to find a summer job as soon as possible. Neil and Carlos had another week of school left, but they too would eventually go to St. Louis and spend part of the summer with the grandparents.

I opened one eye and tried to focus. Cotton balls lined my mouth. When I attempted to speak, James backed away ever so slightly. Oh yeah, there's nothing like morning breath laced with stale red wine to make one turn to the power of *Scope*. I didn't care if my breath offended him; it was my head I was worried about. With every beat of my heart, I felt the spot behind my right eye constrict with the pain of an oncoming hangover-induced headache.

"Baby, please get me a cup of coffee and bring me the bottle of aspirin. Momma's got a fierce headache. I guess I over did it last night." My capri pants were bunched up around my knees. I had slept in my clothes. I pushed back the covers and managed to sit up. James went for coffee and Mark walked out of the bathroom.

He snickered, "What made you think you could drink so much? Your Mom told me you put a hurting on an entire bottle of wine last night. How ya feeling?" His concern threw me off.

"Uh, I'll be alright in a few. It's so quiet. Where is everybody?" The house seemed to have returned back to its normal subdued state.

"Considering it is after 2:00, everyone has already taken off. Headed home. Neil and Carlos are out with their friends and won't be back until this evening. Your parents are the last to leave. I dropped mine off at the airport a couple hours ago. They told me to tell you bye. Pops said he really enjoyed his talk with you and he wished he had it sooner. Funny, Mom said the same thing..." He took the cup of coffee from James and handed it to me. "I don't know what to be more surprised about. I know my Mom can be pretty straightforward and say exactly what's on her mind, but you actually got my Dad to open up? What did you two talk about?"

He was extremely curious. Oh, now I get it. He was fishing about me and his parent's conversation, especially his father's.

"Oh, nothing much. We were just shooting the breeze. That's all…" I sipped the coffee and popped two aspirin in my mouth. I didn't realize I had slept so long. With the jet lag still hanging on, guess I must have needed it. I didn't know how much Mark knew about his parent's past and I surely wasn't going to be the one who broke the news to him.

"Hmmm, that's strange. I got the impression you two had a heart-to-heart talk. I haven't seen my old man smile like that in a while. It was like you had brought up some stuff he'd forgotten about. Hey, it's okay if you don't want to tell me. I can respect that. What about my mother? What deep secrets did she have to share with you?" He appeared genuinely concerned, for he knew his mother very well.

"Mark, your mother didn't say anything more to me than what's she's always said. You and I both know I am not her most favorite person."

I took a large gulp of the coffee and felt an immediate noticeable improvement in my headache. I was probably going through caffeine withdrawal, considering how much espresso I drank in Italy. My body had gotten used to the strong stuff. I made my way to the bathroom, brushed my teeth, straightened my hair and managed to look halfway presentable. I'd take a shower afterwards. I didn't want to hold them up any longer than I already had.

"I need to see James and my parents before they leave. Can we talk later?"

He left it at that. Though he obviously had much more to say, he acquiesced and followed me to the living room where my parents patiently waited.

After we said our good-byes and they made promises to drive carefully, I watched my oldest child take his first steps towards independence. James waved at me, throwing kisses as they pulled out of the driveway. The sting of tears threatened to come, but I pushed them back. Now was not the time to be sad. I had to be happy for him as he embarked on his journey towards becoming a man.

I avoided Mark by heading straight to the bathroom. I peeled last nights clothing from my body and stepped into the steam filled shower and let the water run through my hair, all over my face, down my back. I took my time. There was no hurry to get this conversation started, and yet at the same time, I had let too much time pass and it needed to be done. There was just the two of us in the house. It was now or never…

The shower served its purpose. I was clean and my mind was much clearer. That said, my tummy reminded me that I skipped dinner last night, foolishly drowning my sorrows in a bottle of wine instead of eating. As a result, my stomach growled, grumbled, and threatened to take me down if I didn't put something in it soon. Luckily, there was leftover chicken and spaghetti in the fridge. I expected to be greeted in the kitchen by dishes piled high in the sink and trash covering every conceivable surface. This was not the case. I'm sure I had Mom and Ruth to thank for that. I warmed the food in the microwave and guzzled down a bottle of water in one long gulp. Food in one hand and a second bottle of water in the other, I pulled up a chair to the table, sat down, blessed the food and dug in before Mark dug into me.

I was able to get down a few bites of food before Mark made his way into the kitchen and joined me at the table. I continued to eat while he sat and watched. Either he was waiting for me to speak, or he was assembling his own thoughts and didn't know where to begin. We sat in silence until I had completed my meal. My appetite had disappeared as soon as he entered the room, but not knowing when I'd eat again, I thought it best to finish.

"We need to talk," he stated the obvious. "I want to know what's going on with you. Why did you just up and leave like you did? What the hell were you thinking going off to Italy like that?"

I sat and looked at him. I didn't know what to say—where to begin. I opened my mouth but no words came out. I exhaled, picked up my water, took a long sip and sat it back down. I swallowed. I had to tell him the truth. I finally gathered the courage and the strength to speak.

"Mark, I'm not happy. I haven't been for years. I felt like I had to go away for a little while and sort things out in my head."

"Okay. You're not happy. Let's talk about that. That is what married people do. We talk these things through. Lena, if you needed a break from me and the kids, I would've understood if you wanted to go visit your parents for a little while. You don't go flying off to a fuckin' foreign country for weeks at a time!" He tried desperately to keep his anger in check.

"What bothers you more? That I'm not happy or that I went on a spur of the moment trip to Italy?"

"To tell you the truth, neither one makes much sense. We've been together almost twenty years and you have never said anything at all about being unhappy. Now all of a sudden, out of the blue, you lay this on me. What the fuck is wrong with you?!"

"You need to check yourself and watch your tone. If you want to have a conversation, don't be cursin' and yelling at me!" I knew how quickly this would go south once the yelling began.

"Sorry for yellin'. I'm so confused! I was worried sick about you. The boys were worried sick about you. When you were in the hospital, I didn't know what I'd do if you didn't come around. You're the glue in this family. You keep us all together and you're what makes it possible for me to be who I am!"

"I am sorry for worrying you all like that. I guess I was exhausted and needed to rest. But, don't you get it? I can't always be the one who keeps everything together. I need some help once in a while. I am not Superwoman! Haven't you been paying attention? This isn't the first time that I've told you I'm not happy. I've been saying it for years." I made it a point to not be emotional or this would blow apart.

"Okay, so you've told me this before…. I thought it was because you were having a bad day. I didn't know you meant you were unhappy in general. Is that it or are you unhappy with me?" he asked defensively.

"Let me ask you a question. Do you love me? And before you answer that, I want you to really think about your answer."

"What kind of question is that? Of course, I love you. You're my wife!" He stood up and got a beer from the fridge. He remained standing, leaning against the counter.

"*Why* do you love me?" I asked.

"I love you because you are a good wife and mother. You take care of me and the kids and never complain about it. I don't have to worry about coming home to a dirty house and you are a great cook."

"Okay, go on…." I needed to hear more. So far, he was batting zero out of a thousand.

"Well, you take care of yourself and always look good. You know how to stretch a dollar. And you are so nice. The guys at work are always commenting on how nice you are. I know as long as you are around, I don't have to worry about anything. How's that?!" He seemed pleased with his answers.

"Sounds like you should have married your mother." I replied with no attempt to hide my sarcasm.

"What are you talking about? What do you mean I should've married my mother?"

"Not once did you say how you feel about me. Everything you just said you could have gotten that from hiring someone—a maid, a nanny, or a personal assistant. Or your mother. Do you miss me when I'm gone? Does your heart skip a beat when I walk into the room? Do you desire me and only me? Can you hardly wait to get home to see me, to hold me, to kiss me? Do you think of me as your queen, like I'm the most important person in your life? Do you want to spend the rest of your life with me?" I watched his face cloud over, like I'd asked him difficult questions that required serious contemplation.

Mark stood sipping his beer, silent in his thoughts. Too afraid to speak, too afraid not to. He picked at the label on the bottle, pulling back the four corners until each one met in the center. He worked the label off, balled it up, and tossed it towards the trashcan. He missed.

"Yeah, that's exactly what I thought. You don't have anything to say." His silence answered my questions.

"Look Lena, all that stuff you just mentioned...okay, so I'm lacking in the romance department. That doesn't mean that there's something wrong with our marriage. We just need to rekindle the fire, that's all. Come on baby, we've been married too long for this nonsense. What do you want me to do? You want to go away together? Just the two of us? I'll even take you to Italy for your birthday. I can start helping out more around the house if that's what you want. I promise I'll try to do better. Okay?!" He looked almost desperate.

"No, I don't want to go away together. A vacation is not going to fix what's wrong with us. Face it! You don't love *me*. I don't think you ever did—at least not the kind of love that sustains a marriage." I suddenly felt very, very weary.

"What are you saying?" He sat down in the chair facing me.

I had to ask otherwise I'd never know the truth. "Mark, remember when your mother told you we had a conversation?" I watched him nod. "Well, she blurted out something to me. I don't think she really meant to say anything at all, it just kinda came out."

"All right. You and my mother had a talk. What did she have to say this time?" He braced himself. He knew his mother very well.

"Ruth said you were going to leave me as soon as all the boys were grown and on their own. Said the only reason you stayed this long was because she told you to be a man and own up to your responsibilities and obligations. Did you tell her that?" I sat back and impatiently waited for his response. The tapping of my fingers on the table was a dead giveaway to the feelings I kept bottled inside.

He inhaled deeply, and then slowly let it out. "When I first met you, I thought you were the classiest woman I had ever known. You had a style and grace I had never seen before. I didn't really care that we were as different as night and day. My life was the Army—that's all I knew. I didn't hang with girls, women, like *Ms. Lena*."

He emphasized my name, almost making it sound like a dirty word. I let it slid to hear what else he had to say.

"You were pretty, smart, and you didn't fall down at my feet like most of the women I knew. You made me work for you and I wasn't going to stop until you were mine. Problem was, once I had you, I didn't know what to do with you. And then we had the boys one after another and before I knew it, I was the "family man". Seemed like you loved them more than me, but I didn't trip, cause that's what mothers do. My road dawgs never let up on me because I was no longer one of them. You always had this air about you like you were too good for me. Sometimes, I felt like I didn't measure up to your standards, like I could never take care of you the right way. I kinda let things slide at home and put most of my energy into work where I knew I could measure up. I may have told my Mom, early on into our marriage that I didn't think we were going to work out. I don't remember telling her anything about leaving when the boys were older. If she said I did, most likely I did." He mentioned this as if it were nothing.

"Are you telling me that you feel inferior? Is that why you treat me so badly? You trying to feel better about yourself by making me feel bad about myself?"

"Hell to the no! I don't feel inferior to nobody! Especially you! And I don't need to put a woman down to feel like a man. It's just that you were always so, so, "high sididity" in your attitude. Just cuz you went to school and all…" he added.

"I never thought I was better than you. I can't help how you see me. You knew how I was when you met and married me. I didn't change. I never pretended to me something I wasn't. But you… You're not the same man I met and married. What happened to the man who promised to cherish me forever and give me the world? You pursued me, remember? You told me you would quit drinking, but you've done just the opposite. You can't even get through a day without a drink in your hand. In fact, you drink so much that the alcohol oozes from the pores of your skin. You think I like that?! Mark, tell me the truth. Are you truly happy with *me*? I ask because *I* am not happy in this marriage and it's time for us to do something about it." I felt defeated.

"You want to know the truth, huh? Couldn't leave well enough alone, could you? Always pushing and pushing until you get what you want. You know I was willing to stay in this marriage and raise our boys, putting up with your "wanna-be-miz-high-and-mighty" bourgeois ass! You say you're not happy?! I don't care if you're happy or not. You think I am?! What does being happy have to do with anything anyway?!"

It took every bit of resolve I had to not throw my empty water bottle at him.

He shouted, "Problem with you is you watch too much damn TV. You always thought you were better than me just cuz you got your MBA. Humph! I'm the one who took care of you and supported you when you were going to school trying to get that degree. You didn't even have a job! If it weren't for me, your ass would be on the streets somewhere. You think you something, don't you?! You ain't shit! And you never will be anything without me!" Mark screamed, thumping his chest like some throw back to cavemen days.

"Oh, so you really think you rescued me?! You actually believe I needed you to take care of me all those years?! I gave up so much to follow you around the world. I'm the one who sacrificed so you could be successful and have that career! Who was there to take care of the boys when your ass was laid out on the floor dead drunk?! Who pulled you out of the car to keep the neighbors from seeing you passed out behind the wheel?! How many times have I had to get your ass up so you wouldn't be late for work? *You* wouldn't be where *you* are without me! And now you have the nerves to tell me that I ain't shit?! You must be out of your damn mind!" I stood facing him, feeling the rage from all those years of holding my tongue come to the surface.

He waved his hand in the air, dismissing me and my anger. "You must be delusional!"

I continued, "Don't you think we both deserve to be happy? All these years, you put me last, treating me as if I didn't matter. You treat your friends better than you treat me. I was just someone who took care of you and the kids. You never showed me you cared for or loved me. I was just the maid, the cook and someone to fuck when you needed it. And for all I know, you got some bitch on the side!"

"Oh, c'mon. You're the one who's crazy! Without me, you're nothin'. Just another dependent!" He smirked. "You ain't never had to pick me up off the floor or anywhere else. And if I do have someone else, it's because you haven't been a wife to me in years. Every time I get near you, you pull away. You act like you don't want me to touch you! When we do make love, you can't wait for it to be over! You can't wait to wash me off of you—like I'm dirty or something!" He yelled, eyes bulging. Spit flew from his mouth.

"Well, maybe if it lasted for more than a minute, I'd enjoy it more!" I knew I would hurt him with that last comment, but at this point I didn't care. The damaging, contemptuous words were flying uncontrollably from both our mouths.

"And maybe if you acted like you wanted it, we'd both enjoy it more! You lay there like some cold, dead fish... No, I don't love you and I haven't for years! Is that what you wanna hear? Okay, so now what Lena? *You* gonna leave *me*? Is that part of your plan in flying off to Italy? You got someone better waiting for you?!" He threw up his hands in defeat.

"Yeah, Mark. I do want to leave you. I don't love you anymore. I want a divorce." I managed to somehow finally say aloud the words that had rested on the tip of my tongue for as long as I could remember.

"Fine. Then get the hell out of my house," he said with a chilly calmness in his voice.

Mark turned around and walked out of the kitchen. He uttered not another word. I heard the front door slam, followed shortly by the screeching sound of his tires as he raced out the driveway towards the street. He was pissed and this time didn't care if the neighbors knew. I was relieved that he'd left, yet slightly alarmed at his behavior. It was still early. With everyone gone, the house was unusually quiet. Thankfully, the boys were still out with their friends. I wandered around the house, occasionally peeking through the curtains to see if Mark had changed his mind and come back to continue the argument.

I flipped mindlessly through the hundreds of cable channels, finally settling on the *Discovery Channel.* They were airing a special documentary on the crisis of obesity in America. They had this brother on who must have weighed at least 600 pounds and still gaining. He was so fat he could barely get out of bed to use the bathroom. The only way he could breathe was with the aid of an oxygen tank. This huge man was in denial about the amount of food he took in on a daily basis, so the producers laid out an actual spread of a typical day's worth of meals. The amount of food on that table could have fed a family of four for a week. I was thoroughly disgusted, but couldn't look away. It was like watching a train wreck. After they switched to another story about a woman who could barely walk due to her massive weight, I made myself turn off the television. Enough was enough already.

I went to my closet and opened the suitcase I never got around to unpacking. All at once, images of Giovanni flooded back, washing away the awful blowup with Mark. I slowly pulled out each piece of clothing stuffed inside. I pressed the dress I had worn to his parent's house to my nose. If I inhaled deeply enough, I could just make out the scent of his cologne commingled with my own perfume.

I sorted the dirty laundry from the clean and hung the remaining items in my closet. I was about to put the suitcase away when a piece of paper caught my eye. I slipped my hand into the outer pocket and pulled out an envelope with *Alitalia* written across the front. I opened the jacket and pulled out three one-way tickets from Kansas City, Kansas to Verona, Italy. They were good for one year from the date I left. I sat down and stared off into space.

"Oh, Giovanni! You do love me." When did he have time to buy these tickets and when did he put them in my luggage? I had to speak to him and I was alone in the house. There would be very few opportunities in the upcoming days to call him. Now, where did I put that cell phone? Oh yeah, I hid it in my purse during last night's graduation ceremony.

It was about 1 am in Italy. I didn't think Giovanni minded my calling so late and chances were he was still at *Busco's.* Very few minutes remained on the card. I figure I'd use them until they ran out. I did a quick recheck of the house making sure I was still alone before I sat down to talk. I powered up the cell and hit redial for Giovanni's number. The phone rang twice before he answered.

"Ciao bella. Lena, amore mio." Love colored his voice with joy.

"Giovanni! Baby, I miss you so much! I haven't been the same since I left your side. I feel like I'm moving in slow motion. Like I'm in a fog." I felt the first waves of emotion hit.

"Lena? Is everything okay? You do not sound like yourself."

"That's probably because I'm not myself. I don't know who I am at this moment. James left with my parents today to begin another chapter in his life. He's on his way to becoming a man. My other two boys are out somewhere playing with their friends and I just told Mark I want a divorce. Told him I didn't love him anymore." Funny how I didn't cry when I talked to Mark, but hearing the concern in Giovanni's voice let me know I could confide in him.

"I see. *Va bene.* How did he take the news?" Giovanni was extremely concerned, and rightfully so.

"I don't know. He seemed surprised at first, then he got pissed off and told me what he really thought about me. Before he left the house, he told me to get out."

"I see. Of course he was angry. When are you going to leave?"

"I'm not going anywhere right now... I will leave, but it will be on my terms. I just got back and I really don't have anywhere to go. I think I'll be okay staying here until I can figure things out." At least, I hoped I would.

"Lena, I want you to pack your bags and go to a hotel—perhaps for a couple of nights. I am concerned about your safety. When a woman tells a man she wants to leave him, he will become very, very angry. It hurts his pride more than anything else."

"You know what? I found out from his mother and he later confirmed that it's always been his intention to leave when the boys are old enough. He isn't happy in this marriage either. I think that if both of us want out, then what's the problem? He's not happy, I'm not happy..." Made sense to me.

"*Amore mio*, you are attempting to apply logic to an illogical, emotional situation. You have just told a man you do not love him. No matter what his feelings are for you, he will not take this news well at all. It is a macho thing. Logic and sense do not apply. I want you to seriously consider taking your boys and going somewhere else until he has had an opportunity to cool off." He spoke as if he had firsthand knowledge of this situation.

The seriousness in his voice did manage to catch my attention. "I hear you Giovanni, but I'll be okay. He's never been violent with me. I think his bark is worse than his bite. He won't do anything stupid."

"*Va bene.* Lena, if he harms a single hair on your beautiful head.... Well, let me just say he had better not do anything to you. *Por favore,* I want you to call me everyday and tell me that you are safe. As I told you a few days ago, I will be in Texas next week. If I have to come to Kansas to get you, I will *amore.*"

I heard the front door open followed by laughter coming from my two youngest. I was always amazed by their boundless energy. They headed to the kitchen for snacks.

"Mommy, we're home!" Carlos called out.

"Hold on a moment Giovanni, my boys just came home." I called out to them, "I'm in my room on the phone. I'll be out in a few! Okay, I'm back. I promise you I'll be okay. Don't worry about me. He won't do anything to me as long as my boys are around. And about your trip, let me see what I can do about that. I can't let you come all the way the states and not see you." I smiled at the thought of seeing him again.

"I will trust your judgment. If you tell me not to worry, I will try not to, but I make no guarantees. I want you to call me tomorrow. *Promessa?*"

"Yes, yes, yes.... I promise. Love, I have to go. My boys are looking for me. I'll call you tomorrow. I love you."

"*Ti amo tu.* Be safe my lovely Lena."

"Giovanni, before you hang up... I almost forgot to tell you. I found the three tickets to *Italia* in my luggage. Thank you so much! You are so sweet and thoughtful."

"*Si,* for you I will do anything. I will talk to you tomorrow. *Ciao.*"

"*Ciao,* my love." And with that, I turned off the phone and tucked it back safely inside my purse.

CHAPTER 31

I spent the remainder of the evening talking to Neil and Carlos about their plans for the last week of school. Both were excited about their upcoming summer vacations, which seemed to revolve around sleeping late and eating as much junk food as they could stand. Neil had just gotten his driver's permit earlier this year and wanted to spend as much time as possible behind the wheel. James often took him out so could to get used to being on the road. Unfortunately, Neil equated driving a real car with those in the arcades. I had yet to convince him that *California Speed* was not good practice for being on the road with real drivers. My plan was to put him in driver's training and then let him get his license.

Mark still hadn't made it home, but I wasn't worried. He had stayed out late before, although this time, he supposedly had good reason to. To take my mind off our earlier argument, I joined the two of my boys and watched Tom Cruise play the hero in *War of the World's* on the big screen television. We munched on buttery microwave popcorn. When the movie ended, we all retreated to our respective rooms. In spite of my sleeping half the day away, I felt worn out and needed the rest.

The sound of the garage door opening woke me with a start. I looked at the clock. It was 3:33 a.m. My heart began to beat wildly in my chest. Something was dreadfully wrong. I heard Mark fumble with his keys trying to unlock the door.

He finally managed to get the door open, banging it against the wall as he did. He must have tripped over something in the dark hallway because a barrage of every imaginable curse word he knew spewed out his mouth. I normally don't lock the bedroom door because he usually heads right to the living room sofa to pass out in front of the TV. Not this time. This time, before I was able to get out of the bed, he burst into the bedroom cursing at me. He turned on the overhead light. I shielded my eyes from the brightness.

"Bitch! I thought I told you to get your sorry ass outta my house! What the fuck you still doing here?! You said you wanna leave! So go! Get the fuck out! What you waiting on?! Leave before I throw you out!" He screamed, looking like a man who had lost his ever loving mind. Maybe he had!

I turned over and prayed he would go away and leave me alone. Before I realized what was happening, he punched the lamp on the nightstand sending the phone and pictures flying all over the place.

"What the hell is wrong with you?! You're going to wake up the boys!" I sat up in the bed and tried to grab my robe. I wanted to put as much space between us as possible. This did not look good.

"I don't give a fuck who I wake up! I want you outta here! Now!" He looked around wildly.

"I'm not going anywhere! How you gonna come in here and tell me to leave in the middle of the night?! This is my house too and I'll leave when I get good and ready!"

"Get the fuck out! You fuckin' cunt!" Mark jumped on the bed, pinning me down beneath him, grabbing for my neck.

"Get off me! Let me go!" I struggled to get away from the man who might as well have been a total stranger.

"I'm gonna kill you bitch!" He totally lost whatever little bit of self-control he had since walking in the house.

"Neil! Carlos! Call 911! Your Daddy is trying to kill me! Call the police!" I yelled at the top of my lungs, as I tried my best to get him off. He would not let go. I could smell the alcohol on his breath. He looked like a madman. His eyes were bloodshot red. I almost didn't recognize him at all. "Get off me!" I continued to yell.

"Mom, what's wrong!" Neil yelled, as he came running down the hallway. He opened the bedroom door.

"Call 911! NOW!!!" I screamed.

"Daddy, get off of my Momma!" Neil was almost as big as Mark. He jumped on his back and grabbed Mark's arms. Mark shrugged off Neil's hold like it was nothing and continued to swing.

"Boy, get offa me! This shit is 'tween me an your fuckin' momma!" He slurred his words, but the meaning was clear as day.

Carlos was on the hallway phone talking to the 911 operator. He was crying but managed to give the operator our address and describe what was happening. Mark heard him on the phone. He jumped off of me and grabbed the phone from Carlos' hands. I rolled off the bed, wrapped myself in my robe and ran outside dragging my boys along with me. As I walked towards the door, I listened in amazement as he switched on the charm to the operator in an attempt to convince her that all was well in the Delgado household. She wasn't convinced, for in a matter of minutes, the cops were pulling up in front of the house.

"Ma'am? Are you alright?" asked the young, fresh-faced officer who looked like he just joined the police force that very morning. He couldn't have been a day over 23. A rookie cop. He shined his flashlight first at me and my boys, then towards the house.

"Fisher, you stay here with them. I'm going to go have a talk with him," instructed the much older officer. He beamed his flashlight at Mark standing in the open door looking out at us. He still had the phone in his hand.

I tried to comfort Carlos as I repeated the events of the evening to the officer. Neil, unfortunately, heard most of what his Dad screamed at me. He wanted to hurt his father for hurting me. I hated Mark at that moment. Hated him for all the years of hurt and abuse he put me through.

I remember as a child the old saying of "sticks and stones can break your bones, but names can never hurt you". I knew firsthand how untrue that was. Throughout our marriage Mark had called me every conceivable name in the book—mostly when he was drunk. But there is also a saying that "a drunken mouth speaks the sober mind". He never respected, nor could he have loved me with the words he inflicted upon me. Looking back, it always bothered me that he could say such hurtful things, but I always let it slide. I once told my auntie how he talked to me and she said as long as he wasn't hitting me, I could put up with it.

Up until tonight, Mark had never tried to physically hurt me—he had never laid a finger on me. Tonight was the first time he actually tried to really hurt me. I was afraid for me, as well as my children. I faced the fact that I didn't know what he would do to me when pushed against a wall. Apparently, he decided to literally come out swinging. The older officer switched places with the younger one to compare my version of the truth with Mark's.

"How are you Mrs. Delgado? I just spoke with your husband there and he says you two had a little misunderstanding this evening. Is that true? I want you to tell me what happened tonight. He seems to have calmed down. Probably had just a little too much to drink and needs to sleep it off." He had the fucking nerve to smile. Like this was some damned joke. Very condescendingly.

"Hell, naw that ain't the truth officer!" Neil interjected. "Look what he did to my Mom's eye!" Tears streamed down his face as he tenderly touched the swollen area around my eye.

"Neil, take Carlos inside the house. I'll be alright. I want to talk to the police alone." I didn't want him hearing anymore of this than necessary. Thank you baby. Mommy will be fine. Go on now." I waited until they were both out of earshot before I spoke.

"Listen, officer... uh?"

"Banks, Ma'am. My name is Officer Banks."

"Okay, Officer Banks. Listen. My husband is a Sergeant in the Army and he's used to dealing with you authority figures. I'm not. So I know he's probably told you that we just had a "little tiff" and that he'll handle things. Probably convinced you that I deserved to have my eye blacked too. Am I right?" I felt indignant that the police would so quickly choose his side.

"Did he do that to you ma'am?" he asked in reference to my black eye.

"Yes, he did. Even threatened to kill me. He was so angry— angrier than I've ever seen him before." I looked up at Mark.

"Lena baby. I'm sorry. I don't know what came over me!" He exclaimed, loudly enough for all to hear.

"Officer, I can't stay in the same house with him. He's still drunk and I don't know what he'll do when you all leave." I watched Mark put on the charm too many times. I wasn't going to chance him doing something else to me once the cops left. I did not intend to end up on the evening news.

"Ma'am, I'm going to call an ambulance to check you out. Your eye is beginning to swell pretty badly and we want to make sure there's no permanent damage." He picked up his radio and called it in. "I'm also going to have to take statements from both your children. Is that alright?" asked the officer. Maybe he wasn't so bad after all.

I put my hand to my eye and felt the swelling. My skin was hot, swollen, and tender to the touch. He must have hit me pretty hard. "Yes, yes, that fine."

"Okay, Mrs. Delgado, this is what's going to happen. We're going to take your husband in tonight. He will be arrested and charged with assault. You can press charges or not, but he will be arrested and will spend the night in jail. The soonest he'll be out is tomorrow afternoon."

"Damn. I hope I'm not making a mistake. No, I'm not going to press charges. After all, I did give him some pretty devastating news today. But even so, he had no right to attack me." I pulled my robe tighter to ward off the cool night air.

"That's your option ma'am, but you may want to contact an attorney for legal advice, considering what you told me earlier. His violence could possibly escalate, especially if you begin divorce proceedings. I've seen it go this way too often. Husband calls his wife names every now and then and gets away with it. Soon the verbal abuse turns to physical, and before you know it, the next time I have to bring a coroner along with me." He shook his head.

"I understand," I replied.

"All righty then. Let's all go inside." He led me towards the house to where Mark stood.

"Mr. Delgado, your wife has decided not to press charges, but despite her reluctance, you are under arrest for assault. We have evidence that you assaulted her, so we are taking you into custody on a domestic violence offense." Officer Banks pulled out his radio and reported in as he led Mark towards his patrol car.

Mark looked at me and the boys then hung his head in shame. "Lena, I am so sorry. Damn, look what I did to you." A stream of tears flowed from his bloodshot eyes.

Looked like those weren't the first tears to fall from his face today. Yeah, I'm sure he was sorry, but in his drunken stupor he threatened to kill me and probably would have if my boys weren't there to stop him. I'd seen too many news stories with men crying in front of the television cameras expressing their sorrow for killing their wives or girlfriends. I did not intend to be one of them. No, I wasn't going to press charges against Mark, but actually, it didn't matter if I did or not. He was now part of "the system" and I had unwillingly joined the statistics of those involved in domestic violence. I always knew his years of arrogantly thinking he could charm his way out of trouble would finally catch up with him. Well, that time had come. I felt nothing. Not angry, not hurt, not sorry—I was just numb.

While I sat in the back of the ambulance, the police officers went inside to take statements from my boys.

By now, many of our neighbors had come outside to see what the commotion was. The early morning had turned into a circus of police cars, ambulances and neighbors standing around half-dressed watching my family fall apart. Mark sat in the back of an unmarked police car, handcuffed, head down, looking embarrassed and ashamed.

Neil called a family friend who remained inside with Carlos. A police photographer took a couple of photos for evidence if and when this ever went to trial.

What an awful mess this weekend had turned out to be! In the span of a couple of days, I had celebrated my oldest son's graduation and was now watching my husband being carted off to jail for domestic violence. I laughed inwardly at the craziness of the situation.

Ironically, as I sat quietly listening to the hum of machinery as the EMTs checked my vital signs, I wished more than ever that I were dreaming. How surreal my life now seemed. All I really wanted was to climb back into my bed, close my eyes and find that place where fantasy collided with reality. More than ever, I needed to see Simone, to have her remind me of the lessons I was supposed to have learned. I didn't want to face reality. I wanted to get away and live a life that revolved around me and only me. I wanted to escape back to a place where I was truly loved by a man who cared only for me and wasn't afraid for the world to know.

For a moment, I actually questioned if I *had* spent those weeks in Italy with Giovanni. He felt as far away as the moon and just as unreachable. I began to wonder if it all really was just a dream and I was now living in a nightmare.

One by one, the neighbors drifted back towards their houses, content in the knowledge that their little worlds were still safe. The cruiser with Mark in the back seat pulled off, followed by the backup. I stood in the driveway with my sons as they watched their Dad being taken to jail. I didn't need to ask them what they were thinking for I saw it in their eyes.

The EMT suggested I make an appointment with my doctor the following day, but in the meantime she told me to take Tylenol for the pain and to keep my eye iced down for a few hours. Thankfully, no permanent damage was done.

After the ruckus had died down and mostly everyone else had gone, only the original officers remained at the house. I thanked both officers for their kindness and watched as they drove off. When I finally looked in the mirror, I discovered why everyone else was so upset upon seeing my eye. It looked like I had been punched by Mike Tyson. I was horrified. After further review, I discovered more scrapes and bruises over my body. I felt like I'd just been in a knockdown, drag out fight. Huh, I guess I had. Now I was pissed. How dare he do this to me? What a night!

By the time all had finally calmed down, the sun was beginning to rise behind a cloudy, drizzly sky. The weather matched my mood perfectly. Even though I could barely see out my right eye, I prepared a big hearty breakfast. We all needed our strength.

Both boys wanted to stay home with me, but I convinced them I was okay and sent them both off to school. Before he left, Neil told me that James had called sometime during the commotion to let us know they had made it to St. Louis safely. He filled him in on what had happened and of course, James wanted to take the first plane back, but Neil convinced him I was okay and he'd have me call him first thing in the morning.

That was the first call I made that morning—to my son to let him know everything was going to be alright. The second call was to my supervisor at work letting him know I needed a little more time to recuperate. He said he understood, but reminded me I would need a doctor's note upon returning to work. I didn't know how I was going to swing that one and frankly, I really didn't care. Screw that job! After those two calls, I made myself a big, hot, extra strong cup of coffee, put on a CD of jazz favorites, and sat down to really think.

I must admit, even though I did what I had to do, I felt I had made a huge mess of everything. Opened up Pandora's Box, a can of worms, really stirred things up with my moment of honesty to Mark.

I never in a million years imagined he'd react the way he did. I knew he could get angry, but to actually put his hands on me?! You just never really know who you're dealing with until you put them in certain situations! I knew I didn't love him. I've known it for a very long time—even suspected how he felt about me... But now that I actually know what he's been feeling all those years and to actually have him physically hurt me!

Well, there was absolutely no way we should even consider staying together. Our marriage was over anyway, we were both just biding our time waiting for the right moment to put an end to our suffering. Guess it was time one of us finally did something about it to help move things along. I didn't want it to go down this way. Although I no longer loved him, I certainly didn't hate him. After all, he was the father of my three children.

Well, too late to turn back now. I suppose I was feeling just a little bad with the way things turned out. But it wasn't my fault that Mark went out, got drunk and tried to beat the hell out of me. That was his bad decision and now he had to pay the consequences for his actions. He had his cross to bear and so did I.

I pulled out my laptop and immediately began a job search. If there was any doubt in my mind about what I was about to embark on, last night removed any remaining traces. I typed in "overseas employment Italy" and discovered an entirely new world open to those who wanted to live a real life adventure overseas. I never imagined there was such a market for those who wanted to live and work in a foreign country! I spent the next few hours applying to various U.S. companies with offices located in northern Italy. I even applied with U.S. government agencies for anything that may come up on the military bases. I figured if it was God's will, then that job would find me.

On a whim, just in case, I booked a flight for next Friday to Dallas on Southwest Airlines. If I was able to make it, at least I'd have a seat and if I weren't, I would only be out $105.46.

I cleaned up and tried to make myself look halfway decent. My eye didn't look quite as bad as it did the night before. The swelling had gone down; now it was just horribly discolored. No amount of makeup could cover this, so I would do what so many other woman before me had done—wear sunglasses until the bruising went away. I heard a key in the lock, followed by the door opening. I thought it was Neil. It wasn't. In walked Mark followed by his friend Keith, who must have picked him up from the police station. I stepped aside and waited for him to speak.

"Hey Lena? How's it...." Keith stammered, unable to complete his greeting. He was obviously uncomfortable and understandably so.

"I'm gonna stay with Keith for a little while until we both can cool off. I just came to get some of my clothes." He looked embarrassed when he noticed Keith's reaction to my face.

"Fine." That was all I could say. I was extremely pissed at him and every time I looked in the mirror, I got pissed off all over again.

"Hey, I'm sorry about hurting you. You know I would never hurt you. Don't you?" He tried to touch my arm.

I didn't say anything—had nothing to say. Just turned my head and walked into the kitchen. About the same time he was walking out with his suitcase, Neil came home.

"Hey little man. I was just telling your mother that I'm gonna be staying with Keith for a minute. I'll give you a call later. Okay?" And he hugged his middle child before adding, "I love you guys and I'm really sorry for how I acted. Tell Car I'll catch up with him later." He walked out the house, a defeated man.

"Later Pops," replied Neil. To me he asked, "You okay Mom?"

I nodded my head, gave him a quick hug and watched him go to his room. Loud music wafted down the hall punctuated by my son's ever deepening voice. I felt incredibly awful. Fortunately life goes on...

The following week was filled with end of school year activities. Mark stayed with Keith as he'd promised. I didn't go to work at all. Didn't want to deal with all the questions about my eye and truthfully, I had absolutely no desire to ever return to that place. I had made my mind up on what I was going to do and now I was determined to make my dreams really come true.

Over the phone, Mark and I discussed his returning home. I agreed with the stipulation that I wasn't going to be there over the weekend. I told him I needed some more time alone to think and was going to take a weekend trip to help clear my thoughts. I was going to Dallas for a few days to visit an old "friend" and would return to discuss our future or lack of one. He agreed, reluctantly, but with the threat of pending charges against him, he didn't want any more trouble.

I hadn't talked to Giovanni. I left a message with his answering service that I was okay and would see him in Dallas. That was four days ago. He hadn't attempted to contact me and I was almost afraid to call him. I didn't know what I was going to say to him, nor how he would react once I told him what happened. The last thing I needed was two hot headed men going at each other over me.

Friday morning rolled around quickly. I checked my reflection in the mirror and was thankful the bruising had all but disappeared. All that remained was what could have passed for a smudge of makeup applied with a heavy hand. At some point, I would tell Gio what had happened, but not on this trip. I didn't want anything to spoil our reunion. I told Neil and Carlos that I would be gone over the weekend and that their father would be home when they returned from school. They knew something was going down, just not what. I asked them both to trust me and I would see them in a couple of days.

CHAPTER 32

The flight was quick. By the time I landed, I had learned all about the *Nightclub and Bar Owners Association Convention*. As fortune would have it, I was seated next to a woman also headed to the convention. I noticed the brochure she was reading and asked about it. We introduced ourselves. Her name was Beverly and she was the Midwest territorial manager for a large entertainment corporation. She had been scouting new locations in Kansas City for a chain of nightclubs based out of Dallas. Her job was to gain inroads on the market and determine the type of clientele who frequented those types of clubs. She was headed to the convention to pick up a few new ideas and meet with other people "in the business".

I informed her I was also going to the convention to meet a friend who had a small, but successful nightclub in Italy. I relayed to her some of what Giovanni had taught me during the short time we were together and explained that I was also interested in learning more about what it takes to run a business. Her ears perked up immediately. She seemed very interested and suggested we all meet. Before we were about to deplane, she gave me her business card and information about her company, *McCluskey and Chambers Entertainment, Inc.*

I called all the major hotels and motels in the area within a 30 mile radius of the airport. Due to the convention, they were all booked solid. I couldn't even get a rental car. I was basically stuck at the airport with nowhere to go and no way to get there. Only one thing left to do. I had to reach Giovanni.

My original plan was to get a room in his hotel, knock on his door wearing nothing but a towel and a smile, and see the surprised look on his face. Okay, so maybe trying to surprise him wasn't the brightest idea. I pulled out the Italian cell phone realizing I didn't know his number by heart. I powered up the phone and immediately the low battery warning came on. The phone hadn't been on the charger since I last used it when I returned from my trip. Considering the last time I used it, I'm surprised it came on at all. I searched through my purse only to realize I didn't have a pencil.

I took out my other cell and quickly dialed, not knowing if I could make an international call or not. The other phone went black just as soon as I punched in the last number.

Now he had no way to reach me because I didn't bring that phone's charger. The call would not go through. A very friendly sounding female voice informed me the call could not be completed as dialed and to please try again. I knew what the problem was. I was not dialing the international code for an Italian phone number. I couldn't make a call using my phone. It was on my family's shared plan and would really look bad for me to make a call to Italy while I was supposed to be visiting a friend in Dallas. And it's not like the call would go unnoticed. Even though Giovanni was in Dallas, the call would probably have to bounce all the way to Italy and back before it was connected, therefore, it would probably cost a small fortune to use this phone.

I went to the nearest gift shop. For only $20 I could make a 5 minute call to Italy. Talk about being ripped off, but what choice did I have? I bought the card and went searching for a pay phone. It's amazing how scarce those things are! I actually had to go back and ask the store clerk where one was. I finally found two pay phones located near the baggage claim. The first phone I tried didn't have a dial tone. Luckily, the second one did and the call went through.

Please answer, please answer, I repeated over and over. I was about to hang up when I heard his all too familiar voice answer.

"*Pronto?*" he finally picked up.

"Giovanni! It's me. Lena! Hey baby guess where I am?!" I could not contain my excitement

"Lena! *Mi dispiace.* I almost did not answer my phone. I did not recognize the number. Where are you *amore mio?*" he asked.

"Baby, I'm in Dallas. I'm at the airport!" I felt my heart race at the thought of seeing him again.

"You are here? In Texas? You should have told me you were coming. I would have met you when you landed." Giovanni sounded excited as well.

"I'm sorry. I wanted to surprise you at your hotel." I laughed. "Problem is I don't know where you're staying. I was going to get a room in your hotel and show up at your door, but all the hotels are booked because of the convention." I started to feel like my old self again.

"Oh, my loveable, impulsive, sweet woman. I only checked in my hotel this morning. I want you to get into the first taxi and come to my hotel. I am staying at the Adam's Mark Hotel, room 1111. I do not want to sound presumptuous, but I reserved a suite anticipating you would make it. I hope you do not mind sharing a room with me?"

I heard the one minute warning beep signifying my time was almost up. "Are you kidding? Baby, I am on my way! Hey, take down my cell number in case you need to call me. My other cell phone died on me, that's why I'm using a pay phone. Sweetie, I've got to go, my time is almost up. I should be there in about half an hour. My love, I can't wait to see you. I miss you so much."

"*Si*, so do I. See you in a few. I love you too," he said it for the first time in English.

"*Ti amo tu*. See you soon. *Ciao*," I replied back. The call ended and I ran to the nearest exit to find a taxi.

I waited impatiently in line at the taxi stand behind a family of Pakistanians decked out in wedding garb. To most folks, I probably looked like I had to use the bathroom because I could not stand still. I shifted my weight from one foot to the other and willed the taxis to hurry up.

Finally it was my turn. I jumped in the backseat of a taxi and instructed the driver. "Please take me to the Adam's Mark Hotel and step on it!" I always wanted to say that to a cabdriver. Apparently, he had heard it before because he looked in the rearview mirror and shook his head.

Leave it to Giovanni to stay in one of the most luxurious hotels in all of Dallas. Good thing he invited me to stay with him. After one look at the lobby, there was no way I could have afforded to stay in this hotel. I took the elevator up to the eleventh floor, found Suite 1111, exhaled my apprehension away, and knocked on his door. Giovanni let me in and loved me up and down like no other man ever has or ever will. After we had gotten reacquainted, doing what we do best, I told him about my chance meeting with Beverly. He was interested so I called and arranged for all three of us to meet the next day after one of the seminars.

Over cocktails in the hotel lobby, we spoke at length about the entertainment business and the future of nightclubs in general. In recent years, many of the smaller clubs were being taken over by large corporations, just as with other businesses. Beverly emphasized her company's intent was to merge with local clubs that showed huge potential, and allowed them to keep their own "flavor" while increasing business and overall profits. They didn't want to open up a lot of "cookie cutter" nightclubs.

A lot of what Beverly envisioned fell in line with Giovanni's vision for his next club. The meeting was a success for all! Beverly had spoken to her bosses beforehand about expanding internationally and had mentioned that she had a contact in Italy. After we met, she told them about our conversation on the airplane. They were really interested and wanted to arrange a meeting with Giovanni at his club if he was agreeable.

Giovanni had previously considered expanding on his own, but was willing to discuss a possible joint venture. Of course, he was not going to make any final decisions until he had an opportunity to research the American corporation and discuss this with his brother and partner, Lucio.

As for me, if I were so inclined, I would become *McCluskey and Chambers Entertainment, Inc.*'s newest employee. My position would be assistant manager of their regional office. I would be the company's representative and meet with local Italian nightclub owners. Because of my most recent experience working in Giovanni's nightclub and my eagerness to learn the business, Beverly offered me the job with an impressive salary and extensive benefits to boot. It included an intense three-week training program that focused on all aspects of the business and what my job would entail.

After I successfully completed the Dallas based training, the company would relocate me to *Pordenone,* Italy, about 30 kilometers from *Gorgazzio.* I made sure that the job offer was not contingent upon Giovanni accepting their proposal and Beverly laid my fears to rest. She said she had been impressed with me and thought my talents were being wasted putting together tanks in Salinas, Kansas. No, the offer stood on its own merit and the position was mine if I wanted it. I asked for a few days to think it over, and would let her know my decision within the week. She thought a week's time was fair because moving all the way to Italy was, in her words—not mine, "more than a notion".

We thanked Beverly for her time and parted ways. It was finally time to celebrate. Ever the charmer, Giovanni persuaded the bartender into sending a complimentary bottle of champagne and a plate of fruit and cheese to the room. We had a lot to discuss and not much time to do it.

"A toast," he raised his glass, "to my angel for bringing me in prosperity in business and good luck in love. *Salute!*"

I raised my glass and joined him in the toast. The champagne bubbles tickled my nose but it was oh, so, delicious. "*Salute!* I can't believe how things worked out. I came down here to see you. Who would have thought that by random chance I would be seated next to someone like Beverly? The funny thing is I normally don't talk to people on airplanes. It was sheer coincidence that I happened to be sitting next to her, saw her reading that brochure and ended up talking about your club and my life ambitions. Giovanni, I am leaving Dallas with the prospects of a new job in another country and of starting a new life. A new life that will eventually lead me to you." The bitter sweetness of the moment did not pass me by. When one door closes, another one opens.

"Ah, Lena, you do not believe in coincidences, remember? Everything happens for a particular reason. Part of God's plan? *Si?* What are you going to do? Are you going to accept the job offer? Will you be moving to *Italia?*" he asked.

"I honestly don't know Giovanni. Everything is moving so fast. I need time to think." I sat down and continued to sip the bubbly.

"*Si, si,* this is a big decision and not one for you to take lightly. For tonight, you do not have to think. Tonight is a celebration of our love. After you go, you will have much time to think about what is best for Lena. Not what is best for me, or your husband, or your children. You must think about you. When you make your decision, you know how to reach me. Now come here. I am not trying to sway your decision, but let me remind you of what it feels like to experience love and passion with a man who truly, truly cares about you." He took the glass out of my hand kissing each finger along the way. We made it to that special place where only he knew the roads. We were together and tonight, that's all that mattered.

The next few days consisted of us doing tourist type things. We visited the Sixth Floor Museum at Dealey Plaza, the site where JFK was shot. Touring the museum and seeing how they pieced together the facts, well, it definitely made you wonder how one man could set off a chain of events that changed the course of history. One man acting alone? No wonder so many people bought into the conspiracy theory. To think that one man could do so much damage was unfathomable.

The *Nightclub and Bar Owners Association Convention* was a huge success and in between viewing displays, attending presentations, and making industry contacts, we did a lot of walking, a lot of talking, and a whole lot of eating. Giovanni had discovered Texas barbecue and wanted some form of it every day.

"Now that you have seen a bit of my country, what do you think?" I asked.

We settled upon a local BBQ joint and conversed over a plate of barbecued brisket and ribs, baked beans, coleslaw and corn bread.

"Do you want me to be polite or do you want my honest opinion?" He sat back and loosened his belt. He sipped his ice cold mug of beer, put it on the table and looked squarely at me.

"What do you mean? Why would I want to hear anything but your honest opinion?"

"You do have a point. Well, to be perfectly honest. I find your country very interesting. The first thing I noticed was how big the sky appears. It looks like it goes on forever. But when I look closer, everything looks bigger. The cars, the streets, the buildings, even the people! Food is everywhere! So many restaurants with cars lined up! Look at the amount of food on my plate! It is enough to feed two people!"

"I suppose, you're right. We do love our food! What else have you noticed about the U.S.?"

"Lena, why does everyone here speak so loudly? It appears everyone talks and no one listens. Everywhere I go, there is noise. Loud music, loud voices, bright lights! There isn't any subtlety. I get the feeling that everything and everyone is trying to stand out more than the next person. Who is the loudest and most obnoxious?! Who can have the biggest, noisiest car? Which sign can outshine the other? Whose skirt is tighter, shorter, or brightest? Which restaurant gives you the most food? Where is the biggest, most expensive house? I have visited cities in Germany and now I realize that they are imitating life here in the United States. There is too much excess! In Italy, we are not as "westernized" as other European countries. And from what I have seen here, I must say I do not wish my country to ever change."

"Giovanni look, you are in a major metropolitan city. Dallas is a lot even for me to take! Yeah, this is what you can expect in our larger cities, but all of the U.S. isn't like this. Okay, well maybe it is, but our smaller towns are much more laid back than the cities. If I took you back to Salinas, Kansas, it would be like night and day compared to this. But as far as the competitive spirit, it is alive and well throughout the states. Most of us want to do better than the next—outshine our competition, whether it's neighbors or the business down the street. We actually have a term for it. We call it 'keeping up with the Jones'."

"Is this how you wish to live? Keeping up with other people and trying to out do them?" He bit into a rib and got sauce all over his face.

"No, I didn't say that's how I want to live. For most Americans, it's just matter-of-fact. We are taught to compete from a very young age. You Italians do it too. You're probably just not blatant as we are. Take for instance your club. You're in competition right? You want to bring in customers and those people may be regulars at some other club. So if you offer them more, they're going to bring their business to your club." I took my napkin and wiped the sauce away.

"You are as smart as you are beautiful. Now let us finish our meal so we can have desert in the room later." He kissed me, tasting like Texas ribs and *Shiner Bock* beer.

CHAPTER 33

On the short flight back to Kansas, I didn't have any deep, thought provoking conversations with my fellow passengers. There were no paperback novels or music piped into my ears to push heavy thoughts away. I used the forced aloneness to contemplate the events that had taken place over the past few weeks of my life. In that short span of time, I felt I had lived several lifetimes and my life had changed dramatically as a result. For whatever reasons my mind, my spirit, my soul, had taken me to a place where few people go and those who do are hesitant to admit it out of fear of being labeled "crazy".

I truly believe I had an out-of-body experience which took me to another dimension. How else can I explain meeting and falling in love with a man who was literally the man of my dreams, the love of my life, my future and destiny all rolled into one?

I don't expect I will ever understand how I traveled to Italy while my body lay still in a hospital in Kansas. I just know that it did happen. Giovanni Morelli was—is a real, live person. He was not a figment of my imagination—of this I am most certain. I do believe in miracles, for miracles occur everyday. Perhaps this was one of those miracles. I can't prove it one way or another. And at this point, it really doesn't matter how or why it happened—only that it did. I now have some hard choices to make. My oldest son is out on his own, my two youngest aren't far behind. I had to consider my life and what I wanted out of it. How long should I continue being with a man I didn't love? Was I expected to stay in a marriage until I was no longer able to pursue my dreams or too old to care about them anymore?

One thing is for certain in all of this; I only have one life to live and wasn't getting any younger in the process.

I thought about Mark. Our marriage was over long before either one of us admitted it. There was no love there. It was a marriage of convenience intended to survive long enough to raise our children and send them on their way. After that, as far as Mark was concerned, all bets were off. Well, since last week even that had changed. There was no way in hell that I was going to stay in the same house—let alone remain married—to a man who threatened to kill and could have disfigured my face in the process? Yes, it was over, finally over.

The major issues that needed to be resolved were when and how I was going to leave. And whether or not I was going to take that job.

Was it fate that I happened to be sitting next to Beverly on that plane? Was it by chance that Mark's mother blurted out her son's true feelings for me? Was it God's will that I fell in love with Giovanni, a man I thought only existed in my dreams? There are some things in life that don't require answers, you just have to believe. As Giovanni so eloquently reminded me, there is no such thing as coincidences. There was a reason that everything happened the way it did. I figured it was all part of God's plan. He laid out the plan for my life and now it was my decision how I chose to follow it.

I didn't have any trouble locating my car in the long term parking lot. I had my wits about me this time when I parked. My mind was clear and I knew what I had to do. My time in Dallas was well spent and would prove invaluable in helping me tie up loose ends. Thirty minutes later when I pulled up at the house, Mark's car was parked in the driveway. I opened the door and went inside to face my past, and my present, which would ultimately affect my future.

"Hi Lena. Uh, how are you? Uh, how's your eye?" Mark asked hesitantly, while turning the volume down with the remote. As usual, he was sitting on the living room sofa watching ESPN.

"I'm fine. Where are the boys?" I answered, looking around the house that no longer felt like home.

"Uh, they're outside playing. Do you want me to go?" He didn't want trouble. Neither did I.

"No, no, that's okay. Listen, we need to talk." I uttered the dreaded words no man ever wants to hear from a woman.

"Okay, sit down. How was your trip? Did you see your friend, um, what was her name again?" he asked, trying to be pleasant by making small talk.

"The trip was good. I actually went to a convention. That's part of what I want to talk to you about." I was not going to go into specifics about my trip nor *my friend*. I felt very uncomfortable. I didn't know how this was going to turn out.

"Oh, yeah? What kind of a convention?" He immediately became uncharacteristically interested in my life.

"It was a convention for those in the entertainment industry, you know, nightclub owners and such. I had a chance to meet some very interesting people." My throat was dry.

"Entertainment industry?" He smirked. "I suppose there is a reason why you are suddenly interested in nightclubs. What's really going on, Lena? You got yourself someone else?" Mark still appeared calm.

"No, there's no one else. It isn't about that," I hesitated. "I don't know how to say this…"

"You don't know how to say *what*?" he asked.

"Uh, well, you remember our conversation a few days ago, right? Of course, you do. Well, uh, remember when I told you I wasn't happy. Right?" I decided to quit stalling and just say what I had to say. As much as I wanted to tell him, it wasn't easy. I stood up and put a few feet between us.

"Look, I'm not going to get angry or do anything to you. I learned my lesson from the other night. The last thing I want is for the police to come to my house again. Just tell me whatever it is you have to say." He slowly exhaled.

I took a deep breath and just spit it out. "Mark, I'm not happy and I haven't been for years. I have had a lot of time to think about us and our life together. Things haven't been right between us for so long. We are basically just roommates sharing a house together. I want so much more out of my life. Ya know?! While I was in Dallas, I met this woman who offered me a job with a future. It involves all the things that interest me—interacting with people, travel, responsibility, decent pay… I'm thinking about taking it."

"Cool, I'm fine with you changing jobs. Where is it and when does it start?" He looked as if he were waiting for the other shoe to drop.

I let it fall. "Mark, you're not hearing me. I don't know how to tell you this, so I'm just going to say it. Look, I want a divorce. I'm not in love with you and I don't want to be married anymore." I blurted it out and let the chips fall where they may.

He sat there as if he hadn't heard the last few sentences. His initial reaction was not to react. I watched him suck at his teeth and sigh. He shook his head several times as if he couldn't believe what he'd just heard. I stood where I was, waiting for him to speak. Several minutes passed before he said anything.

"Okay".

I must admit I expected more of a fight considering how he reacted last time. "What? What does "ok" mean?"

"It means alright. I get it. Okay! I agree with you. Maybe that is what we need to do. You're right. You're not happy, well neither am I. If you don't want to be with me, I can't force you to love me. So now what? What are your plans? I assume that's what you've been out doing—planning how you're going to leave me." He was beginning to sound more like his old self.

"Uh, like I said. I'm thinking about taking them up on their job offer. I don't see any reason to prolong this anymore. Neil and Carlos are going up to my parent's house for the summer, if that's still alright with you. Then when they get back, I'll take them to Italy with me." As soon as I mentioned Italy, I remembered I neglected to mention that part about the job offer.

"Italy?! Did you just say you were taking my kids to Italy?! Woman! Are you out of your mind?! You can go to Italy on your own! My boys aren't going anywhere! They're staying right here!" He was understandably angry.

"Look. I'm not going to talk to you when you're like this. We can talk more about this later. I'm going to the store to get something for dinner," I grabbed my purse and headed for the door.

"I don't know how you expected me to act! Not only did you just tell me that you want a divorce, but you throw in that you want to take my kids out of the country. You expect me to just roll over and take that news without being upset?! Did you really think I was going to agree with you on that? Hey baby, if you want to leave, then leave. But don't expect me to let you take my kids because you got some wild hair up your ass!" He stood up.

I needed some air. I felt like I couldn't breathe. I jumped in the car and headed to the nearest Kroger's. I hadn't expected him to say he wasn't going to let me take the kids. I couldn't leave them here. What did I expect? After all he was their father and even if he were hands off most of the time he didn't want them that far away from him.

Someone once asked me what was the best time to pray? Was it at night before you went to bed? Was it before you or a loved one was about to travel? How about when you were sick and wanted a blessing to get well? I replied that I did not know when the best time to pray was. But now I do. The best time to pray is anytime. So that is what I did. I sat in that little car in the parking lot of Kroger's and prayed for strength and guidance in what I needed to accomplish. I don't know how much time passed before I finally went inside the store, but when I came out I felt a whole lot better.

I stood over the stove stir-frying chicken and vegetables for dinner. Mark came in and joined me. The boys were in their rooms doing whatever it is that they do.

"Lena, I've been thinking about what you said. You know, about wanting to split up and you moving to Italy. I thought about it after you left and maybe it's not such a bad idea. I must admit that what my mother told you was true. I have been feeling trapped for a long, long time, but I was willing to stick it out at least until both boys were out of school."

"If you feel the same way, then what the hell was the other night about? Why did you go off like that on me?" I still had my guard up.

"I was drunk. It's a man thing. A pride thing. I was pissed off because you had the nerve to actually say what I felt. You wanted out when I was trying to hold it all together. No man wants his woman to up and leave him. I don't care how badly they get along."

"Is that right? You tried to beat the shit out of me because you were drunk and your pride was injured?! Incredible!" I was not about to let him off the hook. "Okay, so are you going to fight me about taking the kids?"

"As much as I don't want you to take them, I probably can't stop you. Not with a charge of domestic violence hanging over my head and that's not to mention what the Army's going to do with me when they get a hold of me. You do what you have to do. I know you will anyway. You always do…" He grabbed his keys off the kitchen counter. "I'll be back in a couple of days after I talk to my lawyer. Let me know when you plan on taking off." He hesitated before continuing.

"Uh, since we're laying all our cards on the table, you may as well know now. I've been seeing someone else for the past year. So if I have seemed distant, now you know why. Oh yeah. I already told the boys. See you later."

What the fuck?! He's had someone else all along? I watched him storm out the door. I couldn't help but feeling like he had won. Here he was wanting to get out of this marriage for the longest time. I probably did him a favor by calling it quits. Now he could finally be free, free of me and free of the responsibility of being the father he never was to the boys. Free to be with his skank! No wonder he didn't fight me more. He wanted out as badly as I did. Humph! Ain't that a trip?!

Over dinner, I sat down with Neil and Carlos and told them that their Dad and I were through. We were getting divorced. I reiterated that they would always have two parents and our splitting up had nothing to do with them. They would still be loved by the both of us. There were a lot of tears followed by the excitement of going to St. Louis for a few weeks and then joining me over in Italy after I got settled in. I answered their questions as best as I could before sending them off to their rooms. I even let them get away with not cleaning the kitchen. Tonight, I'd take care of the mess.

James called to give me an update on his new life in St. Louis. With the help of his uncle he found a good part-time job and a small, inexpensive apartment near the university campus. He was excited and I hated to rain on his parade, but he needed to know. I told him about me and Mark. He didn't seem surprised at all, in fact, he was okay with it. Said he'd rather have two parents who were happy apart than miserable together.

I plugged the Italian cell phone into the charger, took a deep breath and began a conversation that began the first day of the rest of my life.

"Baby, I'll be there before summers end. I love you and I am looking forward to sharing a life of love, happiness, and joy with you. I waited all my life to meet you and now I'm never going to let you go. You are me, I am you, we are one." I cried tears of joy as I spoke to the man who had shown me what real love was all about.

In spite of the thousands of miles that separated us I had never felt closer to any other person. Ever! And in that moment, I knew my prayers had been answered. Thank you Lord!

~~~~

Journal Entry 1. My New Life in Italia.

How far will you go and what will you do in the name of love? It was truly more than a notion to end a chapter of my life when it was all I ever knew. Was it all worth it? Did I make the right decision? My divorce from Mark was final a few months ago. Me and my two youngest boys moved to Italy and we love it here. Giovanni and I took a romantic trip for two to the beautiful mystical island of Corsica and decided that is where we will be married next spring. All three of my children took an immediate liking to him and they will give me away at our wedding. It's going to be a small intimate affair with both of our families and a few close friends. I am so happy now—happier than I have ever been in my entire life. I found him and he found me.

The love of my life.......finally.

Finito
(The End)